D1296492

Praise for J. R. Ward's Black Dagg

'Now here's a band of brothers who know how to show a girl a good time'
New York Times bestselling author, Lisa Gardner

'It's not easy to find a new twist on the vampire myth, but Ward succeeds beautifully. This dark and compelling world is filled with enticing romance as well as perilous adventure'
Romantic Times

'These vampires are *hot*, and the series only gets hotter ... so hot it gave me shivers'
Vampire Genre

'Ward wields a commanding voice perfect for the genre ... Intriguing, adrenaline-pumping ... Fans of L. A. Banks, Laurell K. Hamilton and Sherrilyn Kenyon will add Ward to their must-read list'
Booklist

'These erotic paranormals are well worth it, and frighteningly addictive ... It all works to great, page-turning effect ... [and has] earned Ward an Anne Rice-style following, deservedly so'
Publishers Weekly

'[A] midnight whirlwind of dangerous characters and mesmerising erotic romance. The Black Dagger Brotherhood owns me now. Dark fantasy lovers, you just got served'
USA Today bestselling author of *Evermore*, Lynn Viehl

J. R. Ward lives in the South with her incredibly supportive husband and her beloved golden retriever. After graduating from law school, she began working in health care in Boston and spent many years as chief of staff for one of the premier academic medical centres in the nation.

Visit J. R. Ward online:

www.jrward.com
www.facebook.com/JRWardBooks
@jrward1

By J. R. Ward

J.R. WARD

THE SAVIOR

piatkus

PIATKUS

First published in the US in 2019 by Gallery Books, an imprint of
Simon & Schuster, Inc.
First published in Great Britain in 2019 by Piatkus

13 5 7 9 10 8 6 4 2

Copyright © 2019 by Love Conquers All, Inc.

The moral right of the author has been asserted.

*All characters and events in this publication, other than those
clearly in the public domain, are fictitious and any resemblance
to real persons, living or dead, is purely coincidental.*

All rights reserved.
No part of this publication may be reproduced, stored in a
retrieval system, or transmitted, in any form or by any means, without
the prior permission in writing of the publisher, nor be otherwise circulated
in any form of binding or cover other than that in which it is published
and without a similar condition including this condition being
imposed on the subsequent purchaser.

A CIP catalogue record for this book
is available from the British Library.

Hardback ISBN 978-0-349-42048-6
Trade paperback ISBN 978-0-349-42047-9

Printed and bound by CPI Group (UK) Ltd, Croydon, CR0 4YY

Papers used by Piatkus are from well-managed forests
and other responsible sources.

MIX
Paper from
responsible sources
FSC® C104740

Piatkus
An imprint of
Little, Brown Book Group
Carmelite House
50 Victoria Embankment
London EC4Y 0DZ

An Hachette UK Company
www.hachette.co.uk

www.littlebrown.co.uk

Dedicated to You:
We are back, you and I.
It is wonderful to be home.

xxx

GLOSSARY OF TERMS AND PROPER NOUNS

abstrux nohtrum (**n.**) Private guard with license to kill who is granted his or her position by the King.

ahvenge (**v.**) Act of mortal retribution, carried out typically by a male loved one.

Black Dagger Brotherhood (**pr. n.**) Highly trained vampire warriors who protect their species against the Lessening Society. As a result of selective breeding within the race, Brothers possess immense physical and mental strength, as well as rapid healing capabilities. They are not siblings for the most part, and are inducted into the Brotherhood upon nomination by the Brothers. Aggressive, self-reliant, and secretive by nature, they are the subjects of legend and objects of reverence within the vampire world. They may be killed only by the most serious of wounds, e.g., a gunshot or stab to the heart, etc.

blood slave (**n.**) Male or female vampire who has been subjugated to serve the blood needs of another. The practice of keeping blood slaves has been outlawed.

the Chosen (pr. n.) Female vampires who had been bred to serve the Scribe Virgin. In the past, they were spiritually rather than temporally focused, but that changed with the ascendance of the final Primale, who freed them from the Sanctuary. With the Scribe Virgin removing herself from her role, they are completely autonomous and learning to live on earth. They do continue to meet the blood needs of unmated members of the Brotherhood, as well as Brothers who cannot feed from their *shellans* and injured fighters.

chrih **(n.)** Symbol of honorable death in the Old Language.

cohntehst **(n.)** Conflict between two males competing for the right to be a female's mate.

Dhunhd **(pr. n.)** Hell.

doggen **(n.)** Member of the servant class within the vampire world. *Doggen* have old, conservative traditions about service to their superiors, following a formal code of dress and behavior. They are able to go out during the day, but they age relatively quickly. Life expectancy is approximately five hundred years.

ehros **(n.)** A Chosen trained in the matter of sexual arts.

exhile dhoble **(n.)** The evil or cursed twin, the one born second.

the Fade (pr. n.) Nontemporal realm where the dead reunite with their loved ones and pass eternity.

First Family (pr. n.) The King and Queen of the vampires, and any children they may have.

ghardian **(n.)** Custodian of an individual. There are varying degrees of *ghardians*, with the most powerful being that of a *sehcluded* female.

glymera **(n.)** The social core of the aristocracy, roughly equivalent to Regency England's *ton*.

hellren **(n.)** Male vampire who has been mated to a female. Males may take more than one female as mate.

hyslop **(n. or v.)** Term referring to a lapse in judgment, typically resulting in the compromise of the mechanical operations of a vehicle or otherwise motorized conveyance of some kind. For example, leaving one's keys in one's car as it is parked outside the family home overnight, whereupon said vehicle is stolen.

leahdyre (**n.**) A person of power and influence.

leelan (**adj. or n.**) A term of endearment loosely translated as "dearest one."

Lessening Society (pr. n.) Order of slayers convened by the Omega for the purpose of eradicating the vampire species.

lesser (n.) De-souled human who targets vampires for extermination as a member of the Lessening Society. *Lessers* must be stabbed through the chest in order to be killed; otherwise they are ageless. They do not eat or drink and are impotent. Over time, their hair, skin, and irises lose pigmentation until they are blond, blushless, and pale eyed. They smell like baby powder. Inducted into the society by the Omega, they retain a ceramic jar thereafter into which their heart was placed after it was removed.

lewlhen (**n.**) Gift.

lheage (**n.**) A term of respect used by a sexual submissive to refer to their dominant.

Lhenihan (pr. n.) A mythic beast renowned for its sexual prowess. In modern slang, refers to a male of preternatural size and sexual stamina.

lys (**n.**) Torture tool used to remove the eyes.

mahmen (n.) Mother. Used both as an identifier and a term of affection.

mhis (n.) The masking of a given physical environment; the creation of a field of illusion.

nalla (**n., f.**) or *nallum* (**n., m.**) Beloved.

needing period (n.) Female vampire's time of fertility, generally lasting for two days and accompanied by intense sexual cravings. Occurs approximately five years after a female's transition and then once a decade thereafter. All males respond to some degree if they are around a female in her need. It can be a dangerous time, with conflicts and fights breaking out between competing males, particularly if the female is not mated.

newling (**n.**) A virgin.

the Omega (pr. n.) Malevolent mystical figure who has targeted the vampires for extinction out of resentment directed toward the Scribe Virgin. Exists in a nontemporal realm and has extensive powers, though not the power of creation.

phearsom **(adj.)** Term referring to the potency of a male's sexual organs. Literal translation something close to "worthy of entering a female."

Princeps **(pr. n.)** Highest level of the vampire aristocracy, second only to members of the First Family or the Scribe Virgin's Chosen. Must be born to the title; it may not be conferred.

pyrocant **(n.)** Refers to a critical weakness in an individual. The weakness can be internal, such as an addiction, or external, such as a lover.

rahlman **(n.)** Savior.

rythe **(n.)** Ritual manner of asserting honor granted by one who has offended another. If accepted, the offended chooses a weapon and strikes the offender, who presents him—or herself without defenses.

the Scribe Virgin (pr. n.) Mystical force who previously was counselor to the King as well as the keeper of vampire archives and the dispenser of privileges. Existed in a nontemporal realm and had extensive powers, but has recently stepped down and given her station to another. Capable of a single act of creation, which she expended to bring the vampires into existence.

sehclusion **(n.)** Status conferred by the King upon a female of the aristocracy as a result of a petition by the female's family. Places the female under the sole direction of her *ghardian*, typically the eldest male in her household. Her *ghardian* then has the legal right to determine all manner of her life, restricting at will any and all interactions she has with the world.

shellan **(n.)** Female vampire who has been mated to a male. Females generally do not take more than one mate due to the highly territorial nature of bonded males.

symphath **(n.)** Subspecies within the vampire race characterized by the ability and desire to manipulate emotions in others (for the purposes of an energy exchange), among other traits. Historically, they have been discriminated against and, during certain eras, hunted by vampires. They are near extinction.

the Tomb (pr. n.) Sacred vault of the Black Dagger Brotherhood. Used as a ceremonial site as well as a storage facility for the jars of *lessers*. Ceremonies performed there include inductions, funerals, and disciplinary actions against Brothers. No one may enter except for members of the Brotherhood, the Scribe Virgin, or candidates for induction.

trahyner **(n.)** Word used between males of mutual respect and affection. Translated loosely as "beloved friend."

transition (n.) Critical moment in a vampire's life when he or she transforms into an adult. Thereafter, he or she must drink the blood of the opposite sex to survive and is unable to withstand sunlight. Occurs generally in the mid-twenties. Some vampires do not survive their transitions, males in particular. Prior to their transitions, vampires are physically weak, sexually unaware and unresponsive, and unable to dematerialize.

vampire (n.) Member of a species separate from that of Homo sapiens. Vampires must drink the blood of the opposite sex to survive. Human blood will keep them alive, though the strength does not last long. Following their transitions, which occur in their mid-twenties, they are unable to go out into sunlight and must feed from the vein regularly. Vampires cannot "convert" humans through a bite or transfer of blood, though they are in rare cases able to breed with the other species. Vampires can dematerialize at will, though they must be able to calm themselves and concentrate to do so and may not carry anything heavy with them. They are able to strip the memories of humans, provided such memories are short-term. Some vampires are able to read minds. Life expectancy is upward of a thousand years, or in some cases, even longer.

wahlker **(n.)** An individual who has died and returned to the living from the Fade. They are accorded great respect and are revered for their travails.

whard **(n.)** Equivalent of a godfather or godmother to an individual.

†HE SAVIOR

CHAPTER ONE

Eliahu Rathboone House
Sharing Cross, South Carolina

I'm going to kill it, that's what I'm going to do."

Rick Springfield—no, not the singer, and could his parents have done a little better on that one?—got up on the queen-size bed and rolled this month's *Vanity Fair* into a weapon. Good thing the Internet was sucking up ads and magazines were shrinking in size because he got a tight roll on the anemic pages.

"Can't we just let the bat out a window?"

The helpful suggestion was posited by the "Jessie's Girl" he wanted to impress—her name was Amy Hongkao—and so far the weekend away had been good. They'd left Philly Friday at noon, both of them cutting the work day in half, and traffic hadn't been bad. They'd arrived at the Eliahu Rathboone B&B around eight, collapsed into this bed he was currently trying to balance on, and had sex three times the following morning.

Now it was Sunday night and they were leaving tomorrow early afternoon, barring any snowstorms up the coast—

The bat came gunning for his head, and it flew in the manner of a moth, all discombobulated flapping with the flight path of a drunk.

Pulling up memories from Pee Wee baseball, Rick got his stance set, hauled back on the *Vanity Fair* slugger, and gave a good swing.

The goddamn bat bobbed out of the way, but his arms kept going, all aim, no target, throwing him into a lurch that was right out of the Concussion Handbook.

"Rick!"

Amy caught him by bracing against his outer thigh and pushing, and he threw out a hand for the first steady thing in his vicinity—her head. As her hair twisted up under his sweaty palm, there was cursing. From him and her.

The bat came back and dive-bombed them, all how-you-like-me-now-douchebag. And in a fit of manliness, Rick shrieked, recoiled, knocked a lamp over. When it crashed, they lost nearly all the light in the room, only a glow at the base of the door offering any frame of retina reference.

Talk about going to ground fast. He hit that bed like a duvet, falling flat and dragging Amy with him. Wrapped in each other's arms, they panted hard, even though there was nothing romantic about the contact.

Nope. This was an aerobic workout to that old school "I Will Survive" song.

"It must have come down the chimney and out of the fireplace," he said. "Don't they carry rabies?"

Overhead, the scourge of room 214 did the rounds at what Rick hoped was, and stayed at, the ten-thousand-feet molding level. And all the flapping and squeaking was surprisingly ominous, considering the damn thing probably didn't weigh more than a slice of bread. The darkness, however, added a threat of death that was primordial: Even though the manly side of him wanted to solve the problem and be a hero—so he looked better than he actually was to a woman he'd just started dating—his fear demanded that he outsource this catastrophe.

Before their first weekend away together became a viral story about how you needed to watch out for bats or you ended up with a fourteen-day course of shots.

"This is ridiculous." Amy's breath was Colgate-minty and close to his face, and her body felt good against his own even though they were in dire bat-stakes. "Let's just make a run for the door and go downstairs to the front desk. This can't be the first time this has happened, and it's not like that's Dracula—"

Their door swung open.

No knock. No sound at all from the hinges. No clear indication how it had become unlatched because there was no one on the other side.

The light from the hall plunged in like a hand of safety to the drowning, but relief was short lived. A shape materialized from out of thin air to block the illumination. One moment there was nothing between the jambs, the next, an enormous silhouette of a long-haired male figure appeared, the shoulders powerful as a heavyweight boxer's, the arms long and muscled, the legs planted like steel beams. With the light coming from behind, there was no seeing the face, and Rick was glad for that.

Because everything about the arrival and the size and that scent in the air—cologne, but not fake, not out of a bottle—suggested this was a dream.

Or a nightmare.

The figure brought up a hand to his mouth—or seemed to. Maybe he was taking a dagger out of a chest holster?

There was a pause. Then he held his forefinger forward.

Against all odds and logic, the bat came to him as if called to a master, and as the winged creature landed like a bird, a voice, deep and accented, entered Rick's brain as if pushed into his skull not through his ears, but via his frontal lobe.

I don't like things killed on my property, and he is more welcome than you are.

Something dropped from that finger. Something red and frightening. Blood.

The figure disappeared in the same manner it arrived, with the abrupt speed of a quick-stepping, panicked heart. And with the light from the hall no longer invaded by the figure, the path of happy-place yellow illumination pulled out from the darkness the guest room's patterned rug, and their messy, open suitcases, and the antique dresser Amy had admired so much when they'd first arrived.

So normal, so regular.

Except the door closed on its own.

As if it had been willed back into place.

"Rick?" Amy said in a small voice. "What was that? Am I dreaming?"

Overhead, footsteps, heavy and slow, crossed the floorboards of the attic. Which should have been empty.

Another memory from childhood now, and not of the city park and its Little League diamond and the striped mini–Yankees uniforms he'd worn with pride. This one was of his grandmother's farmhouse, with the creaking stairs, and the second-story hall that made the hair on the nape of his neck stand to attention . . . because it led to the back bedroom where the girl had died from consumption.

Wheezing. Labored breath. Whispered weeping.

He had woken up to those sounds every night at 2:39. And each time, although he had been roused by the ghostly gasping, although the struggle for air was in his ears and his mind, he was aware upon his sit-up-fast of only silence, a dense, black-hole silence that consumed the echoes of the past and threatened, with its gravitational pull, to swallow him as well, no trace of his younger self left behind, just an empty twin bed with a warm spot where his living body had once lain.

Rick had always known, with the razor-sharp surety of a child's self-preservation, that the silence, the horrible quiet, was the moment of death for the ghost of the little girl, the culmination of an endless, tortured cycle she re-experienced every night at precisely the moment she'd passed, her will losing the battle as her body's functions failed, her long slide into the grave over, her end arriving not even with a whimper, but with a dreadful absence of sound, absence of life.

Scary stuff for the nine-year-old he had been.

He had never expected to feel anything close to that confusion and terror as an adult. But life had a way of special delivering packages that ticked to your emotional address, and there was no refusing the service, no way to not sign and accept them.

The past was permanent in the same way the future was always just a hypothetical, two ends of a spectrum where one was concrete and the other air, and the instantaneous now, the single real moment, was the fixed point from which the weight of life hung and swung.

"Is this a dream?" Amy said again.

When he found his voice, Rick whispered, "I'd rather not know for sure."

✦   ✦   ✦

Upstairs in the attic of the old mansion, Murhder re-formed and walked over to one of the dormers. As a vampire, he supposed his rescue of the bat, who was lapping up the welling blood on his forefinger and incapable of comprehending the breadth of salvation just rendered upon him, could be termed a professional courtesy.

Assuming you went by human mythology.

In reality, there was not much in common to be had. Vampires needed the blood of a member of their opposite sex to be at optimal strength and health—a nourishment he had not had for many years, and a requirement that he had been forced to forage for from lesser sources. Most bats, on the other hand, lived off of insects, although clearly, there was an exception to be made for what he had offered this present mammal. The two species were as separate as dogs and cats, although Homo sapiens had linked them through all manner of books, movies, TV, and the like.

Opening one-half of the arch-topped window, he extended his arm and shook the bat free, the creature winging out into the night, crossing over the shining face of the risen moon.

When he had purchased the Eliahu Rathboone B&B from its original owner, some century and a half prior, he had intended to live in it alone during his dotage. Not how things had ended up. Twenty years ago, as a result of his breakdown, he had been in the prime of life yet the throes of insanity, burned out and very much crazy, ready to wander empty rooms in the hope his mind followed the example and moved out the soul-destroying images that were cluttering up his memory banks.

No such luck. On the alone front, that was. The house had come with staff who needed jobs, and returning guests who wanted the same room for their anniversary every year, and bookings for weddings that had been made months in advance.

In an earlier incarnation of himself, he would have fucked all of it off. With everything that had happened, however, he hadn't known who he was anymore. His personality, his character, his soul, had been through a trial of fire and failed the test. As a result, his superstructure had been collapsing, his building coming down, his once strong and resolute construction of character turning to rubble.

So he had let the humans continue to come and work and sleep and eat and argue and make love and live around him. It was the kind of move someone who was lost in the world made, a Hail Mary that was uncharacteristic and desperate, a maybe-this-will-keep-me-on-the-planet from a person in whom gravity was no longer all that interested.

Dearest Virgin Scribe, it was a horrible lightness to be insane. To feel like a balloon on a string, no ground under your feet, only a thin tether tying you to a reality you were imminently going to slip free of.

He closed the window and walked over to the trestle table he spent so many hours at. No computer on its old, chipped surface, no telephone or cell phone, no iPad or flat screen TV. Just a candleholder with a lit length of beeswax . . . and three letters . . . and a flat envelope marked FedEx.

Murhder sat down on the old wooden chair, the spindle legs protesting his weight with a creaking.

Reaching into the folds of his black shirt, he pulled out his talisman. Between the pads of his thumb and forefinger, the shard of sacred glass, wrapped in bands of black silk, was a familiar worry bead. But it was more than something for an anxious hand to toy with.

On its long silk cord, he could extend it out such that he could see the glass, and presently, he stared into its transparent face.

Some thirty years ago, he had stolen the piece of a seeing bowl from the Temple of Scribes. Totally illegal to do so. He had told no one. The Brotherhood had gone up to the Scribe Virgin's sanctuary, where her Chosen were sequestered, to defend what should have been sacrosanct from invaders who were of the species. The Primale, the male who serviced the sacred females to provide next generations of Brotherhood members and Chosen, had been slaughtered, and the Treasury, with its inestimable wealth, had been in the process of being looted.

As always ill-gotten financial gain had been the *mens rea*.

Murhder had chased one of the raiders into the Temple of Scribes, and in the course of the ensuing fight, several of the workstations, where the Chosen peered into the crystal seeing bowls and recorded the goings-on down on earth, had been crashed into. After he had killed the felon, he had stood among the ruination of the orderly rows of tables and chairs and wanted to weep.

The sanctuary should never have been defiled, and he prayed that no Chosen had been injured—or worse.

He had been about to drag the body out onto the lawn when something had flashed and caught his eye. The sanctuary, being on the Other Side, had no discernible light source, just a glow across its milky white sky, so he had been unsure what had made anything wink like that.

And then it had happened again.

Stepping through the debris and bloodstains, he had stood over the glass shard. Three inches long and wide, in a lozenge shape, it had appeared as a dead combatant on a field of war.

The thing had done it a third time, that shimmer sparking up from nowhere.

As if it were attempting to communicate with him.

Murhder had slipped it into the pocket of his combat vest and not thought of the shard again. Until three nights later. He had been going through his gear, looking for a missing knife, when he'd discovered it.

That was when the sacred glass had shown him the beautiful female's face.

So shocked had he been with what he'd seen that he'd fumbled the shard, cutting himself as he dropped it.

When he'd picked the thing up, his blood had turned the portrait red. But she was there all right—and the sight of her carved a piece of his heart out. She was terrified, her wide, scared eyes peeled open so that the whites showed, her mouth parted in shock, her skin pulled tight over her features.

The vision chilled him to the bone and promptly invaded his nightmares. Was it a Chosen who had been hurt during the sanctuary break-in? Or some other female he could still help?

Years later, he had learned who it was. And failing her had been the final blow that cost him his sanity.

Tucking the sacred shard back under his shirt, he looked at the FedEx envelope. The documents inside had already been signed by him, the inheritance left by a relation he only vaguely remembered renounced and sent further down the bloodline to another recipient, also someone he was only tangentially aware of.

Wrath, the great Blind King, had demanded them be executed. And Murhder had used that royal order as a pretext to get an audience.

The three letters were the thing.

He brought them closer, pulling them across the varnished wood. The writing on the envelopes was done in proper ink, not the stuff that came out of Bics, and the lettering was shaky, the hand wielding whatever instrument had been used palsied and therefore only partially controlled.

Eliahu Rathboone
Eliahu Rathboone House
Sharing Cross, South Carolina

No street address. No zip code. But Sharing Cross was a little town, and everyone, including the postmaster, who was also the postal deliveryman and the mayor, knew where the B&B could be found—and was aware that people at times fancied communication with a dead figure of history.

Murhder was not, in fact, Eliahu Rathboone. He had, however, put an old portrait of himself down in the front hall to mark the property as his own, and that had ignited the false identification. People "saw" the ghost of Eliahu Rathboone on the grounds and in the house from time to time, and in the modern era, those reports of a long-haired, shadowy form had spurred amateur ghost hunters and then professional ones into coming and obtaining footage.

Someone had even added, at some point, a little signage at the base of the frame, Eliahu Rathboone and the birth and death dates.

The fact that he bore only a passing resemblance to the human who had built the house centuries ago didn't seem to matter. Thanks to the Internet, grainy images of antique pencil drawings showing the actual Rathboone were available for viewing, and other than them both possessing long dark hair, they had little in common. That did not bother the people who wanted to believe, however. They *felt* like he was the first owner of the house, therefore he *was* the first owner of the house.

Humans were big proponents of magical thinking, and he was content to let them stew in their folly. Who was he to judge? He was insane. And it was good for business—which was why the staff let the lie lay, so to speak.

The letter writer knew the truth, however. Knew lots of things.

They must have seen the B&B on the TV, though, and made the connection.

The first letter he had dismissed. The second had troubled him with details only he would know. The third had determined him unto action, although he'd not immediately known how to proceed. And that was when the King's solicitor had arrived with news of the inheritance and Murhder had decided upon his course.

He was going to the King for help. He had no choice.

Down on a lower floor, upon the landing of the main stairs, the grandfather clock began to chime the announcement of nine o'clock.

Soon it would be time to go back to where he had escaped from, to see once again those whom he had no wish to cast sight upon, to reenter, for a limited period, the life which he had left and vowed ne'er to return.

Wrath, son of Wrath. The Black Dagger Brotherhood. And the war with the Lessening Society.

Although that last one was no longer his problem. Nor the other two, actually. In the august and ancient annals of the Brotherhood, he held the notorious title of being the only Brother ever expelled from membership.

No, wait . . . the Bloodletter had also been kicked out. Just not for losing his mind.

There was no scenario he had e'er expected to reengage those fighters or that King.

But this was his destiny. The sacred shard had told him thus.

His female was waiting for him to finally do right by her.

Indeed, he bore the weight of many wrongs in his life, many things that he had done to hurt others, cause pain, maim and destroy. A fighter he had been once, a killer for a cause that had been noble but whose execution had been bloodthirsty. Fate had found a way to hold him accountable, though, and now its ruthless will was once again grinding upon him.

Abruptly, the image of a female came to his mind, powerful of body, fierce of will, her short hair and her glowing gray eyes staring at him with a no-nonsense directness.

Not the one in the glass.

He saw Xhex often in his broken mind, visions of her, memories of them together as well as everything that had happened later, the only channel his mental TV was trained on. If he were apprehensive of taking his malfunctioning cognition into the Brotherhood's orbit, meeting up with that female would ruin him, he was quite sure. At least he didn't have to worry about running into her. His former lover had been a lone wolf all her life, and that trait, like the gunmetal color of her eyes, was so intrinsic to her makeup that he had no concern she would congregate with anyone.

That was what you did when you were a *symphath* living among vampires. You kept that part of your DNA a secret from everyone by removing yourself as much as possible.

Even when it came to males you were sleeping with. Males who thought they knew you. Males who stupidly ran up to the *symphath* colony to free you from captivity—only to learn that you hadn't been kidnapped.

You'd gone to see your blooded family.

That noble move on his part, rooted in his need to be a savior, had been the start of the nightmare for both of them. His decision to go after her had permanently altered the course of their lives because she had kept her true nature from him.

And now . . . further repercussions, unforeseen and undeniable, had arrived unto him. At least these, however, might lead at long last to a resolution he could take to his grave in some kind of peace.

Murhder fanned the letters out. One, two, three. First, second, third.

He was not up to this task.

And on the same deep level that he knew he could not handle this pilgrimage of his, he was aware that there would be no returning from the journey. It was time to end things, however. When he had initially come unto this property, he had had some hope that in time, perhaps he would reenter his body, re-inhabit his flesh, restore his purpose and connection to the common reality in which all other mortals dwelled.

Two decades was long enough to wait to see if that happened, and in those twenty years, naught had changed. He was as unglued as he had been when he had first arrived. The least he could do was put himself out of this misery once and for all, and do it in a righteous way.

One's last act should be virtuous. And for the female destiny provided unto you.

Rather like leaving a room clean after its use, he would take care to restore order to the chaos he had unwittingly unleashed before exiting the planet. And after that? Nothingness.

He did not believe in the Fade. He did not believe in anything.

Except suffering, and that would soon be over.

CHAPTER TWO

Ithaca, New York

G ood evening, ma'am. I'm Special Agent Manfred from the FBI. Are you Dr. Watkins?"

Sarah Watkins leaned forward and checked out the badge and credentials the man held up. Then she looked over his shoulder. In her driveway, a dark gray four-door was parked behind her own car.

"How can I help you?" she said.

"So you are Dr. Watkins." When she nodded, he smiled and put his ID away. "You mind if I come in for a minute?"

Out on her quiet street, her neighbor's new Honda Accord ambled by. Eric Rothberg, who lived two houses down, waved and slowed to a roll.

She waved back to reassure him. He kept going. "What's this about?"

"Dr. Thomas McCaid. I believe you worked with him at RSK BioMed."

Sarah frowned. "He was one of the lab supervisors. Not in my division, though."

"Can I come in?"

"Sure." As she stepped back, she channeled her inner hostess. "Would you like something to drink? Coffee, maybe?"

"That'd be great. It's going to be a late night."

Her house was a small three-bedroom on a small lot on a nice-and-normal street of young families. Four years ago, when she'd bought it with her fiancé, she'd assumed at some point she'd hop on that mommy train.

She should have sold the place a while ago. "The kitchen's this way."

"Nice digs, you live here alone?"

"Yes." Inside her gray-and-white kitchen, she indicated the round table with the three chairs. "I've got K-Cups. What's your poison—oh, sorry. Bad phrasing."

Agent Manfred smiled again. "It's okay. And I'm not picky, long as it has caffeine in it."

He was one of those good-looking bald guys, a forty-something who'd stared his missing hair in the follicle and decided not to pretend about his male pattern no-go. His nose was a ski jump that was crooked, like it had been broken a couple of times, and his eyes were a bright blue. Clothes were loose dark slacks, a dark navy windbreaker, and a black polo with FBI stitched in gold on the pec. Wedding ring was one of those titanium dark gray ones, and its prominence reassured her.

"So what's this about?" She opened a cupboard. "I mean, I know Dr. McCaid died last week. I heard it in my lab. There was an announcement."

"What was his reputation at the company?"

"Good. I mean, he was high up. Had been there for a long time. But again, I didn't know him personally."

"I've heard BioMed's a big place. How long have you been there?"

"Four years." She refilled the water tank for the machine. "We bought this house when we moved here and started at BioMed."

"That's right. You and your fiancé. What was his name?"

Sarah paused as she put a mug onto the grate. The agent was leaning back in her Pottery Barn chair at her Pottery Barn table, all no-big-deal. But those blue eyes were focused on her like he was video-taping all this in his head.

He knew the answers to these questions, she thought.

"His name was Gerhard Albrecht," she said.

"He was a doctor, too. At BioMed."

"Yes." She turned back, and put a K-Cup of Starbucks Morning Blend in the machine. Lowering the handle, there was a hiss and then dripping into the mug. "He was."

"You met him when you were both at MIT."

"That's right. We were in the Harvard-MIT HST program." She glanced back at the agent. "I thought this was about Dr. McCaid?"

"We'll get to that. I'm curious about your fiancé."

Sarah wished she hadn't tried to be polite with the coffee offer. "There's not much to tell. Do you want sugar or milk?"

"Black is great. I don't need anything to slow down the caffeine absorption."

When the dripping was done, she brought the mug over and sat across the table from him. As she awkwardly linked her hands together, she felt like she'd been called to the principal's office. Except this principal could level all kinds of charges at you, charges that lead to prison instead of detention.

"So tell me about Dr. Albrecht." He took a sip. "Oh, yeah, this hits the spot."

Sarah looked at her own ring finger. If they'd made it to their wedding, she would still be wearing a band even though Gerry had been dead for two years. But they'd missed what they'd been planning by four months when he'd passed that January. And as for an engagement diamond, they'd skipped that on account of getting the house.

When she'd had to call the venue and the band and the caterers to cancel, they'd all given her the deposits back because they'd heard what had happened on the news. The only thing that hadn't been fully refundable had been the wedding gown, but the people at the bridal shop had not charged her the other half of the cost when it came in. She'd donated the dress to Goodwill on what would have been their first anniversary.

Oh, and there had been the suit they'd bought for Gerry at Macy's on sale. There had been no returns on that and she still had the thing. He'd always joked that he'd wanted to be buried in a "May the Force Be with You" shirt.

She would have never guessed she'd have to honor that request so soon.

That initial year after he'd been gone, she'd had all of the major holidays to get through—his birthday, his death day, and that non-event wedding anniversary. The calendar had been an obstacle course. Still was.

"I'm going to need you to be more specific," she heard herself say. "About what you want to know."

"Dr. Albrecht worked with Dr. McCaid, didn't he."

"Yes." She closed her eyes. "He did. He was hired into the Infectious Diseases division when we graduated. Dr. McCaid was his supervisor."

"But you were somewhere else in the company."

"That's right. I'm in Gene and Cell Therapy. I specialize in immunotherapy for cancer."

She had always gotten the impression that BioMed had really only wanted Gerry, and had agreed to hire her solely because he'd made it a contingency to his own employment. He'd never said as much, of course—and ultimately, it hadn't mattered. Her work was more than solid, and academic research centers around the country routinely tried to hire her. So why did she stay in Ithaca? She'd been wondering that lately and decided it was because BioMed was her last tie to Gerry, the last choice they had made together . . . the dissipating mirage of the future that they had planned on being long and happy and fulfilling.

But which had turned out to be anything save all that.

Lately, she had begun to feel that her grieving process had stalled because she was still in this house and at BioMed. She just didn't know what to do about it.

"My mom died of cancer nine years ago."

Sarah refocused on the agent and tried to remember what his comment was in reference to. Oh, right. Her job. "I lost mine from the disease sixteen years ago. When I was thirteen."

"Is that why you got into what you're doing?"

"Yes. Actually, both my parents died of cancer. Father pancreatic. Mother breast. So there's an element of self-preservation to my research. I'm in an iffy gene pool."

"That's a lot of losses you've been through. Parents, future husband."

She looked at her ragged nails. They were all chewed down to the quick. "Grief is a cold stream you acclimate to."

"Still, your fiancé's death must have hit you very hard."

Sarah sat forward and looked the man in the eye. "Agent Manfred, why are you really here."

"Just asking questions for background."

"Your ID has you from Washington, D.C., not an Ithaca field office. It's seventy-five degrees in this house because I'm always cold in the winter, and yet you're not taking that windbreaker off while you're drinking hot coffee. And Dr. McCaid died of a heart attack, or that's what both the papers and the announcement at BioMed said. So I'm wondering why an imported special agent from the nation's capital is showing up here wearing a wire and recording this conversation without my permission or knowledge while he asks questions about a man who supposedly died of natural causes as well as my fiancé who's been dead for two years courtesy of the diabetes he suffered from since he was five years old."

The agent put the mug down and his elbows on the table. No more smiling. No more pretext of chatting. No more roundabout.

"I want to know everything about the last twenty-four hours of your fiancé's life, especially when you came home to find him on the floor of your bathroom two years ago. And then after that, we'll see what else I need from you."

✦   ✦   ✦

Special Agent Manfred left one hour and twenty-six minutes later.

After Sarah closed her front door, she locked the dead bolt and went over to a window. Looking out through the blinds, she watched that gray sedan back out of her driveway, K-turn in the snowy street, and take off. She was aware of wanting to make sure the man actually left, although given what the government could do, any privacy she thought she had was no doubt illusory.

Returning to the kitchen, she poured the cold coffee out in the sink and wondered if he really did take the stuff black, or whether he had known he wouldn't be drinking much of it and hadn't wanted to waste her sugar and milk.

She ended up back at the table, sitting in the chair he'd been in, as if that would somehow help her divine the agent's inner thoughts and knowledge. In classic interrogation form, he had given little away, only plying her with bits of information that proved he knew all the background, that he could trip her up, that he would know if she were lying to him. Other than those minor factual pinpoints on whatever map he was making, however, he had kept his figurative topography close to his chest.

Everything she had told him had been the truth. Gerry had been a Type 1 diabetic, and fairly good about managing his condition. He had been a regular tester and insulin administrator, but his diet could have been better and his meals were irregular. His only true failure, if it could be termed as such, was that he hadn't bothered to get a pump. He rarely took breaks from his work and hadn't wanted to waste the time having one "installed."

Like his body was a house that needed an air conditioning unit or something.

Still, he'd managed his blood sugar levels pretty well. Sure there had been some rocky crashes, and she'd had to help him a couple of times, but on the whole, he'd been on top of his disease.

Until that one night. Almost two years ago.

Sarah closed her eyes and relived coming home with Indian food, the paper bags swinging from flimsy handles in her left hand as she'd struggled to open the front door with her key. It had been snowing and she hadn't wanted to put the load down in the drifts as the garlic naan and the chicken curry had already lost enough BTUs on the trip across town. She herself had been on the hot and sweaty side, too, having been first to her spin class, the one she did every Saturday late afternoon, the one she'd wished she could make time for during the workweek, but never quite managed to leave the lab in time.

Six thirty p.m. Ish.

She could remember calling upstairs to him. He had stayed home to work because that was all he did, and although it felt wrong to admit now that he had passed, his constant focus on that project with Dr. McCaid had begun to wear on her. She'd always understood the devotion to the subject matter, to the science, to the possibility of discovery that, for both of them, was always just around the corner. But there had to be more to life than weekends that looked exactly like the M–F's.

She'd called his name again as she walked into the kitchen. There had been annoyance that he didn't answer. Anger that he probably hadn't even heard her. Sadness that they were staying in, again, not because it was winter in Ithaca, but because there were no other plans. No friends. No family. No hobbies.

No movies. No eating out.

No holding hands.

No sex, really.

Of late, they had become just two people who had bought real estate together, the pair of them walking paths that had started out on the same trail, but had since diverged and become parallels with no intersection.

It had been four months until the wedding, and she could recall thinking of "postponing" the date. They could have pumped the brakes at that point and people could still have gotten their money back for airline tickets to, and hotel reservations in, Ithaca. Which had been the site of the ceremony and reception because Gerry hadn't wanted to take the time off to travel to Germany, where his family was, and with both her parents gone and no siblings, Sarah had nothing left of where she'd grown up in Michigan.

As she'd put the bags of takeout on the counter, she had been struck with a profound immobility—and all because she needed a shower. Their bathroom was upstairs off the master bedroom, and to get to it, she would have to pass by his home office. Hear the ticking of his keyboard. See the glow of the computer monitors flashing molecular images. Feel the coldness of the shut-out that was somehow even more frigid than the weather outside of the house.

That night, she'd reached her adaptation threshold. So many times she'd walked by that makeshift office of his since they'd moved in. In the beginning, he had always looked over his shoulder as she had come up the stairs and he'd beckoned her in to show her things, ask her things. Over time, however, that had downshifted to a hello over his shoulder. And then a grunt. And then no response at all, even if she said his name when standing behind him.

Sometime around Thanksgiving, she'd taken to tiptoeing up the stairs so as not to disturb him, even though that was ridiculous because in his concentration, he was un-disturbable. But if she made no noise then he couldn't be ignoring her, right? And she couldn't be hurt and disappointed.

She couldn't find herself in the unintended, unfathomable position of questioning their relationship after all their years of being together.

That night, as she had stood frozen at the kitchen counter, she'd been unable to face the reality of her deep unhappiness . . . yet she'd no longer been able to deny it, either. And that conundrum had trapped her between her desire for a hot shower after exercise and her head-in-the-sand position on the first floor.

Because if she had to walk by that office one more time and be ignored? She was going to have to do something about it.

Eventually, she'd forced herself to hit the stairs, a marching band of don't-be-stupid's drumming her ascent.

Her first clue that all was not well had been the empty swivel chair in front of his computers. Further, the room had been dark, although that was not all that unusual, and Gerry's monitors had offered plenty of light with which to navigate around the sparsely furnished space. But it wasn't like he got up all that often.

She'd told herself that he wasn't where he should have been because nature had called and she promptly resented the hell out of him for his need to pee: Now, she was going to have to interact with him in the bathroom.

Which was going to make cramming her emotions back into the Don't Touch Toy Box even harder.

Special Agent Manfred had gotten the death scene right. She'd found her fiancé sitting up on the tile against the Jacuzzi's built-in base, his legs out straight, his hands curled up on his thighs, his MedicAlert bracelet loose on his right wrist. His head had lolled to one side and there was a clear insulin bottle and a needle next to him. His hair, or what was left of the Boris Becker blond strands, was messy, probably from a seizure, and there was drool down the front of his Dropkick Murphys concert shirt.

Rushing over. Crouching down. Begging, pleading, even as she had checked his jugular and found no pulse underneath cold skin.

In that moment of loss, she had forgiven him all transgressions, her anger disappearing as if never been, her frustrations and doubts gone the way of his life force.

To heaven. Assuming there was such a place.

Calling 911. Ambulance arriving. Death confirmed.

The body had been removed, but things were hazy at that point; she couldn't remember whether it had been taken by the paramedics or the morgue or the coroner . . . . Similar to someone who had sustained a head injury, she had amnesia about that part, about other parts. She remembered clearly calling his parents, however, and breaking down the

second she'd heard his mother's accented voice. Crying. Weeping. Prom-
ises by his parents to be on the next trans-Atlantic flight, vows to be
strong on her side.

No one to call for herself.

Cause of death was determined to be hypoglycemia. Insulin shock.

Gerry's parents ended up taking his body back to Hamburg, Germany, so that he could be buried in the family cemetery, and justlikethat, Sarah had been left here in this little house in Ithaca with very
little to remember her fiancé by. Gerry had been the opposite of a
hoarder, and besides, his parents had taken most of his things with
them. Oh, and BioMed had sent a representative to take the computer
towers from his home office, only the monitors remaining.

After the death, she had closed the door to that room and not reopened it for a good year and a half. When she finally did venture across
the threshold, chinks in the all-is-forgiven armor she'd girded herself
with had appeared the instant she'd seen that desk and chair.

She'd shut things up again.

Remembering Gerry as anything other than a good, hardworking
man had felt like a betrayal. Still did.

Sarah had been through this post-passing recasting of character before with her parents. There were different standards for the quick and
the dead. Those who were alive were nuanced, a combination of good
and bad traits, and as both full-color and three-dimensional, they were
capable of disappointing you and uplifting you in turns. Once a loved
one was gone, however, assuming you were essentially fond of them, she
had found that the disappointments faded and only the love remained.

If only through force of will.

To focus on anything but the good times, especially when it came
to Gerry, felt just plain wrong—especially given that she blamed herself for his death. On their second date, he had taught her how to identify the symptoms of insulin shock and use his glucagon kit. She had
even had to mix the solution and inject it into his thigh on three different occasions while they'd been in Cambridge: His cousin Gunter's

wedding when he'd drunk too much and not eaten. Then when he'd tried to run that 5k. And finally after he'd taken a big dose of insulin in preparation for a Friendsgiving dinner and they'd gotten a flat tire on Storrow Drive.

If she hadn't stood there in front of the goddamn Indian food in the kitchen and been angry at him, could she have saved him? There was a glucagon kit right there in the top drawer by the sink.

If she had gone right upstairs for her shower, could she have used it in time and then called 911?

The questions haunted her because her answer was always yes. Yes, she could have turned the insulin crash around. Yes, he'd still be alive. Yes, she was responsible for his death because she had been condemning him for loving his work and finding purpose in saving people's lives.

Reopening her eyes, she looked over at the counter. She could remember, after the body was removed and the police and medics had left and the phone call to Germany made, she had told herself to eat something and shuffled toward the kitchen. The silence in the house had been so resonant that the screaming in her head felt like the kind of thing the neighbors could hear.

Entering the kitchen. Stopping dead. Seeing the two paper bags full of now utterly cold and congealed food.

Her first thought had been how foolish to worry about putting them briefly in the snow to unlock the door. They had been destined to lose their warmth.

Just like Gerry's once vital body.

Weeping again. Shaking. Jelly legs going out from under her. She had hit the floor and cried until the doorbell had rung.

BioMed security. Two of them. Coming for the computers.

Returning to the present, Sarah shifted around and looked through the archway, past the living room, to her front door.

She had been honest with Agent Manfred. She had told him the whole story—well, minus the emotional bits like the stuff about calling Gerry's parents and her Cold Indian Takeout Food Breakdown.

Also the part about her feeling responsible for the death—and that was not just because she didn't want to share the intimate details of the loss with a stranger. Bottom line, it didn't feel smart to even hint to a federal agent that she believed she might have played a role, however unintentionally, in the very thing Manfred had come to talk to her about.

Other than those two omissions, both of which were non-factual, she'd hid nothing about the natural death that had tragically occurred to a Type 1 diabetic after he had no doubt kept on his insulin schedule but forgotten to eat all day long.

Utterly heartbreaking, but a totally common, garden variety way for someone with Gerry's condition to die.

Frowning, she thought about her statements to Manfred. Relating the this-then-that-after-which-this-other-thing-happened to the agent had been the first time she had relived Gerry's death from start to finish. In the intervening two years, she'd had plenty of flashbacks, but they had been out of sequence, an unending supply of discordant, invasive snapshots unleashed by all manner of foreseeable and unforeseeable triggers.

But tonight had been her first full replay of the horror movie.

And that was why she now wondered, even though she had spent too many hours to count ruminating on the natural death of her fiancé . . .

. . . how it was that BioMed had known to come pick up those computers before she had told anyone at the company that Gerry was dead.

CHAPTER THREE

The Black Dagger Brotherhood Mansion
Caldwell, New York

Born in a bus station. Left for dead. Rescued from the human world by a stroke of luck.

If John Matthew's life had been required to carry ID, some kind of laminated card detailing its vitals, those would be his birth date, height, and eye color.

Listed also would be mute and mated. The former didn't really matter to him as he had never known speech. The latter was everything to him.

Without Xhex, even the war wouldn't matter.

As he entered the King's study—that pale blue French sanctuary which suited Wrath and the Black Dagger Brotherhood about as well as a ball gown on an alligator—he found the four walls and the silk furniture crowded with big bodies. They were all there waiting for the King, these prime males of the species, these teachers and smart-asses, these fighters and lovers.

This was his family on such a deep level that he felt like he should caboose that particular f-word with "of origin."

Not everyone was a Brother, however. Still, he and Blay fought side by side with them in the war against the Lessening Society, and so did Xcor and the Band of Bastards. There were also trainees in the field and females. And the team had a surgeon who was a human, for godsakes. And a doctor who was a ghost and an advisor that was the king of the *symphaths* and a therapist who had been taken out of time continuum by the Scribe Virgin.

This was the village that had sprung up under Darius's old roof, all of them living here on this Adirondack mountain, *mhis* protecting them from intrusion, time's passing marked by the collective purpose of eradicating the Omega's *lessers*.

Squeezing past Butch and V, he zeroed in on a spot in the corner. He always hung back, even though nobody asked him to last-row-it.

Leaning against the wall, he adjusted his weapons. He had a belt with a matched pair of forties and six full clips around his hips. Under one arm, he had a long-bladed hunting knife, and on the other side, he had a length of chain on his shoulder. Before he went out into the field, he'd throw on a leather jacket, either the new one Xhex had just gotten him or the old one that was beat to shit, and the wardrobe addition was not because it was a howling winter's night out there.

If there was one thing he'd learned in the war? Humans were like toddlers. If there was something that could kill them, they would beeline for that mortal event like the gunfight/knife fight/hand-to-hand was calling their name and promising free Starbucks.

One rule in the war. One common ground between the Lessening Society and the vampires. One single, solitary issue on which both sides could agree.

No human involvement—and not because anybody cared about collateral casualties of the noisy and nosy variety. What neither Wrath and the Brotherhood nor the Omega wanted was the bees' nest of Homo sapiens rattled. On so many levels humans were inferior: not as strong, not as fast, not as long-living—hell, *lessers* were immortal unless you stabbed them back to their black gasbag of a master.

Humans did have one big bene going for them, however.

They were everywhere.

This was something that, back when John Matthew had assumed he was one of them—or rather, a super-scrawny, mute version of one—he hadn't noticed. Then again, humans tended to believe they were the only species on the planet.

According to their myopic point of view, there was nothing else that walked upright on two legs, had hyper-deductive reasoning, gave birth to live young, etc. And the only things with fangs were dogs, tigers, lions, and the like.

Everybody wanted to keep it that way—

Wrath entered the room and a hush came over the conversation as the King made his way to the throne, a.k.a. the only piece of furniture properly sized for what was going to sit on it. And even though John had been around the great male for how long now?, he still was awed. Sure, all the Brothers were enormous, products of a now-defunct— and thank God for that—breeding program instituted by the Scribe Virgin.

But the King was something else.

Long black hair falling to his hips. Black wraparound sunglasses to hide his blind eyes. Black leathers and shitkickers. Black muscle shirt even though it was January and the old mansion had more drafts than lawful inhabitants.

More power in those muscles than a wrecking ball.

Tattoos of his lineage running up the insides of his forearms.

At his side, like a first grade schoolteacher next to a serial killer, a golden retriever kept pace with those heavy strides, the fine leather harness that connected canine and master telegraphing all manner of communication, of which, first and foremost, was absolute loyalty and love on both sides. George was Wrath's sight, but also—not that anyone would bring this up because hey, who needed to be stabbed, right?—the King's comfort dog.

Wrath had been so much better with George around—which was to say, he probably lost his shit and screamed at people only two or three times a night, instead of using his booming voice, epic impatience, and brutal communication style every time he opened his mouth. Still, in spite of his nature, or perhaps because of it, he was utterly revered, not just in the household, but out in the species as a whole. Gone was the Council, that ruling body of the *glymera*, those aristocrats who had tried to overthrow him. Gone was also his birthright to the throne. Now, he was democratically elected and his leadership, although gruff at best, and at worst downright scary, was spot-on in this most dangerous era in the war—

"You, sir, are a bag of dicks."

Lassiter, the fallen angel, broke the silence with that little ditty. And at least he wasn't talking to Wrath.

John Matthew leaned to the side to see who was the recipient of the cock-ticular call-out, but there were too many heavy shoulders in the way. Meanwhile, people jumped in with all kinds of shut-the-fuck-up, what's-wrong-with-you, are-you-stoopid, as well as an at-least-they're-big-dicks—that last one clearly from the accused.

Lassiter had joined the household ranks a while ago, and talk about indelible impressions. The blond-and-black-haired angel with the David Lee Roth zebra tights and the questionable taste in television seemed to enjoy his role as cutup, counter-cool anarchist. John Matthew wasn't fooled. Underneath the pecker cracks and the *Golden Girls* marathons, there was a watchfulness that seemed to suggest he was waiting for something to happen.

Something of H-bomb magnitude.

Wrath settled on his father's great chair, the ancient wood accepting his weight without a groan. "A civilian died last night on the streets and didn't stay that way. Just like the others. Hollywood was there. Rhage, do your thing."

John listened to the Brother make a report that was not a news flash. For eons, the war with the Lessening Society had pitted vampires against de-souled, paled-out humans who stank like baby powder and followed the Simon-says of their bus-exhaust leader, the Omega. Not anymore. Something else was stalking the night, prowling the back alleys of Caldwell's downtown, picking off vampires, not humans.

Shadows.

And not of the Trez and iAm variety.

These new entities were literally shadows and they were deadly, lashing out, killing mortal flesh while leaving clothes intact, their victims dying and being reborn into some other plane of existence out of the Zombies-R-Us playbook. The Brotherhood had so far found the reanimated victims before any humans did. But how long was that good luck going to last?

Nobody wanted BuzzFeed to sink its viral teeth into "The Zombie Apocalypse Is Real!!!" Or for Anderson Cooper to remote report from a zip code full of snap-jawed, rotting corpses. Or for there to be front-page stories on the National Guard battling an army of leg draggers.

Although knowing humans, it would probably be good for tourism in Caldie.

After Rhage finished sharing the details, all kinds of questions came from the Brotherhood. *What were the shadows? How many were there? Were they a new soldier for the Omega?*

"I don't think so," Butch said. "I can sense that shit, and there is nothing to them that rings that bell for me."

The former cop from Boston with the Fenway Park accent and the Fendi/Prada clothes would know. He had the Omega *inside* of him. He was the *Dhestroyer* Prophecy manifest. He would, someday, or so people said, end the war.

Pretty good source of intel, in other words.

There was more talk, and then someone came and stood next to John, although he was so into what was being discussed that he didn't look over.

Eventually, the King wrapped things up. As the rotation schedule was reviewed, something that scented of spring, not winter, tapped John's attention on the proverbial shoulder.

Zsadist was the one who'd joined him. Not a surprise. The scar faced Brother with the silent and deadly M.O. also liked to be out-of-the-way in a crowd. And he was working on . . . a blast from the past.

The Brother had unsheathed one of the black daggers that were strapped, handles down, to his chest, and he had taken the sharp blade to the skin of a green apple. Round and round, in his large, sure hands, the ribbon of skin spiraled down, the white, tart flesh exposed.

It made John remember another apple that that dagger had been applied to with such paring skill.

They had been on the bus about to leave the training center. John Matthew had been a pretrans smaller than all the other boys in his group, an outsider thrown not only into the program, but into the vampire world, by virtue of a birthmark that was on his left pectoral. Lash, the class bully, had been picking on him.

Something the fucker had been doing since John's first day of "school."

This had been before Blay and Qhuinn had become John's best friends. Before he had gone through the transition and come out on the other side of the change enormous, bigger than all he'd been smaller than before.

It had been before Wellsie, the only mother he had ever known, had been murdered.

He'd had such a hard time in the training program at first. So much weaker than everyone else, so uncoordinated, so shunned and ridiculed by all the trainees except for Blay and Qhuinn.

But an apple had cured all that.

Some nights after his entry into the program, maybe it was only a couple, but it had felt like a lifetime, John Matthew had gotten on the bus, and dreaded the ride home from the training center because of the bullying that was going to come his way. Just before the doors had closed, something huge and threatening had mounted the steps, its weight so great, the load had tilted the vehicle's suspension.

Zsadist was the Brother all of the trainees had feared the most. That scar that ran from his nose down to distort one side of his mouth was scary, but his black eyes were the true terror. Flat, unemotional, and disarmingly direct, the Brother's stare didn't pass right on through you. Instead, it consumed whatever it was trained on, eating you alive, owning you and your future.

It was the stare of a survivor of horrors, of torture, of depravity, for whom there were no unfamiliar cruelties.

The stare of a stone cold killer.

When Zsadist had sat down beside John Matthew on the bus, and had taken out a black dagger, John had figured his nights were over . . . but all the Brother did was peel the green apple in his hand.

Just as he'd done now.

Back then, Zsadist had offered a piece to John. And taken one for himself. And then again for John. Until there was nothing but the thinnest core left, whittled down to the brown seeds.

A clear message that John was protected by people who could make the lives of asshole trainees a living hell.

"—and for that, it's going to be just the Brotherhood."

John Matthew refocused on the King and wondered what he'd missed.

Wrath stroked George's boxy blond head. "There's no way of knowing what game Murhder is playing here so no nonessential personnel will be present."

Nonessential. Okay, ouch. But it was what it was.

When Zsadist cleared his throat, John Matthew looked over. A piece of apple was waiting on the black blade, the tart white flesh tempting.

John Matthew bowed his head in thanks and accepted the share. Then everyone was leaving, which was confusing until he realized that Wrath had no doubt arranged for the meeting with the insane Brother to be done at the Audience House. Made sense. There was no way the King would risk the females, young, and staff in this mansion by inviting that kind of loose cannon here.

No reason to open your front door to Heath Ledger's version of the Joker.

Zsadist and John funneled out of the study together, consuming the apple as they had the one on the bus, trading off on pieces. At the head of the grand staircase, they finished it off, nothing left but for that surgically pared down core, thin as a twig in the middle between the ends.

Z gave him the last piece.

As John accepted the simple gift, he tried to ignore how hard it was to be different from those around him. No voice. Not a Brother. Here by a stroke of luck that could just as easily have not connected him with Tohr.

Which meant he would have died during the transition without the blood of a female vampire to sustain him through the change.

As Zsadist nodded his head in goodbye, John did the same, but instead of going immediately to his and Xhex's room for his jacket, he walked over to the balustrade and stared down at the foyer below.

This mansion, full of elegance and grace, had been his father Darius's dream, or so John had been told. The Brother who had died by a car bomb just before John might have met him had always wanted the King and his elite guards under one roof, and had built this extensive house specifically for that purpose over a century ago. The *Field of Dreams* setup had been vacant for much longer than it had been currently lived in, however.

Those fallow eons had been a waste of a magnificent palace. The foyer was so lush it was more Imperial Russia than anything American and twenty-first century. With columns that were either malachite or polished claret marble, and flourishes made of gold-leafed plaster, and enough crystal to twinkle like the galaxy, John could remember stopping in his tracks when he first walked in. For a kid who had been raised in an orphanage—and then followed all that luxury up with living in a shithole apartment while working as a dishwasher and contemplating suicide—it had been a Daddy Warbucks situation.

Little Orphan Johnny.

Below, on the gorgeous mosaic floor, the Brothers were churning around Wrath, those huge bodies charged with aggression. Everyone hated when the King was exposed to risk, and the pull that John felt to be with them, to protect the last purebred vampire on the planet, to serve a male he respected with all his being, was so strong that his eyes prickled with tears of frustration.

He refused to let the emotion show.

That was a pussy move. Besides, who the hell was he to demand he be nominated to become a Brother? They had chosen Qhuinn for that honor, and it wasn't like Blay was bitching about being shut out.

John reached up to the left side of his chest. Through the skintight muscle shirt, he could feel the ridges of scars that formed the circle on his pec.

The Brothers all had the same marking in the same place. He'd always assumed his was a birthmark, and it was because of the strange pattern in his skin that he'd been brought into the training center. Everyone had wanted to know why a pretrans had one.

Later, he had learned that the inductees received them as part of a secret ceremony.

As his heart ached, he rubbed the uneven scars and wished he was not an outsider.

Thank God for his Xhex, he thought. At least he knew he could talk to her about all this and she would listen and not judge.

After all, there were no secrets between them.

CHAPTER FOUR

As Murhder rematerialized within the Caldwell city limits for the first time in twenty years, he was across the street from a Federal mansion in the wealthy part of town. He knew the house well, and had not been surprised to be directed to its address.

Darius owned the place and lived in it. The Brother had always liked the finer things, and Murhder had stayed in its basement bedrooms a number of times. Dearest Virgin Scribe, it seemed like both less than a week and more than a lifetime since he had last walked through its door, and shared a meal with D, and crashed either underground, or upstairs in that room with the twin beds.

Knowing who was waiting for him inside made him feel like he had lost more than just his mind. He'd lost his family.

It was going to be hard to look into Darius's eyes again. One good thing about insanity was that you didn't mourn all you no longer had. You were too busy trying to figure out what was real and what was not.

Murhder told himself to step off the curb. Walk across the snow-packed street to the front door. Knock to announce his presence— although surely the Brothers were staring at him even now. There were no lights on inside, which meant those fighters could be stacked ten deep in front of any piece of glass and no one could see them, know their numbers, assess their weaponry. He had to wonder if some were not outside, too. They would be careful to stay downwind so he couldn't scent them, and they would be silent as snow falling on a pine bough if they shifted their positions.

Murhder had not brought an overcoat. A jacket. Even a pullover. The oversight, coupled with the fact that he didn't even own a parka, seemed a revealing symptom of his mental disease.

But he hadn't forgotten everything. The three letters were in the back pocket of his slacks and the FedEx envelope with the documents was tucked under one arm. The former had been his priority as he'd departed. The latter he had left without and nearly hadn't gone back. Wrath's solicitor was expecting the papers, however, and knowing the King, there would be no letting that one go.

No coming back, either. Murhder fully intended to get what he needed and never see any of them again.

Bracing himself to step off the curb, he—

◆   ◆   ◆

The biomedical facility was about the horizontal, rather than the vertical, and from Murhder's hillside cover, he memorized the layout of interconnected, single-storied buildings, all central core with radiating spokes. No windows, except for at the entrance, and even there the glass was tinted and kept to a minimum. Parking lot was mostly empty, what cars there were congregating close to the way in.

Finally, *he thought.* I've found you.

There was no one walking around outside.

Nowhere to walk around, really.

The forest surrounding the remote site crowded in tight, another unbroken stretch of wall, the pines bough-to-bough blockers of access. There was a perimeter fence as well, the concrete barrier some twenty feet high with a curl of barbed wire at the top and a single gatehouse that appeared to be fitted with bulletproof panels of glass.

If you were a human, and you didn't have the right credentials? You weren't getting on the property much less inside the place.

Fortunately, he had other options.

Closing his eyes, he concentrated on calming himself, his respiration slowing down from the fast-pump of his impending attack to a far more steady, easy rhythm. As soon as he was able, he dematerialized, proceeding forward in a scatter of molecules. His entry point was an HVAC exhaust fan on the flat roof of one of the spokes, and in his invisible, mostly-air-state, he easily penetrated the aluminum mesh that covered the chute and continued through the duct work.

The interior layout was unknown to him, and that made re-forming dangerous. If he chose the wrong environment to materialize into, he could do damage to himself on things that weren't going to grow back.

But he was not worried about his own personal safety.

Vents. More ductwork. Filters he was able to get through because there were no steel components to them.

He came out through a furnace, reestablishing his physical form in a pitch-black room that smelled like desert-dry air and motor oil. The instant he was corporeal, his presence triggered a motion-sensitive light and his eyes burned in the glare. Bracing for an alarm, he palmed one of his guns and sank down into his thighs in case someone threw open the door that was before him.

When no one came in, he glanced back at the industrial furnace, took a deep breath, and dematerialized through the thin seam under that door.

Re-forming again, he found himself in a break room. Two maintenance men in dark green uniforms had their backs to him, the pair of them sitting at a table and watching basketball on a black-and-white TV as they smoked.

"Pardon me, gentlemen," he said dryly.

The humans jumped and whirled around. Before they could call for *help, he reached into their minds and paralyzed them where they stood. Then he chose the one on the right, and started popping the tops off the man's mental canisters, peering into all kinds of memories.*

Okay . . . wow.

The guy was cheating on his wife and worried he'd caught a venereal disease from his girlfriend. He had tremendous guilt over the betrayal, but he couldn't fathom his life without the other woman and he was obsessed with knowing who else the woman was sleeping with. Was it Charlie from Engineering—

Totally not what Murhder was looking for, but brains were not like a library full of books. There was no Dewey decimal system with a corresponding card catalogue to go by. Things came up in order of importance to the individual, not the temporal trespasser.

He switched to the guy on the left and hit the jackpot.

This one had just gotten promoted and was eager for the union-mandated break to be over so he could get back to work. He liked having some power around the place.

Much better, Murhder thought.

Moments later, he had the information he needed: Yes, there was a top secret laboratory, and it was not far.

Murhder wiped their memories clear of his interruption, and then inserted orders for them to sit back down and resume watching the game.

No reason to kick up complications until he absolutely had to.

Out in a corridor now, and there was no dematerializing anymore. He was way too hyped, his senses far too alive, and as a master would unleash a hound, so he released the most animalistic part of himself to carry forward: Ambulation was no longer a conscious coordination of limbs but an autonomic process serving the greatest good.

These humans had vampires imprisoned here. And they were doing unholy things to them.

He knew this down to his soul, and he was going to get it right this time. No distractions. No mistakes. No emotions.

All of which had led to his failure before.

When he rounded a corner and came upon two human males in white laboratory coats, he snapped their necks and left the bodies where they fell. Innocent victims? Not fucking hardly, and if time hadn't been of the essence, he would have taken their death knell pain to new levels—and not stopped with just this pair.

He would murder every single living, breathing entity in this torture chamber.

Instead, he kept going, pounding down corridors, passing in and out of the views of security cameras mounted in the ceiling.

The alarms sounded just as he stopped before a door that was made of steel, the one metal that vampires could not dematerialize through.

And they'd sealed the walls of whatever was on the far side with steel mesh.

These humans knew how to keep their victims on their premises, *he thought.*

Thank fuck they hadn't had the foresight to secure the entire facility that way—no doubt because they were more concerned with escape rather than rescue.

The explosives he carried were in his backpack, and he set up a quick wad of C4, shoved a detonator into its compliant form, and stepped back. Boom! was an understatement. *And before the smoke cleared, the door fell away from its jamb, landing on the floor inside like a tomb slab.*

Murhder jumped forward with his daggers palmed. No guns. He didn't want to kill any captive victims with stray bullets—

It was a full-blown medical laboratory with shelves full of supplies, an operating table that made him want to throw up, and all kinds of microscopes and monitors on counters and desks.

He slaughtered the lab workers in seconds. Three of them, all men in white coats. They offered no coordinated resistance to his attack, wasting time screaming and trying to run, and he went for the one who picked up a phone first. As he slashed their throats, those lab coats turned red down the front, and the laminated ID cards they wore around their necks got a pink stain.

As he dropped the last of them, he wheeled around and confronted a pair of mesh-covered cages. They were some six feet wide, fifteen feet long, and six feet tall, and through the densely woven steel that had been wrapped around them top to bottom, he saw a male on the left, naked with a food bowl and a container of water like he was a fucking animal.

There was a female in the other pen—

Dearest Virgin Scribe, she was heavily pregnant.

And as her eyes, hollow and haunted, stared out at him through the weave of steel bands, her mouth opened in shock.

Reality warped on him.

The face in the sacred glass. From the seeing bowl.

This was the female!

"You can't touch the bars," the male said over the din of the alarms and through the dissipating smoke. "They're charged."

Murhder shook himself back to attention. The male was up on his feet, but so emaciated, he was probably going to have to be carried out. And the female with the young was in even worse shape—she was on her knees, and he worried that was all she could do.

"Over there," the male said as he pointed to an electrical box mounted on the wall. "There's the circuit breaker for the cages."

No time to fuck around with fuses. Murhder traded one of his daggers for a gun and plowed six shots into the metal panel. Sparks flew and there was a minor explosion, more smoke with a metal bite to it released into the lab.

"Stand back," he ordered.

The male knew what he was thinking, and the poor guy got his fragile body out of the way as Murhder pointed his gun at the locking mechanism on the cage. The bullet he discharged split the casing, releasing a set of mechanical internal organs onto the floor.

The prisoner pushed the door wide and stumbled out on pin-thin legs that trembled so badly, the knobby knees knocked together. His hair had been shaved and there were electrodes attached to his skull.

Murhder focused on the pregnant female. "We can't leave her." The sprinkler system came on, water raining down on them, triggered by the release of smoke. "I need to . . ."

But he couldn't carry both of them and still have a hand free for a gun. And it went without saying that in their weakened states, neither one of them could dematerialize.

"I'm going to save her." His voice didn't sound like his own. "It is my destiny."

As Murhder approached the cage, the female dragged herself over to the hinged panel in front. Behind the steel mesh, her hands clenched on the bars, her mouth moving, her voice too weak to register through the alarm, the sprinkler, that internal screaming inside his head.

Her hair had been shaved off, too. She had bruises on her shoulders. To spare her modesty, he didn't look any further down.

"She won't make it out alive," the male said in a voice that cracked. "She's about to give birth."

"Fuck that," Murhder said as he reached for the latch. "I'll carry her out and then we'll get her medical attention—"

Security guards skidded into the doorway, three men in blue uniforms who were armed with autoloaders. Murhder shot at them as he pulled the male behind his body and moved for cover. Flipping a worktable over, he yanked a portion of glass-fronted metal shelving on top of the thing, all kinds of beakers and test tubes crashing as the front panels broke open and let loose its contents. Changing clips, he kept shooting, but it was without aim.

The male let out a bark. "I'm hit!"

More security guards at the door. Murhder looked at the other cage, at the female. She had flattened herself in the far corner as best she could, her big belly out to the side, her eyes locked on him as if she knew he was her one chance to get out of a nightmare.

He looked at the male, and did the risk benefit analysis in his head. Twice.

There was no chance of getting her out of that cage safely now, and as long as he was in the lab, bullets were going to continue to fly.

"I'll come back for her. I'll bring the brothers with me. I swear on my honor."

Another lead slug whizzed by his head. Two more went into the table and the shelving, the dull, metallic impacts belying the flimsy nature of their cover.

They both looked over at the female. She hadn't been hit, yet, and it was clear she could read what was on their faces. That mouth of hers opened wide as she clawed at the bars, at the mesh, her frantic eyes revealing the depths of the hell she was in—

◆   ◆   ◆

A car horn, set at the precise pitch of that terrified female's scream, brought him back to the present. He had stopped dead in the middle of the snowy street, and as he turned toward the sound, he was blinded by headlights. His arm went up to shield his eyes, but he didn't think to move—

The car hit him solidly, its tires locking on the snowpack, its mass times acceleration utterly unabated on the slippery road—and his body slammed into the hood and rolled up the windshield. He caught a quick passing survey of the clear winter sky as he passed over the roof, and then he hit the road on the far side facedown and in a jumble of limbs.

With a curse, he gave his body a second to register any complaints, and besides, the cold snow felt good against his hot cheek. Dimly, he noted the sound of car doors opening—three of them?

"Aw shit, my father's gonna kill me—"

"You shouldna drive high—"

"What the fuck, Todd—"

Murhder cranked his head around and focused on the three young human boys standing near the back end of a very expensive BMW.

"I'm okay," he told them. "Just go."

"You serious?" one of them said.

And that was when he caught a scent he hadn't smelled in years and years. As tears came to his eyes, he closed his lids.

"If he's fucking dead," he heard Xhex say in her hard-ass voice, "I will kill each one of you. Slowly."

CHAPTER FIVE

Xhex shouldn't have been anywhere near this car accident for a whole lot of reasons. First, she was supposed to be down at shAdoWs, keeping the humans in line as the club's head of security—and considering it was midnight on a Saturday, the fun was just getting rolling down there at work. Second, she didn't have any invitation to be at the King's Audience House for this Brotherhood-only business.

And third, she didn't actually want to see Murhder.

Be all that as it were, however, she was now in this shitshow way too deep to pull out.

Naturally, the trio of stoner idiots who'd gotten out of Daddy's motherfucking BMW was staring at her like she was their favorite wet dream upright in leathers. Which made her want to slap some sense and manners into them on principle. But there was no time for that. The Brother she'd never thought she'd cross paths with again was lying facedown in the middle of the road like he was paralyzed or had broken something seriously material to ambulation—and considering that the house he was in front of was crawling with vampires and this was a ritzy human neighborhood where people had security guards on their prop-erties and were themselves iPhone'd up the ass, it was more important to clear the scene.

"Get the fuck of here," she ordered the boys. "Or I'm calling the police."

Todd I, II, and III looked at each other like they were either com-municating telepathically or so stoned and dumbfounded at her appear-ance, they'd lost the ability to speak.

"Now!" she barked.

The three slipped and slid in their loafers to get back into the car, and whoever was behind the wheel hit the gas so hard, tire treads of snowpack pelted her lower legs.

As she turned back to Murhder, she had hope he'd be getting to his feet. Nope. He was still lying on his stomach with his face turned to the side—and his eyes were closed, his dark lashes low on his prominent cheekbone.

Dropping herself to her haunches, she swallowed hard as she tried to get a read on his condition. Even though it was dark, there were peach-colored streetlights at regular intervals down the lane, the whole neighborhood glowing sure as if the wealth of its homeowners had been brought out to the curbs in gold bars. And she tracked every nuance of him in the man-made gloaming.

At least he was breathing, and as soon as she saw that, she took note of other things: His black hair was still long and streaked with red. He was still a very big male. And his scent hadn't changed.

God . . . so much. She and Murhder had been through so much to-gether, too little of it any good.

"Do you require medical attention?" she said hoarsely.

Like she was addressing a stranger who had been struck. Instead of a male she had been to hell and back with.

Well, actually, that hyperbole wasn't exactly true. She had rejoined life. He had not.

"Murhder? Are you dead?" As she whispered the words, her breath came out in puffs that were carried away in the cold air.

"Strange question to ask someone," came a croaking reply.

As her eyes stung with relief, she glanced in the direction the BMW had sped off. "So I take it the answer's no."

Murhder popped his lids and looked up at her. A sheen of tears made the peach of his irises shimmer. "You look the same."

As they made eye contact, the impact of their shared past was so great, she was knocked off her crouch, her ass hitting the cold snow, her brain unable to deny the onslaught of memories: Him breaking into that room up in the *symphath* colony, thinking he was rescuing her from an abduction. His shock as he realized she had come willingly . . . to see her blooded family.

Which meant she was not as she had portrayed herself to be.

And then her relations streaming in and realizing that she had lied to them, as well.

Symphaths and vampires did not mix in those days. Still didn't.

What had happened after the truth had come out had been one nightmare after another. Her relatives had tortured Murhder in the way only *symphaths* could, getting into his subconscious and making hash out of every part of who he was as a male, as a vampire, as a mortal entity. Then they had cast her out of the colony—and not as in banishment. As in selling her to humans as a lab animal to be experimented on.

And the story hadn't ended there.

"I shouldn't have come," she said roughly.

When John Matthew had texted her that he was going out into the field with Blay because the Brotherhood had a special meeting at the Audience House? She should have just sent back her regular response of "Be safe, love you." Then she should have put her phone in her back pocket and continued to monitor the crowd at the bar, on the dance floor, in the rear hallways where the bathrooms were. She should have stuck to her own lane because she, like any other person who wasn't a Brother, had no goddamn reason to be here.

But as a *symphath*, she had sensed the unrest in the Brotherhood's household for the last several nights. The anxiety had been the deep kind, the soul kind, and each one of the Brothers' emotional grids had registered the same upset. There was only one explanation, and even though she had pledged to herself she would not use her species' tool-box among the vampires who were now her family, she had lifted the lid on one of the warriors.

Murhder was coming from South Carolina—

Male voices caught her attention and she looked up. Members of the Brotherhood were streaming out of Darius's old place into the snow, their heavy bodies covered with loose coats to hide their weapons.

"Help is on the way," she said as she got to her feet.

"Don't leave."

Guilt stung as she turned away, and it wasn't on account of leaving him in the street. "Good luck with your Brothers."

"I'm not one of them anymore."

As she dematerialized, she hated that she'd been seen. The Brothers all knew what had gone on between her and Murhder back before she'd headed up to the colony that final time, and she'd just as soon they not know she'd been anywhere near the male in the present.

And as for John Matthew, yes, he was aware of the who, what, where, and when of her time with Murhder, but she'd just as soon things stayed on that newspaper article level. After all, she'd—what did they call it—she'd "processed" what had happened, including what had been done to her and how Murhder had lost his mind and everything the male had done afterward.

It was over. Finished. In the past, moving on, focusing on the future.

So there was no reason to reopen anything—

And yet she had come tonight. To see him.

She was surprised he was still alive.

The fact that John didn't know she had sought out another male—even though it was, obviously, not to have sex or bond or feed or anything like that—felt like a betrayal of her mate because it was an admission that, much as she hated it and wished it were not true, there was unfinished business between her and the Brother who had been kicked out for insanity.

Business that threatened every part of the life she held so dear.

◆   ◆   ◆

This was not the way he wanted to return the fold, Murhder thought: Face-down in the street. Eyes leaking. Throat choked.

As Xhex dematerialized and the Brotherhood approached in fighter formation, he reflected it was also not the way he wanted to see that female again—although he would have been hard-pressed to define exactly under what conditions he would have chosen to meet up with her. She was the fulcrum of his downfall, the eye of the storm that had taken him into madness, the catalyst, although not the precise cause, of his disintegration.

All things considered, it was a relief to have to face the Brothers—which was saying something, as he had no real interest in seeing them, either.

As he pushed his torso off the snowpack, and rolled over to sit up on his ass, he measured the males who came unto him. He recognized all but two, and noted two were missing: Wrath wasn't among them and neither was Darius, no doubt because the latter had stayed inside to guard the former.

When he tried to get to his feet, he became aware that his right thigh bone was probably broken. The pain that registered as he moved his leg was a chainsaw that rode up his spine and slashed through his brain, his vision going in and out as he attempted to put weight on it. He ended up back on his butt.

So he was stuck looking up at all of them as they formed a circle around him.

Like they didn't trust him to behave himself.

Made sense. With his brain the way it was, thanks to Xhex's people, he was far from on their level functionally speaking, and he didn't resent the tacit reminder of reality.

Fuck knew he was used to being crazy.

"Someone mind giving me a hand," he said dryly.

Not a request. More like an if-one-of-you-assholes-doesn't-help-me-up-we're-going-to-still-be-here-at-sunrise kind of thing.

A palm presented itself directly in his face, and he took what was offered without caring whose it was. The hoist up was slow and steady, and after he balanced on his left foot, he dragged in a deep breath and met a pair of glowing yellow eyes.

He should have known it was Phury. He'd always been a decent guy, like Darius and Tohr.

"Welcome back to Caldwell," the male said.

The "my brother" was left out because it was no longer applicable. And somehow, that hurt more than his leg.

He couldn't look at any of the others.

"Let's get this over with." Murhder nodded at the house. "Wrath in there, I take it?"

In lieu of an answer, Phury stepped in close and hitched a hold to Murhder's waist. "Lean on me."

"Ordinarily, I'd argue with that."

"This is not ordinary."

"Wait, someone needs to pick up that FedEx envelope over there." Actually, he didn't give a shit if they left the thing in the street. "It has the papers Wrath wants."

As somebody did the duty, he and Phury made a slow pace toward a snowbank that would have been a short leap to get over pre-impact, but now presented itself as a Mini-Everest. On the far side of their ascent and descent, Murhder needed to breathe through the pain for a minute before they could continue.

When they resumed their progress, moving toward the elegant house's shoveled walkway, he was acutely aware that no one was speaking. No one was touching him, other than that which was medically required. No one was too close.

And they all had their hands on a weapon that was discreetly held by the thigh. Some were guns, some were those black daggers that he had once had strapped to his own chest.

Jeez, you go rogue once and slaughter a bunch of humans after they torture your girlfriend, and suddenly you're a leaper.

Up the front walk that had been cleared and de-iced with rock salt, the wind that whistled through bare branches making him want to cover his ears. The pitch was too close to that scream he heard all the time in his head.

Up steps that had been de-iced as well. Onto a porch that was long as the front of the mansion and bare of fine wicker furniture, no doubt in deference to the inclement weather.

Now they were at the broad front door, which he could recall going in and out of countless times with Darius.

Phury stopped and unhitched his hold. "We have to search you."

"I got guns, two of them. That's it—no, I also have a hunting knife in my ass pocket. Do *not* remove those letters."

Murhder stared straight ahead at the wood panels as his weapons were taken off him. And then someone patted him down.

He closed his eyes and lowered his head. "I didn't lie. Christ."

"Come on." Phury opened the way in. "We're going to the right."

"The dining room."

"You remember."

"I practically lived here with you, do *you* remember?"

Thanks to all the walking, Murhder's thigh had hit red-hot-poker-pissed-off on a pain scale where one was a splinter, and ten was red-hot-fucking-poker. Sweat broke out across his chest and rode up his throat to his face, and goddamn, he was glad he hadn't eaten before he'd come or there would have been one hell of a mess to clean up.

Was Fritz still the butler in this house? he wondered.

"Over this way—"

"I know," he snapped.

The growls that percolated up behind him were easily ignored. If they were going to kill him outright, they never would have let him in the house. They'd have thrown him into the trunk of a sedan to take him to a more remote location.

The double doors to the dining room were closed, but he could sense Wrath's presence on the far side—and what went through his mind was that this was a return to the Old Ways, to the private guard function of the Black Dagger Brotherhood. Previously, it hadn't been needed because Wrath had always refused to lead his people.

Something big had changed.

"I'm going to have to ask you to keep your hands visible at all times," Phury said. "No sudden movements—"

A male voice interjected coldly. "I'll fucking rip your head off if you go anywhere near him."

Murhder smiled and glared over his shoulder, meeting a set of diamond eyes that were sharp as blades. "V. Always with the sentimentality."

The Brother with the icy stare and the tattoos at his temple had added a goatee to his face. Other than that, he was unchanged, his intelligence radiating outward as much as his urge to kill. And oh, look, he still smoked.

"I don't give two shits about you," Vishous said on an exhale.

"Same brand of Turkish tobacco. You still get it from that head shop down on Market?"

"Fuck you."

"You always wanted to—"

Phury jerked Murhder back around. "This is *not* helping."

The doors flew open, and there was the King, standing in the center of the dining room, under the chandelier where the long mahogany table should have been.

The wave of sadness that hit Murhder was so unexpected, he weaved on his good foot, and he blinked his eyes quick even though no tears came. It wasn't that Wrath was different—hell, it would have been a shock if anything had changed about the autocratic leader of the species. And it wasn't that Murhder was in the house of his old friend,

Darius, and nervous about seeing the male again. And it wasn't even that this could be a foolish rabbit hole he was going down.

There was a ring on Wrath's forefinger.

Ancient, and fitted with an enormous black diamond, there was only one that had ever been like it.

The male had never worn the thing before. Had refused to bear the mantle of his birthright. Had shunned all manner of what his father and his father's father, and his father's father's father, had done with such great humility and effect.

Wrath, son of Wrath, truly was the King.

And for the first time, Murhder got a sense of all he had missed. Years had had no meaning to him as he had stalked that old attic down in South Carolina: Nights had run into nights that had become weeks and months and years . . . and decades . . . and none of that had mattered. He had had absolutely no cause to mark any passage of time as significant, so great had been the depths to which he had fallen.

Now, staring at that ring, the inexorable march of mortality had a bright light upon it, although it was not his own loss that devastated him.

Murhder took the letters out, and spoke before formally addressed. "I need you to help me find this female."

CHAPTER SIX

John Matthew proceeded down the sidewalk, his shitkickers crunching through that which had been slush at some point during the day, but was now refrozen ice-fossils of boot prints. On either side of the one-way street, there were apartment buildings that had been new seventy or eighty years ago, the five- and six-story brick walkups showing every scratch and dent of wear and tear, their shutters half-missing and off-kilter, their slate roofs gaping with vacancies, their concrete stairs to dingy front doors un-railing'd and uneven as mountain passes.

He had patrolled this area many times in the last couple of years, and he thought of the summer months when the trash rot threw off gaseous clouds of nasty and the humans were out in greater numbers. It was a toss-up what was worse, the cold with the bad footing of the Decembers and Januarys or the complications and the stench of the hot months.

"Two more blocks," Blay said next to him.

Then we go west, John Matthew signed.

"Yup, west."

This was the "bad" part of town, where the drug dealers were plentiful and the good people stayed inside unless they really had to go somewhere. And he supposed their precise location within the twenty-block zone of narcotics violations should have registered before now. He wasn't even sure why it hadn't, although he was feeling off-kilter, some premonition dogging him and making him tense, the existential equivalent of oysters that gave you nightmares.

He stopped abruptly in front of one of the buildings, and stared up at its decaying exterior, counting the windows so he got the floors right.

"What is it?" Blay asked. "You see something?"

Not officially, no. Just where he had stayed when he'd been working as a dishwasher. In fact . . .

He walked forward a couple of feet. Yes, here. Here was the curb where Tohr had picked him up, where his few belongings had gone into the Brother's black Range Rover and they had driven off, to a new world, a new home . . . a new family.

Where Wellsie had known that his touchy, pretrans stomach could only handle ginger and rice. Where he had slept feeling safe for the first time in his life. Where he had found others like himself.

Even though he had previously assumed that if he were among humans, that was true enough.

"John?"

He jumped as Blay said his name, and he meant to respond. His brain was jammed. Something was tapping on his foundation, testing the strength of his concrete, and he could not figure out why—

The vibration that went off at chest level was the reality check he needed, and he went for his phone. The text was from the newly instituted emergency alert system, where calls from civilians were routed through a team of volunteers manning a central number 24/7.

911 for the species.

"Shit," Blay said as he looked at his own screen. "We got another one."

And it was right by shAdoWs, where Xhex was.

With the Brotherhood otherwise occupied on the Murhder thing, he and Blay were the only buck-stops-here available, and they dematerialized to the cluster of clubs in the old warehouse part of downtown.

As they re-formed one block over from the location that had been given, they got out guns and proceeded in silence to an alleyway that allowed them to visualize the precise address.

In war, you could never be too sure who was calling what in, and the last thing they needed was to get capped by a squad of *lessers* that had somehow gotten the number and set a trap—

The scent of vampire blood was thick in the air.

Keeping himself tucked against the brick wall, he had his forty up and double-palmed as he let his gun lead the way. Instincts prickling, body tensed for anything, it was a relief to get out of the headspace he'd been in.

Yup, far better to run the risk of being killed by the enemy than to dwell in his existential swamp.

At the intersection of the alley and the street proper, he stopped and used his ears. Something was shifting in the snow, the soft sounds of limbs churning on top of winter's cold ground cover barely carrying over the distant thump of shAdoWs's music. The smell of vampire blood was even stronger, but there was no other scent mixed with it, no sickly sweet baby powder of *lessers* or the cologne/soap/shampoo-infused calling card of humans.

John swung around the hard-cut corner of the brick building, gun pointed at the sound/smell combination.

Tragedy had struck.

About fifteen feet away, a civilian male was flat on his back and clutching his chest with one hand. The other was clawing at the dirty snow as he moved his legs like he was still running from what had mortally wounded him.

"I'll cover," Blay said.

John ran over and dropped down. The first thing he did was assess the clothing. Nothing torn, not the fine cashmere coat or the fine cashmere sweater underneath. But there were bloodstains on the chest.

"Help me . . ." There was a gurgle to the words, as if the civilian's airway were blocked. "Help . . ."

Those eyes struggled to focus, and the hand that was digging into the snow grabbed onto John's leather jacket, bringing him closer.

"I don't . . . feel right . . ."

Alerted by a scent, John looked up sharply, his senses firing. A split second later, another civilian male, in nice clothes as well, came racing around the back of the club—with Xhex and a bouncer right behind him.

As the trio came up to John, his *shellan* was clearly surprised to see him, and signed, *You need help?*

The other civilian started talking fast. "We were supposed to meet friends out here, and we were waiting—all of a sudden this black shadow comes from out of nowhere—"

Take him out of the way, John signed. *We don't want him seeing what happens next.*

"Hey," she said to the male, "let's you and I go back into the club—"

"He's my cousin! I can't leave him—"

Xhex stared at the civilian, her dark gray eyes steady, fixated. Hypnotizing. A moment later, the civilian nodded and followed behind her, a train that had changed tracks. The bouncer, who was also of the species, covered them both.

Just before they went around the corner, Xhex looked back at John. Her face was drawn and pale. But death did that to people, even the strong ones.

John signed, *I've got this. Don't worry.*

She nodded. And continued out of sight.

Meanwhile, the wounded civilian was getting more frantic with his movements, as if he knew his end was coming closer, and he was racing against his demise in the only way his broken body could. To offer compassion, John moved his own lips, speaking in silence things that he hoped would have been comforting if he'd been able to speak and the victim able to hear.

But the male was beyond that now. His eyes rolled back, the whites flashing, and his breathing became even more labored.

John quickly screwed a suppressor onto the muzzle of his gun, and he was aware that his own lungs stopped working as he took the weapon and put it directly to the temple of the dying male—

"What are you doing—what the fuck are you doing!"

John looked up. Two human men had come around the back of the club, and even though they were weaving in the still night like they were in a stiff wind, they were sober enough to recognize where the business end of a gun had been pointed. Too bad they didn't understand that this was none of their fucking business.

The men rushed forward, all Good Samaritans in savior mode, but Blay was on them—or would have been, if the sickly sweet stink of the enemy didn't waft over from the opposite direction, the worst kind of party crasher ever.

John cursed to himself as Blay dematerialized, clearly to get on the slayer who was somewhere close by.

"What the *fuck* you doin'!"

The human man was in his mid-twenties, tall and lanky as if he either did a lot of coke or was an organic, non-processed foodie with a vegan slant. His buddy was along the same lines, man-bun'd and hipster-clothed, but unlike the guy in front, he was a true New Yorker who didn't want to get involved in shit that wasn't his problem: He was staring at the ground, shaking his head, slowing down.

When he finally did glance over, he recoiled and changed flight paths completely.

"I'm out of here," he muttered as he turned away.

His friend grabbed him. "Get your phone—I lost mine. Call nine-one-one—make a video! This needs to be on video! We need to go—"

As John Matthew straightened to his full height, the human with the big plans quieted down a little, proof positive that the survival mechanism hadn't been completely eradicated by all those chemicals he'd taken in at the club.

"I'm not afraid of you!" he shouted.

Considering the guy knew there was a gun with a suppressor involved here, that seemed like bluster over brains, but John was done dealing with the interruption. With a force of will, he entered the human's mind, burrowing into that gray matter, shutting down memory function and rewiring—

"Fuuuuuuck . . ."

Something about the tone of that curse got John's attention and he paused in the middle of his erase job. The other human, who'd been on the way out, was staring over John's shoulder, his face showing the kind of horror a person would feel if they came up on a dead body.

Or, as it turned out, if a dead body came up on them.

The mortally injured civilian was back on his feet, but not because he had magically rebounded from his injuries. His eyes had stayed rolled back, nothing but white showing between those lashes, and his mouth was open and snapping, fangs fully descended.

Clap. Clap. Clap.

The lock of that scissor bite as the jaw reflexively opened and closed was piranha and then some, and even though the reanimated corpse shouldn't have been able to see, he somehow focused on John.

The damn thing lunged without warning, and there was none of that *Walking Dead* uncoordinated shit. The corpse's hands went for John's throat like it had been trained in the art of strangulation, and when John ducked the hold, there was no break in the assault. Those snapping jaws rerouted to his shoulder, his upper arm, the just-dead-a-second-ago like a banshee unleashed with hellfire in its veins and the strength of ten thousand linebackers in its muscles.

John punched his palm forward, catching the thing in the center of the chest and holding it out of bite range. Then he plowed his gun into the gut on an upward angle and squeezed off four rounds. The corpse jerked in time to the shots, onetwothreefour—

And kept right on coming at him.

Not a pain receptor in sight, evidently.

As he wasn't sure whether a bite from the thing would welcome him to the reanimation club, John lunged to the side, grabbed the corpse by the waist, and went discus on the sitch, slinging his undead attacker into bricks and mortar.

It didn't even register the impact.

But John had time to point-blank a shot to its head.

There was a screeching sound that made his ears sing, and then the corpse went deadweight, falling through the cold air and landing like a tabletop in the snow.

John stepped over, put two more bullets into its brain, and then waited, his breath leaving in locomotive-puffs of condensation—

Abruptly, he remembered the peanut gallery of those two humans. Glancing over his shoulder, he erased their memories, wiping things clean and sending them away.

As they wandered off and nothing moved at his feet, he commenced a frantic self-assessment, checking for breaks in his skin under his leather jacket.

The jacket had been nailed a number of times, those twin punctures of fangs giving him a case of the cold sweats—

"John!"

Blay came stomping around the corner, the black blood of slayers spattered on his face and his jacket, his dagger traded for a pair of guns.

I'm okay, John signed. *But we need to get this moved.*

"I'll take one end," his old friend said.

The two of them hand-and-foot'd the now-immobile-and-please-God-stay-that-way body and carried the civilian further into the alley, a trail of bright red blood staining their boot prints in the dirty city snow. Laying the male facedown again, John took out a set of handcuffs and clicked the corpse's wrists together.

The sound of Blay texting was a series of *tip-tip-tips* that made John's nerves shimmy. Not that they needed the help. Standing over the remains with his gun out and pointed at the leaking head, he felt sick, especially as he looked at the stain that marked the path of the carry.

As of now, there was no additional scent of *lesser.*

Please, God, let things stay that way. Because the slayers used to work in squads, back when there had been more of them.

"I just texted Tohr," Blay said as he put his cell away. "They're going to send the surgical unit, ETA from the garage bunker is three and a half minutes."

John could only nod. Even if one of his hands wasn't busy holding his Smith & Wesson, he didn't have anything to add.

He focused on the handcuffs that were biting into the flesh of those wrists and then on the back of the head. Ordinarily, if you were detaining someone and they were lying facedown, you wanted to make sure they had an air source. Not a problem here. The civilian's nose and mouth were right in the snowpack, but it didn't matter.

A great wave of sadness hit him as he thought about the *mahmen* and father who had brought this male into the world however long ago. In the vampire species, to have a successful live birth was a blessing given the incredibly high numbers of maternal and fetal deaths. The parents must have been so thrilled, assuming mom lived as well.

And yet all that ended here, in a shitty alley, in a rough part of town, facedown in the snow with fucking restraints on the corpse because no one was sure whether the term "dead" as applied in this case counted as a permanent thing.

I'm sorry, he mouthed to the body.

It struck John how random fate was with both its blessings and its curses. How he'd won a nick-in-time jackpot back as a pretrans whereas this poor male had gotten short-straw'd in the most terrifying of ways.

Who made those decisions, he wondered. *Who doled out such cosmic wins and losses?*

People said it had been the Scribe Virgin, but V's mom was long gone now. So who was there to pray to when an innocent male died in such a gruesome way?

Maybe, like the arrangement of stars in the night sky, it was all just random, with only the minds of the afflicted and the affluent alike trying to make sense of the great swings of pain and grace . . . while the disinterested universe churned on through relentless, infinite time, on a journey to nowhere.

Who the fuck knew.

CHAPTER SEVEN

M urhder waited for Wrath to walk out of the dining room, but the King stayed where he was, under the chandelier. The Brotherhood were the ones who moved. They closed ranks and formed a wall facing their "guest."

Impressive. Like being in a forest. Where the trees were made of tigers. And you had sirloin steaks as clothes.

"I signed the papers you wanted," Murhder called out to his King through the breathing barricade. "And now you have to help me."

Wrath didn't reply to that, not that it had been a question. And in the crushing silence of the foyer, Murhder got impatient with the game—

"I don't have to do shit for you," Wrath said.

Ah, yes, that deep voice. Still autocratic in tone. Still aristocratic in the drawl.

Still with the vocabulary of a trucker.

The King was staring straight ahead, his black wraparounds positioned toward no one in particular—and the disconnect between focal point and head direction suggested that Wrath's poor eyesight had faded into a true blindness.

To confirm this, Murhder tilted his body to the left. And indeed, that cruelly handsome face did not follow the movement.

Those nostrils flared, however, the King clearly testing his scent. "I want to see him alone."

Big surprise, the Brotherhood voted no on that idea, a chorus of grunts and creative curses bubbling up those thick throats.

Not his problem. "Where do you want me."

"Let him through, boys." When none of Wrath's guards complied, the growl that came out of the dining room sounded like someone had started a Ferrari. "Let him in, right fucking now!"

"You're not seeing him alone—"

Murhder wasn't sure who said that, but PDQ, the opinion didn't matter. All of a sudden, a cold blast came from out of nowhere, as if a door to the outside had been opened—no, wait. The arctic chill was emanating from Wrath's body, and even Murhder felt his butt pucker in warning.

The Fence of Ferocity broke in the center and parted, the disapproving guards moving away, letting him pass. And as he limped for the open doors, he could feel the stares on his back and decided it was a wonder he wasn't knocked on his face again just from the death rays.

The second he was through the archway, the dining room's great wooden panels slammed shut, and that was when he noticed the dog. A golden retriever was cowering behind Wrath, its head lowered, its big body tense as it sought protection from the vampire it was using as a shield.

"Relax, Murhder," Wrath said dryly as he bent down and picked up the one hundred pounds of blond fur. "You're freaking out my dog."

"Me? You're sure it's not that private guard of yours?"

Wrath turned in a deliberate way, as if he were orientating himself by memory rather than sight, and then he walked toward the fireplace. As he went, he stroked the dog, who put his front paws on each of the King's shoulders and nestled his muzzle deep into all that long black hair. The way those kind brown eyes squeezed shut suggested the animal was trying to find his happy place.

Wonder if there's room for two there, Murhder thought.

The King settled his weight into one of two armchairs, and positioned the dog on his lap. "George doesn't like me to raise my voice."

"Then he must be anxious as hell most of the time."

Wrath let his head rest on the high back of the chair. His hand, the one with the King's ring, went up and down on the retriever's flank.

"Tell me why you think any problem of yours is a problem of mine," he said.

"I need your help."

"Doesn't answer my question."

"It's the truth."

"Twenty years, and you show up here with a demand. So like you. I take it you're back to your old self again."

"I just have to find this female—"

"Do you have any idea the kind of problems you caused? On the way to your whatever the hell it was—your breakdown?"

Murhder closed his eyes and muttered to himself.

"What was that?" Wrath cut in sharply. "Are you suggesting I'm not allowed to have an opinion, after we cleaned up your fucking mess?"

"I didn't ask you to do anything for me."

"Bullshit. You disappeared on us for two months, and then showed up from out of nowhere obsessed with shit that had nothing to do with the war against the Lessening Society." Wrath leaned to the side and picked a folder up off the floor. "You burned one biomedical firm down. And then went to another and did *this.*"

With a toss, the King sent the folder and its contents flying, the color photographs inside fanning out in a slide show that ended at Murhder's feet.

Bodies. Staked to the ground. Their internal organs removed.

He didn't need to be reminded of the images. He'd seen the massacre up close and personal—which was what happened when you were the one responsible for the carnage.

What he was *not* responsible for was that fire in the first facility.

That had been Xhex going back and taking care of business for herself—and he would never forget the sight of her standing against the backdrop of the flames, vengeance in the flesh. But he had protected her secrets back then and he was still going to protect her now.

If the Brotherhood had it wrong and blamed him? What the hell did he care?

"You're right, you didn't technically ask us to clean up the mess," Wrath said. "But what you did to those humans made Hannibal Lecter look like an amateur. You made things really goddamn complicated on your way to the exit."

Murhder's knees popped as he squatted down and gathered up the glossies. "It was less than they deserved—"

"You field dressed seven scientists on the grounds of one of the country's foremost medical research companies."

Murhder shoved the eight-by-tens back into the folder. "They were experimenting on our kind, Wrath. On a male and on a *pregnant* female. What did you expect me to do, leave them a strongly worded letter?"

There was a period of silence. "That wasn't the way to handle it."

"I tried to get both of those vampires out." Murhder cleared his throat as his voice cracked. "But I had to . . . leave the pregnant female behind because everything went wrong."

A barrage of images blinded him . . . all things he couldn't bear thinking about: After that emaciated male got shot, Murhder himself was drilled in the side by a bullet. More humans came. Complete chaos with all the gunfire. Then the male died in his arms.

Murhder had been left with no choice but to dematerialize out of there before he himself lost too much blood.

By the time he'd returned the next night, after having fed from a Chosen and gotten his strength back, the pregnant female had been moved.

That was when he'd lost it and gone on the hunt for those scientists. The first white-coated lab worker he'd come to? He'd searched the man's memories and discovered he had been in on the top secret project—and

Murhder had intended to delve further to find out where the female had been taken. His hands, however, had taken over, his brute strength fueled by vengeance and unchecked after what the *symphaths* had done to him. He'd choked the human unconscious and dragged him to the next human he'd found. And the next. And a fourth.

All of them had worked in the lab where the vampires had been held.

Seven of them.

Murhder had lived up to his name that night. Had stacked the men like logs and then carried them out via a receiving dock. Which was where he'd found the iron stakes. And the mallet.

He'd used his black dagger only after he'd immobilized them.

The men had regained consciousness screaming. And as other humans had come running, he took control of their minds and froze them where they stood. By the time dawn had come, he had an audience of a hundred stupor'd sentries, all staring in zombie-like trances at the work he did. Wrath called it field dressing. But that was just the end result.

He had experimented on those seven. Taken his time and staggered his attention, working on one for a while, before leaving him alive and moving to the next. And the next and the next. Until the final . . . after which he'd returned to the first. His victims had heard the suffering and begging of their ilk—all the while knowing their turn was coming again soon.

It was what Xhex and that male and that pregnant female had been through.

Payback. Yet it had cost him. Unhinged as he was, he had not gotten the information he needed, did not know where the female had been taken, had no other way of finding her location. And he had realized this only as he had returned to Caldwell.

Coming back to the present, he cleared his throat. "I've had to live for the last twenty years with the knowledge that I left one of ours behind. Who was pregnant. Do you have any idea what that's been like? I had to see her through the bars of a fucking cage, screaming for me to help her, to not leave her, to not let them continue to torture her—and she was in labor. Do you have *any* concept of what that has done to me . . ." He rubbed his stinging eyes. "I know you think I'm insane for what I did to those doctors. I know that was why I got kicked out of the Brotherhood. You couldn't trust me anymore. I get that. But it was the right thing to do and I will not apologize for my vengeance."

"Of course not," Wrath muttered. "Why would you."

Murhder shook his head. "Balance is what the Scribe Virgin demands, right? It's a universal law. And I made sure I took the suffering of our kind out of the hides of those who had been responsible. You used to be an eye-for-an-eye kind of male. I saw what you did to slayers. You think the way you treated our enemy was just because you wanted to save our race? Bullshit. You watched your parents get slaughtered in front of you by *lessers*. So you know *exactly* what I was doing when I took my damn time with those humans."

Wrath lowered his head, as he would have if he were looking at his dog. And his hand shifted to the retriever's silken ear.

"I got these letters." Murhder put the folder of photographs on the floor and took the correspondence out of his pocket even though the King couldn't see the envelopes. "The first one came about six months ago. Then a second. Finally, last week, the third. They're from the pregnant female. She must have lived, somehow, and then gotten away from them. This is my chance not to fail her, Wrath. Finally, I can do right by her."

The King's head lifted. "How do you know it's her?"

"In the final letter, she describes exactly what happened when I broke into the lab. I haven't told anyone those details."

"And you want us to find her for you?"

"I don't have those kinds of intel resources. I wouldn't even know where to start." Murhder wanted to fall to his knees, clasp his hands and go into straight-up implore mode. "I just need to know where she is so I can help her."

"What does she want you to do for her?"

Murhder opened his mouth. Then closed it. The female wanted him to go after her son, who was apparently still with the humans, and nearing his transition. If there wasn't another vampire of the opposite sex available to him, he was going to die during the change. Assuming the humans hadn't killed him already.

Revealing that mission, given Murhder's track record for destroying things and causing headaches for the race in laboratory settings? Not smart.

He focused on his intent rather than the details because undoubtedly Wrath's keen nose would pick up on it if he lied or tried to hide anything.

"I just want to be whatever she needs. It's all that matters in my life."

CHAPTER EIGHT

W hich bathroom did John go into?"
        As Xhex put the demand out there, her number two
        pointed to the back of the club. "Boss man's, I think. He
took the stairs up."

"Thanks—and handle shit for me, will ya? I'm taking twenty minutes."

"Yeah, sure. I got you."

Xhex headed across the dance floor. It was an even-Steven on
whether it was faster to cut around the edges where there were fewer
people, but more distance to cover, or plow through the packed, stacked,
and jacked clientele who were grinding on each other like God was
going to outlaw intercourse first thing in the morning.

She'd never had any problem playing bowling ball to their tenpins,
however, and as she shoved the bodies out of her way, she was rougher
than usual.

God . . . what a scene out in that alley. It had to be more of those
shadows. She'd heard the Brotherhood talking at the dining room table
about what happened to this new kind of victim, the wakeup call from

some unholy place reanimating that which should, however tragic the deaths were, stay cold and stiff. Apparently, the only way to keep the corpses down was to shoot them in the head with hollow-tipped bullets filled with water from the Sanctuary's fountain.

Fucking Omega. New games, new tactics. Then again, the war was coming to an end, the Brotherhood finally getting a leg up on the slayer population, so of course the enemy was going to get desperate and therefore inventive.

And on top of all that? There was another reason she wanted to see her mate, other than a garden variety are-you-okay, God-that-was-awful, man-this-war-sucks kind of thing.

As the congestion of the dance floor cleared, Xhex nearly broke out into a run when she had a clean shot to the stairwell. And as she ascended and went for the door to Trez's second-floor command center, her heart was pounding so hard, she forced herself to stop, regroup, and take some deep breaths before she entered.

Closing her eyes, the image she got on the backs of her lids was not one she was happy about.

But shit, Murhder was exactly the same as she remembered. Even facedown in the snow, it was obvious his body hadn't changed. He was still built as the Brother he had been, all long legs thick with muscle and broad shoulders and heavy arms. And damn, his hair . . . all that black and red stuff had been fanned out in the snow, the streaks that ran through the midnight parts still not ginger colored, like Blay's, but barn red. Blood red.

She'd assumed he colored it when she first met him. Nope.

No clue what genetic mutation was responsible for that combo, and she certainly hadn't seen it on anyone else.

Speaking of which, she had never expected to see him again. After she'd learned he was at that B&B down south, she had sent him the address of her hunting cabin, but he had never sought her out. She didn't blame him. There wasn't much to say between them, was there.

Not after she'd lied to him. Not after what her bloodline had done to him. Not after what he had done after that.

Rehvenge, now king of the *symphaths*, had been the one who arranged for Murhder's release from the colony. She'd still been in captivity at BioMed at that point, but she escaped not long after he'd been freed. Sometime later, she'd heard about him going to another BioMed facility and doing brutal things. At first, she'd wondered how he'd found them. And why he'd gone after them at all.

But then she remembered. When she'd returned to burn down where she'd been tortured, she had sensed she was being watched.

It had been Murhder. Somehow, he'd found her, yet he hadn't interfered.

The idea he had kept going after that company, even after she had stopped, seemed a noble, although ultimately fruitless, pursuit—but then he had been permanently changed by her kin. He was not the same male, and when it came to the Brotherhood, all they knew was that he had lost his mind. He'd apparently never told them that he'd been held against his will and tortured in the *symphath* colony.

She'd never understood why he hadn't revealed the truth to them, even if it had meant exposing her half-breed status—something that back then hadn't been common knowledge. But maybe the Brothers would have understood. No one could get under a person's skin like a *symphath*. No wonder Murhder had ended up insane.

And it was all her fault.

"Enough," she muttered to herself. "Stop it."

Coming back to the present, she opened the door to Trez's office, and got hit with a whole lot of no-one-home. The desk was empty, the computers shut down, the black leather couches without occupants. No lights on, either. The only illumination came from sporadic bursts of filtered purple lasers, the dance floor's beams blunted by the tint of Trez's wall of glass.

No, there was another source of light.

Turning away from the observatory, she tracked the glow over to the corner. "John?"

The bathroom door was shut, and as she came up to it, she hesitated—and didn't like the reticence. She never knocked to announce herself to him.

"John?"

No running water. No toilet flushing.

She knocked. "John?"

He opened the door while pulling a long-sleeved shirt into place on his shoulders. *Sorry, I need a quick shower. Do you think Trez will care if I borrow this button-down?*

"No, of course not," she said. "So how did it go outside. Did you take care of the civilian? I sent his cousin to Havers after the male fainted on me."

As his hands moved through sign language positions that she knew well, she didn't track the words he was making.

The button-down wasn't buttoned down yet, and the muscle shirt below it was so tight that the real estate of his torso was on display even though his upper body was covered: In the light that flooded down from the ceiling fixtures, his pecs and his abdominals looked like they had been deep-carved by a master hand, and the prominent wings of his hip bones rose up out of the waistband of his leathers.

Smooth skin. Powerful strength. And she knew every inch of him by touch and taste.

John seemed new to her tonight, however, and that was another thing—like the way she'd hesitated in front of the closed door—that made her uneasy. She could not ignore the fact that she was assessing the torso of her mate as if seeing it for the first time.

Something about Murhder had reset her.

What's wrong? John signed.

That got through to her. Or maybe it was the worry in his face, his eyes narrowing.

She wanted to tell him nothing. That it was nothing, nope, she was fine, all good, hunky-fucking-dory. But she didn't think he'd be fooled by that cascade of denial.

Instead, Xhex stepped into him. Placed her palms inside the two of halves of that shirt. Stroked her way around his torso to the small of his back.

Instantly, his bonding scent flared, and she was aware of a pang in the center of her chest. If she'd asked him what was wrong? His "nothing" would have been honest, and the dark spices surging into the bathroom proved it.

Her lips found the column of his throat. And as she brushed the skin over his jugular, he clapped his hands on her hips and squeezed. Hard. Like he wanted her badly—and she loved that about him. Her mate was always ready-to-go-now, and in this, they were compatible.

One of many ways they worked, she reminded herself.

Her tongue licked across his collarbone and then she dragged one fang over the swell of his pec beneath the muscle shirt. In response, his body shuddered, and she knew what that felt like, the prickling of sexual tension, the hypersensitivity to touch, the heat that kindled just under the skin. The anticipation. They had shared all of it so many times, and yet as she got down on her knees in front of him, she recorded his arousal on fresh mental pages and tracked the flush on his face and the thickening behind his fly with new eyes.

Oh, God, he mouthed as he threw out a pair of brace-myself hands, the tight confines of the bathroom giving him good anchors with the wall behind the sink and the door to the toilet's cubicle.

Xhex ran her tongue on a meander across his lower belly, about an inch above his waistband. He was so leaned out from his workouts and what he did for a living in the field that there was just thin skin stretched over taut sinew and vein, everything so tight, it was like licking marble that happened to move.

Her fingertips skipped up his bulging thighs, the heat he was throwing off making the leather warm to the touch. The contours of his muscles were a road map of his heavy running while carrying weight, the ropes of strength offering ridges and valleys to explore.

Talk about ridges. There was one particular ridge she was interested in, and it didn't have shit to do with his legs.

Behind his button fly, his cock was ready for airtime and then some, the erection so big and so demanding, she knew he had to be in pain from the tight squeeze.

Guess she'd have to help her male out.

One by one, the buttons of that fly came free. Top. Next. Next. Next . . . and final.

His arousal barged out and she looked up from the floor at him as she took the shaft in her palm.

John's eyes glowed and his chest was pumping from ragged inhales. As he breathed heavily, the sight of those abdominals flexing and relaxing under the falling light was so erotic, she almost forgot what came next.

Nah, she remembered. She just liked the view.

Parting her lips, she extended her tongue and licked her way from his heavy sac all the way up the underside of his erection. And she liked his clenched jaw and flaring eyes so much, she did that again, taking her time.

Annnnnnnnnnnd how about one more for good measure.

❖   ❖   ❖

Holy. *Fuck.*

As John braced his arms and prayed like hell that his legs continued to hold him up, he stared down at Xhex as she crouched at his shitkickers, her gunmetal-gray eyes low-lidded and sexy, her hand wrapped around his arousal, her mouth—

Oh, God, she was going to lick up his cock again.

He wanted to watch. He really did. But more than the incredible visual of her pink tongue taking its sweet time as she tilted her head to the side and looked around his erection—

Wait. What was the question?

Coming. That was the problem. If he added what things looked like down there to the sensations of wet and warm on his sac and on his underside and the would-she-or-would-she-not take his head into her mouth? He was going to orgasm—which, okay, fine was the point to all this, but he didn't want it to stop.

He needed this powerful distraction. After what had gone down with that civilian, he needed this so-intense-he-didn't-have-another-thought-option, this total, primordial priority, this incredibly hot nothing-else-matters.

All there was in the world was he and Xhex. Sure, there was a crowd of five hundred humans downstairs, and there was music thumping, and please Lord don't have Trez come into his own bathroom right now—but none of that really registered. Just like he didn't think about the reanimation and the fight . . . and the way Manny had come over in the mobile surgical unit, and John and Blay had loaded the civilian's corpse into the back still handcuffed—

John popped opened his lids. The instant he saw his mate's mouth hovering a thin inch away from his head, all the stuff that had come back to him was evac'd out a side door.

Xhex was all that he knew.

She led with her tongue, and treated him to a swirl that made his toes curl, the tip of his erection getting the kind of attention that made his sac tight. Then she sucked him down, her whole throat somehow opening, his entire length disappearing into her lips.

Warmer. Wetter.

And she started to suck.

With her hair so short, there was nothing in the way, nothing tangling around her face or his sex, nothing blocking him from watching everything: The way when she retracted, his shaft glistened in the light from overhead. The way when she came forward, her mouth stretched thin to accommodate his girth. The way she teased him with her tongue when she popped him free of her pressured hold.

It was frustrating not having a voice. He wanted to tell her that he loved this. He loved her. He loved them being together like this, clandestine, semi-public, on the verge of discovery if the Shadow happened to enter his office.

But he wasn't going to move his planted palms so he could sign. Nope. He'd be liable to fall on her.

The rhythm started slow, and did not stay that way—and he knew she was getting ready to finish him because she slid her hand back onto his shaft. Deep in her mouth. Almost out with a twist of her hold. Down again, her lips touching the skin of the front of his hips. Almost out again, twist of her hand, and a lick this time. Back down, all the way down, the whole shaft inside of her.

It made him think of the other places on her he could get into. Leave something of himself behind.

Faster now. And he had to close his eyes again because goddamn, as much as he wanted to come, he didn't want to come. The suspension between the hyper-charged almost-there and the sweet sting of release was an addiction that was deadly.

Because the top of his skull was surely going to blow the fuck off if she kept this up.

He started to pant with sawing breaths that went in and out of his mouth as his cock went in and out of her mouth.

Faster again. And then she gripped his sac and squeezed—at the very instant she popped his cock out of her mouth and opened wide.

As jets shot out of him, he watched himself come into her. At least until his eyes squeezed shut of their own volition—because it was either that or they popped out of their sockets, ping-ponged off the closed door behind her, and ended up on the floor.

Making moaning noises in the back of her throat, she finished him off nice and slow, sucking him in once more, helping him ride out the tides of pleasure that ebbed and flowed for what was about ten minutes.

Vampires males made big messes.

Fortunately, she liked cleaning up after him.

When things eventually wound down, she licked her lips, her pink tongue making a lazy round of her mouth like she had enjoyed the taste of him—and holy hell that was nearly enough to get him going again. But he was dry. At least for the next ten minutes.

His cock was known to rally quick.

As she sat back and stared at him from under those low lids, he wanted to thank her. Instead, he bent down and drew her up to her full height. Putting his lips to hers, he kissed her in the hopes he could communicate in that way how much it had meant to him.

In fact, he was glad his hands were shaking too much to sign. If they had been in good working order? Well . . . then he might have started to explain himself with words, and he would have been unable to keep from her the true reason for his gratitude at her erotic distraction.

He would have had to tell her that he'd been bitten by that reanimated corpse.

The cursory examination he'd given himself in the field had not been thorough enough—and on some level he must have known that because he had raced up here after the surgical unit had removed the civilian's corpse from the scene. He had intended to check properly in this private bathroom only to relieve his mind.

But paranoia had proven to be prescient.

And he had the twin rings of teeth marks to prove it.

Keeping the injury from Xhex was wrong, but it made him feel like it hadn't really happened. That he hadn't seen the marks in his shoulder. That he hadn't pulled a borrowed shirt closed so she didn't see the wound.

Keeping it from her . . . meant he didn't have to admit to himself that he was terrified he'd been infected with something evil.

CHAPTER NINE

The following morning, Sarah Watkins looked out her bedroom window without disturbing the venetian blinds. Given that the slats were closed, all she had to go on was the inch and a quarter vertical gap next to the molding. It was enough if she contorted her neck.

Across the street and down three houses, there was a car parked facing her property. American make. Pale, nondescript color. No parking or gate pass stickers on the windshield. Nothing hanging from the rearview mirror.

There was a person in it. She couldn't tell whether it was a man or a woman, and that didn't matter.

Looked like her hunch was correct. The question was whether the FBI was watching her from the back, too, but she wasn't going to waste time answering that hypothetical.

Finally, it was light enough. She had never been a let's-savor-the-sunrise kind of person. Daybreak had always been late, in her opinion, its inevitably lazy arrival meaning that she could finally go back to work, her brain always chomping at the bit to return to whatever she'd had to quit the night before.

Prior to coming to Ithaca, she had liked that Gerry had been the same. Romance in their relationship had been rooted in mutual intellectual support; as a couple, they were a think tank that each could come to and vet ideas and solve problems in. To her, progress on research had always been so much better than bunches of flowers or lingering gazes in the moonlight.

So much more practical and important.

But BioMed had changed that, although not the part about her wanting someone to think work through with. No, Gerry had stopped talking to her about what he was doing, and had not given her any opportunity to share her own trials and triumphs. Once that previously two-way street had been closed off? Everything had fallen apart.

And she did judge him for that. She also still to this day had no idea what changed for him.

Straightening, Sarah pulled her sweatshirt back in place and padded across the carpet to her bedside table. Back when Gerry had been alive, they had each had their side of the bed. Hers was the one closest to the door because she had an irrational fear of burning to death in a house fire and couldn't settle unless she was close to the exit. He hadn't been picky.

Now that he was gone? She slept all over the place.

Too bad it felt rootless rather than an expression of mattress freedom.

As she picked up her cell phone and double-checked the time, she glanced over at where he would have lain. There were no pillows where he'd put his head. She'd had to stash his two away in a closet. She'd also bought all new bedding, down to the mattress pad, the bed skirt, the headboard. When she'd still not been able to get a good night's sleep, she'd gone out and gotten a new mattress.

Nothing had worked. Even now, she tossed and turned.

Refocusing on her phone, she realized she'd looked at the time and not seen the numbers at all. Eight thirty. And given that it was a Saturday, she had nowhere she needed to be.

Out in the hall, she flipped the switch that turned on the overhead light.

The closed door to Gerry's study was wood paneled, and not in a fancy way. It was just your bog standard, fairly cheap but serviceable, Home Depot special.

Facing off at it, she felt like the damn thing was a locked vault without a combination.

Her hand trembled as she turned the knob and the hinges creaked softly in a way that made her spine shiver. Musty air escaped like the oxygen molecules were getting off a crowded subway car.

It was darker than she remembered, and that was a problem. She didn't want to turn on the crane-armed desk lamp given that nondescript car down on the street. But like the Feds knew the layout of her house? As if they'd see the light come on and suss out that she hadn't been in this room for how long because it was where Gerry did his work for BioMed?

Besides, it was her damn house. She could go wherever she wanted to in it.

Stepping over the threshold, she nonetheless kept the lights off, leaving the door wide to let in as much illumination as possible from the hall.

As her shadow fell across the dusty desk, her head and shoulders created a blackened cutout in the middle of the fake wood surface. When the two security guards from BioMed had come to take Gerry's computers, they'd left the monitors, the keyboards, the printer, the modem, all the wires. The discord and vacancies left behind in the workstation made her think of a corpse that had had its organs removed, the vital parts that had engineered life gone, the connective tissue and ancillaries all that was left behind.

Now useless.

Flipping on her phone's flashlight, she made a fat circle with the shallow beam. Amazing how much dust there was. Probably meant she needed to change her furnace filters. Or clean, of course.

The chair Gerry had spent so many hours in was turned away from the desk, the seat and arms facing left. She could picture him pivoting with his feet, standing up . . . going to the bathroom. Had he felt odd? Had the need for insulin intruded on his concentration because he was hungry and about to eat?

But she couldn't lose herself in all that.

Time was wasting. Although she wasn't sure how she knew that.

Pushing the chair out of the way, she got down on her knees and looked under the desk. In her Nancy Drew mind, she imagined an envelope taped to the underside with her name on it. When she opened the thing, there would be a note from Gerry, in his messy handwriting, telling her what to do in the event of his death. Whether to be suspicious or not. And maybe at the end, there'd be an apology for him being so distracted and withdrawn toward her.

Nothing.

She sat back on her heels. Then she gave the chair an examination worthy of a proctologist, getting into all kinds of nooks and crannies of the padded seat, the undercarriage, the rollers.

Nothing.

There was a set of file cabinets off to one side and she opened each of the drawers, training her cell phone's light inside them. For all of Gerry's orderly thinking, he had sucked at the basics of life, like remembering to pay bills and file taxes and get car insurance, and the anemic collection of folders that had been laid down flat, instead of suspended properly on the slides, seemed like a symptom of his my-priorities-are-elsewhere. Going through the layers, she found his employee orientation packet from RSK BioMed as well as his first set of ID credentials that had given him partial access to the facility.

Seeing his face in the little picture made her breath catch.

God, he looked so young, all clean-shaven, smiling, and bright-eyed.

The image bore little resemblance to the second ID he'd gotten, the one that went with his top secret clearance. In that photograph, he'd been grim, his eyes narrowed and baggy'd, his face drawn from stress.

Where were those credentials, anyway? she wondered. He'd kept them with him always, even when he was in here.

Their disappearance hadn't seemed relevant before now.

The rest of the documents in the cabinets formed a chronology of their major purchases. The titles to their cars. The contract and then the mortgage for their house. Brochures for the honeymoon to Europe that they had considered signing up for. There were also copies of the taxes for the years they had been in Ithaca. A term life insurance policy on her that was still good. A term life insurance policy for Gerry for which he had been preliminarily approved, but, because he'd never gotten the physical done, was not in force.

She could remember nagging him about that and getting nowhere. At first, he'd put it off because they'd been too busy getting settled in the house. Then he'd been too busy getting settled at work. And then they hadn't really been speaking.

Sarah shut the bottom drawer and went over to the closet across the way. Opening the lever doors, she shined her light in.

Nothing but a bald hanging rod with two pant hangers on it and a set of shelves carrying a light load of Harvard-related paraphernalia of the academic variety: textbooks, notebooks, old laptops. She was about to close the doors again when she saw the pair of boots down on the floor.

Crouching, she picked one of them up, and as she saw the mud still caked in the tread, her eyes filled with tears.

Gerry had been as outdoorsy as an orchid. He burned to a crisp in any sunlight. He hated bug bites and bee stings and anything with more than two legs and an upright ambulation. Grass and trees were things to be regarded with suspicion, as they were nothing but housing units for creepies and crawlies. And bodies of water, particularly those with more than three feet of standing or rushing H_2O? Forget about it. Somewhere he had heard that there were sharks at the mouth of the Mississippi that were capable of surviving in freshwater.

So therefore, it was possible that a mutant version of one could show up in the Finger Lakes of New York. Or Lake Champlain. Or Lake George.

And yet he had gone camping with her the first month they'd arrived in Ithaca. The pair of them had invested in hiking boots and a tent and some sleeping bags. She had promised him it would be a good time. He hadn't exactly been thrilled, but he'd known she wanted to go and had been determined to make the best of it.

The weather had been terrible for late August. Rain both days.

They'd laughed about sharks falling from the sky. And this had been before the first *Sharknado* had come out.

Looking at the dried mud on the sole, it seemed unfathomable that he was gone. That this boot that had been worn so casually and then put away without any mindfulness was now in her hand as a symbol of everything that had been lost when he'd died.

She was touching both their history and their unfulfilled future. And the feelings that came up for her, the sadness and mourning, were so powerful, it was just as the pain had been in the beginning for her, the raw absence of him incomprehensible.

According to the calendar, she had had two years to get used to the death. Why then did it still hurt this badly?

Sarah turned the boot over in her hand—

Something fell out and bounced on the carpet.

Frowning, she pointed her little light source at it, and the warm glow of metal was a surprise.

A key. It was an odd-shaped key.

CHAPTER TEN

The painting of a French king slid back on the wall of Darius's drawing room, revealing, just as it always had, a set of narrow, curving steps that disappeared into earth. A torch, mounted on the stone wall, frothed quietly, casting liquid yellow light over the descent. The smell was the same, candle wax and lemon.

As Murhder stood at the threshold, he told himself to go down, take the bedroom on the right, crash in the bed that he'd used before.

Instead, he looked back over his shoulder. Vishous was at a computer at the receptionist's desk in the room beyond, the Brother's black-haired head bent forward in concentration, the hand-rolled between his teeth releasing a faint tendril of smoke, the tattoos at his temple distorted from his frown.

Off in the distance, low voices percolated. And there was the smell of bacon. Someone was making a snack.

Four of the Brothers had stayed behind after Wrath had left. Vishous, Rhage, Phury, and some dark-haired, stocky male who had a scent reminiscent of the King's. Had to be a blood relation, but other than that, Murhder didn't know anything. Not even the male's name.

Vishous had been at the computer for hours now, the three letters that had been handwritten and sent to Murhder fanned out next to him. Naturally, they had been read, and in retrospect, he'd been foolish to think he could hide the request that had been put to him from the people he was asking help of. But at least no one had argued about him searching for that son.

Yet.

Murhder had been mostly in the waiting area, his ass getting numb in spite of the cushioned chair he'd been given. Fritz, Darius's ancient butler, had been as kind and solicitous as ever, insisting on delivering food which Murhder had eaten without tasting. But that had been how long ago?

The chiming of a grandfather clock, slow and laborious, began out in the foyer. Nine in the morning. With all the drapes in the house pulled and the inside shutters in place, it was impossible to tell day or night.

Murhder looked down the stone steps. Took another deep breath through his nose.

Then he stepped back into the drawing room and retriggered the release on the painting, watching the full-length portrait slide back into place.

Pain lanced through the center of his chest, the grief both unexpected and not surprising. "When did Darius die."

When there was no answer to his non-question, he walked over to the waiting area's desk. "Well?"

Vishous sat back in the swivel chair, taking a drag and then tapping the ash off the tip into a mug of cold coffee. "Who says he's dead?"

"His scent isn't anywhere in this house. Not even down where he sleeps."

V shrugged. "Fritz is good with a vacuum."

"Don't play games with shit like this."

The Brother regarded the glowing end of his hand-rolled. "Fine." His diamond eyes swung up and met Murhder's. "It's none of your fucking business. How's that."

"He was my brother, too."

"Not anymore." Vishous shook his head. "And before you get on your high horse and go all right-to-know on me, I'll remind you that you left the Brotherhood."

"I was kicked out."

"You chose to slaughter those humans. Do you have any idea what the cleanup was like? We saw it on the news after the humans found your little party out on that lawn. It was a national fucking incident. It took us two weeks of stripping memories to calm that shit down, and spare me the eye-for-an-eye shit. You created a lot of problems for us. Thank God the Internet hadn't been like it is today or God only knows what would have happened—"

"How did Darius die?"

Vishous narrowed his eyes. "How do you think."

Murhder looked away. The war with the Lessening Society was such bullshit. "When?"

"Three and a half years ago. And that's all I'm going to say."

"You don't have to be an asshole about everything."

"Oh, right. I'm supposed to give a male who has a history of poor impulse control and mental instability details about someone who has nothing to do with his life."

Murhder leaned forward and bared his fangs. "I fought with him for over a century. I've earned the right—"

Vishous shot up out of his chair and slammed his palm down on the letters. "You haven't earned *shit*, and if you think we're wasting one more fucking man hour on this stupid fucking MacGuffin of yours—"

Big bodies entered the room on long strides and the next thing Murhder knew, Phury was pulling him back.

"Get your hands off me," Murhder snarled as he shoved the Brother away. "I'm not going to do anything."

"How do we know that?" V taunted as Rhage blocked his flight path.

"Shut the fuck up, V," someone said. "You're not helping."

"The hell I'm not. I've found his fucking female."

◆   ◆   ◆

Sarah left her house with her sunglasses on. Which was ridiculous. It was cloudy, the overcast sky clearly considering the idea of dumping more snow on the ground, the wintery landscape not that bright, blinding kind, but rather an all over gray. More than all that, however, there was no fooling anybody who was watching her house.

She was about to get in her car and drive off, and a pair of Ray-Bans wasn't going to disguise that. Although given her line of thinking, maybe she needed to hat-and-dark-glasses her Honda.

Yup, she was straight-up 007 material.

She tried to look casual as she got behind the wheel, backed out, and headed for the main drag. The unmarked nothing-special that had been three houses down two hours ago was gone, but there was another now, in a slightly different position, and her dark lenses were useful as she went by the navy-blue sedan. Keeping her head straight, she shifted her eyes over.

There was a woman with short dark hair in the front seat, staring forward.

Looks like everyone is wearing sunglasses today, Sarah thought.

The local bank she and Gerry had their accounts in, one for household bills, the other for savings, had branches all over town. They'd only ever been to the one at the strip mall a mile and a half away from the house, however, and it took her no time to go over there, find a parking space, and get out.

As she came up to the glass doors of the entrance, she made a show of rummaging through her purse like she was looking for something. Then she took out her checkbook and nodded, as if she were relieved she hadn't forgotten the thing.

Inside, the bank was warm, and there were two tellers behind the counter, several darkened offices, and a manager talking to a customer.

Sarah went up to the teller who wasn't helping someone at the drive-thru. "Hi, I'd like to get some cash but I forgot my check card. Have to do it the old-fashioned way."

The man smiled. He was on the young side, with a name tag that read "Shawn." "No problem. Do you have your driver's license?"

"I do, yes." As she took out her wallet to slide her ID free, she passed the key that had dropped out of the boot across to the guy. "And can you please tell me if this goes with one of your safety deposit boxes?"

Shawn leaned in. "It looks like it."

Sarah took her sweet time putting her name on the check and writing out "one hundred and no/100." "My fiancé and I have a joint account here—I mean, he's passed, so everything came to me. Can I get into the box? I brought with me the power of attorney I got as executor of his estate just in case it's only in his name."

Over at the door, there was an electronic *bing* as someone entered—and she wanted to wheel around to see if it was the brunette with the sunglasses that had been parked on her street. But that seemed like a rookie move for somebody trying to be covert.

"Let me check on your account," Shawn said as he started entering things into his computer from her driver's license. "If it was joint, then you'd have right of survivorship, and I believe that would carry over for any safety security box that you got as a service when you both opened the account. Do you remember signing for a box at that time?"

"No, I don't."

"Okay, let me see what I can do." More typing on his keyboard, quick and sure. And then Shawn smiled. "I need to check with my manager, hold on a second."

"Take your time. I write slow, anyway."

Or at least she did today, turning the check over and printing "for deposit only" like she was carving the letters in hardwood.

Shifting her position, she looked across at the man who had entered. He was waiting for the other teller to finish up with the drive-thru customer. As with the woman in the unmarked, he was staring straight ahead. Jeans. Buffalo Bills parka. Sneakers that had snow on them.

Impossible to know if he was undercover or not.

Yeah, like she had anything to go by in making that assessment.

"So my manager—oh, sorry. Didn't mean to startle you."

Sarah forced herself to ease up. "It's okay. Too much coffee this morning."

"My manager said she'd be happy to help you in her office."

"Great." Sarah almost packed up her fake withdrawal. "Oh, here. All made out."

Five twenties and a no-thanks-I-don't-need-the-receipt later, she was sitting down across from an early thirties woman who looked about halfway through her pregnancy. Her tag read "Kenisha Thomas, Branch Manager."

"These are totally sufficient," she said, after she entered some things in her computer and reviewed, then scanned, the notarized POA. "I'd be happy to let you in. It looks like your fiancé simply signed for the box associated with the savings account by himself. You weren't billed because it was a free service that came when you started banking with us, and you would have had access if you'd just come in with him and your ID."

Sarah turned the key over in her hand. "I guess he forgot to tell me about it."

Bullshit, she thought.

"Happens all the time," the manager said as she passed the POA back.

Does it really?

"Come with me."

As Sarah followed the manager back out into the open area, she looked for Buffalo Bills guy. He was gone. Maybe she was just being paranoid.

The safety deposit boxes were way in the back, in a vault that must have weighed as much as the rest of the entire strip mall. After a little manila envelope was taken out of a narrow filing cabinet, Sarah was invited to sign on one of its vacant lines.

She froze with her Bic. The sight of Gerry's signatures was like those boots with the mud in the treads, but worse: Without her knowing, he'd been in and out of the box seven times over the twelve months before he'd died . . . seemingly at random as she noted each of the dates.

The last one really got to her.

The Saturday he'd died. As she blinked away a wash of tears, she imagined him coming here as she had just done. Which spot had he parked in? Who had he talked to in the branch? Which of the staff took him over here to sign this little envelope?

What had been on his mind?

And like her . . . who had been watching him?

"Why wasn't there a notice when he died?" Sarah asked. "I mean, why didn't I get a notice that I needed to switch this to my name?"

The branch manager shook her head. "My guess is that because it's a joint account, there was an assumption that you'd signed as well."

"Oh."

"Just right there at the bottom," the manager pointed out gently. "That's where you sign."

"Sorry." She focused on the initials beside each of Gerry's John Hancocks. As they were just a squiggle, she couldn't read them. "Is that you?"

"No, my predecessor. I took over this branch about nine months ago."

"Oh, okay." Sarah scribbled her name. "I was just wondering."

The bank manager initialed and then they were inside the vault, looking for 425 in the rows of rectangular doors. Twin key turns later, and Sarah had a long, narrow metal box in her hands.

It was light. But there was something in it, a shifting weight and soft clink being released as she turned and went into a private room with no windows or glass.

The bank manager hesitated before closing the door. As she put her hand on her round belly, her deep brown eyes were grave. "I am very sorry for your loss."

Sarah put her palm on the cold metal of the box and focused on the manager's engagement ring and wedding band set. It was hard not to think that if Gerry hadn't died, maybe she'd be where the other woman was. Then again, if Gerry had lived, who knows where they would have ended up, given how things had been between them.

God, she hated thinking like that.

"Thank you," she whispered as she sat down in the chair.

Sarah waited until the door was shut before she lifted the latch and opened the half lid. Her whole body shook as she looked inside.

A USB drive. Black with a white slide.

And a set of BioMed credentials she'd never seen before.

Frowning, she put the USB drive into the zipper pocket of her purse. And then she inspected the credentials. The laminated card had the BioMed logo on it, and the bar code that got scanned by security whenever anyone entered the facility. There was also the strip on the back that you swiped through the door lock readers, a seven-digit phone number written in permanent marker, and the holographic image pattern that ensured authenticity.

But there was no photograph, no name, no rank.

Sarah tilted the box forward to make sure she hadn't missed anything on the far end. Then she stuck her hand into the cramped space, feeling around.

Nothing.

She sat back in the chair. As she stared at the blank wall ahead of her, she realized that she'd once again expected a letter from him. Something sincere and heartfelt, along the lines of a last missive that helped her put everything into a good place.

Re-closing the box, she put the credentials into her purse.

As she stood up, she hesitated.

Then she got the USB drive and the credentials back out, and stuffed both of them in her sports bra.

Good thing she was relatively flat-chested. Plenty of room in there.

CHAPTER ELEVEN

Longest, lousiest day of his life, Murhder thought a couple hours later.

Okay, fine, so maybe only the first part of that was true. But shit.

As he limped around Darius's drawing room on his bum leg, he was surprised he hadn't worn a path in the nap of the rug, his footfalls making a wear pattern that wound in and around the antique furniture.

God, it was difficult being so frustrated with something that didn't care about his emotional state.

And no, he wasn't talking about Vishous.

The issue was the sun. That enormous, glowing death ball did not give two shits about how pent-up he was. The sonofabitch was just meandering its way from east to west, and the fact that it had been snowing since about eleven in the morning didn't help. Vampires were incompatible with daylight in all its forms, and even for somebody as loosely held together as he was, there was no risking even tangential exposure.

At least it was winter in Upstate New York. That grandfather clock had announced it was three in the afternoon a while ago, and darkness would start falling at about four thirty.

If it had been July? He'd have gone insane—

More insane, that was.

One more hour and he was free. Maybe he could get away with leaving in forty-five minutes.

Entering the empty waiting room, he stopped by the desk. Vishous, that supercilious shithead, had done in a number of hours what Murhder had failed to do in twenty years—and the answer had been medical records.

Murhder reached out and turned each of the three letters around so they faced him. He knew them by heart. The handwriting in the first two was painfully imprecise, the words scripted with a shaky pen. The final one was all in the symbols of the Old Language, and they were likewise drawn by a frail hand.

There was also a single piece of paper on the blotter by the computer, and Murhder picked it up. Nothing precise here. Just a bunch of dates scribbled on a timeline. Creating the chronology had been the only piece of teamwork he and V had performed.

Murhder had provided the start date, the night that he had gone back to the second facility, looking for the pregnant female. Working from there, they had traced the events the letters detailed, she being moved to another location, as she had given birth to her son, the years the two had spent together, her escape when the scientists had been transferring her away from her young.

Separated from her son, she had tried desperately to find him, searching every night for the hidden lab. With few resources and no money, she had never gotten very far, and she had another thing working against her: The final letter noted that she was in poor health.

And that was how V had found her. Havers, the race's healer, had long kept records on his patients, and recently, the files had been transcribed into a database the King had access to. The search function had been complicated and inefficient, especially as they had no idea what she might have had to see the healer about. Because she had given birth, however, Vishous had started with that and managed to identify a pool of females who had come in with issues common to those who had at some point been on the birthbed. From those patients, he had further isolated those who had been born of a son.

Case by case, the Brother had looked for details that might match what Murhder knew and what the female had revealed, tacitly or through implication, in the letters. It had been a long shot more likely to yield frustration than an answer. But then V had found a patient presenting with a vaginal prolapse from a birth ten years before. Follow-up care had been provided to her at her home.

Which was in the same town the letters had been mailed from.

Reading deeper into the records, Vishous had discovered that the female was unmated. The son was not with her. And she had extensive internal abnormalities associated with surgeries not performed by Havers.

As well as a prominent display of PTSD around medical intervention, about which she would not expound on.

It had to be her. It was the only explanation.

And Murhder was going to be knocking on her door approximately two seconds after nightfall.

"You realize you can't go alone. If you're allowed to go at all."

Murhder looked up from the letters. Phury had come to stand in the archway, and his yellow eyes were apologetic as he stated what he apparently thought should have been obvious.

"No, I'll take it from here," Murhder said. "This is private."

The Brother shook his head, his long blond-, gold-, and brown-streaked hair moving on his shoulders. "Not anymore—"

"A bunch of Brothers shows up at her door with me, and you're just going to scare the shit out of her. She's had enough of that, trust me. Besides, she asked for my help. Not the Brotherhood's or the King's."

It was easier for him to keep his voice down when arguing with Phury. The two of them had always gotten along because how could you not? The guy had been chasing after his twin Z since he'd rescued the male from the hell of being a blood slave. There had been nothing to be in conflict with, because Phury had always had total decency running through his veins.

"I'm not going to hurt her," Murhder muttered. "For godsakes, what kind of monster do you think I am?"

Bad question to put out there, he thought to himself.

"It's not just her we're worried about," Phury hedged. "Your history with this kind of thing is not the best."

How politic, Murhder thought.

"Listen," he said to the Brother. "Would you have wanted anyone else to go in to save your twin when he was a blood slave? Would you have trusted anybody but yourself to do what had to be done to get him to safety and make things right?"

Phury's frown was deep enough to shadow his eyes. "I'm not getting personal here. And neither should you."

"This is my wrong to right, Phury. You've got to understand that. I failed the female. I left her behind, in the belly of the beast. I haven't been able to live with myself since I made that decision. It's been killing me. I *have* to do this."

"It's official business now. If you'd wanted it to stay otherwise, you shouldn't have come here."

"What choice did I have?"

"That's not the point. It's where we all are now. We'll keep you posted—"

"Wait a minute—are you suggesting I'm not even going?"

When there was only silence, Murhder felt a rage ride up on him that was so great, he was liable to tear Darius's fucking house down.

"Fuck that."

Before the Brother could stop him, he grabbed the letters, lunged around the guy and went right for the front door. Even though it wasn't fully dark out. Even though he was just going to toast up. Even though—

His hand was almost on the old-fashioned, fist-sized knob, when a thick arm locked around his throat and hauled him back with such power, he popped off his feet and went flying. As he landed face-up on a very nice Oriental, his back reminded him that it was the second time in the last twenty-four hours that he'd hit the ground hard. But he didn't give a shit.

He pushed Phury off him and, in spite of his injured leg, went right back for the—

Brothers everywhere: Vishous in front of the door, looking like a brick wall except with daggers in both hands. Rhage racing in with a bagel shoved in his mouth and a pair of guns out. Phury back on his feet and ready to attack again. And then there was the one he didn't know, who seemed like he was hoping things got stupid so he could hit something.

As Murhder faced off at them all, he knew, if he played his cards right, he could commit suicide right here and now. With a couple of well-timed aggressions, he could force them to kill him, and there was a cowardly relief in the idea of that option.

He was tired. So tired of his broken head. And what had happened in that lab. And what he had done afterward. He was bone-achingly exhausted with where he had ended up, kicked out of not just the Brotherhood, but the lives of the males who had been his family.

When he'd disassociated from reality, the loss of them all had been but a passing blip on his radar, way off to the side. Now, he felt his outsider status like an open grave calling his name.

He'd had pride, once. Just as he'd been sane for a good portion of his life. But both were commodities that had proved to be expendable.

He didn't bother to hide his suffering as he opened his mouth and spoke in a hoarse rush. "Please, I promise I won't go off the rails again. Just let me go to her." He reached into his shirt, which made them all jump. Taking out the piece of sacred seeing glass, he showed them his talisman. "I've seen her face. It's been shown to me. For twenty-five years."

As some of those expressions softened, he jumped on the opening.

"Look, my life is over. Do you think I don't know that? Even if I do right by her, even if I find her son, I'm not going to make it, but at least my eternity will be less like the hell of my mortal nights. I beg of you, please, let me take care of her."

Abruptly, through a magic he could not understand, the seeing glass warmed between his fingers. Looking down with a frown, he realized the shard had started to glow—and there she was, the face he had seen for so many years, staring back at him.

Shoving the image outward, his hand shook as he tried to get them to see what he did. And they must have caught it because slowly their weapons lowered.

Then suddenly, he knew what the solution was.

"Xhex," he breathed. "If you don't want me to go alone, let Xhex come with me. The female will be comforted by her presence, especially when she says she's a survivor, too."

After a moment, he added dryly, "And we all know that Xhex can take care of any kind of business that comes her way. You can trust her to make sure I stay in line."

CHAPTER TWELVE

Sarah did not make it back to her house until just after three in the afternoon. Under the assumption she was being tailed, she had followed the routine that her Saturday's had taken on. Pick up dry cleaning. Go to vegetable market. Go to butcher's. Go to supermarket. The fact that it was snowing had slowed things down, and she would have worked out, but not with what she was carrying inside her sports bra. As she went through the motions, she wondered if the fact that she wasn't going to a gym, but was dressed in running tights, Brooks, and a parka, counted against her.

Except she had to be overthinking that one. Half of America was in Lululemon 24/7.

As she parked in her driveway, she checked out her street. No deceptively non-event cars parked in the vicinity. So she probably had been watched.

It took her three trips to get all her bags into the house, the snow squeaking under the treads of her running shoes, the flakes falling from the sky getting into her eyes as the cold wind swirled around. After locking up her car and locking herself inside, she went into the kitchen, waded through the bags and put stuff away. Her grocery purchasing in-efficiency had never registered before, but now she saw her three differ-ent stops as an adaptive behavior to waste otherwise empty hours.

On the weekends, the less time she had to stare at the walls of her little house, the better.

Of course, now that the FBI seemed interested in her, she had something to focus on. Not exactly the distraction she had been looking for, however.

On that note . . .

Setting her security alarm, Sarah went down into her basement. Other than the washer and dryer and the water heater, there wasn't much, just a couple of boxes of her university papers and some leftover dorm room stuff that hadn't gone well with her and Gerry's this-is-real-life furniture upstairs.

The old laptop she was looking for was in a Rubbermaid tub next to the futon she'd used for all four years of college and her postgraduate work. "Old" was a misnomer for the Dell. She'd bought the thing only about five years ago, and it was fully functioning—"obsolete" was a bet-ter term given the speed of technology's changes.

Sitting on the futon, she plugged the charger in and opened the lap-top. Boot up didn't take long and she entered her password.

As she inserted the USB drive she'd taken from the safety deposit box, she was aware of her heart pounding, and her eyes flipped up and surveyed the basement. Nope, still no windows. And no one was creep-ing down the cellar stairs. Or staring over her shoulder.

The drive's directory was not password protected, which was a sur-prise. Then again, Gerry had stored the thing in a safety deposit box only he could get into. Scrolling down the list of files, she found dozens of differently titled entries and a variety of programs used, all of the lat-ter standard for medical research, from Excel spreadsheets to Word documents to images.

What was the same in every single entry? They had all been added the day before Gerry's death.

Sarah closed her eyes and thought about the last of his signatures on the safety deposit box envelope.

Then she refocused. One by one, she went down the list of files. The identifying numbers and combinations of letters seemed to follow the same system she and everyone else used at BioMed to identify research protocols. Accordingly, there was nothing that gave away any hint of the subject matter if you were a layperson—or a professional one unaffiliated with the project, for that matter.

Three hundred and seventy-two files.

When she came to the final listing, she rubbed the pain behind her sternum. Once again, she had expected something with her name on it, a sign that he had left this drive not just for anyone, but for her to find. Instead, it looked like he had copied these for himself.

As she prepared to start opening things, her scientific brain insisted on finding order, and when there wasn't an obvious one in the directory, she started at the top.

Lab results. From a complete blood panel.

Except . . . the patient in question had readings that made no sense. Values for liver function were completely off. Thyroid. White and red blood cell counts made no sense. Plasma was . . . she'd never even seen a reading like this. Iron was so high the patient should have been dead.

She read the values twice and then tried to get a bead on where the rundown had come from. No patient name. No ordering physician name. No laboratory or hospital logo, not even a BioMed one. All there was was an eight-digit reference number, which she guessed identified the patient, and a date, which was about six months before Gerry died.

The next file included images from a CAT scan series of the upper torso—

"What the . . . *hell* . . . is this?"

The heart appeared to be six-chambered, not four-. And yet the ribs, lungs, stomach, liver, and other internal organs and spine were recognizably human.

It was conceivable that a patient, somewhere on the planet, could have a mutated heart like that. The surprise was why Gerry, as an infectious disease researcher, would have the files pertaining to a case like that.

Would have *stolen* the files to a case like that.

Sarah frowned and went back to the CBC results. The eight-digit reference number on that report . . . yup, it matched the one on the CAT scan series.

In quick succession, she opened the next six files. All medical results. But then came the seventh, and by the time she was finished reading that one, she had to sit back and take some deep breaths. When that didn't help, she put the laptop aside and rubbed her eyes.

She literally couldn't breathe right.

Those medical results? All normal screening tests on a male patient with totally abnormal readings. Urinalysis. Cardiac catheterization. Stress test with echocardiogram, where she watched that six-chamber heart beat.

But the seventh file was so disturbing, she'd had to read the document three times. At first, it appeared to be a fairly standard report on a patient, with a review of the test results that seemed to be the ones she'd just opened. Then words like "major histocompatibility profile assessment" and "immunosuppression protocol" jumped out, and she recognized the names of anti-rejection drugs that helped transplant patients' bodies accept the new organs they'd been given.

All of which were topics well familiar to her and close to her field of work.

And just as she'd wondered why Gerry hadn't mentioned all this work to her, given the synergies with her own efforts, she read the following line: "Intravenous administration of the ALL cells occurred at 15:35."

There was only one thing that ALL stood for in Sarah's world.

Acute Lymphoblastic Leukemia.

If she was reading this right, and she was hard-pressed to come up with an alternative interpretation, someone at BioMed had injected a human patient with cancer cells after they deliberately depressed his immune system.

They were torturing someone under the guise of medical advancement.

◆   ◆   ◆

As John Matthew came out of the hidden door under the Black Dagger Brotherhood mansion's grand staircase, he smelled First Meal being prepared off in the kitchen wing—and attempted to ground himself in the familiar.

This was just like any other night. Nothing unusual. No out-of-whack going on anywhere.

It was an okay enough pep talk and one he'd been giving himself all through his workout down in the training center. The goal was to convince the warning bells in his head that they were wasting their time with all that high-pitched ringing.

Too bad his success rate was zero. Like a tour guide taking a group past a dead body and going, "Nothing to see here, we're walking, we're walking."

Crossing over the mosaic depiction of that apple tree in full bloom, he hit the blood-red runner that went up the ornate staircase and felt like he was dragging a car behind him as he ascended. He hated the fatigue. The fact that he'd put himself through a brutal series of dead lifts and then run sixteen miles in under an hour and a half didn't matter. His motivation in the gym had been to prove to himself that the bite on his shoulder wasn't a systemic issue, and the exhaustion he was now feeling made him worried that it was.

Of course, the answer to that debate was to get the wound checked out by Doc Jane or Dr. Manello in the clinic, but he was still undecided on that one. The edges of where those teeth had sunk in seemed the same. At least . . . well, they were mostly the same—

Who the hell was he kidding. The irritation was bigger, the swelling worse, and the pain unrelenting.

Abruptly, he stopped at the top of the stairs. Xhex was standing in front of the open doors of the King's study, her body fully weaponized with autoloaders and knives, her face pale and tense. Behind her, inside the room, the King was at his desk with Tohr beside him, the pair of males looking out at John as if they weren't sure whether he was going to need restraining.

What's going on, he signed.

"I need to talk to you," Xhex said quietly. "Can we go in here?"

As she nodded over her shoulder, John frowned. *What's it about.*

Not a question. Jesus, had they found out about the bite? He hadn't told anyone—

"Murhder."

He recoiled. *Who's dead? Someone got killed?*

"No, the, ah, the male. Murhder."

John looked back at his King. Then at Tohr, who was, for all intents and purposes, the father figure John had never had. Clearly, the latter had been called in for whatever issue this was.

Without a word—natch—John went over to the doorway and waited. When Xhex followed, they both stepped inside together, and as the doors closed of their own volition, he was aware of an oppressive feeling across his chest.

Up until now, he hadn't been worried about the former Brother's re-arrival. But if it had something to do with his female? Especially if she was looking as tense as she was?

"G'head, Xhex," Wrath muttered as he petted George's boxy head.

Even the golden retriever looked nervous, although that, at least, wasn't unusual.

"I have to go out tonight," she said as she stared John straight in the eye. "And help Murhder with a problem."

Okaaaaaay, John thought.

Generally speaking, bonded males didn't like their females being around members of the opposite sex. And that was a nice way of putting the issue. John had never subscribed much to the truism, however, believing that he and Xhex were part of a new generation of vampires that didn't fall into that macho bullshit.

It was a nice theory.

Unfortunately, it was also one that was thrown right out the fucking window as a curling aggression clenched his nuts and made him want to hunt down and kill a male he'd never met before. Still, he forced himself to think of what Mary always said about emotions. You weren't responsible for them and you couldn't control them, but you were in charge of your response to them.

And he refused to be the hothead who went Cro-Magnon on something like this.

John narrowed his eyes. *What kind of problem? And why would you be the one helping him?*

Xhex cleared her throat. Then she started to pace, her eyes trained on the Aubusson carpet.

"I told you that at one point I had a brush with some humans."

Brush? he thought. She'd been kidnapped and tortured by researchers in a clinic somewhere.

To this day, he didn't know many details of what had been done to her—similar to the situation with Lash, she never talked much about the horror of it. He had always wanted to help her, but he'd had no choice except to respect the line she drew and the privacy she kept.

"Murhder took that personally." She stopped by the fireplace and stared into the yellow and orange flames. "And started some kind of crusade."

As those warning bells John had tried to bribe off with that all-normal shit went straight-up cathedral on him, he decided he was becoming clairvoyant.

And when she didn't go any further, he whistled to bring her head up and around. *As part of his role as a Brother, right,* he signed. *He was avenging the species instead of you specifically.*

John knew damn well there was more to it, given the pair's previous relationship, but he tossed that ditty out there in the hopes he was wrong.

"No, it was personal." She refocused on the fire. "I told you about him and me."

John exhaled long and slow. Okay, he thought. He could deal with this. This was not new information, for one thing. But more than that, she was with him now.

Xhex continued, "After I escaped from the lab I'd been in, he kept hunting for humans who were experimenting on vampires. I didn't know he was doing this—not that that's relevant. Anyway, he found another site with members of the species in captivity. One of them was a pregnant female, and though he tried to get her out, he ultimately failed. After two decades, she reached out to him, and long story short, he's going to see her tonight. Because of his . . . instability . . . it's not a good idea for him to be out in the world unsupervised, so I'm going with him to see the female. Plus, you know . . . I get what happened to her."

John closed his eyes as he thought about the horrible things the two females had in common. Then he looked to Tohr. The Brother had his arms crossed over his tremendous chest, his navy-blue eyes grave, the white streak in his dark hair out of its cowlick because he'd clearly been dragging a hand through the stuff.

"Murhder needs an escort," Tohr said. "And given the fragility of the situation, it does make sense for Xhex to go with him."

"The female has been through a lot," Xhex said. "And so has Murhder."

Okay, and I'm going with you, too, John signed. *Give me ten minutes to shower—*

"No," Xhex said. "We don't need anyone else."

John narrowed his eyes. *The hell you don't. And I'm not pulling a bonded male thing here. If Murhder is so unstable that he's been kicked out of the Brotherhood, and you don't trust him to go see a female alone, why do you think it's okay for you to be the only one on backup?*

"She won't be," Tohr interjected. "The Brotherhood will be on standby in the area. He puts one foot out of line and we'll be all over him."

All right. So then I'll be with the Brotherhood.

"We're good, John," Tohr said as he shook his head. "We've got this."

One more on the fringes is not going to hurt.

When Tohr didn't respond, John trained his eyes on Xhex, and waited for her to speak up. Surely she'd want him there. Surely she'd understand how badly *he* wanted to be there.

When his mate just went back to staring at the fire, John looked at Wrath. The King was sitting tall on his throne, his wraparounds hiding his eyes, his jaw clenched—but when was that mandible ever relaxed?

I'm not going to attack the guy, John signed. *If that's what you people are worried about. Bonded male or not, I can control myself. And if he throws shit at me, I'll handle it.*

When Tohr didn't translate to the King, John motioned toward Wrath and stamped his foot. After a moment, Tohr dropped his head and murmured to the great male.

Say something, John thought at the King. *Tell them they have to let me go because I'm a damn good fighter and this is my mate and I deserve to be there. This may be Brotherhood business, but it involves my shellan, so it's mine, too.*

As silence stretched out, somebody laughed outside in the hall, and then there were voices, muffled but distinct enough for him to recognize. Rhage, it was Rhage. And he was talking with Qhuinn, no doubt as they both hit the stairs to go down for First Meal.

Brothers, now, even though they did not share blood.

John turned and started for the door.

"John." Tohr spoke up. "This about Murhder. It's not a reflection on you, I promise."

There was no responding to that because he either railed against not being in the Brotherhood, which was a bitch move, or he came across as not trusting his mate, which was also a bitch move.

Or wait, there was a door number three: He could admit that he wanted to kill another male for no good reason. In which case he was no different than Murhder because that shit was crazy.

Out of the study, he headed down the Hall of Statues, passing by the Greco-Roman masterpieces in their various poses.

Footfalls, quick and nimble, rode up on him.

"John, please—"

As Xhex took his arm, he jerked out of her hold and turned around. Suspicion, as insidious as any disease, had taken root in his heart and it colored her as she stood in front of him. Even as nothing about her, or them, had technically changed, everything felt different.

Of all the people he'd expect to advocate for him, Xhex hadn't had his six, and he had a feeling he knew why.

She didn't want him to come. That was why she hadn't said anything.

"This won't take long," she maintained. "We're just going to go talk to the female and see if we can help her. She's looking for her son."

Those gunmetal-gray eyes, the ones that he felt like he'd spent a lifetime looking into, were steady as they held his, and she certainly seemed sincere in this noble quest vibe she was rocking.

Good move, throwing a kid into the mix, too, he thought. Made everything even harder to discount. Made him seem, on the surface, all the more unreasonable for throwing a hissy fit.

John's hands started signing before he could stop them. *When was the last time you saw Murhder?*

"There is absolutely nothing going on between him and me."

Not the question I asked.

She looked away. Looked back. "Last night. I saw him last night."

John took a deep breath. *Before or after that blow job you gave me.*

"Really. You're going there."

I'm going nowhere, apparently. John took a step back. *Do your thing. I'm the last person to order you around and I thought that was why we worked. Tonight? I'm thinking it makes me a pussy.*

"You're out of line on that one."

The fact that you think so makes me feel like I'm not. You don't want me to go with you, and you're hiding behind the Brotherhood-only bullshit so you don't have to admit it. If I were you, I'd ask myself why that's so hard to cop to and why you want to be alone with him. I know those are the questions on my mind right now.

"This is not about you."

Yeah, that's the party line lately, isn't it. He touched his chest. *Let me tell you that on my end, this feels very much about me.*

"Murhder is highly unstable, and that makes him dangerous—"

John threw his head back and laughed mutely. *Are you really trying to toss around the it's-for-my-own-safety shit? You know how well I can defend myself. You can't possibly be worried about me fighting with him. I think it's more like you don't want me to see how much he cares about you, or you don't want me to see how much you care about him.*

This time, when he turned away, she let him go, but he could feel her eyes boring into his back as he headed down to the bedroom they shared.

This was not how he'd expected the night to start. Not even close.

And hey, there were so many dark hours left.

God only knew what was going to go tits up next.

CHAPTER THIRTEEN

Hepatitis C. Bacterial pneumonia. Viral pneumonia. Seven different kinds of cancer including melanoma, adenocarcinoma, and neuroblastoma.

Sarah sat back on the futon. Then she put the laptop aside and rubbed at the hot spot it had left on her lap.

She had read or reviewed every single file, and God only knew how many hours it had taken. What emerged, as far as she could fathom, was a research protocol that had involved administering various diseases to a living patient housed at BioMed. The monitoring that followed was intended to measure the systemic response.

Which seemed to be none. Whatsoever.

But that had to wrong. There was no way a human being could be exposed to that kind of virulent disease, on top of a suppressed immune system, and not be overcome with the cancer, the viruses, the bacteria. The whole thing defied logic—and ethics. What person would consent to such a thing? And didn't that raise alarm bells: When you had to ask that question, the underlying assumption was that it was a rhetorical because nobody would.

Nobody would *ever* agree to this. So had the patient been lied to? Or worse, were they being held against their will?

No. That couldn't possibly have happened ... could it?

The whole thing was like falling into a Michael Crichton novel, except it appeared to be actually happening.

Sarah glanced over at the computer screen as she thought through, for the hundredth time, the images she'd looked at—the PET scans, the CAT scans, the MRIs, the results of blood tests, the cardiac imaging.

She could explain none of it. Not the protocol, which violated every ethical standard in medicine, not the patient's response, which was inexplicable, and certainly not BioMed's participation in a study that would expose the corporation to probable criminal liability as well as problems with the federal government, the FDA, the AMA, and all kinds of professional groups.

She also could not explain Gerry's role.

It was clear that this was a protocol run out of BioMed's Infectious Disease division. On one of the reports, both BioMed's logo and the IDD's notation had appeared at the bottom, as if a document template had been used out of habit. Clearly, none of the study's lead researchers wanted their name anywhere, and they had taken care to remove all other identifiers of the lab. That one had slipped through, however.

And Gerry obviously had gained access to the study at some point. Probably when his security clearance had been increased. But did he participate in the unlawful practices?

The mere idea of that made Sarah want to vomit.

She thought of his boss, Dr. Thomas McCaid. Tom McCaid had been the one who'd hired Gerry, and she'd told that FBI agent that the man had been a lab supervisor—which was true, but there was more to it. McCaid was the only researcher with that ranking who reported directly to the CEO, Dr. Robert Kraiten.

Not that McCaid was reporting to anyone, anymore.

Sarah had never met the fabled Dr. Robert Kraiten in person. Her hiring had been coordinated through her lab supervisor. But she'd seen the man speak, both at company-wide annual meetings, and on the Internet. He had a TED Talk which had been widely circulated throughout BioMed, on the limitless horizons of bioengineering.

"We are still in the dark ages of medicine . . ." was how he'd opened his speech. After which he'd gone on to point out that things like organ donation with its immune system problems and Draconian chemotherapy protocols for cancer patients were going to be akin to the leeches, tubercular sleeping porches, and lack of sterilization of the past. Fifty years from now, he maintained, replacement parts for the human body were going to be grown in labs, cancer was going to be battled at the molecular level by the immune system, and aging was going to be a matter of choice rather than inevitability.

Sarah could see some of what he was saying. What she hadn't liked about him was his messianic affect, like he was a self-proclaimed pied piper with all the answers, leading a drop-footed, dumber populace to the promise land of science of which only he was aware.

Then again, the man was worth how much? Having billions could make a megalomaniac out of anybody.

Given that McCaid had been head of the IDD lab, he had to know about this research. And by extrapolation, if McCaid reported directly to Kraiten, then the CEO had to know about this research.

In fact, a strong conclusion could be made that both men had promoted it, one by doing the work and the other by providing the funding and facilities.

Unless she was missing something. But how else could you explain it? Kraiten either had unethical experimentation being conducted in his lab by a rogue researcher with unlimited access to restricted-use MRI machines, PET and CAT scans, and X-rays as well as a blood laboratory and a fucking patient . . . or Kraiten was paying for the research to occur and keeping a lid on everything.

Even if it meant killing the scientists who were doing the work.

And God . . . what happened to the patient? Was he even alive anymore? The files were all two years old.

Sarah brought the laptop back into place and reviewed the directory one more time. She knew what she was looking for, knew that the hunt was stupid and fruitless. Knew that she was bound to be disappointed.

And she was.

Nothing from Gerry. No directions as to what to do with all this. No recounting of why he'd lifted all of this data.

Most importantly, no indication of what his role was in the protocol.

The Gerry she knew would never have endangered the life of a patient in the pursuit of scientific knowledge or advancement. He believed in the sanctity of life and had a commitment to the alleviation of suffering. Both were the reasons he'd gotten into medicine.

But this was his Infectious Disease division. And he obviously had not gone to the authorities with any of this—otherwise, all of BioMed would have been shut down.

On that note, the FBI was asking questions about the deaths, not the work.

Or maybe they were probing the corporation and she just didn't know the depth of what had triggered their investigation.

"What happened to the patient?" she said aloud while she rubbed her aching eyes.

As she closed her lids and leaned back again, from out of nowhere, a memory of her hanging up the phone in her teenage bedroom came to mind, and she saw everything so clearly: the messy floral bedspread she'd been sitting on and her Smashing Pumpkins posters across the walls and the blue jeans draped on the back of her desk chair.

Bobby something or another. She couldn't remember what his last name had been and didn't that seem odd, given the momentous bomb he'd dropped on her.

Total devastation: He'd told her he was taking someone else to senior prom forty-eight hours before the dance. And not just anyone, either. He was escorting her good friend, Sara, a.k.a., No-"h", because Sarah had been with the "h". Talk about your sniper invites. Bobby had been relatively new to school, having arrived the year before as a junior when his dad took a job with the metro government. Sara and Sarah, on the other hand, had known each other since kindergarten.

That phone conversation had been quick, the kind of thing that he'd rushed through because he felt bad, but his mind was made up.

It wasn't like Sarah didn't get it. No-"h" was a knockout, or had been ever since her body had gotten its curves on the summer before. She was also funny and friendly, the kind of girl you looked forward to sitting next to at lunch because there was always going to be a good laugh.

She was not a mean girl. But this was a surprise.

Sarah would have thought, even if Bobby had had the bright idea, that there would have been a no-way from No-"h."

Her prom dress had been hanging off her closet door, and she could recall how she'd looked over at it and started to cry. Her dad had taken her shopping two weeks before in what had been yet another in a whole line up of awkward I-wish-Mom-were-here kind of interactions. Like when Sarah had gotten her period for the first time. Or when she'd wanted to start shaving her legs. Or how about worrying whether she could get pregnant after she hooked up with Bobby for the first time, even though they hadn't gone all the way.

The dress had been form-fitting and a deep red. Her father had approved of neither, but she'd wanted to come out as a woman for the first time.

No more girl stuff. No pastels. No frills. No big bows.

As she'd stared at the gown, she'd thought about how every night after she turned the light off, she looked at it and smiled, imagining all kinds of prom moments with Bobby, him in a tuxedo, her enshrined in red, the pair of them grown-ups at a big blowout. Dancing together. Making out. Maybe sealing the deal in what would be, for her at least, the first time.

Now? She could still go, sure. But the prom was just two days away and everyone was paired up.

And then there was the joy of realizing that they'd all gone in on the limo, eight couples, including No-"h".

Who apparently had broken up with her boyfriend.

As the trickle-downs to the phone call played out—including the cringer that maybe Bobby had liked Sara all along and he'd just been waiting for the break-up to happen and the corollary sting that Sara should have called but probably wouldn't—all Sarah had wanted was her mom.

Sometimes, you needed to bear your soul's pain to somebody who had walked a mile in your sparkly high heels.

It wasn't that she didn't love her father. But he was a resource for other things.

The yearning for her mom, so familiar, so mournful, so ultimately going-nowhere, had just added to her crushing despair.

Sarah felt shadows of that now.

There were questions she needed to ask. Fears she wanted allayed. Choices to discuss. And not just with anyone. With Gerry.

She needed to talk to him about this. Ask him what he knew and what he had done. Demand to know whether he was the good man she had believed him to be or someone else entirely.

But he was gone, and there was nowhere to go with any of it.

She was alone with a baseless yearning, once again.

After so many years of being in this isolated spot, you'd think she'd be used to it.

Some destinations were ever new territory, however, no matter how well you knew their town squares.

CHAPTER FOURTEEN

No, it wasn't Siberia.

But as Murhder re-formed at the outer fringe of a forest, the winter landscape before him seemed both cruel and pervasive. The snowdrifts across the meadow's open acreage were like waves upon a restless arctic sea, the top layer carved into drifts by relentless cold winds. What trees there were seemed tortured by the cold, their bare branches like claws retracted in pain, their trunks starved and ragged. Overhead, a thick cloud cover suggested another blizzard's battering was coming, the weather seeming to hate the earth.

About three hundred yards away, on the far side of the bare field, the shack cowering in the midst of a grove of stubby pines was not the cozy haven of a postcard. There was no wisp of cheery smoke rising from its tilted chimney, no glow of candlelight and warmth in its paltry windows, no strong refuge against the gales, given its frayed siding.

Maybe this was the wrong address.

Maybe V was mistaken—

As Xhex materialized beside him, Murhder shifted in the snow even though he'd been prepared for her appearance. Still, her scent in his nose was a strange shock.

Glancing over, he measured her grim profile. Her hair was even shorter than it had been when he'd known her. Her eyes seemed even darker—but that could be the situation. The rest of her was exactly as he remembered, powerful and sure.

They had said little before they'd left Darius's former house together. And he had the sense that he wasn't going to get another chance to talk to her. Ever again.

"Thank you for coming with me," he said roughly.

She shook her head, and he figured she was going to it's-not-about-you him. When she didn't say anything, he frowned.

"What," he asked.

It was a while before she answered him. Then again, given their history and all the things they had never discussed? Lot to choose from.

"Why did you keep going after them?" She looked at him. "That lab. Those scientists. Those humans. Why did you hunt them?"

Murhder recoiled. "Are you serious?" When she just stared at him, he cursed under his breath. "How could I not. They hurt you. They nearly killed you."

Xhex refocused on the meadow ahead. "We weren't like that, you and I. I wasn't a mate to *ahvenge*."

"On my end, we were."

"I lied to you."

"I know."

As she exhaled, her breath came out into the cold as a haze that dispersed quickly. "I'm sorry. For everything. For not telling you what I am. For my bloodline and what they did to you up in the colony. I'm really sorry."

Murhder opened his mouth. He intended to tell her it was all okay. That he was fine. That he . . .

But they both knew that wasn't true, and he refused to lie. At least out loud, that was.

"I never blamed you for that," he said roughly. "Not telling me about the *symphath* in you, I mean."

"Why?"

"You were protecting yourself. As a fighter, I get that."

Back then, no one with mixed blood would have ever come forward for fear of getting deported. And he assumed that was the same now—although so much had changed since he'd been around, who knew.

Abruptly, she turned to him. Her eyes were shadowed and not just because there was no moon out. They were filled with pain, and he knew what that felt like.

As the cold wind blew his hair around, and sadness darkened the night even further, he realized that even though the pair of them were not destined to be together, they would never fully be apart, either. Their relationship had carved runes in the bedrock of their souls, the suffering on both sides longer lasting than any resonant joy could have been.

"You make me ashamed of myself," she said hoarsely. "You kept going after those humans. I stopped. Otherwise, maybe I could have saved this female. And her young."

Murhder shook his head. "Don't blame yourself. There's no right answer when it comes to healing from tragedy. You took care of yourself. That is what matters."

Okay, so that was some serious bullshit. He hadn't healed a damn thing in himself, so he really didn't know what he was talking about when it came to recovering from anything more serious than a broken bone. Still, he wanted to ease her conscience. After everything that had been done to her, she deserved freedom, and not just from that cage she'd been kept in.

"You were there the night I burned that lab down, weren't you." As he nodded, she continued, "How did you know where I was?"

He closed his eyes and fought against going back to the past. And if it hadn't been for the rock-solid conviction that they were never seeing each other again after this, he probably would have let it all go.

Instead . . . he found himself answering, the words bubbling up his throat and coming out of his mouth on shaky syllables.

"When your people gave you over to the humans up at the colony, I broke free and tried to save you. I saw you get put into a van with blacked-out windows and there was a logo on it. I would have followed, but . . ." Well, her relatives took control of his brain again and that had pretty much ruled his roost. "After Rehv got me out sometime later, I searched for the laboratory that matched the logo. It was dumb luck that I happened to find it the night you lit that fire."

Dumb luck . . . or part of the Scribe Virgin's grand plan. If you believed in that kind of thing.

He touched the shard of seeing glass through his shirt. That van had been how he'd eventually found the other two vampires. As he had watched Xhex against the flames she had started, a vehicle that he had not thought much about at the time had driven off. Only later, after he had decided to leave Xhex alone and had dematerialized away from the site of the blaze, had he recalled it had been the same van from the night she'd been taken from the *symphath* colony.

That was how he'd suspected there were others being held.

And he'd been right.

"I didn't know there were others at the lab." Xhex cleared her throat. "I mean, while I was there, they kept me alone, probably because I attacked them every time they came at me."

Murhder closed his eyes and shook his head. "That should never have happened. To you, or anybody."

"I don't blame you at all for keeping your distance from me. But what I can't understand is, why did you tell the Brotherhood you were the one who burned down the lab?"

"Does it matter now?"

"Yes. I mean, it wasn't until tonight that I figured it all out. That they blamed you for all of it. First that fire and then the slaughter at the second site."

He shrugged. "By the time the Brothers linked what you'd done to all my wrongs? It was a drop in a bucket. I decided you didn't need any more trouble than you'd already found and God knew I was in deep enough as it was."

"They know about me. About what I am."

"I figured that out. Good on them for accepting you—"

"I'm mated now."

"Congratulations," he heard himself say.

"He's a good male."

He better be, Murhder thought. *Or I'll kill him with my bare hands.*

When she didn't say anything further, he waited for feelings of jealousy and possession to bubble up in his chest. Something did kindle, deep inside, but it was too quiet an emotion for him to process. He was very sure it was not a bonded male reaction, however.

"I didn't come back here to make problems for you," Murhder said. "It's really all about the female."

"Any way I can help, I'm there." Xhex looked away to the cabin. "I owe her, even though I don't know her."

Murhder didn't mean to reach out, but his arms extended before he could think about it one way or another . . . and the next thing he knew, Xhex was in his arms, the pair of them holding on to each other, the invisible winds of their pain and suffering turning them into the eye of a hurricane.

It was what he had wanted to do the night of that fire, but he had lacked the nerve.

"I'm sorry, too," he said over her head.

"What are you apologizing for?" she asked.

"Everything."

◆   ◆   ◆

John Matthew was downwind from Xhex and Murhder as they embraced in the shadows of a stand of pine trees.

The ugly grunt that came out of his throat was low and dangerous to his own ears. And then there was the fact that his palms had somehow managed to find both his daggers and unsheathe them from his chest holster.

The crack of a stick directly behind him was the only thing that stopped him from rushing out into the meadow and attacking the former Brother.

As John wheeled around, Tohr loomed behind them. "Damn it, John. What the hell are you doing here?"

All John could do was breathe. His raging bonded male was so dominant that the instinct to attack, protect, defend took over his higher reasoning. Or at least most of it. There was still enough to remind him that he did not want to hurt his surrogate father.

"Son," Tohr said, "don't do this, okay? Don't do any of this."

The image of Xhex stepping in against another male, a former lover of hers, a Brother, was like gasoline on the fire of his temper. And Tohr must have known he was about to act because the male locked a hold on John's right shoulder—

Directly on the bite wound.

If John had had a voice that worked, he would have cursed loud enough to bring snow from the storm clouds overhead.

The unholy pain that lanced through him was so intense it was probably the only thing that could have overridden his bonded male. Pitching forward, temporarily blinded, he fell into Tohr, who caught him before he hit the ground.

"Are you injured? John!"

Tohr rolled him over and laid him out flat on the snow, and as his nervous system struggled with the sensory load plowing through him, his daggers were stripped from his hands and the Brother's face appeared above his.

"Talk to me, son, what's going on?"

With sloppy reflexes, he fumbled around the area of his shoulder, trying to push the Brother's hold away from what was killing him—

Okay, that was a bad choice of words right there.

With a swift yank, Tohr opened his leather jacket.

"You're not bleeding." The Brother took out his phone and turned the light on. "Let me pull your shirt—"

As strung out as John was, he knew the second when Tohr saw the bite wound through the straps of the muscle shirt. The Brother's face froze, composure slamming down on his features. He actually seemed to lose concentration for a split second.

When he came back on line, his voice was falsely even. "When did this injury happen and why haven't you told anyone?"

John just shook his head, the snow underneath his skull creaking from the cold—which made him wonder dimly why he didn't feel the wintery temperature. Actually . . . he wasn't feeling anything all of a sudden, not the weight of his body, not the buzz of his aggression, not even the pain.

At least that last one was good news.

Other voices, now. Deep and quiet. Tohr had called for someone(s), but John didn't bother trying to see who it was.

Instead, he stared straight up at the gray sky overhead. Funny, back before his transition, he had thought he had good eyesight—or maybe it had been more like he hadn't had bad eyesight. Near or far, he'd gotten what he needed in terms of visual information.

After the change? It was as if a cloudy film had been removed, his ability to notice minute details about objects and people from a football field's distance away in near pitch darkness such a shock, he could remember thinking surely it was a superpower.

Now, as he watched the sky, he could see the different shades of gray in the storm's underbelly, the currents of wind swirling in slow-motion banks of snow-swollen clouds. The effect was quiet, beautiful . . . calming, like silk billowing in an open doorway.

Xhex and that male felt miles away. Then again, so did his corporeal form, even as his vantage point suggested he wasn't having an out-of-body experience.

Am I dying, he asked mutely.

When no one answered, he wasn't surprised. They couldn't hear him, and even if they could have, he couldn't connect with whoever was around him.

Sadness washed through him. He didn't want to leave things with Xhex like this.

Even if he was the only one who knew they were estranged.

CHAPTER FIFTEEN

Murhder and Xhex stepped back from the embrace at same time, and as he stared down at her, he figured out what his emotion had been when she'd told him that she was mated to someone. It had been a quiet relief. A door closing not with a slam, but with a click.

Not that he'd come back here thinking they had any future together. It was just a resolution he had not expected to find, and yet valued more than he would have guessed.

"If he ever hurts you," Murhder said, "I'll skin him alive."

"John, you mean?" She shook her head. "He's a prince of a guy. I think you'd like him, actually."

God, it had been so long since Murhder had thought in terms of liking or not liking another living being. But that was what happened when you were all about survival. And when your brain was an unreliable mess.

"Let's do this," he said as he looked across the snow-blanketed meadow.

Xhex nodded and they started off side by side, her boots and his heavy treaded shoes punching through the icy top level and compressing the softer flakes underneath with muffled crunches. Before leaving Darius's old house, the Brothers had given him a heavy parka and thick snow pants as well as gloves and the shoes. No weapons. Not that he'd asked for his own back.

Looking around, he saw nothing but trees on the periphery. Talk about sitting ducks. As the pair of them crossed this open area, they were completely without cover, but he wasn't worried. There were no foreign scents on the cold wind, and the Brothers were no doubt on the fringes and playing nursemaid. If anyone rode up on them?

Shit was going to go down.

The closer they got to the farmhouse, the worse the structure looked. Between its swaybacked roof, distorted windows, and loose clapboards, the place looked like it was on its last legs—and he felt a renewed sense of guilt.

Not that regrets over this female had ever needed help getting over his fence and into his backyard.

If only he'd been faster at that lab. Or if that male hadn't gotten shot. Or if—

"How did she find you?" Xhex asked.

"Eliahu Rathboone." His breath left his mouth in puffs as he spoke. "My B&B. She said she saw the portrait of me on TV."

As a cutting wind came up against them, Murhder put his gloved hands into the borrowed parka's pockets and thought about Fritz providing the insulated clothes. The butler had not been surprised to see him and had offered the same wrinkled smile he always had. In his eyes, though, the *doggen's* sadness had been evident and Murhder got it. Back in his old life, he'd crashed so many times at Darius's, he'd been a member of the household. Now? Being an outcast meant he was worse than a stranger.

He was family with bad baggage.

And on top of that? Darius, the Brother who had brought that butler and Murhder together, was now dead, the conduit between them gone, one more emptiness to register on the long list of people who were no longer there.

Speaking of which . . . they were about twenty yards away when the dark windows of the shack made him worry. He'd expect any exterior glass to be shuttered during the daylight hours, but the sun wasn't a problem now. Why no interior lights? Eyeing the anemic wires that came out of the forest and attached to a corner of the roof, he worried that she'd lost power.

Or what if she'd moved from where she'd received Havers's surgical aftercare, but stayed in the same town? The fact that the female hadn't included her home's location or a phone number had made sense to him because she hadn't been any surer of where he was than he had been of her identity. And as vampires living in a world dominated by humans, everyone was careful.

Especially someone like her who had been tortured by the other species.

But now, he wondered. Was this all a ruse? Except then how had she known what had happened as he'd broken into the lab?

These questions burned up the short distance to the front door, and out of the corner of his eye, he noted that Xhex had discreetly taken out a handgun.

Curling up a fist, he knocked to announce their presence—and did not like the way the panels rattled in the frame. When there was no answer, he knocked again.

The door had an old-fashioned iron latch instead of a modern knob, and as he lifted the weight, he expected the metal to fall right off its mounting. Instead, he got resistance as he tried to push and then pull things open.

He knocked a third time. And then his training and experience as a Brother took over. This position at the door was too much exposure, sentries in the woods notwithstanding.

Murhder turned his shoulder to the flimsy barrier and busted through it, his momentum carrying him into an ice-cold center room.

Silence.

Taking out a penlight, he moved the thin beam around, fine dust turning what was a spotlight into a flood. There was a threadbare sofa. A TV, which surprised him until he recognized it as being from the nineties. A desk with . . .

Walking across the floorboards, he trained the light on a letter that was partially written on paper that was the same as the missives that had been sent to him. And sure enough, in the same hand, the salutation was to Eliahu Rathboone.

He didn't bother reading the two and a half paragraphs.

"She's here. Or she was—"

The moan was so soft, a creak of the floor beneath his feet nearly drowned it out. Hurrying toward the sound, he went into what looked like a cold-water kitchen, everything painfully neat on the pitted counters, the old seventies-era refrigerator making a rhythmic choking noise.

The bedroom was in the back on the right, and now he could scent a female. But she had a terrible visitor with her.

Death.

The acrid and achingly sad scent of the dying was heavy in the still, frigid air, and as Murhder breached a narrow doorway, he clasped the shard of seeing glass once more.

"You found me," a weak voice said.

In the glow of the penlight, a bed was revealed, and upon it, under layers of handmade quilts, a female was on her side facing him, her skeletal visage on a thin pillow. Wisps of hair, gray and curled, formed a halo around the stark bones of her features, and her skin was the color of fog.

Murhder went to her, dropping to his knees.

As her sunken eyes sought his, a tear escaped and dropped off the bridge of her nose. "You came."

"I did."

Strangers they were. And yet as he reached for her hand, it was a family connection.

"I have no more moons left," she whispered. "And my night skies are going starless."

"I will do what you need me to do." He rushed the words, in the event she passed right now. "I will find your son, and I will get you medical help—"

"Too late ... for me."

He looked over his shoulder at Xhex. "Get the Brothers. Bring them here to help her—"

The hand in his own squeezed. "No, it's all right. I know you will not fail ... I cannot hold on any longer, and I do not want my beloved son to see me like this."

Xhex disappeared, and he was relieved. She would bring aid.

"What is your name, female?" he asked as those lids lowered.

"Ingridge."

"Where are your people?"

"I have been shamed. Leave them be ... I told you where my son is. Go, rescue him, make him safe. He would have come unto me here if he had escaped. He knows of this place. We were to meet here if e'er we were separated."

"Ingridge, stay with me," Murhder prompted as she fell silent. "Ingridge ... stay ..."

"Find my son. Save him."

"Don't you want to see him again?" Murhder was aware he could not promise such a reunion, but he would say anything to keep her on this side of the grave. "Hold on, help is coming—"

"Save him."

Beneath the faded quilts, her body jerked and she inhaled sharply as if a sudden pain had gripped her. And then came an exhale that lasted as long as eternity.

"Ingridge," he choked out. "You need to stay here ..."

As he tried to find words to compel her unto life rather than death, he thought about the testimony of *wahlkers*, those who had come up to the brink of death yet returned unto the living, those stories of a foggy landscape that parted to reveal a white door. If you opened the door, you were lost from the earthly world forever.

"Do not open that portal," he said sharply. "Do not step through. Ingridge, come back from the portal."

He had no clue whether the command made sense or even if she could hear him. But then her eyes popped open and she seemed to focus on him.

"Natelem is his name. I told you where to find him—"

"No, you didn't—"

Ingridge switched over to the Old Language, the syllables muddled in places, the words running together. "*Upon my bed of mortal demise, and with the Virgin Scribe watching o'er me, I hereby grant you all rights and responsibilities o'er my young, Natelem. I seek your acceptance of this precious gift upon your honor as a male of worth.*"

Murhder twisted around. He wanted to see Brothers rushing in with a medic.

Not happening.

On to plan B.

Yanking up the tight cuff of the parka, he didn't get far enough so he ripped off the jacket, and pulled his shirtsleeve up to reveal his wrist.

"Swear it," she begged. "So that I might die in peace."

"I swear it." He met her eyes. "But you're going to live."

As she exhaled in relief, he bit into his own vein and then brought the puncture wounds to her mouth. "Drink, take from me and . . ."

She was still exhaling, her eyes closing, her body loosening, but she opened her mouth prepared to accept what he offered—

"Ingridge," he said sharply. "Ingridge, take from me."

His blood, red, warm, vital, dropped onto her lips. Yet she did not respond. There was no turn toward the source, no seal of her mouth upon his vein, no response whatsoever.

Murhder's heart pounded. "Ingridge! Wake up and drink."

With his free hand, he awkwardly reached under his extended arm and gently shook her body. Then he did this again, more forcibly—

She rolled off her side onto her back, but the movement was like blocks falling from a stack, not anything that represented volition.

She was gone.

"No . . ." Murhder swallowed hard. "Don't go. Not now . . . *please.*"

As he argued against the reality before him, his eyes clung to her hollowed face and he prayed for some kind of rousing, his blood slipping down the back of her throat and entering her body, reviving that which was animated no longer.

Instead, she remained still. And the contrast between the vital red of what he wanted her to take from him and the pasty, deathly white color of her immobile lips made his soul scream at the unfairness of life.

With a shaking hand, he reached up to her mouth. He wanted to leave his blood where it was, but he couldn't bear the idea that she looked unattended in her death. Forgotten. Uncared for.

Wiping the stain away as best he could, he whispered hoarsely, "*I shall get your son, and I shall make sure he finds a safe home. This is my vow to you.*"

Pulling the quilts up higher on her neck, as if he could stave off the cooling of the body, he was crushed even as he remained whole. And though she was nominally a stranger, it was impossible not to think of her as blooded kin, the two of them united by events that forged a bond ne'er to be broken.

Bending over the bed, he covered her fragile remains with his strength, the shield of his support too late in coming, the sword of the Reaper having already done its work.

Why was he always too late? Murhder thought as he gathered her in his arms.

Despair, a familiar swamp, drenched him in its swill of sadness, and he retreated deep into his mind as he began to weep.

I will find your son a proper father, he vowed silently. *It will be the last thing I do before I join you unto the Fade.*

CHAPTER SIXTEEN

Xhex ended the call to the training center's clinic and looked across the meadow. The Brotherhood was somewhere in the trees and she waved her hand to catch their attention. Figuring they'd know what the signal meant, she went back inside the farmhouse, treading over creaking boards, walking through cold, still rooms.

When she got to the bedroom, she stopped short in the doorway. She had intended to go in.

She did not.

Across the cold, barren space, a tapestry of mourning tore at her soul, and told her all she needed to know about the futility of medical help. Murhder had covered the female's form with his own body, and the shuddering of his shoulders as well as the scent of tears was such a private moment that she backed off.

Lowering her head, she covered her mouth with the palm of her gloved hand and put her other arm around her middle. Sometimes in-the-nick-of-time was still not good enough, and it was impossible not to put herself in Murhder's position.

God, that male had been born under a dark star. He seemed destined for suffering.

She was standing in the middle of the main room when Rhage and Vishous came up onto the shallow porch.

"What's going—" Rhage didn't finish the question. The scents in the air said everything. "Shit."

"She's dead. The female is dead." Xhex glared at V. "And no, he didn't kill her."

The Brother cocked an eyebrow. "Did I say anything?"

"I can read your grid." She pointed to the center of her chest. "*Symphath*, remember?"

"How can we help?" Rhage interrupted. "What can we do?"

Xhex glanced over her shoulder. As she blinked, she saw Murhder crumpled over that corpse, and wanted to scream at destiny that the poor bastard deserved a break.

"Nothing," she muttered. "There's nothing to be done."

"We can't just leave a dead body here." V took out a hand-rolled. "We're gonna have to—"

"Don't you fucking light up in here."

That diamond stare narrowed. "Excuse me?"

"Have some respect—and if you point out she's dead, I will have your throat in my hand before you get the final word out. This is still her house, goddamn it."

As V's icy eyes flashed with aggression, she hoped the Brother came at her. She wanted to fight with something she could physically strike. But instead, he turned around and headed back for the door. The muttering was under his breath. The f-bombs were nonetheless still audible.

Xhex ripped off her hat and rubbed her short hair. Talk about emotional grids. With the amount of anger she had in her, she was dangerous and not a value add in this highly charged situation. And the last thing Murhder needed was more drama.

Marching over to the open door, she leaned out. V had set up shop against a column and was blowing a stream of smoke into the night.

"I am sorry I took your head off," she said roughly. "This is a shitty situation."

The Brother looked across at her. His inhale on the hand-rolled was long and slow, the tip glowing bright orange. As he exhaled, he talked through the smoke. "You're right. I shouldn't be lighting up in someone else's crib. It's rude."

Xhex nodded. Vishous nodded.

When she went back inside, she stopped short. Murhder had come out from the back bedroom, and other than bloodshot eyes that gleamed too bright, you wouldn't have known he'd just lost it.

Good male, she thought.

Him showing any weakness around the Brothers did not seem like a good idea.

"I wrapped her up in quilts," he announced in a hoarse voice. "Let's shut this place up tight. The cold will preserve her body for the Fade Ceremony."

◆   ◆   ◆

Murhder knew his mouth was moving and he guessed that he was communicating things which made at least nominal sense because Xhex and Rhage were nodding back at him. His mind was somewhere else, however.

I told you where to find him.

Except she hadn't.

And he had already tried to find out if there were any other spin-off labs. Over the years, when he'd gotten particularly antsy, he had searched the Internet for signs that such research could still be going on. The original pharmaceutical company had shuttered its doors, and there were no more facilities registered under the name. He had taken that as a good sign, and tried to use it to ease his conscience—

As conversation swirled around him, his eyes went to the desk.

Murhder ran across the bare room like that half-written letter was the way out of a three alarm fire.

Picking the piece of paper up with shaking hands, he read the Old Language symbols—and exhaled in relief. Okay. All right. She had told him after all.

He knew where to go. Ithaca. There was a rebranded laboratory associated with the original one doing work in Ithaca. She'd found it after scouring PETA websites that tracked pharmaceutical companies with animal rights violations.

Opening his mouth, he turned to Xhex—and then shut things up tight. Rhage was looming in the corner, a big blond mountain who was chewing a grape Tootsie pop like a Great White.

Best to keep this quiet, Murhder thought as he slipped the letter into his pants pocket.

"Where's her son?" Rhage asked as he chewed. "We can help bring him here."

Murhder shook his head. "He's dead. He didn't make it. She told me this right before she died."

The Brother lowered his head and cursed. "I am so sorry."

"Me, too. It's so much tragedy." He was aware of Xhex frowning as she looked at him, but he refused to acknowledge her. *Symphaths* always knew too much. "I guess we should just go, then—"

"We can't leave her here." Rhage went over to the flimsy front door and gave it a shake. The thing had been left open on a why-bother because the inside of the shack was the same temperature as the great outdoors. "This isn't strong enough, even if you lock it."

"To keep out the wind, it damn sure is."

"There are wolf tracks all over these woods, and we scented a pack while we came across the meadow. Go around back. You'll see that they've been sniffing the property already."

Murhder rubbed his eyes to get the grit out. "We'll tie it shut. The door. The front door."

He had no idea what he was saying.

Xhex spoke up. "Rhage is right. She's not safe here. Let's take her back to my cabin, and Murhder, you can stay with her the whole time. You can do the Fade Ceremony there. The place has been shut down for the winter, so it will be cold, and it's solid."

Damn it, just let me go, he wanted to yell. He needed to find the exact location of the rebranded lab and case the place. There was no way he was fucking up his last chance with a haphazard attack. And he needed weapons. Supplies. A plan.

"You can make sure she's taken care of," Xhex said flatly. "You don't want to run the risk of her remains being desecrated."

Before he could reply, Vishous stuck his head into the farmhouse. "Xhex. I need you to come back home with me right now."

The heartbeat of silence that followed took Murhder back to his Brotherhood days. There were some combinations of words spoken in certain tones of voice that you didn't want to ever hear.

And that right there?

Was one of them.

CHAPTER SEVENTEEN

John sat naked on an exam table down in the training center's clinic, hands on his thighs, fingers fiddling with the stitched edge of the blanket he'd wrapped around his waist. Doc Jane and Dr. Manello, a.k.a. Manny, had stepped out into the corridor to talk, and on the patient side of the door they'd closed, he tried to translate the low murmurs.

It was like reading tea leaves. Just vague hints.

He was dead bone tired, but he was not going to lie back. He'd tried that, and had felt a rolling panic, sure as if he were trapped or tied down. Yup, sitting up was better.

The fact that the two docs, whom he considered friends, had put some distance between themselves and their patient for their little chat, suggested they didn't know what the fuck was going on with the bite mark. Which was just awesome considering a black stain had developed in the last two hours, what had been red and swollen when he'd checked it at the gym now looking downright corroded—

As his instincts pricked, John sat up straighter and looked toward the door. Then, right on cue, a dark spice emanated from his body, the rich scent a calling card that, for once, he was not interested in sporting.

Xhex plowed through the exam room door at a dead run, all but wiping out on the tile floor as she pulled up short, thanks to the snow that was on her boots. Those gunmetal-gray eyes went to his shoulder. Narrowed. Stayed there.

"What the hell happened?" she demanded.

She was still dressed for out in the cold, her cheeks windburned red, her hair even spikier than usual. The fact that she did not carry another male's scent suggested that she and Murhder had left things at an embrace, but he wondered how long that would last.

"John?" she said. "Are you okay?"

He watched her as she approached the exam table, and when he didn't respond, she waved her hand in front of his face like she was thinking he'd fallen into a vertical coma.

To distract himself, he looked toward the door that was slowly easing itself shut. Evidently Vishous had come to the training center with her, because the Brother was outside in the corridor talking to the doctors. Made sense. He was both a medic and the son of the great Virgin Scribe.

They would be asking about the Omega, John was quite sure.

"John?"

He lifted his hands, wincing as his shoulder let out a holler. *I saw you two together. You and Murhder—and don't you dare bitch at me for following you to those woods. The fact that you went into a clinch with the guy totally justifies my—*

"There's nothing going on between us—"

Don't tell me there's nothing happening. I saw the way you looked at each other. John shook his head. *I'm such a goddamned fool. I wasn't even worried when people talked about him coming up here. I figured I had nothing to be concerned about.*

"It's not like that."

The door burst open and Vishous came steaming in like he was about to go to battle.

"Let's see what you got, son," the Brother said. "I have a way with these things."

For the first time, John resented the "son" thing. He was a grown-ass male who had seen real action in the field. Not some pretrans getting bullied by his classmates.

But he told himself nothing would come from starting a fight with anybody.

Besides, he was abruptly distracted by Xhex stepping aside, crossing her arms and staring at the tiled floor. You didn't need to be one of her kind to judge her mood; she was a black hole off to the left, the toxic load of her emotions such that she nearly dimmed the overhead light.

Good, John thought. Even though that made him a bastard. But he was abruptly done with being the nice guy. He was always following the rules, doing the right thing, watching out for others. And what did it get him?

"Don't be alarmed."

As V spoke up, he glanced at the Brother—and recoiled. Vishous was taking off the lead-lined black glove that always covered up his curse, his glowing palm revealed in all its deadly glory.

Goosebumps prickled in warning all down John's arms and his guts churned. That thing was capable of incinerating whole buildings, part blowtorch, part atom bomb.

To hell with your finger-of-God shit. V had been born with the Big Fucking Bang.

And the guy was extending it toward John.

"I'm not going to touch you," V said grimly. "I just want to have a conversation with that wound."

Oh, great, John thought. *Let's pull up a couple of chairs and watch the layers of my skin melt off like that guy's face in* Raiders of the Lost Ark.

Doc Jane and Manny entered the exam room, but stayed back, the two white coats standing in identical arms-across-the-chest poses, literally pillars of medical knowledge and experience.

"Just breathe through it, John," V said as he closed the distance between his hellfire curse and the bite mark.

John flinched. He couldn't help it. And then warmth, like you'd feel when you were almost too close to a banked fire, radiated into his shoulder. As the heat intensified further, he had to fight not to pull away—except suddenly that wasn't possible, even if he'd wanted to. Some kind of metaphysical lock had occurred between the brilliant white light glowing in V's hand and the blackened wound, tendrils of energy emanating out of that palm and butterflying around the infection.

A grunting sound got John's attention. V was straining, beads of sweat breaking out over his forehead, his chest pumping up and down, the muscles in his throat, shoulders, and chest bulking up—

Like a rubber band snapping, the connection was broken and Vishous careened back, slamming into a glass-fronted cabinet, breaking all kinds of things in a car crash way. John was also thrown to the side, and as strong arms caught him, he latched on.

To Xhex.

Her face was pale and she trembled, even as she had the strength to keep him from hitting the floor.

V cursed and pried himself off the busted shelving. Glass was everywhere—especially in his skin—and he peeled off his black muscle shirt.

Doc Jane went over and turned him around. He had several big shards sticking out of his back, like a porcupine.

"I'm going to have to deal with this," his *shellan* said.

"We got bigger problems." V unceremoniously pulled out a piece of glass and tossed the blood-tipped stabber on the floor. "That is *not* the Omega. And I don't have a fucking clue what it is."

◆　　◆　　◆

Hours passed, and Xhex stayed with John the entire time. She worried he'd make her leave, but even though things were tense between them, he didn't. Watching the medical team do their thing—taking samples to culture for bacteria and test antibiotic resistance, conferring with Havers, talking with Ehlena, the clinic's nurse, having Payne come down for a healing assessment—Xhex relied on her *symphath* side to read the emotional grids of not just the team, but her mate.

The clinical staff, including V, were alarmed.

John was less so. Because his heart was breaking about Murhder, and that was the main thing for him.

And didn't that just kill her.

"So here's where we are." Doc Jane stepped up to the exam table and put her hand on John's knee.

Manny was right beside her. So was Ehlena. Vishous was off to the side, his back bandaged, his shirt on once more, the glass on the floor from the busted cabinet swept up a while ago by Fritz, the butler.

Xhex listened with half an ear to "no signs of infection," "infiltration beyond the first layers of skin," and "concern about the spread that's occurring." She was more interested in the doctor's emotional grid. Jane was flat-out panicking. Underneath her calm demeanor and even voice, her emotional superstructure—which appeared to Xhex's *symphath* side as a system of three-dimensional girders, like the shell of a skyscraper—was lit up in areas at the very core of her consciousness. Generally, the further out from that center, the more superficial the emotions, and the colors and pattern indicated what sector: happiness, sadness, anger, or fear.

What that doctor was currently feeling? Straight-up hot red terror as well as deep purple anger at herself for not having better answers. And the shit was at the very heart of her.

Do I have to stay here? John signed.

"No," Doc Jane said. "You're free to go. But we don't want you on rotation until we know what's happening."

"What's going to change?" Xhex asked. "About how much you know, I mean. You've looked into everything."

Was that black stain going to take him over? Kill him? Or worse . . . ?

"That's a fair question. The Chosen Cormia is going up to the

Scribe Virgin's library as we speak. She's going to search the volumes with all of the other sacred females. If there is something in them, it will be found."

"Okay. That makes sense. But what if there isn't?"

"We'll cross that bridge when we get to it."

More conversation, none of it material. All Xhex wanted was a minute alone with her mate. An hour alone. A lifetime.

When they were finally by themselves again, he lay back on the table. Then instantly sat back up.

"John." As she said his name, he looked at her. "No matter what happens, I'm with you. I got you. I love you."

Shifting his eyes away, her *hellren* stared down at the floor and took a deep breath. As the silence stretched out, her anxiety climbed and she found herself breaking a cardinal rule. Out of respect for him, she did not read his grid—usually. Some things should be private, and she'd always wanted him to share of himself what he chose to, a gift given instead of a secret pilfered.

Now, she read him as she had read everyone else in the room.

Heartache. Utter and complete heartache. He didn't seem to be concerned about his health in the slightest, but then that was a bonded male for you right there. Always thinking of his mate, and not just because it was the right thing to do. The single-minded focus was in their breeding, literally a part of their DNA.

As worried as she was about that shoulder wound, at least she could do something with his broken heart.

"I can prove to you there's nothing going on between Murhder and me."

John looked back over and she hated the wariness in his eyes.

"No, really." She nodded. "I know just what to do."

CHAPTER EIGHTEEN

The following evening, Sarah tied the laces on her running shoes, first on her right foot, then on her left. As she stood up, things felt nice and cushiony under her soles.

There were also good treads down there. Just what you'd want if you had to make a sprint for an exit.

Pulling on her parka, she picked up her backpack, one-strapped it and grabbed her keys. At the door out into the garage, she looked over her shoulder and wondered if she was ever going to see her house again.

She had spent the daylight hours scrubbing all the bathrooms, vacuuming the rugs, taking out the trash, mopping the kitchen floor. It was, she supposed, a reflex, like making sure before you left for a long trip you had clean undies on.

Just in case you were in a car accident.

Before she lost her nerve, she turned the alarm on, exited and locked up. Backing her Honda out, she tried to make like this was no big deal . . . just another Sunday night heading into work to check ongoing research results. Fortunately, she had done this before. Not all the time, but depending on where she was in her work, she had often headed into the lab on off-hours. Off-days. Even holidays like Christmas Eve, New Year's Eve, Fourth of July.

Although in the last two years, those trips had mostly been to distract herself from the loneliness of her house. Her life. Her future.

Heading down her street, she stared straight ahead. There didn't appear to be any deceptively nondescript sedans around, but who knew where the Feds were.

As she passed by familiar houses in the neighborhood, made familiar turns as she came to intersections, and stopped at familiar lights, she decided this was a bizarre experience. Most people didn't know that they were saying goodbye when they did something for the last time. It was only in retrospect, after things changed forever, that they realized a period in their life, an era, had come to an end.

Considering what she was going to do? There was a good chance she was not coming home.

She had called no one.

No one to call. Nothing really to say.

As she'd developed her plan, she had made sure to keep her schedule exactly as it always was on Saturdays and Sundays with bedtime and wake up, the cycle of lights inside what she usually clicked off and on.

Nothing out of place. Out of sync. Out of order.

Her heart was pounding as she continued along the route to BioMed, and when she pulled up to the gatehouse at the facility, she wanted to throw up.

Instead of giving into the heaves, she put her window down and smiled in anticipation of the security guard opening his sliding door. As the partition pulled free of its jamb, she braced herself for a gun to be pointed at her head.

Instead, the guard smiled. "Hey, Dr. Watkins. How you doin'?"

"Good, Marco, good." She handed him her ID and prayed he didn't notice that her hand was shaking. "It's cold tonight. You warm enough in there?"

"Oh, you know it." He put a scanner on the barcode underneath her picture and the device let out a beep. "Just watching the Heat play the Bulls."

"That'll keep you toasty."

"Sure will." He gave her the credentials back. "I'll see you on the flip side."

"I'll just be an hour or so. Checking on things."

"Good deal."

He closed his door. She put up her window. And then the twenty-foot-high chain-link gate trundled off to the side and the arm bar rose.

The lab compound was located a distance back from the guardhouse, and as she proceeded forward on the plowed two-lane drive, everything seemed both totally familiar and completely out of place. There was still this brilliantly lit road in with speed bumps every twenty yards or so and concrete barriers on either side. Still a vast, single-story complex connected by pediways. Still two parking lots to choose from, with spaces for a hundred or so vehicles.

As she headed to the right to leave off her car, one of BioMed's roving security cops went by her in his marked sedan. She waved to him. He waved back.

And meanwhile, her mouth went so dry she couldn't swallow.

There were a dozen or so cars, many of which she recognized, all of which were parked as close to the entrance as possible. She chose a spot she could drive through and face out.

God, she'd never had to think about making a getaway before. Then again, given the security here, if things went badly, like they were going to let her get back out here to the parking lot?

Disembarking with her backpack, she shut her car door and almost walked off without locking things. Her heart was still doing a sprint and a half behind her sternum, and the puffing of her breath into the cold air was so pronounced she looked around to see if she were being followed by anyone who would become suspicious. Could the FBI even get onto the property?

Probably not without a warrant.

A path had been shoveled and salted up the wide marble steps leading to the entrance, and as she got to the top landing, there was a familiar clunking sound as the lock was released upon her approach. Inside, she stopped in a vestibule that was heated and offered her card to the officer who was sitting behind a desk.

"You watching the Heat?" she asked as she heard a squawking under the counter.

"Sure am." There was another beep as the guard scanned her ID. "They makin' you work late again, Dr. Watkins?"

"Sure are." She forced herself to smile casually. "What can you do."

"Big boss man's here tonight, too."

Sarah hesitated as she put the lanyard around her neck. "Dr. Kraiten?"

"Yup. He came in with a couple of guys in suits."

The FBI? she wondered.

"Well, it'll be a party then." She forced a smile. "I'll see you on the flip side."

She had no clue what she was saying or what he replied. And it took everything in her to wait calmly for the unlocking before she could enter the lobby of the facility.

Marble floors, white walls, long corridors in three directions. Security cameras everywhere.

As she walked off straight ahead, she was aware of the photographic portrait of Dr. Robert Kraiten that hung between an American flag and the New York State flag. He had famously started his first company with his roommate while still at MIT forty years before, and there had been many incarnations since, the mergers and acquisitions morphing the biotech firm into a global leader in pharmaceutical and medical device research. Kraiten, now in his early sixties, was probably worth a billion dollars, and he was showing no signs of slowing down. His original partner, on the other hand, hadn't made it out of his forties.

She could remember Gerry telling her that the guy had come to a gruesome end when one of the labs had been burned down twenty years ago.

And didn't that make her wonder now.

Kraiten, on the other hand, was most certainly thriving, even if she personally found his public persona cold and aloof. But maybe that was the secret to his success. Remaining detached from everything no doubt spared emotions when you had to make hard corporate decisions.

Without meaning to, she rerouted and stopped in front of the picture in its large silver frame. The black-and-white image did little to improve the severity and calculation of the man's stare.

All she could think about was Gerry. And what secrets he had taken to his grave.

No, there was one other piece. She wondered who had put him up to it.

It required every kind of discipline for her to turn away and keep her pace slow and steady as she followed the corridors to her lab. As she went along, she was aware of every security pod in the ceiling, and she passed by a number of different research divisions. The office/lab set-ups were all the same, walls of frosted glass glowing with diffused light and preventing wayward eyes from divining anything of the work being performed behind coded doors.

There was no transparency anywhere. Even within the company, security clearances and access were parsed out like the place was the Pentagon and everyone was a spy. Hell, even the labs themselves were not titled by division names at their entrances, but rather a code of numbers that she still, four years later, didn't completely understand.

Her own division was in the eastern corner of the complex, and she swiped her ID at the card reader by the steel door. As her clearance was accepted, there was the sound of an air lock releasing and then she was inside the front office portion of the layout.

This section looked like your bog-standard office space, cubicles with gray partitions lined up in a row, a conference table and a little break area off to one side. Her desk was over on the right and she went across and put her backpack on it. She had spent so many hours here in her chair, at her corporate computer, on her corporate phone, talking about her research, her discoveries, her clinical trials on how cancer cells could be killed by the immune system under the right conditions. Her contacts included colleagues, researchers and oncologists around the world.

She had done good work, she realized. In spite of everything that had happened with Gerry.

But she had already left, hadn't she. As she looked around at her fellow BioMed employees' cubicles, she saw pictures of husbands, wives, children, dogs. Knickknacks. Mementos. *Dilbert* science jokes. Internet memes.

There were a lot of Einstein riffs.

Her cubicle? Nothing. After Gerry's death, she hadn't been able to concentrate with pictures of him around, so she'd stashed them in the bottom drawer of her desk.

Taking a deep breath, she turned away and walked across the gray carpet to another set of frosted doors. Using her pass card again, she gained access to the laboratory itself, the temperature-controlled, largely sterile, stainless steel and white-tiled area full of microscopes, refrigerators, testing equipment, centrifuges.

One thing that had always been true of BioMed was that they spared little expense when it came to equipment.

For a moment, she forgot why she'd entered. Then she looked at one of the storage units of pathology slides. It was full of tumor and blood samples from patients who were the true heroes of the effort, the real ones that mattered, the pioneers braver than Sarah would ever be.

Although considering what she was up to tonight?

Well, she was certainly woman-ing up in a way she never could have foreseen.

◆   ◆   ◆

As darkness finally fell, Murhder woke up in an unfamiliar room, although it took no time at all to recognize the modest contours of Xhex's hunting cabin. He had slept upright in a chair in the little central room that he imagined would, were he to pull back the blackout drapes that covered every window, provide a view of the mostly frozen Hudson River, the wintered-up shores of the waterway, and Caldwell's twinkling downtown buildings and highways on the far side.

He groaned as he sat forward, his spine having worked out some kind of intimate relationship with the back of the chair that it apparently did not want to end. Everything else on his body cracked and popped as he got to his feet, but he forgot about the aches and pains as he looked to the closed door of the bedroom.

Ingridge was in there. On the bed. Wrapped in clean white batting.

It was twenty or so degrees Fahrenheit in that part of the cabin, only the main room, bathroom, and kitchen winterized and currently heated. She would hold.

At first, he had been frustrated by how long it had taken to get transport for the remains to be taken out of the farmhouse. But then Rhage had let him borrow a cell phone, and it was then that he had done his research on the lab that Ingridge had named in her partially written letter—said Internet search performed under the guise that he was reading the *New York Times* online as the Brother snoozed in a corner.

Murhder had been careful to delete his website history when he returned the phone. And then the high-pitched whine of snowmobiles had cut through the meadow's silence as surely as they ruined the mostly undisturbed snow cover.

The body had been put on a sled, and the Brothers had done Murhder the honor of allowing him to drive her the twenty miles through the woods to where a blacked-out van awaited at the side of a rural road. By the time they had gotten things settled here at the cabin, it had been too close to dawn for him to head out to the location he'd confirmed on that phone. He'd had no choice but to spend the night. Meanwhile, Xhex had not returned from wherever she had gone, and Rhage had insisted on playing surrogate host by turning on the heat in this section of the cabin and getting the water running. And making sure there was food. Drink. A burner phone with the Brother's number in it in case Murhder needed anything.

The kindness had been unexpected and yet not a total surprise. Rhage had always been the Brother with the most voracious appetites, but he'd also had a good fellow side to him. As well as a chatty nature. As he had gotten things all set, he'd filled Murhder in with regard to all kinds of things that had happened in the last twenty years.

The fact that the male had gotten mated had been a shock, given his history with the ladies, and yet he'd seemed happy. At peace.

He even had a daughter he loved.

And that wasn't all. The King had a queen. Z had even settled down. Vishous, too.

That Tohr's Wellsie had been killed made Murhder's eyes sting. That the Brother had found another mate was a miracle, a gift from the Scribe Virgin.

Who, as it turned out, had abandoned the race.

There were too many other things to count. Times had changed. The Brothers had changed.

And yet Murhder himself had stayed the same, stuck in the past, in his madness.

Shaking himself into focus, he went into the bathroom, used the facilities, and decided not to waste time on the shower. Before he headed out to the lab, he had to go down to the Rathboone house to get weapons from his stash there. Ammo, too. And this time, he was wearing a goddamned Kevlar vest when he infiltrated.

Except he didn't want to leave this cabin. Sure as if Ingridge were alive and cognizant of being in a strange place, all alone, he felt the need to stay with her.

Reaching into the front of his shirt, he took out the shard of sacred seeing glass. As he stared into its reflective surface, he waited for the image to appear. And there it was. Ingridge as she had been before age and illness took her life, her face youthful, her hair pulled back, her eyes looking right at him in that widened surprise.

Compared to how she had been at the end, there was almost no likeness, and that struck him as tragic.

The sound of the back door creaking brought his head up.

Before he could find a makeshift weapon, Xhex stepped in out of the cold. She was in the same parka and her cheeks were bright from the frigid wind. She looked intense.

"Hey," she said. "Sorry I bailed on you last night. And before you deny it, I know you're going after the son, and that you know where to find him. I also need you to meet someone."

She stepped aside.

The male that came in behind her was enormous. Clearly a Brother, although Murhder didn't recognize the face—and that was when the unfamiliar ended. The blue stare that nailed him like a sucker punch froze him where he stood, and not just because they were hostile. There was something about the way they narrowed, the flash of aggression, the energy emanating out of them.

"I know you," Murhder said softly.

All at once, the male started to shake, and that big body listed forward as his arms and legs jerked and his eyes rolled back as if he'd been electrocuted.

"John!" Xhex yelled as she caught her mate.

CHAPTER NINETEEN

Sarah fiddled around in the office part of her division, sitting in her cubicle, ostensibly checking order forms for new slides and for the upgraded microscope they'd gotten cleared to buy the week before. What she was really doing was trying to assess in her head whether Kraiten's presence on-site meant she should pull out. In the end, she decided she could not reasonably make any statistical assessment of the probability of her success under current conditions, as her data was insufficient.

Or in layman's terms, she was in the dark about so much, and so patently out of her depth, that "utterly clueless" would be an improvement.

At ten minutes to ten p.m., she casually went over to her backpack and took out her meal card, making sure that it showed on the security cameras. What she kept hidden was the credential badge from Gerry's safety deposit box.

That she slipped into the pocket of her hooded sweatshirt.

One-strapping her backpack, she left her lab, striding quickly down the corridor. Gerry's division had two levels of clearance, the only lab at the firm that did. When it had come time for his level to be increased, she could remember him commenting on how he'd had to go down to Personnel and sign a bunch of documents. He'd also been fingerprinted, drug tested, and, as he'd said, all but microchipped like a dog at the vet's.

The cafeteria was halfway between Sarah's lab and the Infectious Disease division, and she steamed right by it. Security changed shifts at ten, something she'd learned from previous late nights, and she wanted to do her figural breaking and entering during the handoff.

When she came up to the IDD lab, her palms were sweating and she was breathing heavily. Taking the credentials out, she felt time slow to a crawl, and a part of her was all *No! Don't do this!*

Because there was going to be no going back. Her face, her infiltration, was going to be recorded, and if she were wrong, if what she'd seen on Gerry's USB drive was incorrect or if the program had been discontinued in the past two years, she was going to be fired and prosecuted for trespassing. And she was never going to work in her chosen field again because no research program in the country wanted to volunteer for a whistle-blower who'd cried wolf.

Plus she was going to be busy pulling an *Orange Is the New Black* for a while.

But then she thought of those scans. Those reports. All that cancer being pumped into a human being—

Her hand moved with a decisive swipe, and the nanosecond that followed took forever.

The light turned green. The air lock hissed.

She wasted no time going through the office part of the space and the layout was exactly the same as it was for her division, which was helpful. In the rear, over on the left, was another sealed door, and she swiped again, figuring it had to be for the lab.

That lock released as well for her, and as she pushed the heavy steel wide, she stopped.

Now, things were different, the orientation of clinical workstations and equipment not what she was used to. Didn't matter, she told herself as she entered. Walking in between the stainless steel counters and shelving, she looked into every nook and cranny, the whirring sound of the nitrogen cooling units a familiar white noise in the background.

Everything was sparkling clean, from the microscopes to the stacks of supplies to the workstations. Nothing was out of order. Nothing was unusual.

She started to think she was nuts.

But come on, what had she expected? Secret panels sliding back to reveal a clandestine lab?

God, she might well accomplish nothing except career suicide tonight.

After she went through the space three times, she focused on the isolation unit. Behind panels of heavy clear glass, she could see the suit-up anteroom as well as a decontamination area, and beyond, an airlocked chamber with hazmat markings all over it.

The pass card got her into the suit room and she put on the protective gear quickly, pulling a baggy blue isolation suit over her backpack, covering her head and neck with a hood, and latching gloves on that went up nearly to her elbows. After making sure everything was attached correctly, she entered the work area with its negative airflow, its InterVac hood stations, and . . . nothing else.

The sound of her breathing in the echo chamber of the head protection only increased her anxiety and the clear plastic panel she had to look through made her feel like she were underwater.

To hook herself up to the oxygen feed, she pulled one of the tethers away from its ceiling mount and clicked the hose to an aperture on the back of the suit. Instantly, plastic-smelling air flooded the hood, and the artificial smell of it made her gasp for breath.

Telling herself to get over it, she went around the twenty-by-twenty room.

Sarah found the keypad on the far side of the workstations, and at first, she almost overlooked it, as the thing didn't seem tied to any portal. But then she saw the ever-so-faint seam in the wall.

It was a door.

◆   ◆   ◆

John was used to the seizures. He'd been getting them on and off ever since he'd entered the vampire world. His first one, that he had a concrete memory of at any rate, had happened when he'd seen Beth. There had been others, of course, but the one that had occurred when he'd first met his sister, the King's *shellan*, had been truly significant.

This particular shake-and-shimmy, now that he was coming out of it, rang that highly important bell again—although he couldn't understand why.

The electrical storm in his nervous system retreated much like any thunder or snow front, the intensity diminishing, calm returning, a damage assessment the first stop on the back-to-normal road. As John's eyes opened, he didn't immediately record what was around him. He was too busy performing an internal check-in, and when the all-good got sounded, his vision provided him with the details of the two people leaning over him.

Xhex was a relief. The male with the long red-and-black hair? Not so much—and not just because John wanted to go for the guy's jugular as a matter of principle: The mere sight of Murhder's unusual hair, his gleaming peach eyes, the cut of his jaw and the heft of his shoulders, was enough to make the buzz come back, all kinds of nerve endings firing.

But John was able to beat that shit back.

Even as Murhder's voice, which sounded strangely familiar, said, "You remind me of an old friend."

John sat up and studied everything about the male. Then he signed, *Have we met before?*

Murhder's dark brows lifted at the ASL. "I'm sorry, I don't understand—"

Xhex, who had been staring at John as if she'd seen a ghost, seemed to shake herself back into focus.

"My *hellren* is mute." She repositioned herself on her knees with a wince. "And, ah, he wants to know if you've met before."

Murhder narrowed his eyes. "Sure feels like it."

Okay . . . weird. Even though it didn't make sense, John felt his bonded male ease off. It was rare for him to trust anybody at first blush, but this former Brother, crazy though he was rumored to be, felt like someone he could put his faith in.

But maybe that was just the seizure talking. Maybe his self-preservation sectors weren't back on line yet.

"I wanted John to be able to . . ." Xhex said roughly. "Shit."

John was about to ask her what was wrong, except there was so much to choose from. And on that note, he focused on the former Brother—and reminded himself that instincts about other people were all well and good, but the reality of the situation was that he didn't actually know the guy.

I don't want to have to kill you, he signed.

Murhder looked at Xhex. "What did he say?"

"He doesn't want to kill you," she muttered.

John didn't give a crap that he was only halfway back online. If the other male had an aggressive response to that translation, in any way whatsoever, he was going to go for the fucker's throat and chainsaw the goddamn thing with his fangs—

The smile that slowly came over Murhder's face was a bittersweet one. "I'm really glad you feel like that." He looked at Xhex. "You deserve nothing less and I'm happy for you. It's been a really long . . . hard road, and you're more than due a good life."

John turned to his mate. Her eyes were watering as she stared across at the other male. But there was no regret in her face; he had no sense that she wished she'd ended up with the former Brother.

They were more like two family members who'd survived a house fire that had destroyed everything.

John lifted his hands to sign. But then he just extended his dagger palm, offering it to the other male.

Murhder's shake was firm. "Good. Thank you."

Xhex cleared her throat. "Okay, enough of this. You're not going to that site by yourself. The two of us are coming with you—and don't waste our time trying to argue."

John squeezed the other male's hand, trying to communicate that he was in. Whoever that female had been, wherever her son was, if Xhex was going, John was coming with.

Murhder looked to the closed bedroom door.

"You know it's safer this way," Xhex said. "And you're more likely to succeed."

"Do the Brothers know?"

John shook his head, and mouthed, *It's just us. Promise.*

CHAPTER TWENTY

Sarah stood in front of the keypad in the isolation unit, aware of seconds passing. She could try a bunch of numerical codes, but what were the chances of getting the correct one when she didn't even know how long the sequence could be? And then she could get locked out if she got too many wrong in a row.

"Shit," she breathed, looking around through the hazmat suit's plastic visor.

But like they'd put a sticky note with the combination on the side of a cabinet?

If she turned around now and left, at least she had a chance of not getting into trouble. No alarms were going off, and maybe if security saw her on any of their monitors, they'd assume she had proper clearance—

Sarah looked down at the credentials. Then turned the laminated card over.

On the back, written in permanent marker, were those seven digits she'd assumed were a telephone number.

Leaning down to the keypad, she entered them one by one, the bulky glove camouflaging how badly her hand was trembling.

Nothing happened.

As she waited, heart pounding and throat choked, sweat dripped into her eye, and she went to wipe it away, batting at the hood with the glove, making things worse—

Pound key.

When she punched the pound key, the little light turned from red to green and an air lock released.

A door-sized panel disappeared into the wall itself, revealing a shallow stainless steel room that was about ten feet long and five feet wide. Egg crates lined the floor and they were full of a disorderly supply of nonperishables: canned soup, boxes of pasta, cereals, bags of Doritos and pretzels. Shallow shelves mounted on the vertical held shampoo, soap, toilet paper, Kleenex.

The sliding door began to shut behind her and she caught it with her hand. There was another keypad on the inside, and although she considered propping things open, she was worried that an alarm would go off. She just had to take the chance the code would work on the exit.

Releasing the air intake connected at the back of the hazmat suit, she let the hose fall free and then she was closed in.

The second the door she'd come through relocked, another panel opposite from it slid back, revealing a bright white light.

Swallowing hard, she took two steps forward and then stopped in the doorway.

The wave of revulsion and indignation was so great, she nearly vomited.

Across a clinical space, in a large cage that had some kind of mesh around it, there was a figure dressed in what appeared to be a hospital johnny, lying on a pallet facing away from her. Some kind of water source was off to the side, hanging from a hook, and a tray of empty plates had been pushed out onto the floor through a trapdoor. Behind the cage, medical monitoring equipment beeped and whirred.

Sarah reached out blindly for the wall as the world listed on her—

What the hell? The walls and ceiling were covered by the same mesh as the cage. And the floor . . . oddly, the floor was stainless steel.

The patient in the cage sat up and turned toward her—and Sarah lost her breath as if struck in the chest.

It was a child. A frail, thin little boy.

Overcome with horror, Sarah stumbled forward. Fell to her knees. Slumped as the inner door slid back into place and locked them in together.

With hands that shook so badly it was as if she were having a seizure, she tore off the gloves. Ripped the hazmat suit's hood off. Gasped for air.

As she looked up, she found that the child was staring across at her with wary eyes. But he didn't make any sounds of protest, and he didn't move from his spot on that pallet.

He had obviously learned that nothing he could do would stop what was being done to him. He was helpless. Trapped. At the mercy of those who had so much more power than he.

Minutes ticked by and the two of them continued to stare at each other, though the mesh made it hard to see him with total clarity.

"Are you here to give me my next shot?" he finally asked in a thin voice. "They said it would be at midnight. But it's only ten."

Two years since Gerry died. And they'd been experimenting back then. How long had they been torturing this *child*?

"Hello?" he said. "Are you okay? You're not my normal technician."

Sarah swallowed hard. The implications were so enormous they were incomprehensible. But rather than waste time sorting through the morass, she focused on the immediate issue.

"Sweetheart, I . . . I need to get you out of here. Right now."

The child bolted to his feet. "Did my mother send you? Is she alive?"

At that moment, alarms started going off.

✦   ✦   ✦

Murhder had done this mission before, and he was glad his practice run from twenty years ago had stuck with him even though two decades had passed between the infiltrations. He also had some serious backup this time: He, Xhex, and John had suited up with weapons and Kevlar that the couple had brought with them to her cabin in an SUV. And then they'd dematerialized, one by one, out of Caldwell, to this remote site in Ithaca.

Entry through the rooftop vents of the sprawling facility. Just like before. Interception of a security guard. Just like before.

It was then that he began deviating from the past. This time, he compelled the guard to take them down to the top secret part of the facility, a tour guide who had no will of his own.

So many unadorned corridors. So many unmarked doors in walls made of frosted glass.

So many security cameras.

Murhder had a handgun down by his side as he stayed behind the zombie guard. John was right beside him. Xhex was in the rear and walking backward, making sure no one came up on them. The research complex seemed vacant of clinicians and staff, a benefit to Sunday nights in the human world. There were people on-site, however—their scents were distant and dimmed by all the fake air being pumped in through the HVAC system, but Murhder's vampire nose detected them.

As they came up to a branching of halls, the guard didn't skip a beat. He went straight on, striding like an automaton.

Murhder glanced over at John. The male was totally focused, moving with sure footing, gun down at his thigh as well.

Eerie. Even though they'd just met, Murhder could have sworn that they had done this kind of thing together countless times.

John glanced over. Nodded—

And all hell broke loose.

From over on the left, a frosted glass door opened into the hall, and a human male in a suit with an open collared shirt stepped out. He appeared to be in his mid-sixties, with a full head of salt-and-pepper gray hair, a trim build, and eyes that had the dead sheen of sea glass.

The guard in the trance stopped, his training overriding even Murhder's mind control.

"What's going on here?" the man in the suit demanded.

With the kind of authority that suggested he owned the place.

Xhex was on it, jumping forward and shoving the muzzle of her gun into his throat as she twisted his arm around behind his back and cranked him into a hold.

"Stay quiet and I won't shoot you," she said in a quiet voice. "Dr. Kraiten."

The man looked back at her and seemed to pale. "You."

"Surprise. Didn't think you'd see me again? Well, I'm back to finish what I started with your partner. Who knew I'd be this lucky and find you so soon."

As Xhex spoke, her mate bared his fangs, John's upper lip curling back like a wolf's—and Murhder was tempted to let the pair of them do whatever they wanted to the guy. Clearly, Xhex was familiar with the human from her previous imprisonment, and it was hard not to argue with her right to *ahvenge* herself. But there was no time for that kind of delay.

"Walk on," Murhder commanded the guard.

"You're not going to get away with this," the man in the suit— Dr. Kraiten?—said. "I will lock down this facility right now and—"

"Walk on," Murhder snapped at the guard as he pointed his gun at the man in the uniform.

The guard winced like his temples were singing with pain. And then he turned away from his boss and continued onward. As they started forward once more, Dr. Kraiten's words were cut off, no doubt from Xhex pushing that muzzle directly into his voice box.

They'd gone about ten yards when alarms started to sound.

"Sonofabitch," Xhex muttered. "Fucking Apple. Give me that goddamn watch."

Clearly, the man had triggered something at his wrist, and Murhder looked over his shoulder as a struggle started. John ended up grabbing the back of the man's head and shoving him face-first into the expanse of frosted glass, those features mashing up under the pressure, blood smudging as the nose started to bleed.

The man was stripped of whatever had been on his wrist, and then John cuffed him and shoved a bandana into his mouth as Xhex provided cover.

Once more with feeling, Murhder thought as they resumed their trek for a second time. Dr. Kraiten continued fighting against the hold on him, but there was no doubt Xhex would handle it.

Some distance further, the guard stopped in front of a door and took out a pass card. One swipe and they were inside some kind of office space, nothing but desks in cubicles and a conference table and a little break area.

"Goddamn it," Murhder muttered. In a louder voice, he said to the guard, "No, we want the research lab where they keep the—"

The sound of an air lock releasing brought everyone's head around to the right. And then Murhder's heart stopped in the center of his chest.

Two figures broke into the office area at a dead run. One was a pre-trans boy with dark hair and bony arms and legs showing from the hems and sleeves of a pale blue hospital johnny.

And the other . . .

. . . was a human female in what appeared to be some kind of bright blue protective gear. She had her hair pulled back from her face, and as she looked across at Murhder, her beautiful eyes widened in fear.

Dearest Virgin Scribe, he could not breathe.

All these years . . . he had been wrong.

Hers was the face he saw in the sacred glass.

This was the female he was destined for.

CHAPTER TWENTY-ONE

Sarah could not believe what she was looking at, and she instinctively put her body in front of the boy's so she could shield him.

For some completely inexplicable reason, her brain was telling her that, just as she was wondering how in the hell she was going to get the child out of the facility, three commandos dressed in black and draped in weapons showed up not only with a security guard who looked like he was hypnotized, but Dr. Kraiten himself handcuffed, gagged and in a chokehold.

The good news? The military types seemed equally surprised to see her—so much so they didn't even point their guns at her. But she had a feeling that was a "yet" kind of thing.

Were they from a foreign . . . government looking . . . to raid secrets . . .

Abruptly, her brain went offline, all her cognition just grinding to a halt.

The commando with the red-and-black hair was what did it. Even though there were all kinds of reasons to stay completely plugged into the present danger, some part of her took the wheel of her mind and trained all of her awareness on him and him alone. He was incredibly tall and well built, and that hair was amazing, long, thick and obviously professionally colored—although why a soldier would spend time on his physical appearance she had no idea. And his face . . . he was arrestingly handsome, a Jon Hamm type, with bold features that nonetheless weren't coarse.

And then there were his eyes. His astonishing peach eyes were staring at her as if, for some unknown reason, he recognized her—

"You're my kind." The child stepped out from behind her. "My mother, did she send you here?"

As the little boy spoke over the alarms that were going off, his voice woke everyone back up, Sarah jumping to attention, the commando shaking his head as if he were clearing it.

"Yes," the commando said roughly. "Your *mahmen* sent us, and we need to leave—"

Sarah put her hand on the boy's shoulder and restrained him from running off. "The only place he and I are going is to the proper authorities—"

"No," the commando interrupted. "He has to come with us."

"Then show me some proper ID." Maybe they were SWAT, just unmarked? "Are you from the FBI, then?"

Dr. Kraiten spit out the gag in his mouth and added his cold, cutting tone to the party. "Dr. Watkins, what are you doing in this restricted access area!"

Leave it to a guy like him to worry about his precious security clearances rather than the fact that he was clearly a hostage.

On that note, fuck him very much. "What the hell have *you* been doing with this child," she yelled. "You know they're pumping him full of disease! You know everything that goes on here—"

Kraiten hollered right back over the din of the alarms. "I'm going to put you in jail for trespassing! You don't have clearance to be here—"

Cue the slow motion.

Before Sarah could stop herself, blind fury at the fact that the man hadn't denied they'd been torturing a child set her in motion. On a running leap, she threw herself at him without knowing what she was going to do. Punch? Kick? Yell some more?

And the attack was about more than just the secret, unethical medical program.

Gerry had been involved.

Gerry, so brilliant, so kind, so principled, had come here, worked here . . . and fallen into something that either changed him fundamentally or entrapped him into doing the unthinkable.

She would never know which was the case.

But goddamn it, she could physically hurt Kraiten.

And she did. Sarah Watkins—scientist, semi-nerd, all-around good girl who had colored inside the lines her entire life—threw an airborne right punch directly at Robert Kraiten's face.

She'd been aiming for the nose.

She nailed him straight in the eye.

That was as far as it got. The next thing she knew, Kraiten was bent at the waist and cursing, and she was being drawn back with gentle, but firm hands.

Sarah knew who had taken hold of her without having to look. And Red-and-Black's cologne was something else. Dark, sensual spices, the kind of thing she had never smelled before, got into her nose and didn't stop at her sinuses. The scent somehow went through her entire body.

"We'll take care of him," the commando said into her ear. "Don't you worry."

She looked up over her shoulder. Way up.

His peach eyes were too bright, and not in the sense that he was high. More like they were backlit by an ethereal energy, the blue/green irises capable, it seemed, of glowing in the dark.

It was as she stared into that incredible color that the combination of words he had spoken caught up with the language center in her brain.

We'll take care of him.

Everything about the man, from the Kevlar vest across his chest to the weapons on the rest of his body, suggested that whatever all that meant, going through proper legal channels was not going to be part of it. And the end result was bound to include a headstone and a deep hole into the earth.

And what do you know, that outcome was not something she was inclined to protest.

"Who are you?" she breathed.

"We came to rescue the boy," the man said in a hoarse voice. "He's been here too long."

"Are you with the government?"

"We're private actors. But we'll keep him safe, I swear to it. No harm is ever going to fall upon him if I'm around. It was my vow to his *mahmen*."

Her instincts told her to trust him. But what about those instincts? She'd been on the verge of marrying a man it turned out she didn't know at all—and she'd worked here at BioMed for how long and they'd been hiding this horrific secret? How could she put any faith in her sense of anything—

Justlikethat, time snapped out of its stupor and started rolling again, the female commando speaking up.

"Where's your fucking car?"

Sarah spoke up. "It's out in the parking lot—"

"Not yours." The female yanked Kraiten upright. As he sputtered through the blood that ran down his face, she gave him a shake. "His."

◆   ◆   ◆

Murhder was struggling to focus. The female he was holding so close to his body was taking up a tremendous amount of his mental bandwidth, in spite of the life-or-death situation at hand: With every breath he took, he was captivated by her fresh, clean scent. Between each blink of his eyes, he was registering new details about her, from her brown and blond hair, the high color on her cheeks, the curve of her face, the pale honey color of her eyes. She was wearing a loose blue bag of protective clothing, and he wondered what her body was like underneath. But whatever she looked like . . . he was going to want her.

Because he already did.

Except shit, he had to get with the program or this already chaotic situation was going to go nuclear.

"Answer her question," he snapped at the suited man with the attitude and the now swollen eye.

Man, he'd loved the way that woman had swung her fist like that. Good follow-through. Excellent aim. And who could argue with the damage, given that blood flow? The bastard was going to have a helluva shiner in the morning—if they didn't kill him outright after they got a vehicle.

Abruptly, Murhder wondered why in the hell he was wasting time with voluntary answers. Plunging his will into Kraiten's gray matter, he popped the tops off all kinds of memories—and was horrified by what he found . . .

"You sick fuck," Murhder whispered. "You motherfucker."

As everyone looked at Kraiten, the man's eyes peeled wide, like he knew his secrets had been revealed and he had no idea how. But enough of that.

"Take us where we need to go to get out of here," Murhder commanded as he inserted the order into the man's brain and put the gag back in his mouth.

Kraiten mentally fought the impulse, a sign of his intelligence. But he inevitably folded, bested by a higher power than he, as a human, possessed: Wordlessly, he turned around and stared at the door of the office space like it had his name on it.

"You," Murhder said to the guard. "You tell the others it's a false alarm on your radio. Then you go to the system and delete the security camera feeds that we're in. You make it so that none of this ever happened."

As Murhder spoke, he erased all kinds of things in the human's mind and replaced them with images of an empty office area, an inexplicable alarm malfunction, and absolutely no strangers in black cruising the halls or removing a small boy from a lab or taking this guy Kraiten hostage. In response, the human rubbed his temple like it hurt. Then he shook his head and went for the shoulder communicator mounted on his uniform's lapel.

"Five-ten to base, five-ten to base. I have an all clear on that IDD alarm. Repeat, I have an all clear. Returning to base now, over."

Like a robot, he marched out of the door and took a left.

The human woman spoke up sharply. "How did you do that? What did you . . ."

Murhder glanced at Ingridge's young. "Come on, son, let's take you out of here."

And then he looked at the woman. Did they scrub her memories and leave her? Or take her with them?

Either way, her mind would have to be dealt with later—he didn't have time to do that now. They had to move.

"You're not safe here," he told her. "You've got to know this. You need to go underground. We can help."

Anything to get her to come with them.

"Are you with PETA?" she asked.

Given that she seemed relieved at the idea, he nodded.

"We gotta go," Xhex said.

"I'm coming with you," the woman blurted as she put an arm around the young.

Perfect, Murhder thought—with a surge of possession that frightened him.

As Xhex gave Kraiten a shove, the man in the suit led them out the door and to the right. Motley group they were, three heavily armed fighters, a young in a hospital johnny, the human woman and Mr. Bleeder. As they passed beneath the mounted security cameras on the ceiling, Murhder prayed like hell that the security guard did a good job with his erasing.

This was a highly unstable situation, Murhder thought. Sooner or later, some other security personnel was bound to catch them on camera and wonder about the weapons and the cuffs.

It looked like a kidnapping.

'Cuz it was.

Good news came as Kraiten stopped in front of a door that was not frosted glass, but stainless steel. There was a red sign over it reading "EXIT," but as Murhder punched the bar, the thing refused to open.

"Give me the code or your card," he demanded of Kraiten.

When the guy started shaking his head like a little bitch, Murhder had just about had it with delays. Taking two steps back, he kicked the goddamn door with such force, it exploded out of its lock.

It took all he had not to turn around to Kraiten and flip the man off.

As he jumped through into a concrete stairwell, he glanced back. The human woman was staring at him with those wide eyes again and the young was looking up at him like he was Superman. Xhex, on the other hand, was chuckling under her breath like she knew the truth.

So what, he wanted to say. *I wanted to show off for the woman. Sue me.*

"We had to get through the goddamn door," he bitched at Xhex.

"Sure," she said with a wink. "And look, we did."

When he turned back around, he could have sworn she tacked on "He-Man," but he wasn't going to follow up on that. Because he was blushing, damn it.

The group started to follow him down the stairs, moving faster and faster, clomping a descent toward some underground area.

They'd gone a good three levels down when the woman said, "Wait, stop."

At the sound of her voice, Murhder's body jerked to a halt, sure as if he had a choke chain around his throat and she held the leash. Worried that someone was hurt—other than Kraiten, that was—he looked over his shoulder . . . and had an eerie sense that he would never be the same.

As Xhex held on to Kraiten, and John guarded them all with his guns, the human woman crouched down next to the pretrans. The young was trembling and seemed suddenly weak, and Murhder kicked himself for not considering what it would be like for the kid to be rushed through the facility by strangers, even if he knew they'd been sent by his mother.

His now deceased mother.

The woman took the young's fragile hands and murmured to him. Her words didn't carry far. Her compassion went around the world: There was a sheen of tears in her own eyes as she reached up and brushed his hair back. After a moment, he nodded.

In response, the woman wrapped her strong arms around him and picked him up, sitting him on her hip. As the young held on to her shoulders and tucked his head into her neck, Murhder knew that the simple act of kindness to a frightened young in the midst of a nightmare was . . .

Well, it was the sort of thing that told you everything you needed to know about her character, didn't it.

Unconsciously, Murhder's eyes dipped to the ring finger on her left hand. Humans marked their matings in that manner. Hers was bare.

That was a treacherous relief.

"You got him?" Murhder asked softly.

Her honey-colored eyes shifted up to his. "Yes. I do."

Well, brace yourself, he thought. *Because I'm very sure you got me, too.*

CHAPTER TWENTY-TWO

Murhder refocused and shoved at Kraiten's shoulder, reigniting the march of descent, the lineup moving down the concrete stairwell with more shuffle than alacrity. At the bottom, Kraiten stopped and seemed to want to speak.

Murhder ripped the gag out of his mouth. "What."

"I need . . ." Given that the man was still fighting the commands he'd been given, his voice was slurred. "Credentials."

"Where are they?" Xhex said.

"My breast pocket."

The female shoved her free hand into Kraiten's suit jacket and came out with a black alligator-skin wallet, key fob for a car, and a pass card. She swiped the last one through the reader next to another steel door, and after the lock released, they broke out into an underground loading dock and delivery area.

A black Lexus SUV gleamed under the caged fluorescent lights, and as Xhex pointed the fob at it, its running lights flashed.

Thank God it isn't a two-seater, Murhder thought.

Leading the young and the woman over, he settled them in the backseat, and then looked at Xhex and John.

"I'll get these two out," he said. "Kraiten's yours to play with."

The man in the suit started blurting all kinds of threats, his survival instincts partially overriding the mind control.

Murhder stepped up and clapped a hold on the guy's throat. Leaning in, he put his mouth to the human's ear. "I could tear your beating heart out of your chest and eat it for what you've done." He eased back and measured the true terror in those eyes. "But I'm going to leave you to them—especially her. What she is capable of will be much, much worse."

As he felt his fangs elongate, he wanted to take a hunk out of the side of the man's throat, but he was aware of the woman in the car. She was watching him through the glass as she held the pretrans tight.

Backing off, Murhder nodded at John and Xhex, and then he took the car key from the female, the pass card—and for good measure, the wallet. Turning away, he went around the hood of the SUV and got behind the wheel. Glancing up to the rearview mirror, he found the young and the woman holding each other and staring at him.

God, that face, he thought as he focused on the woman. He had been looking at it for twenty-five years . . . and now she was with him.

It was as if a ghost had become real.

But why did she have to be human? And why did they have to meet like this?

"Buckle up," he told them. "And you're going to have to tell me where to go."

He started the vehicle and put it in drive as everyone clicked in.

The woman leaned forward. "I know where we are. Go that way."

As she pointed to a metal garage door, he hit the gas. The panels rolled up as they approached, and then they were out in the night, on the plowed lane that went around the facility.

"Take a left . . ."

She was efficient with the directions, helping him to navigate the route to the single point of entry onto the site. The good news? No flashing lights on the buildings. No security guards coming after them. No human police arriving in a rush.

"That's the gatehouse up ahead," she said. "I don't know how we're going to get through security, though."

"I'll take care of it."

They approached the checkpoint and slowed down. The fencing system that surrounded the property was worthy of a federal penitentiary, some twenty feet tall and mounted with security cameras. As he hit the brakes and prepared to come to a complete stop, he prayed the alarms didn't start going off just as he dealt with the guard's mind—

The gatehouse's sliding door opened on their side, and an arm extended out from the sentry point, giving a little wave-through. Then the gates began to part.

But of course. The SUV's windows were all tinted and up tight against the cold—so whoever was on duty was just assuming the CEO was behind the wheel.

As Murhder cruised through, he stared straight ahead and lifted his hand as he guessed Kraiten might have. Then he beat feet out of there.

As they came off the property, he went to the right and sped away.

"Everyone okay back there?" he asked roughly.

"Yes, we're good," the human woman said.

"All good," the pretrans echoed.

Murhder started to smile.

He'd done it, he thought as he squeezed the steering wheel. He'd fucking *done* it. The young was out of that hellhole, and nothing was going to happen to the kid now.

He hadn't let Ingridge down.

All at once, this strange energy entered not just Murhder's body and mind, but his soul. After everything he had been through with his unreliable thoughts and his swirling craziness, it was hard to trust the rush. But damn, it was as if sunshine had entered him on the inside, the dark spaces between his molecules illuminated with a heavenly glow, whole sectors of his personality, previously eclipsed by penetrating sadness, now bathed in a healing warmth.

With the same abruptness as it had failed, his switchboard seemed now fully operational and ready for business again, his circuits up and rolling, his wires uncrossed, his functioning returning to a normal that he had previously taken for granted, as the healthy and whole always did.

That smile pulled hard at the corners of his mouth. And then, like an athlete after a warmup, his lips stretched wide. Sure, he was in an arguably stolen vehicle, which was owned by a man about to die in a grisly way, and he had an orphan and a human woman in the backseat who both needed his protection.

But after two decades of being in an insane wasteland, he felt like himself.

Fuck that, he felt like a goddamn superhero.

"Are you taking me to my *mahmen?*" the boy asked.

Murhder's eyes flashed up to the rearview. As he met that hopeful stare, he felt a piercing pain in his heart, and all his optimism collapsed.

"We need to talk, son," he said grimly.

◆　◆　◆

In spite of all the reasons Xhex had to slaughter Kraiten where the bastard stood, she decided not to go that route. It was too easy. He had earned a much worse fate and she was just the *symphath* to give it to him.

"Hold him for me?" she asked her mate.

As John nodded, she transferred Kraiten over into what turned out to be a vicious headlock—and yup, she had a moment of reconsideration. Her *hellren* had bared his fangs and was looking like he was ready to make a meal of the guy.

Except she had a better plan.

"John," she said, "you gotta loosen that hold on his neck. He's turning blue—there you go. Respiration is a good thing for the living."

Certain that John was in control of himself, in spite of that bloodthirsty snarl of his, she calmed herself and entered the human's brain.

Kraiten's emotional grid was interesting, and one not uncommon to sociopaths: He had little to no registry around the core of his superstructure—which meant that nothing affected him deeply. Everything was superficial to him, with the ego sectors the only thing that were lit up elsewhere.

He was very protective of his position of superiority.

Well, that was going to change. And she was also going to teach him a lesson in what it was like to be out of control.

Using her *symphath* side, she set the man upon a path that was going to make him insane, and as she worked, she thanked the higher powers for the opportunity to ruin him. She had never expected to run into the guy, and this was such a bonus to getting that young free.

After she was done, she erased his memories of the infiltration, the hostage taking and the rescue, making sure that he would have no recollection of any of this. Then she nodded to John and he let go of the human, shoving him in the direction of the door to the stairwell. They both watched him stumble and then start pounding on the door.

No doubt the first time he had been locked out of his own business.

"You ready to go?" she asked her mate.

John's hands were quick to sign, *Tell me you did enough.*

"More than enough." She leaned into him and kissed him on the mouth, lingering with the contact. "Thank you for coming with me. And for believing me when it comes to Murhder. We have a shared history, but not a shared future. It's you who I love like that. No one else."

The small, secret smile she was used to seeing appeared on his face. It was his special one. The expression that he never gave anybody but her. It was how he said "I love you" without using his hands.

Abruptly, she felt a relief and gratitude so enormous, she had to blink quick. "Let's go."

One after the other, they dematerialized, leaving the loading dock through the tiny gaps in the garage door's slats. They re-formed on the perimeter of the lab property, in the snow field on the far side of the high concrete wall. No alarms. No signs that the infiltration had been noted or responded to. There might be some confusion for the security folks when they saw the video feeds, but with any luck, Murhder's guard took care of all that.

John tapped her on the arm. *Are you sure you're okay leaving like this?*

As Xhex exhaled, her breath left her in a white cloud. It was impossible not to measure this departure against her previous, toast-your-marshmallows-and-then-some one. And the truth was, she was never going to be perfectly okay with any of it. Not what her bloodline had done to her or to Murhder. Certainly not what had been done to her body at the hands of that human she'd just scrambled the brains of.

But burning this lab down and slaughtering a bunch of innocent humans working security detail was not going to bring her any greater measure of peace.

Besides, she had taken care of things when it came to the drug company. Kraiten had a special project he was going to work on over the next couple of days.

"Yes, I'm all right."

She turned and faced her mate. As a cold breeze ripped by, like it had discovered a zip code that wasn't frigid AF and was determined to take care of that oversight, John's hair ruffled on one side.

As she reached up to smooth things, he captured her gloved hand and kissed the center of her palm.

She thought of him meeting Murhder—and the seizure he'd had. Then she thought of what she knew, but had not told him, about his emotional grid. And of the scar on his pectoral, the one that he said he had been born with.

John whistled in an ascending sound, his way of asking what was up.

Xhex glanced over to the lab's wall and wondered if they shouldn't get moving. But what did it matter. If any humans came after them, they could just dematerialize away.

Or kill the bastards.

It was more than time for her to say this, and why not here? "John . . . you belong in the Brotherhood. And not just because you're a good fighter."

He frowned. And then shrugged.

"I know, it's not your decision or choice. But . . . you recognized Murhder, didn't you." Yes, that was a leading question. "In your heart, you know him. You know all of the Brotherhood. Have you ever asked yourself why that is?"

John shrugged again and let go of her hand. *It just is the way it is. I get along with them.*

"It's more than that. And you've sensed this."

Her beloved mate had a total anomaly when it came to his emotional grid. In fact, she'd never seen anything like it before. The structure of his emotions and sense of self were perfectly normal, the norths and souths, easts and wests of his feelings in an orientation that was exactly as it should be. What was not? The fact that there was a shadow grid directly under his own, an echo of his pattern that precisely reflected whatever he was feeling, like she were seeing double. She had often wondered if maybe he'd had a twin who had died . . . but there was no way of knowing that because the details of his birth and the whereabouts of his *mahmen* were unknown.

And more to the point, she would have seen this construct before if it were associated with twins.

There was only one other explanation, and even considering it made her feel like she was going *Conjuring* on the situation.

It wasn't like the ghost of a deceased Brother had taken up residence inside of him—and manifested that star-shaped scar on his pectoral.

That just was nuts.

I'm not sure what you're talking about, John signed. *But I really hope someday that . . .*

You already are a Brother, she thought to herself.

She kept that to herself because the yearning in his face broke her heart—and made her angry at the Brotherhood. Why couldn't those males just do the right thing? And not, like, fifty years from now or some shit. John was a helluva fighter. He deserved the recognition and the honor.

"Come on, let's head to the safe house," she said. "It's cold out here."

CHAPTER TWENTY-THREE

As Kraiten's SUV slowed and the commando behind the wheel turned them in to a driveway, Sarah frowned out of the side window in back. They were about an hour outside of Ithaca, to the north, and the fact that she hadn't been in the area before wasn't a news flash. It wasn't like she and Gerry had traveled a lot upstate.

Scratch the driveway part. This was more like a lane, the curving, plowed passage winding its way through snow-draped evergreens that crowded up close.

Some two or three hundred yards in, the definition of cozy made its postcard'd appearance, the brick house and its smoke-curled chimneys like someone had made a model for a Christmas ad.

Sarah looked down into her lap as the SUV stopped at the front walkway. The boy had tucked in and fallen asleep, his head a warm weight on her leg, his arms crossed, his hands folded under his chin. She had been tempted to offer him the hazmat suit as a blanket, but the heat was up high, and he'd been out like a light almost as soon as they'd hit the highway.

The fact that she was sublimely uncomfortable because her backpack was still on under the protective gear and the leg he was using as a pillow had gone numb didn't matter in the slightest. All she cared about was that the child got some rest.

She was worried he had a fever. His skin felt hot.

"He's sleeping hard," the commando said softly.

She glanced at the driver. He had twisted around and was staring down at the child with a sadness that made her worry about what he was going to have to tell the boy. She wanted to ask if the mother was indeed dead, but she already knew the answer, and she didn't want that conversation to be what woke the boy up.

"We need to get him to a doctor," she whispered.

"We have people we use."

"When are they coming?" She thought of those scans. "He's been . . . experimented on."

God, how had it all happened? Her brain just could not get wrapped around any of it. Had they abducted him? Or . . . had he been sold like a commodity? Born in the lab?

"And I need to use a phone. A landline."

"Are you calling your mate?" the commando asked.

"Mate?" She shook her head. "Oh, sorry. No, I have no one I need to get in touch with for myself. But I have things the FBI needs to see."

Except she wasn't sure the boy was on that list. He had been through so much, and she wasn't convinced that tossing him into the foster care system was a great plan if the father wasn't an appropriate custodian. But maybe he had relatives. Nice, normal relatives, like an aunt or uncle, who had a house just like this one.

"Come on," the commando said as he disembarked, "let's get you both inside."

The boy stirred when the man opened their door and cold air burst in. And then Sarah was reluctantly handing her precious load over to the commando because there was no way she could carry him up to that front door with her leg as numb as it was. And then she worried about him catching pneumonia from the cold—

He'd already had pneumonia, she reminded herself grimly. Two years ago.

Cursing to herself, she shuffled out and nearly fell when she put weight on her left foot. Before she could catch herself, the commando threw out a hand and grabbed her arm.

His strength was . . . astonishing. Even with the boy in his arms, he kept her from hitting the snowpack like she weighed nothing at all, his body not even registering the load she represented. He was like a damn oak tree.

She thought of him kicking that steel door in like the thing was part of a dollhouse—as opposed to a reinforced metal panel locked into a jamb with a dead bolt.

Sarah pulled at the collar of the hazmat suit as a flush of warmth went through her. She had only ever dated fellow geeks, her three or four boyfriends conscientious, serious, and arguably ever so slightly on the scrawny side—hey, Mensa members could be hot, okay. But this man? With that . . . body?

Unfamiliar territory.

That had a topography which made her wonder if he were this powerful on the vertical, what the hell could he do to a woman on the horiz—

"Hello?" he demanded urgently. "*Hello?*"

As if he had been trying to get her attention.

Sarah shook her head. "Sorry, I'm . . ."

Wondering if you're good in bed, she finished to herself.

The commando's eyes peeled wide and he recoiled.

"Oh . . . dear God," she breathed as she winced. "Please tell me I didn't just say that out loud. Actually—don't answer that. Forget you know me—you don't know me, actually. You don't know my name—*I* don't know my name at this point—hey, it's a party!"

She muttered all of that as she stepped around him and hit the shoveled path like she'd hammered two pints of beer and the only bathroom on the planet was up ahead.

"The door should be unlocked," the commando said behind her.

"Fantastic, because I'm unhinged." She pivoted around. "I'm Sarah, by the way. Dr. Sarah Watkins."

Well, crap. The slow smile that hit that handsome face was more sexual than the best orgasm she'd ever had.

"Should I call you Sarah or Dr. Watkins."

Call me anytime, she thought.

"Sarah's fine. Good. I mean, yes. Please."

Fuck.

Sarah jumped up onto the quaint front porch, and as she tested the door and discovered he was right, the glow from inside the house, the warmth, the homeyness . . . was pretty much the last way she'd expected her night to end.

Not that it was ending here.

It wasn't like she was staying with the man and his hard-ass friends—although props for decorating, she thought as she looked around. Instead of a bunker for war, the place was kitted out in early Americana: woven rugs on the floor, hanging quilts as wallpaper, and a stuffed sofa that was totally book-nook material.

"Is this your house?" she said as she held the door open.

"No. It's a friend of mine's."

Okay, that made sense, she thought. He would live in a bunker—so was this his girlfriend's? Wife's? No, wait, mother's.

Had to be Mom's. She could practically smell the apple pie in the oven. And the idea that he liked his momma enough to bring two fugitives home? Well, didn't that just melt the cockles of the heart.

Certain she was losing it, Sarah closed them in as the man put the child on that sofa and covered him with a blanket. The fact that the boy didn't stir at all made her paranoid that he was dead—but no, that painfully thin chest was going up and down.

Too much color on those cheeks, she thought as she reached out and put her hand on his forehead.

Sarah shook her head as she straightened. "We really need to take him to a hospital. He's got a temperature."

"I'll call someone in."

On cue, the couple that had been with him at the lab came down from upstairs. The man and woman had just showered, going by their wet hair, and they wore clothes either the same or identical to what they'd had on before.

They both still sported guns at their waists, too.

"I'll text Jane," the woman said. "She'll come right away."

"Is she a fully trained doctor?" Sarah asked sharply. "An internist?"

The woman nodded. "She treats all of us. She's a surgeon, actually."

"Look, this child has been deliberately infected with—"

"I know," came the terse reply. "They did the same thing to me."

Sarah blanched and glanced at the boy. Then she stared at the woman in alarm. But there was no eye contact to be had there. The female commando was stepping away into the kitchen, and her boyfriend/husband/partner went with her.

"You're awake."

She refocused on the child as the man spoke. Those eyes were opening slowly, the boy's thin limbs stirring under the blanket.

"Where's my *mahmen?*"

The man looked over at Sarah. "Can you give me a minute with him?"

A powerful impulse to stay right where she was—or, even better, take the poor child into her lap again—hit her like a message from God. But something in the way the pair of them stared at her suggested they had a history.

"Are you his family?" she asked the commando.

"Yes," he said. "In all the ways that matter right now."

Sarah nodded and backed her way into the hall. She went all the way down to the archway of the kitchen, and then could go no further. Leaning against the wall, she crossed her arms over her chest and felt like her heart was breaking as she watched the two of them from afar.

She couldn't hear anything that was said as the man rubbed his face, cracked his knuckles . . . and then sat down on the sofa to look the child right in the eye.

The man's mouth moved again, and the expression on the boy's face tightened into a mask. The boy asked something. The man answered.

There was another question.

Another answer.

The boy looked down at the quilt that had been pulled over his little body. As he began to cry, the man seemed exactly as heartbroken as Sarah felt.

The commando took the child into his strong arms and held him.

As those oddly glowing eyes lifted to Sarah over the boy's dark head, she put her hand over her mouth. And wondered exactly how much more anyone that young could take.

Hell, most adults couldn't handle half of what he'd lived through already. It was so unfair for anything to be added to his burdens.

"—about to go through the change. So we need to get a Chosen here before day breaks just in case."

Sarah frowned and glanced over her shoulder. The female commando was talking urgently into a cell phone.

Change? Sarah thought.

◆　　◆　　◆

When the Brotherhood's physician arrived ten minutes later, Murhder retreated to the kitchen so that "Doc Jane," as the female was called, could sit with the young privately.

Dr. Sarah Watkins was alone at the table, the blue bag of that hazmat suit halfway off of her, a backpack set off to the side. She had a cup of coffee in front of her, her stare floating somewhere above the mug. As he entered the room, however, she looked up at him.

And kept looking.

Had she really wondered what he was like in bed? Holy shit, that was hot. And what do you know, his libido was demanding he take this opportunity to show her firsthand that yes, he'd always been good at sex, current two-decades-long mostly dry spell notwithstanding.

But instead of wading into naked waters, he said, "How you doing?"

"I can't seem to get my brain to work," she murmured. "It's the strangest thing."

He sat down across from her, and fought the urge to try to pull her into his lap so he could hold her. They were, after all, strangers.

"Totally understandable." He attempted to make sure his tone was gentle because sometimes you could hug someone without touching them, right? "You're not used to anything like tonight."

"I'm just a scientist." She leaned to the side, as if she were checking on the young in the front room. Then she looked back at the mug. "Or I used to be. After this, I don't think anyone's going to be hiring me. The whole breaking and entering thing, stealing information, going to the authorities—it's kind of frowned upon on any résumé to Big Pharma."

"No one is going to know about this."

Her eyes shot back up. "Are you kidding me? Kraiten will cover up that secret lab and call the police."

"No, he won't."

"No offense, but don't be naïve. And besides, I'm going to turn everything over to the Feds. As soon as I finish this coffee, I'm calling the agent who came to see me two days ago."

"Kraiten's not going to be a problem anymore."

"Exactly. Because I have proof of what was being done in that lab of his." She shook her head. "And if I'm finished in my field, it's fine. I'd lost my passion for the work anyway. Time for me to find something else to do with my life."

He traced her face with his eyes. She had a little mole on her cheek. And flecks of green in those pale brown eyes. She had taken her hair out of its ponytail, and the naturally highlighted weight was spilling onto her shoulders.

She smelled like a summer meadow to him, and her voice was hypnotic. He literally could spend an entire night just watching her mouth enunciate random syllables, his ears full with the sounds she made, his skin prickling with sensual awareness of every minute move she made.

"What exactly do you do?" he blurted, aware he'd been silent for too long.

"I'm a molecular geneticist. I work on curing cancer using the body's own immune system." Her eyes swung back to him. "We need to tell that doctor what they did to him. And I have scan results and information on the protocols—granted, they're from two years ago. But after I go to the Feds, I'm sure they can get the most recent studies. There must be records—I mean, I'm assuming they didn't stop. They gave him terrible diseases and—"

"The doctor knows what they did to him."

Dr. Watkins—Sarah—blinked. "Does she know about the woman fighter, too?" When he didn't reply, she prompted, "She said they'd done it to her as well."

"The doctor knows everything."

"Is there any chance Kraiten's illicit program is doing that to anybody else, somewhere else?"

Murhder thought about what he'd seen when he'd tapped into that CEO's mind. "The young was the last one he had left. He's been trying to get more but has failed."

The woman tilted her head. "You have the strangest way of saying things. And that accent of yours. It's not French, it's not . . . well, I know it's not German. What part of Europe are you from? My fiancé was from Hamburg."

Murhder stiffened in his chair. "Fiancé? You're engaged?"

Sorrow suffused her face. "Was. He passed."

The fact that he was relieved made him feel like a total asshole.

"I offer my sincerest condolences at your loss." He eased the tension in his body. "May I inquire what happened?"

She sat back in the chair. Pivoted to the side again to check on the young. "Where did the couple go?"

"I'm sorry?"

"The man and the woman who were here with you?"

Footsteps sounded overhead and Murhder looked up. "I guess they are settling in for the night."

"Oh." She put her hand on the backpack and went to stand up. "I need to make that call and get those files to the FBI."

That cannot happen, he thought.

Murhder reached out and put his hand on hers. Instantly, a bolt of electricity rode up his arm . . . and continued on to places that had not been awake in a very, very long time.

"The doctor isn't done yet," he pointed out as he shifted in his own seat. "Let's hold on until she's finished in case she needs to ask us anything."

The woman retracted her hand. Rubbed it on her thigh. Clearly, she had felt the connection, too: Her arousal scent flared, and it was heavenly in his nose, an erotic combination of bergamot and ginseng.

He wanted more of it. He wanted it all over his naked skin, as he entered her sex and felt her claw into his back—

Murhder ducked one hand under the table and discreetly rearranged the sudden and very inappropriate erection that had punched his cock into the fly of his pants.

"Why are you smiling?" she asked.

Because I didn't know the damn thing still worked, he thought.

"I'm sorry." He pushed his heavy hair back. "It's nothing."

"God, don't apologize." She sat down again. "I could use a good joke, that's all. This has been a rough couple of days."

Even though there was so much more to worry about, he found himself needing to know what was under the baggy blue plastic suit she had on. What her hair would look like fanned out over his bare chest. How she would sound as he pleasured her.

Crazy, all of it.

Because she needed to go back to her world, without any memory of ever having met him.

First, however, he had to get those files she was talking about.

CHAPTER TWENTY-FOUR

I t was hard to pinpoint exactly when Sarah's brain began to send out
warning signals that all was not as it appeared—or exactly what
tripped up her suspicions.

But as she leaned to the side for a third time, and looked down the
hall to the front room, she knew something was way off. As she watched
the doctor take a bog standard stethoscope out of an old-fashioned
physician's bag and place it on the young boy's chest . . . as his blood
pressure was taken with a proper juvenile cuff . . . as the woman in
scrubs checked his pupils with a penlight and looked into his ears . . .
none of it felt right.

The doctor and patient talked the whole time, their voices so quiet,
Sarah couldn't hear what they were saying. And she could not find fault
with the attentiveness of the clinician. The woman was solely focused
on the boy, her face grim, her body turned to him.

But this just was not right.

Sarah shifted her eyes to her commando—*the* commando, she corrected. "An ambulance is coming, right? They're taking him to a hospital."

"Yeah. Sure."

"Which one?"

"It's a private clinic."

Sarah frowned and shook her head. "Okay, you need to get real with me. What the hell is going on here."

The commando shrugged his powerful shoulders. "As you see, he's getting checked out by a doctor."

She thought of the six-chambered heart. The bizarre CBC readings. The test results that indicated profound disease resistance even in an immunocompromised state.

One of the things they taught residents in medical school was that when you heard hoofbeats, don't think zebras. In other words, don't immediately assume a bump was malignant, flu-like symptoms were Ebola, a cough was the Black Death.

For the most part, it was good advice. Right up until the symptoms you were presented with turned out to be cancer or the plague.

She leaned into the table. "That child should be dead right now. He should have died two years ago, assuming that the files I found were his scans, his reports. None of this is adding up."

At that moment, the doctor came into the kitchen. She was a good-looking woman, with short blond hair and deep green eyes, and you had to appreciate the gravity with which she seemed to be taking the situation. But there was something . . . well, off about her.

Like she had a different energy source or—

"He's been through a lot," the physician announced. "But he's in physically fine shape. Other than . . ." She glanced at Sarah. "Anyway, I'd like to bring him in for further testing—"

"I am going wherever he goes." Sarah got up. "I am not leaving his side. And will someone please explain to me why we're not on the way to law enforcement and a medical center right now?"

The doctor gave the commando a look like he was accountable for something. Then the woman said, "I'd like to check John before I go."

"He's upstairs." The commando also stood. "And I'll take care of things down here."

"Take care of what things?" Sarah asked sharply as the doctor went to the bottom of the stairs and called up.

"I'm sorry," he whispered.

"Sorry about what?"

Loud footsteps came down the stairs, and Sarah glanced through the hall to the see the male half of the couple shirtless and clearly worried . . . as he presented a nasty shoulder wound for the doctor's inspection.

"Sarah? Will you look at me?"

Reflexively, she glanced at the commando—only to recoil at the intense expression on his face. At which point, from out of nowhere, a strange, piercing pain hit her temples, as if she'd eaten ice cream too fast—

"This is getting worse," she heard the doctor say off in the distance.

Breaking eye contact with the commando—something that was strangely difficult to do, as if their stares had formed a tangible tie— Sarah leaned to the side and looked down the hall again. The doctor was palpating that shoulder—and before Sarah could help herself, she burst up and walked down to the two of them.

The doctor seemed surprised at the intrusion—and Sarah didn't bother with reading anyone else's expression. She was fascinated by the wound. It was unlike anything she had ever seen before—and jeez, talk about ugly. There was a blackened erosion of the first and second layers of skin along the edges of an infected area that extended from the top of the shoulder down onto the pectoral.

"Have you tried antibiotics?" Sarah asked. "What have you done so far to treat this?"

When they all stared at her and the commando came in from the kitchen, she glanced around at the group—which now included the girlfriend/wife who had come down the stairs.

"I'm sorry." She took a step back and looked up at the patient. "I don't mean to be pushy, but I'm a molecular geneticist. I specialize in the immune system and I'm just curious about what's going on here for you.

Your body's clearly fighting off something, and the researcher in me wants to know what it is and what you're doing to help yourself?"

She was surprised when the man lifted his hands and signed, *I was hurt fighting. We haven't treated it with antibiotics because it's not that kind of infection.*

The girlfriend/wife cleared her throat. "He really doesn't want to talk about this—"

Sarah signed back, *What kind of infection is it?*

◆   ◆   ◆

Smart was sexy.

It was also incredibly inconvenient when you were trying to get into someone's brain, take over their thoughts, erase their short-term memory . . . and send them back to the human world where they belonged.

Murhder had a lot of experience wiping memories and replacing them with different versions of events, but he'd never started the process and had his target break away from the mind control and latch onto something else so completely that their consciousness locked him out.

Hello, Sarah.

And P.S., he loved her name.

As she and John signed back and forth, Murhder was very aware he needed to get into her skull again, and not just finish the scrub job, but start the damn thing all over. Instead, he just stood there like a planker, enjoying the sight of her as she communicated with John, her hands flipping smoothly through positions.

Lot of nodding between the pair of them.

Then Sarah looked at the doctor known as Jane. "I don't have to know the details of how it happened. I can respect his privacy. But I don't understand what the infection is—any more than you all do, evidently. I have a feeling you are not going to take him to a medical center, and no, I am not going to make trouble for you guys." She glanced around. "But I can help if you want someone who knows a helluva lot about immune response to take a stab at it."

Xhex spoke up from the stairwell's bottom step. "What kind of help?"

"I'm not going to lie," Sarah replied. "I don't have any treatments immediately in mind. But I don't like to see patients in pain or scared about their future. I deal with cancer patients, and trust me, after having lost both my parents to that disease, I know too well how hard it is to be terrified about your health. I'm motivated by all that, but also the researcher in me is fascinated. I want to know what the tissue looks like under the microscope. I want to see what his white blood cells are doing. I want to go down to that cellular level and find out what's happening. There's no easy solution, of course. Immunotherapy is still new science and it's not like there's a magic pill or shot that I can recommend that will make him better. I would love to help, though, and it is my area of expertise."

Murhder waited for the Brotherhood's doctor to pump the brakes on the idea. Then he glanced at Xhex and figured she'd be shaking her head. Finally, he checked out John and expected him to no-thank-you the offer.

When none of that happened, he tried not to get excited. Failed.

And had to remind himself that ultimately it was not going to work. Sarah couldn't stay in their world, and the longer she was involved with vampires, the more memories she gathered, and the more difficult and painful it was going to be to clean her out.

Short-term stuff was one thing. Long-term was a different story.

Sarah shrugged. "Besides, after tonight, I'm out of a job anyway. Likely out of a career when I come forward with what I know."

The Brotherhood's doctor spoke up. "What was your name? I'm sorry, I didn't catch it."

"Dr. Sarah Watkins." She put her palm out. "As I said, I specialize in immunotherapy for cancer patients and I am about to have a lot of time on my hands."

"I'm Jane." The two shook hands. "Dr. Jane Whitcomb."

"Pleased to meet you." There was a long pause. "Do you mind if I make some phone calls first?"

Murhder stepped up. "Sarah? Look at me, please. Just for a moment."

This time, without her incredible intellect distracted by the thing that interested it most, he found getting into her consciousness and staying there much easier.

Images rose from out of the depths of her memories, sunken boats floating to the surface of her own private sea. He saw a lot of a human man and guessed it was her fiancé—no surprise, he had an instant dislike of the guy. He also saw a lot of the inside of a laboratory not unlike the one they had infiltrated at the site. He further saw a simple house, with simple furnishings, and a bed that was messy only on one side.

He also caught the recollections of an FBI agent showing up on the doorstep of that simple house . . . and how she had made the man a coffee and sat down with him to answer questions about her dead fiancé.

Sarah had been unnerved by the whole thing.

Murhder slipped a patch over those memories associated with the FBI agent, effectively disappearing any mental trace of that visitor and his line of inquiry. Gone. As if she'd never met the man.

As he withdrew from her consciousness, she winced and rubbed her temples. "Does anyone have a Motrin? I've got a heck of a headache."

"I'll get you some," Xhex said as she turned and went back up the stairs.

Murhder took a deep breath. "Sarah, exactly how open-minded are you?"

It wasn't exactly a question.

More like a prayer of his.

CHAPTER TWENTY-FIVE

As Doc Jane went off somewhere with her phone up to her ear and her voice at whisper level, and Murhder and the human researcher went back to the kitchen, John turned to the sofa and looked at the pretrans who was sitting under a quilt and watching everything with wide, exhausted eyes.

John lifted his palm at the kid.

"Hi," the boy said back. "You don't talk?"

John shook his head and went over to a rocking chair. When he sat down, the thing creaked like it might lose its structural integrity under his weight, but somehow the antique managed to hold him.

"What happened to your voice?" the young asked. "Were you hurt?"

John shook his head and then shrugged.

"You were born like that and you don't know why." When John nodded, the kid seemed sad. "I'm sorry."

John shrugged again and put up his palms, all what-can-you-do. Then he pointed into the other room, to Doc Jane, and gave the boy a thumbs-up.

"You trust her?" John put his hand over his heart, closed his eyes, and nodded. "You trust her with your life."

John gave the a-okay sign. Then pointed to the kid and made the a-okay sign.

"You think I'm going to be all right?"

John nodded, made the cross in front of his chest, and then pointed his finger like a gun, put it to his temple and pulled the trigger.

The young smiled. "Cross your heart, hope to die."

John jammed a thumb toward his eyeball.

"Stick a finger in your eye."

John made the a-okay sign again.

The boy got serious. "I knew my *mahmen* was dead. Last night, I was asleep in the cage, and all of a sudden, I felt someone shake me awake. As I sat up . . . I felt like she was sitting next to me, the way it used to be, the two of us together. It made me miss her so much. And then the feeling went away. It was like she visited me on her way unto the Fade."

John nodded and put his hand over his heart, rubbing.

"Thanks. I appreciate that." When John nodded again, the young took a deep breath. "I told the doctor what the last month has been like. The humans at the lab, they were getting excited because my readings are all messed up. My *mahmen*, she told me if I lived this long that I had to watch for signs that my change was coming. She also told me that I had to get out of that lab before the transition hit. The humans weren't going to know what to do to get me through it."

John shook his head. Then he exposed his watch, tapped it, and pointed at the young.

"How old am I? I'm twenty. Or at least I think I am that old. Sometimes I'm not sure whether I count the years correctly. It's kind of messed up in my head. My *mahmen*, she told me I'd go through the change at about twenty-five, but that stress could add or subtract from that."

John let the kid talk it all out and decided that one good thing about being mute was that he was able to give people a lot of space to share what was going on for them. And the more the kid chatted to him, the more he returned to his own past, to when he'd been scrawny and living in that rat hole, calling the Suicide Prevention Hotline, praying for Mary's voice on the other line.

This young was just as lost as he had been.

And like John, he'd been found in a nick of time.

Jesus, it made him sick to his stomach to think of what would have happened to the pretrans if he hadn't been rescued tonight—because the kid was right. Those humans couldn't have gotten him to a female of the species—hell, they probably didn't even know they had to. And if he'd hit the transition without the proper vein to take, he was going to die outright.

Unfortunately, sometimes the young died anyway. Even if they had help.

A powerful worry took up root in John's chest as he stared across the safe house's sitting room. For some reason, he didn't want anything to happen to this young.

Funny, how what you had in common with a stranger could turn them into family so quickly.

"Were you scared when you went through the change?" the young asked.

John nodded. And then he pointed to himself and flashed the thumbs-up.

"But you made it. And you're big and okay."

As John nodded again, the kid took a deep breath. "Do you think they'll let the human woman stay with me? And the big male?"

John nodded, even though he wasn't sure what was going to happen. But come on, surely the Brotherhood would give the young a break? And he was very close to the transition. John could scent it.

"I just don't . . ." Those eyes gleamed with tears. "I've been alone for a really long time and I'm scared."

John pointed to the kid. Then pointed to the center of his own chest. Then he curled his upper lip and tapped his fang with his finger. After that, he made a slashing motion in front of his own throat.

"You were alone, too? In the human world."

John nodded grimly.

"Really? I thought I was the only one." The boy took a deep breath. "It's kind of a relief to know that isn't the case."

When John nodded once again, the kid half-smiled. "No offense, I'd rather we have winning the lottery in common."

The two of them laughed, the young with sound, John without.

Not that the difference mattered.

◆   ◆   ◆

In making the immunology pitch, Sarah had played the only card she had. Her instincts were telling her that her time with the group was ending. Somehow, they were either going to disappear on her, or disappear her—although not in a mortal sense: At no time had she felt threatened or fearful for her life. But this secretive enclave of . . . she didn't know what . . . had resources, talent and intelligence, and clearly liked to stay under the radar.

She thought of the security guard at BioMed. Kraiten, himself. She couldn't begin to explain how the commandos had seemed to take control of those men. And the fact that she didn't understand so much of what had happened made her want to know more about them. Was it the researcher in her?

Or maybe something more primal?

Across the kitchen, leaning back against the counter, the commando with the red-and-black hair was looking at her with the kind of speculation usually reserved for women who were not like Sarah. And no, she didn't mean that she wasn't attractive. But those hooded eyes, the fixated stare, the erotic air around his big body, were more often directed at those who put their sexuality on display and encouraged the currency exchange of sex and attraction with men.

Meanwhile, she was looking like a hot mess over here in the damn hazmat suit.

Unless, of course, he had a fetish thing for weather balloons.

"You've never told me your name," she blurted. When he hesitated to respond, she had to smile. "Top secret, huh."

"Is it important?"

"It's where most people start when they want to get to know each other."

Abruptly, his voice dropped low, the tone deepening. "Do you want to know me?"

The words were simple. The question behind the curtain of those syllables was anything but.

Sarah glanced down at her hands. It had been so long, she thought.

"Sorry," he muttered.

"Yes," she said without looking up. "I do want to know you."

That scent, that cologne he wore, returned to her nose, and she swore the smell of it gave her a contact high: All at once, she was floating in her own body.

"Sarah."

Taking a deep breath, she shook her head. "I'm not good at this."

"Good at what."

She wanted to tell him that she hadn't been with anyone since Gerry died, but she didn't want to dwell on that. People were allowed to move on, weren't they? And it had been two years since he'd been gone. Two years . . . which had been preceded by a lot of lonely nights.

And it was funny, in the midst of this drama, this storm of incomprehensible scope and unprecedented magnitude, she found herself wanting to break free of everything: Her humdrum life, her complicated grief, her sense that she had somehow missed her future because nothing had ended up as it was supposed to.

Gerry gone. Her alone. Now her job likely over—because she'd trespassed at her goddamn research facility, busted out a hostage patient, and gone on the lam with a bunch of commandos who were so far off the grid, they had their own medical team.

"Lam"? Or was it "lamb"? She didn't even know what the proper term/spelling was.

Because, hello, the closest she had ever come to committing a crime was parking too close to a frickin' fire hydrant.

Sarah rubbed her aching head. Hell, maybe the tossing sea of emotion she was in was part of her attraction to this stranger. He represented an anonymous outlet for all the energy she couldn't seem to hold inside her skin—

When a floorboard creaked, she looked up.

He was standing in front of her, this incredibly tall man with that hair, those peach-colored eyes . . . that body . . .

Okay, fine. The attraction was also probably his body, she decided. He would look amazing laying naked in messy sheets, all those muscles on display and his . . . sword of love . . . all erect and—

Sword of love? Had her brain *really* just spit that one out?

And please, God, let her have kept that to herself.

"Sarah . . ."

The way he said her name was a caress, something tactile as opposed to just sound through air. And as she allowed her eyes to travel down his chest to his hips, it became abundantly clear he could more than follow up on the sexual tension between them.

He was fully aroused. And not bothering to hide it in the slightest.

"Yes," she said.

As she spoke, she was aware that she had answered the question that arousal of his was asking: She didn't know where and she didn't know when, but she and this stranger were going to be together.

The doctor came into the kitchen. "Okay. Let's bring you in. Let's do it."

Yes, Sarah thought to herself as she got up from the table. *We're going to.*

CHAPTER TWENTY-SIX

Throe, son of Throe, sat at a Louis XV bureau plat in a canary-yellow parlor in a mansion he had inherited from a distant relative because of a murder.

Or at least that was how he had come to frame his largesse. In reality, he had no official property rights to the home and he'd had no relation to the deceased other than sharing the social status and DNA common to all aristocrats. Still, he had possession of the structure, and that was not going to be challenged by rightful heirs because no one knew the previous owner was dead.

Fine, he had previously shared such status. But the genetic ties were immutable.

And he did have a blood connection to the male of worth who had been stabbed.

Throe had ordered the murder to be committed.

Looking around at the damask wallpaper, the Aubusson rug, the oil paintings of distinguished males and winsome females, he felt an existential calm bloom within his body. He had been on the outs for so long, his forced tenure with the Band of Bastards a period in his life he would sooner forget: That centuries of fighting and surviving in the Old World with Xcor's group of rogue soldiers had been an aberrant interruption of where he had started and where he was now, a bout of existential flu, a passing infection that his destiny had managed to surmount and cure itself of.

He put his hand on the Book. "Isn't that right, darling."

As his palm made contact with the ancient tome's leather cover, he felt a shimmer travel up his arm to his heart—and the resulting resonance in the center of his chest was rather like the warmth one felt when complimented or hugged, a reassuring glow of happiness, a subtle charge of well-being flaring where one needed it most.

His ambitions were finally gathering momentum once again and it was all because of the Book. Courtesy of its powers, he had conjured weapons from thin air.

Shadows which did his bidding.

The ghostly forms were the perfect fighters, capable of killing at the slightest direction from him and requiring no armaments, no ammo, no food or rest. And just as significant, they had no independent will or aspiration. They were content to serve him as he saw fit, with no chance of argument or threat of mutiny.

They were hellaciously effective, too. He had staged a number of attacks downtown, the targets chosen with care: sons of the *glymera* in their prime. With the aristocrats already enraged by Wrath's disbanding of the Council, the upper class was disaffected and unstable. Add to that simmering discord the fact that the Black Dagger Brotherhood and the King could not protect their precious male progeny?

It was the perfect social unrest, a kettle about to o'erboil—and Throe was in the best position to seize upon the fear and anger, and leverage them into a claim on the throne.

His first foray unto that goal had failed. This time? With his shadows? With his Book?

He was going to get what he wanted, rising above the ridicule and the shame from the centuries before, reclaiming his rightful place in the *glymera*.

And the idea that the Band of Bastards, now aligned with Wrath, would suffer? Well, that just gave him additional satisfaction. Granted, overtime, he had fallen in with them, believing those males to be his family. But that had been a ruse created by circumstance. Forced proximity to their brutish ways did not equate with true kinship.

All he needed was the Book and his shadows, and his future was secure.

Opening up to a random page, he stroked the symbols of the Old Language that had been inked into the parchment, and in response, they shifted ever so slightly as his fingers passed over them—

In the back of his mind, he was aware that that was not right.

Images imbedded through an inking's permanent stain should not move, and people in their right minds did not talk to inanimate objects as if they were in a relationship with them.

In a foggy, rambly series of recollections, he remembered going to that psychic's shop and having the Book materialize unto him, its seductive power calling him forth and deeming him worthy of its many gifts. He recalled opening the cover and being unable to translate the runes upon its pages—except then, before his very eyes, the ink had rearranged itself into the Old Language which he could read.

In a series of vivid snapshots, he remembered coming back here, and conjuring his first shadow . . .

All at once a flush went through him, the heat reaching his brain and unscrambling his thoughts.

No, it is fine, he told himself. *All is well. All is as it should be.*

"I have my faith and my faith has me," he whispered. "I have my faith and my faith has me . . ."

As the mantra came out of his mouth, over and over again, he focused on the desktop. On it was a seating plan for twenty-four in the formal dining room. The guests had been chosen with deliberation, each one of the couples not just from the *glymera*, but with *hellrens* who had been members of the Council that Wrath had seen fit to do away with.

As if aristocrats didn't know best.

Everything was set for the party. The *hors d'oeuvres*, the menu, the wine pairings—and most especially the entertainment.

Following all those targeted deaths downtown, it was now time for him and his shadows to take it up a notch. At the appointed moment, the party was going to be "infiltrated" with the terrifying new enemy of the species, the scourge of downtown, the mystical killer of the *glymera's* young.

And there would be no Brotherhood, no Wrath, to save them. Just as there had been no Brotherhood, no Wrath, to save their sons.

Instead, Throe would be the one who vanquished the threat. Protected them and their *shellans*. Placed himself voluntarily in grave bodily danger in order to ensure their safety and survival.

All of which were no big deal when you were actually in control of the attack.

All of which positioned him nicely as a one-of-them leadership alternative to Wrath's throne.

Throe stroked the Book as he imagined himself in a position of true power, no longer the fallen-from-grace also-ran of a fairly good family.

Instead, the King.

Without the Book, none of this would be possible, he told himself. So whatever oddities occurred with respect to its pages, whatever things he could not explain about how it had come to him—or him to it, as it were—whatever concerns he might have about sometimes not feeling as if he were in control of himself, none of these mattered as long as he dethroned Wrath, son of Wrath, sire of Wrath—

No, his inner voice insisted. *None of this was right, none of this made sense*—

The Book cover flipped open, casting his palm away. Pages turned at a frenetic pace, the blur faster than the eye could track, continuing longer than there were folios set within the binding.

"Now, darling," he said. "Let us not do this."

The pages slowed.

"Forgive me my wayward thoughts." Slower the sheaths turned. "It is never my intent to offend."

Finally the Book stilled.

"I do not want to quarrel—"

Leaning over, he frowned at the pages facing up at him. The characters of the Old Language upon them were beginning to swirl around a fulcrum in the center of the open binding. Faster and faster they turned, a galaxy forming and then tightening into a black hole so resonant and intense, Throe could have sworn a three-dimensional sinkhole had been created, one that was so vast, there was no comprehending its terminal—or perhaps it had no terminal at all.

He leaned closer.

Staring into the void, his eyes adjusted to the dense blackness . . . and that was when he recognized a contouring around its edges. The pattern that was uneven and yet predictable.

Stones, he thought. It seemed as though stones had been mortared together in a circle that plunged into the earth.

A well.

Throe . . .

At the sound of his name echoing up to him, a surge of fear had him pushing back against the desk, and for a split second, the pull of that voice, of whatever was at the base of the void, latched onto him and held him in place.

Sucking him in—the vortex was sucking him in—

The seduction snapped like a tether that had reached its limit, and he was suddenly free and falling back into the chair with a slam that nearly toppled him backward onto the carpet. As he threw out his hands to steady himself, his heart pounded and his head swam, sure as if he'd just caught himself from a deadly fall, his life saved by a split second and a stroke of luck.

When he looked up, all four of his shadows were in front of the desk.

"What are you doing here?" he asked roughly.

It was the first time they had moved of their own volition.

CHAPTER TWENTY-SEVEN

As Sarah sat in the back of a van with blacked-out windows and bench seats, she was aware she needed to go to the authorities about BioMed and the secret lab. But every time that impulse went through her head, a ringing pain cut her thoughts off. She had proof, however. Proof that had to be given over to some kind of official someone.

She wasn't exactly sure whom to go to. The New York State police? Or maybe the FBI. Yes, the FBI—

As the sharpshooter in her frontal lobe returned, she distracted herself from the discomfort by looking around the inside of the van. It was the boy, the commando, and the doctor sitting with her on padded seats that ringed, not row'd, the rear compartment. Early on in the trip, she decided it was like the inside of a cargo plane and they were all going to parachute out of the rear doors when they reached ten thousand feet.

She didn't know who was driving. Where they were going. Or what exactly was going to happen when they reached their destination.

But the boy's head was in her lap, and someone had given her a really good Reuben sandwich and a Coke before they'd left, and there was a nice warm heater breezing up her ankles.

There would be time to go to the Feds. Or whoever. Just not tonight.

As they continued along what had to be a well-paved road, different things drifted through her mind, none of them landing on her proverbial tarmac for very long: the fact that she was still in the hazmat suit, the weird headache, the way the commando continued to stare at her.

Okay, that one did stick.

By all accounts, she should have been terrified to put her life in the hands of these strangers with their guns and their secrets: There was nobody at home to miss her. No family who was expecting her to call. No friends to check in. And didn't all that make her feel like a ghost in her own life, P.S.

Work, however, would miss her—although considering what she had done? Breaking and entering, evac'ing the boy, taking Kraiten's own SUV, for godsakes . . . there was going to be chaos at the company tomorrow and her absence would be noted.

So maybe this little side step wasn't a bad thing. It might give her some time to think of a plan to confront the mess she'd left behind. The real question, she supposed, was how Kraiten was going to spin things. After all, it was hard to go to the authorities and demand the laws be used to defend your own illegal practices.

Kind of like a drug dealer calling 911 when his stash gets stolen.

But Kraiten had tremendous resources—and not all of them were of the "proper authorities" variety, she was willing to guess. Hell, she'd heard his private security were ex–Israeli Defense Forces soldiers.

Abruptly, she thought of Gerry. Of Thomas McCaid, his dead boss. Of Kraiten's own partner, who had met a grisly end two decades ago.

Anxiety, of the mortal kind, curled around her heart—

"What's wrong?"

As the commando spoke, she snapped her head up. The sudden movement caused the boy to stir, but she stroked his thin arm and he resettled. His name was Nate, she'd learned. Or at least that was his first name. Last hadn't come up. Yet.

Surely he had family somewhere.

"Tell me," her commando said in a soft voice.

Sarah glanced over at the doctor. The woman was deep into her phone, sending some kind of text message. "Oh, it's nothing."

"Tell me anyway."

The van slowed. Stopped.

"Are we here?" she asked.

"It's the gates. We still have a while to go. Answer my question."

I'm so over my head, she thought. *With all of this. The kid, that patient with the wound, what we did at BioMed . . . what I know about that company.*

"I won't let anything happen to you."

Had she spoken all of that aloud again? She wasn't sure.

Shaking her head and looking down at the boy, she fell silent and concentrated on the stopping and going of the van. After a while, there was a descent, as if they were coming off a hill or going underground. And then the van finally halted, the engine was turned off, and the rear doors opened—

Sarah did a double take as she saw four or five men, in tactical gear, standing around the back of the vehicle.

What the hell, she thought. *Did they have a hydroponic farm somewhere and grow these big boys from test tubes?*

The soldiers—and that was absolutely what they were—were all like her commando, huge, calm, and surprisingly welcoming as they peered in at her and the child. That being said, she did not want to get on their bad sides.

Look at those weapons.

"Hi," the blond one said. "You need a hand there?"

As he smiled, she blinked like she'd been hit by a beam of sunshine. Between his brilliant blue eyes, his gleaming teeth, and that too-handsome face, he should have been in Hollywood.

The guy made Chris Hemsworth look like a candidate for recon-structive surgery.

"I've got him," she murmured as she gathered the boy in her arms.

Crab-walking out the back, Nate stirred when they got hit by the bright lights of . . .

It was a parking area. They were in a professional grade, municipal parking garage, on what appeared to be its lowest level.

"This way," another soldier said as he went across to a reinforced steel door with no markings on it.

Okay, that man had long, multi-colored hair and incredible eyes that were lion-yellow and impossibly kind, especially as they rested on the boy.

Sarah stayed put, however, even as the doctor hurried off through the entry like she had another patient to see. Instinctively, Sarah waited for her commando to get out and come alongside of her, and then the pair of them walked into the facility together with Nate still in her arms. The boy woke up properly halfway down a long hall that had con-crete walls, a tiled floor, and fluorescent ceiling lights that were as bright white as the moon on a clear winter night.

Big money, she thought as she passed by numerous closed doors. *These facilities were on a par with BioMed's.*

So who was the Kraiten behind all this?

Up ahead, a dark-haired man in a white physician's coat stepped out of a doorway. With his scrubs and that stethoscope around his neck, he seemed right out of central casting.

"And here's our patient," he said as they stopped in front of him. "Hey, buddy, what's up? I'm Dr. Manello, but you can call me Manny."

As he extended his hand to the boy, Sarah turned so Nate could put his tiny palm in the man's.

"My name is Nate," the child said. "It is short for Natelem. I am the proud son of Ingridge."

Such a strange formality, Sarah thought.

"Well, Nate, welcome to my humble abode. I understand you're going to be staying with us for a little while." He looked at Sarah and smiled. "And you're Dr. Watkins. Welcome."

"Thank you."

"You want to bring him in here? I have a sumptuous suite prepared for his use."

The doctor swept the door open and revealed a hospital room that had every piece of monitoring equipment you could want for a trauma patient—and even though that confused the hell out of Sarah, she felt instantly better for the boy.

She glanced at her commando. He was staring at her with hooded eyes, as if he were waiting to see what she was going to do.

"Let's get you settled," she said to Nate as she went in. "And maybe fed. How's that sound?"

◆   ◆   ◆

The Brotherhood had certainly taken things up a notch or twelve down here, Murhder thought as he followed Sarah and Nate into the hospital room.

Darius's old digs in the Richie Rich part of town were nothing compared to this underground stuff. The Brotherhood had what looked like an entire hospital down here, and God only knew what else.

Not that he was paying a huge amount of attention to the facility.

Nope, his gray matter was trained on the human woman. Every move she made. The nuances of her expression. The sound of her voice—

Okay, fine, maybe he was also ever-so-slightly, kinda-sorta, possibly-a-little interested in where the Brothers were and what they were doing. Like, oh, say, how close they were getting to Sarah. Whether she seemed to notice them or they her. If any of them were taking down her phone number.

Which, P.S., he didn't have.

Ten-digit vacancies aside, and fortunately for his possessive nature, none of what he was worried about—initial attraction turning into lust that transitioned into a lifelong bonded love and adoration between Sarah and Rhage or Phury or Tohr—seemed to be happening as she took the young over to the hospital bed: The Brothers were keeping it all strictly professional, and if anything, the only carbon-based life form his woman seemed to notice, apart from the young, was Murhder himself.

But eternal vigilance and all that—although, really, what was he going to do if he saw something he didn't like? It wasn't as if the woman was his to claim—

As his upper lip twitched and his fangs threatened to drop down, he tried to reason with the male beast inside his skin—and didn't get far. It was kind of like throwing a math problem at a grizzly bear: You got frustrated and the bear didn't give a shit.

"—rest for a little while," Manny, the human doctor—human?— said. "I'll be right back with some eats for everyone. You want anything in particular, Dr. Watkins?"

"Whatever you have is fine for me. And it's Sarah. Just Sarah."

As the doctor smiled and then left, Murhder shook himself back to attention. The Brothers had stepped out, the young was lying down against the pillows, and the woman who was not his was removing the blue bag of plastic from her body.

And what do you know. As she finally stepped out of the loose, flapping outer shell she'd had on, what was revealed was beautiful to him— although not because of what it necessarily looked like, but because it was *her*. Those long legs, the graceful curves of her torso, the proportion of shoulder to hip, all of that could have fit together in any particular way, been any-whatever-size, had more or less in any place, and he still would have wanted to touch her, taste her, take her.

"I'm scared," Nate said.

Murhder and Sarah both turned to the young, and Murhder became very aware that he was the only one who knew what the boy was talking about. The change was coming to him. Soon.

"Would you like me to stay in here with you?" she asked the young.
"Yes, please."

When Nate looked over at Murhder, the answer was easy. "Sure," he said. "I'll stay with you, also."

There were two chairs along the long wall opposite the bed, and Murhder let Sarah choose the one she liked first. He wasn't particular because either way, he was going to get to sit close to her. As they settled in, he wanted to hold her hand. She looked worried.

Especially as she stared at Nate. The young did seem wiped out, his skin too pale, his breathing shallow, his eyes fluttering to a close so hard, the tortured wince turned his face into a death mask.

That was the transition for you.

"God, what they did to him in that lab," she muttered under her breath.

Yes, he thought. But it was also what the young was about to go through—and as the reality of Nate's impending transition really hit, Murhder wondered how the hell all this was going to work when it came to Sarah. She was bound to learn about the race now, either from her trying to treat John Matthew's wound or from what was going to happen here in this hospital room very soon.

And then what? Was she going to be repulsed by it all?

By Murhder, himself?

Without conscious thought, he did reach for her hand—and it wasn't until he felt her warm palm against his own that he realized what he'd done. Glancing over, he met her eyes and waited for her to pull away, look away . . .

She squeezed his hand and held on.

As a feeling of warmth spread throughout Murhder's chest, the two of them went back to staring across at the young, so small and fragile in the big, clinical bed. Sometime soon thereafter, food was brought in by a *doggen* in uniform, steak and steaming potatoes for him and Sarah, white rice with ginger sauce for the young's sensitive stomach.

The pair of them ate in silence—Nate couldn't seem to tolerate anything, not even that signature fare for those about to go through the change—and the next thing Murhder knew, the trays had been cleared, the young was back asleep, and he and Sarah were staring at each other.

He knew exactly what was on her mind. It was what was on his.

But now was not the time for sex. And here was not the place—

"Will you tell me what's going on with this?" she said quietly. "All of you. These facilities. The staff. This is not a casual, cobbled-together operation, and I want to understand what the hell's happening here."

Okay . . . so maybe they weren't thinking about the same thing.

CHAPTER TWENTY-EIGHT

As Sarah put the demand out there, she didn't expect her commando to answer with total honesty. Something as extensive as all this? Something as *expensive* as all this? They didn't want to be known, and they had the resources to keep it that way—so he wasn't going to spill any secrets to a woman he'd just met. But . . . dayum.

And there was another reason she'd asked. She wanted to hear his voice, have that strange accent of his in her ear . . . watch his lips move as he enunciated his words.

Like he was doing right now.

Shoot, she needed to pay attention.

"—take care of our own, that's all," he said with the kind of finality that suggested he wasn't going to go any further with the discussion.

Before she could do any kind of follow-up, Nate tossed and turned over on the bed, his frail legs moving under the blankets, his head going back and forth on the pillow. Just as she was wondering if she shouldn't go and get help, he resettled, seeming to sink back into sleep.

"Who are you, though," she said absently as she stared across at the boy. When there was no reply, she looked back to her commando. "I mean, what group are you affiliated with?"

The man looked down at his hands. "Does it really matter?"

"I just want to know who you are," she said. And funny, as she spoke, she wasn't sure what worried her more: whatever his answer was going to be—or how desperately she wanted to know it.

She thought of Gerry and shifted uneasily in her chair.

"Can you tell me your name at least?" she asked.

At that moment, there was a knock on the door, and they both said "enter" as quietly as they could. What came in was . . . utterly unexpected.

The woman was tall and slender, and instead of being dressed in street or even hospital staff clothes, she was draped in a fall of white fabric that started at her shoulders and went all the way down to the floor. With her dark hair swept up and away from her face, and her hands tucked into the sleeves of the robing, she seemed like something out of a religious ceremony. From Greece or Rome. Back in, like, 1500 BCE.

A vestal virgin.

But that wasn't the half of it. She had an ethereal, unnatural beauty, her skin seeming to glow, an aura surrounding her and somehow charging the air with heavenly electrons.

A saint.

Abruptly, the woman stopped just inside the doorway, recoiling as she saw the commando.

"'Tis you." At that, she bowed very low, such that Sarah could see the complicated twist that her hair had been wound into on the top of her head. "Sire, you have returned."

Her voice had the timbre of a concert violin being played by a master, her speech not so much words, but musical notes.

An angel.

The commando cleared his throat. "How are you, Analye. And this is Sarah."

There was a brief pause of confusion. And then the woman bowed again. "Mistress, it is my honor to serve. May I please approach the young?"

Sarah stiffened in her chair.

"Yes," the commando interjected. "And maybe we'll just give you guys some privacy."

As he went to stand up, Nate's voice cut through the awkwardness. "I don't feel well."

Sarah frowned as the woman went over to the bedside. That unnatural glow seemed to intensify, surely as if that robe with its strangely iridescent threads had been hit by a theater light instead of the dull fluorescent panels in the ceiling. And then Sarah had to rub her eyes because clearly her vision was off. A distortion, like heat rising off hot pavement in the summer, created waves in the air between the woman and the boy, warping that which should have been static such as the wall behind them, the bed between them, the pillow his head was on—

The commando stepped in front of her, blocking her view. In a low, grim voice, he said, "We need to leave now."

A strange tingling had Sarah pulling up the sleeves of her fleece and looking down at herself. Both of her arms were alive with goosebumps, the skin bearing a chill that could not be explained from a drop in temperature in the room.

The door into the hall opened wide and the female doctor leaned in. She took one look at the boy, and then stared hard at the commando.

"You need to get her out of here. Now."

Sarah knew damn well she was the subject of that order. But she shook her head. "I'm not leaving him. I don't know what the hell is going on here, but I am *not* leaving him—"

"I don't feel right," Nate said roughly. "I don't . . ."

Sarah burst to her feet. "We need a crash cart!"

The woman in the robe calmly looked over at the commando. "It is time, sire. It is upon him."

"What's wrong with you people?" Sarah glared at the doctor. "Do something! He looks like he's seizing!"

For godsakes, if she were a clinician, rather than a researcher, she would jump up on that bed and start chest compressions—or do whatever had to happen to stabilize him. Meanwhile, everyone else just stared at the child as his small hands gripped the sheets and balled up wads on either side of his body. Arching back, he opened his mouth and let out a sound that didn't seem human at all.

It was the cry . . . of an animal.

As the high-pitched wail faded in the bald room, Sarah felt the blood leave her head, a sudden warning rising up through her consciousness.

She thought of those lab experiments. Of the results that were inexplicable. Of the strange accents, this secret lair, that female in the robe.

Losing her balance, she fell back into the chair and stared up the commando's powerful body.

Abruptly, she realized she had been asking the wrong question.

It was not "who."

"What are you?" she breathed.

◆   ◆   ◆

Murhder drew a palm down his face. This was getting in way too deep, way too quickly for the human woman. He'd thought they'd have some time before the transition came unto the young, time for her to get a good look at John Matthew's wound, time for her to weigh in on that, time for Murhder and her to . . .

Explore their attraction.

After which, she would have to return to her life in the human world.

Instead, the change had arrived and there was no stopping it—no doubt the stress of the escape and coming here had jump-started the process. Or maybe Nate's body had always meant for this night to be the one.

What the hell did it matter.

"I need to feed him," the Chosen said urgently. "May I have your consent as guardians?"

Murhder swallowed hard. Then looked to Doc Jane. Part of him wanted to order the female healer to give the permission. He certainly didn't feel like anything close to fit-parent material. But he had to remember what he had promised Ingridge.

"Yes, you have my consent," he heard himself say.

Doc Jane spoke up. "Get her out of here. She can't be a part of this."

Nate's bloodshot eyes popped wide, and he looked around frantically. "I want Sarah! Don't make her go!"

It was the last comprehensible thing he spoke.

As he fell into a state of mumbles, Sarah narrowed hard eyes up at Murhder. "You will have to take me out of this room in pieces. Am I making myself clear?"

Murhder sat back down and rubbed his palms on his thighs, up and down, up and down. As he felt Doc Jane's glare, he muttered, "I'll take care of it."

Doc Jane cursed. "This is not right and it is not good. For her."

On that happy note, the physician backed out of the room—and in the wake of her departure, he was very clear on why Sarah staying and watching this had bad idea written all over it. The more vivid the memories, the harder they were to scrub. But like he wasn't going to have to patch over whole sections of her recollections now, anyway? What was one more thing?

Okay, based on his life story, that was probably the wrong question to pose to destiny.

"What is she doing?" Sarah whispered. "Oh, God . . . what is that woman doing?"

Murhder looked over to the bed, even though he didn't need visual confirmation to know what was going on. The Chosen had pinned up her left sleeve within the folds of the robing and brought her wrist to her mouth—and now she was puncturing her vein with her fangs.

Meanwhile, Nate was definitely in the thralls of the change. The poor kid was thrashing on the bed, his body contorted by the pain inside his skin, the hunger in his marrow, the need for his cells to have a sustenance only members of the opposite sex could provide him—

Except then the scent of that blood hit the young's senses and he froze even in the midst of his suffering. In slow motion, his head cranked toward the Chosen.

There were no pupils to his eyes. They were nothing but white in the midst of his wide lids.

Fixated, he opened his mouth and released that high calling sound again, like a bird of prey about to be provided fresh meat.

"*For your sustenance,*" the Chosen said in the Old Language.

The sacred female extended her wrist over his open lips, and as the first drop of blood hit the young's tongue, his body started to shake so hard, he levitated off the mattress—

Murhder felt a slap on his own arm and then pinpricks of pain.

Sarah had grabbed onto him, probably without even realizing it, her nails piercing his skin. Meanwhile, her other hand was braced against the wall, her face drawn in lines of horror.

Shit, he really should have gotten her out when he could.

The Chosen lowered her vein directly to the young's mouth and Nate grabbed onto her hand and forearm, as if he were afraid the source of his very life would be taken away before he got what he needed.

"What are they doing . . ." Sarah's voice trailed off weakly. "What . . ."

Murhder hung his head and wondered what the hell he had been thinking, allowing the human to come here, be a part of this, see what for all intents and purposes could not be unseen. Selfish. So selfish.

The problem was that after so many years of drowning alone in his insanity, he had missed feeling grounded and connected—and not merely to everything around him, but to one special person in particular.

This was going to cost the human dearly, however.

Yet another in his long list of regrets.

CHAPTER TWENTY-NINE

After Sarah's decade or so of medical science education and training, she was very well acquainted with the way the human body functioned, how the mechanisms of sight and hearing worked, how the channels of information gathering and processing ran along neuropathways, how the brain managed the flows of sense and thought.

All of that academic crap went out the window as she stared across the hospital room and watched a boy open his mouth and latch on . . . to a woman's wrist.

He was drinking.

Blood.

She could see his throat working as he swallowed again and again.

Simple logic told her she needed to stop what was happening. There was never a reason for a human to give their blood orally to another person. This was both dangerous, given all of the blood-borne pathogens that could be carried, and unnecessary.

But she returned again and again to those scans.

"What are you," she repeated without taking her eyes off the bed.

She was dimly aware that she was gripping the commando's arm—and there was no letting go of it. In some strange way, she was convinced the connection was the only thing keeping her on the earth.

And then things began to happen to the boy.

Things that . . . could not possibly be explained.

The first sign of what was to come was a popping sound, like that of a finger joint being cracked. Then there was another. Louder this time. Like a vertebra during a stretch after someone had not moved for a while.

After which began the transformation: Under the sheets, down where Nate's feet were, something was moving—and not as in back and forth. As in growing longer.

Sarah's eyes got even wider as beneath the thin blankets, his toes began to extend down the bed. At first, she told herself it was just because the pain he was in had made him point his foot. But that could explain only so much.

More pops. Even louder now.

And his feet moved still further . . . as if his legs were growing.

Sarah looked up to where he was gripping the arm of the woman and holding the source of the blood to his mouth. Before her very eyes, she saw his elbow distort under his skin, the bony protrusion seeming to curl into a fist and twist before—snap! It was in a different position.

The same thing happened to his jaw. Initially, she assumed the disfiguration of his face occurred because his mouth was wide open due to being latched onto that wrist—but soon she realized that whatever was happening to his legs and his arms was affecting his entire body. He was growing.

Not by millimeters. By leaps and bounds—

Abruptly, his forehead seemed to bubble forward, his brow ridge undulating under his skin, his ears moving outward.

More popping.

Sarah felt something wet on her hand and looked over at where she had gripped the commando's bare arm. Her fingernails had sunk so deeply into his skin, his blood welled in crescents.

When she looked at him in alarm, his eyes were remote. As if what was going on across the room was no mystery at all—but her reaction was what concerned him.

Sarah snapped her hand back and wiped it on her pants.

She had spent all her professional life on the lookout for revelations about the mysteries of the human body, her days and nights devoted to the pursuit of breakthroughs in knowledge and lightning strikes of hyper-deductive reasoning that ultimately relieved suffering and cured disease.

She had never, ever expected that the biggest discovery of her career would not be about humans at all.

◆   ◆   ◆

Sarah had no idea how long it took. Hours could have passed. Days. Who knew.

But she sat through the entire . . . whatever it was . . . not feeling the chair under her, not caring that she had to go to the bathroom, not aware of anything other than the boy's maturation process.

That was the only framework into which she could fit what she witnessed.

Nate had started out looking like a nine or ten year old boy. Then some kind of craving had come over him, and that woman had arrived. She had bit herself in the wrist, put the open wound to his mouth . . . and somehow as he drank from her, his arms and legs grew by inches upon inches, and that wasn't the only change in him. His face became that of a man's, growing a jawline and brows. His hands elongated, his shoulders widened, his throat thickened. His chest doubled, then tripled in size, until it split the small hospital johnny down the middle.

There was incredible pain. Horrible pain. Then again, it was clear that the process wasn't coordinated, some bones and muscles growing before the joints did, others lagging behind. It was impossible for her to tell what was going on internally, but his organs—his heart, lungs, stomach, intestines, liver and kidneys—had to be doing the same.

Sometime in the midst of things, the woman took her wrist from Nate and seemed to seal the raw wounds with her own mouth. Then she bowed deeply to the commando and removed herself from the room. She appeared exhausted, her skin pale to the point of snow, her gait a shuffle rather than a walk. As she stumbled out the door, there were people waiting in the hall to catch her, and soon thereafter, the medical staff came in and checked on Nate. They listened to his heart, took his blood pressure, ran an IV—for fluids? Sarah wondered.

No one said anything. Everybody was tense.

Instinct told her it was a dangerous time, given how nervous the doctors were. And then hello, there was all the obvious stress on his body.

After the woman left, Nate continued to change on the bed, his legs sawing as they kept growing, his torso twisting and flopping back, curling in and releasing.

At one point, he gasped and threw his head to the side—and this time, as she caught sight of his eyes, he had pupils again now. Pupils that stared out of a man's face.

And they locked on her.

"Help . . ." he said in a rasping voice that was a full octave lower than it had been at the lab. At the farmhouse. In the van on the way here. "It hurts . . ."

A tear escaped, rolling out and trailing down the cheek that was no longer that of a child.

The boy was still in there, though. And he was begging for her to go to him, even though there was nothing she could do for him.

As he implored her for help, time slowed down—and in the swirl of her own confusion and panic, a thought crystalized with the clarity of church bells ringing through a foggy night: If she went to him, if she sat with him, if she tried to ease his suffering, she was going to lose a part of herself forever.

Because she did not belong in this world. In his world.

She was not supposed to be here. She was not supposed to know any of this. And somehow, she wasn't sure exactly how, they were going to make sure she went back to where she belonged with all her previous ignorance front and center.

There was no way she was going to be allowed to keep this information, this experience. All she had to do was remember their escape from the lab and the way the commando had seemed to put that guard in a trance, and control Kraiten, and make things happen with people's minds.

He was going to end up doing the same to her.

Except . . . she was willing to bet emotional ties were not going to be as easy to get rid of. And there was nothing more powerful for the heart than the mother/child bond—which was the way Nate implored her now.

He was a child. He was in pain. And he needed somebody to nurture him.

What are you going do, Sarah, she thought.

"You don't have to," the commando said gruffly.

Sarah gripped the arms of the hard chair and slowly stood up. As her legs let out creaks of protest, her muscles stiff from however long she had been sitting, she thought of what Nate had been through—was still going through.

She looked down at the commando. "I know what you're going to do to me." When he opened his mouth, she shook her head. "Just stop. Don't lie to me. You think I'm not aware of how you work? The only thing I ask is just warn me when you're going to take my mind over and let me say goodbye to him before you make me leave."

The commando's eyes dropped. "Sarah . . ."

"Swear it."

He took a deep breath, his chest expanding. Then his beautiful peach stare lifted to her. "I swear. On my honor."

Oh, God, she was right. She had guessed correctly.

Sarah cleared her throat and looked over at the bed. "Just let me say goodbye to him."

Straightening her spine, she walked over and gingerly eased her hip on the mattress. As another tear escaped Nate's eye, she reached out and snapped a Kleenex free from a box. Even though she dabbed ever so carefully, he winced as if she had struck him with barbed wire.

"Your skin is sensitive?" she whispered. When he nodded, she nodded back. "I would imagine it is—"

"You think I'm a monster."

As his deep voice came out of his mouth, her heart stopped, and she had to catch herself before she recoiled. It was all just so hard to comprehend. But what she was clear on? None of this was his fault or something he had volunteered for.

She shook her head. "No, I don't think you're a monster."

"Yes, you do. I can see it in your eyes."

She refused to lie to him. "I just didn't know . . ."

"About us."

She wanted to ask what exactly "us" was, but she had a feeling she knew. And the reality frightened her.

"I won't hurt you," he said, as if he read her mind. "I promise."

"Now, that I completely believe."

"I might still die," he mumbled. "It's not over yet. I just . . . I'm scared."

"What happens now?" God, she was suddenly terrified for him, and she took his hand in her own as if she could keep him alive by the contact alone. "Do you need the doctors?"

"I don't know."

The commando got up from his seat. "I'll go get somebody." Something in her expression must have gotten through to him because he just shrugged helplessly. "Sometimes things just stop working. All we can do is wait and see what happens."

As he left, the door eased shut.

Left alone with Nate, Sarah leaned up and brushed his hair back. It was darker, thicker . . . wavier. A man's hair, not a boy's. And his eyelashes were the same, longer and thicker. And he had the shadow of a beard.

"It happens to all of us," Nate said. "This is how . . . it happens."

She nodded because she wanted to calm him down, but under her skull, her brain was racing. "You're different from me."

"I am."

"But that does not make you a monster to me." Strength entered her voice. "Do you understand—you are *not* a monster."

He stared at her for the longest time. Then he took a deep breath of relief. "You didn't know about us, did you."

"No."

"So how did you come and get me?"

She thought of Gerry, and felt a fresh bolt of anger at what he had done, what he had been involved in. "I, ah, I found some of your lab results. They weren't meant for me to see, but . . . once I did, I couldn't not investigate. I couldn't not . . . try and find you. I wasn't even sure where . . . to go with any of it."

"I'm glad you came. And I'm glad they let you stay with us."

Sarah nodded. "Try and rest."

"You're not going to leave, right?" Before she could reply, his eyes narrowed shrewdly. "Of course, I want you here. Even if you're not one of us, you came to get me out when no one else did. I trust you."

"Do you trust them?"

"You mean, do I trust the male with you. That's what you really want to know."

"Do you read minds?"

"Not really. I'm just putting myself in your position. And to answer your question, yes, I do, and you can, too. He's bonded with you. He will not let anything bad happen to you and he will die trying to protect you."

This time Sarah could not hide her reaction. She felt the shock hit her face—and was aware that something else was with it. Something closer to . . .

The door reopened and the commando came back in with the female doctor.

Sarah stepped back from the bed to give the physician a little room. And as she looked at the commando, she was not surprised that he was staring at her, the remote expression on his face suggesting he knew exactly where her head was at.

"—ask you both to step out for a minute?" the doctor said. "I'd like to do a full exam on him and I think we're going to need some privacy for that?"

As Nate looked up at Sarah, she took his hand and gave it a gentle squeeze. "I'll just be outside in the hall. And then as soon as it's over, I'm coming right back in. Okay?"

When he squeezed back and nodded, she gave in to an impulse she didn't think was necessarily appropriate: She leaned down and kissed him on the forehead.

As if he were her child.

Even though he was most certainly not.

CHAPTER THIRTY

Murhder held the door open for Sarah, and then they were out in the corridor together. Crossing his arms over his chest, he leaned back against the concrete wall and looked to the right. There were a number of doors that were closed. And then a bank of them all at once that suggested there was a gym or something down there. Distantly, he caught a whiff of chlorine, as if there were a pool somewhere in the facility.

No one else was around. No . . . that wasn't right. He could pick up scents of males, females, but they were far off. Behind all those shut doors.

Good thing. He had a feeling what was coming.

Sarah's eyes burned as she stared at him, but he couldn't look her in the face. He just couldn't. He didn't want to see something he wasn't ever going to forget: Disgust. Horror. Revulsion.

He had enough bad luggage to haul around with him already.

"Explain to me what happened in there," she said.

Annnnd here we go. "That is how we become adults."

"So I was right," she murmured. "That is the maturation process. So tell me, what exactly are you?"

"You know what we are."

"Do I?" When he nodded, she shook her head. "I'm afraid I don't. I know that you've got six-chambered hearts. Strange white and red blood cell counts. Different responses to things like cancer and bacterial and viral disease. But I—"

"Vampire." Now, he looked at her. "We are . . . vampire."

Ah . . . there it was. Yup, exactly what he'd wanted to avoid.

Her eyes stretched wide and she covered her mouth with a palm, as if holding in a scream. But he was done lying to her, and she might as well get the full reveal.

Retracting his upper lip, he willed his fangs to elongate, feeling them tingle as they extended below his front teeth.

The fact that she got pale was right out of Bram Stoker land. But he wasn't a soulless defiler of virgins, and she wasn't a Victorian damsel in distress. As unreal as this was to her, as much of a shock as it clearly was, the reality didn't bear much resemblance at all to what humans had made up, and he prayed she'd be open-minded enough to give him a chance to explain.

"I'm sorry," he said roughly.

He figured he'd best lead with that Old Reliable. There was, after all, so much to apologize for: The fact that she was here at all, for one. And then that she had seen Nate's transition.

Oh, and there was still the erase job he was going to have to do to her.

Let's not forget that door prize, he thought.

Under the rubric of in-for-a-penny, in-for-a-pound, he said, "We evolved parallel to humans. We don't prey on your kind for blood. We can't bite you and turn you. We aren't half bat and the swooping cape thing doesn't happen, either. We just want to live our lives in peace, and the only way to do that is through secrecy. It's not that mysterious."

As bitterness crept into his tone, he stopped there. Him getting all defensive was not going to help things.

"Look, I'll take you back at nightfall," he told her. "And you're right, you won't remember any part of this. From time to time, you might have a strange dream, but it will never be enough to matter much."

She blinked. Then rubbed her face like she was trying to get things straight. As she seemed to formulate her thoughts, he had no choice but to wait for the avalanche of shit to fall on his head—

"First of all," she announced, "I'm not going anywhere until I know Nate is safely through whatever happened to him and I have a chance to assess that wound from an immunology standpoint. If that takes a day or a week, I don't care. And secondly, how is it possible that you've kept all of this a secret—" She stopped. "Mind control. You've used that mind control a lot."

"It makes things easier."

"Obviously."

After a moment, her expression changed. Then her eyes traveled from the top of his head, down over his chest . . . his lower torso . . . his legs.

And that was when it happened.

That was when . . . her scent changed.

Instantly, his body flared to life in response, the sexual impulse thickening his blood, swelling his muscles.

Swelling other places, too.

"Yes," he said in a low growl. "We do that in the same way humans do. And yes . . . I want you."

Her eyes flared again, but it was not out of fear. Far from it.

Shit, he thought. She wanted him, too.

Or . . . maybe he shouldn't go that far. Maybe she was just curious. Either way, he was desperate enough for her that he didn't care.

"Talk to me, Sarah."

He kept his voice way down. He was already in deep shit with the powers that be for so many reasons, past and present. The last thing he should be adding to this situation with her was anything erotic, but if she wanted a demonstration on how a vampire made love?

He would be her guinea pig. And then some.

Murhder turned his body to her, and did nothing to hide the erection that was straining at his hips. "Tell me what you want from me. Whatever it is, I'll give it to you."

She closed her eyes and took a deep breath. "I don't know . . . what I'm doing right now."

"Yes, you do. I can scent it. You know exactly what you're doing."

She shook her head. "Maybe this is all a dream."

"It's not." Then he added tightly, "It will be someday, but it is not tonight."

Abruptly, she looked at him.

No, that wasn't quite right. She was looking at his mouth.

Knowing damn well he was playing with fire, he extended his tongue and ran it over his lower lip.

"I'll make it good for you," he said softly. "I'll make it so good for you that you won't regret it."

Her hand lifted to her own mouth. And as she brushed her finger over what he wanted to kiss first, she jumped as if the contact surprised her.

Then she frowned and the scent of her arousal was cut off. "Are you putting this thought in my mind right now? Are you doing to this to me—making me want you."

Murhder shook his head. "No, I would never do that. That is a total violation."

"But how do I know that for sure." She nodded at his hips. "I mean, you're . . . aroused, and it would get you what you want."

"I am turned on. In my mind, my hands are on your skin, my mouth is on yours, I am on the verge of entering you." Murhder smiled a little and then got serious again. "But no, I'm not making you feel this way. Your reaction is all your own body's, it is every bit your free will and nothing else—and trust me, the fact that you want me of your own volition? It's the hottest thing about you right now."

◆   ◆   ◆

Sarah didn't have time to respond to any of it. Not what her commando had revealed about himself and his . . . kind. Not the currents of sex that ran between them. Not her questioning him about the mind control.

Before she could go any further, the doctor came out of Nate's room, and instead of letting the door close slowly on its own, she pulled it shut.

"I think he's doing well. You can't beat that Chosen blood. But we'll be monitoring him."

As the woman smiled, Sarah focused on her teeth. No fangs.

She shook herself back to attention. "How does that process work? At the cellular level, for example—I just don't understand any of it."

The doctor looked at the commando. Looked back. "Their pituitary glands take about twenty-five years to properly mature, and during that time, their bodies and organs are fairly nascent. When the pituitary reaches its proper size and functioning, their version of growth hormone is secreted all at once, triggering a firestorm of cellular activity and change that can be lethal to them. As adults, they require regular feeding from the opposite sex, and he will have to do that from now on to remain healthy and strong."

"'Their'? So you're not a . . ."

The doctor smiled again. "No, I'm not. Listen, I'm going to go check on John again. Do you want to join me? Take a look at him? You might as well while you're here."

As Sarah's inner scientist woke up in a big way, she glanced at the door to Nate's room. "Someone will come and find me if he needs anything?"

"You got it," the commando said.

Before she headed off with the doctor, she glanced at the commando. He was watching her with those hooded eyes, his big body throwing off waves of heat that surely the doctor felt, too?

The fact that his hands were loosely linked in front of his hips, over his erection, made her flush.

"It's okay," he murmured.

She wasn't sure what exactly he was reassuring her about. But for some reason . . . the fact that he cared enough to try warmed the center of her chest.

Forcing her mind away from . . . well, everything, she focused on the doctor and then walked away with the woman.

"How long have you been . . . here?" Sarah asked.

"Awhile now." The doctor pushed open an unmarked door. "It's a long story."

As they entered another clinical room, the tall commando—um, vampire—with the shoulder injury looked up from the exam table. He had his shirt off, and he was poking at the nasty black stain on his skin.

It was much larger, Sarah thought.

"It's bigger," the doctor muttered.

The solider looked over and nodded grimly.

Sarah approached the man—vampire—oh, God—and leaned in for a closer inspection. "It's like cellulitis." She glanced over at the doctor. "And you've tested it for fungus?"

"I've tested it for everything."

All at once, Sarah's researcher brain came fully online. Sure as a football stadium would turn its lights on at night, section by section, her mind blazed with questions, thoughts, observations, ideas.

Dimly, she realized she had been on autopilot at work for quite a while, going through the motions at the lab, being competent, although not extraordinary.

It was only now as her enthusiasm got her buzzing that she recognized the slump she'd been in.

She straightened and addressed the doctor. "I want to see everything you've got."

The blond woman looked at the solider. "John, would you consent to—"

When he nodded vigorously, the doctor smiled a little. "Come on, Sarah, let's go to my computer. We can start there."

CHAPTER THIRTY-ONE

Xhex strode through the subterranean tunnel that connected the Brotherhood mansion to the training center at a fast walk. She wanted to run, but she didn't have the energy for that, even though her nerves were live wires under her skin, her body was a tuning fork for anxiety, and her head was a cocktail blender full of Holy Fuck Frojitos. She had only gone back to her and John's room to shower and change, but even that felt like too much time away from him.

When she came up to the entrance to the training center, she put in a code, the lock sprang, and she stepped into a supply closet that had OfficeMax written all over it. On the far side of all the shelves of printer paper, Scotch tape and Bic pens, she exited through the facility's office and hit the corridor.

Only to stop short.

Murhder was halfway down to the parking area. Leaning against the wall. Arms crossed, one foot over the other. Head lowered.

Resuming her stride, she approached the former Brother, and he looked over, his red-and-black hair fanning across his shoulder.

"How we doing with the young?" she asked.

"Nate's good. Well, good as can be expecting. Expected, I mean." He rubbed his eyes like his head hurt. "Jane and Sarah are in with your male. Two doors up."

Xhex still wasn't sure how she felt about some random human messing around with the single most important person in her life. But it wasn't like anyone on the vampire side had a bright idea about what could be done. And everything would be vetted first. Or rather, it better be.

As Murhder went back to staring at the concrete floor, she was struck by how familiar that pose of his was to her. This was what he'd always looked like when he was working through shit in his head.

Even though she wanted to get to John, she eased back against the cold concrete wall, crossing her arms just as Murhder had.

"Are you going to ask if the woman can stay?" Xhex rubbed her nose as it itched from the underground. "Does she want to?"

"Well, if she can find a way to help John . . . maybe she won't have to leave?" He shrugged. "I mean, there are humans all around here now. The rules have clearly changed from my time."

Yes and no, Xhex thought.

"So, are you planning on hanging around, then," she prompted.

As he opened his mouth, but closed it quickly, she had the impression he hadn't thought any of this through: not his obvious attraction to the human woman, not his presence here in the Brotherhood's orbit, not the longer term of anything.

"I don't have a role here anymore," he said after a moment.

"You were really effective on that lab infiltration."

"Old habits." He glanced over. "I'm going to go back to South Carolina. After . . . I mean, as soon as . . ."

"You'll take her with you, then?"

"Ah . . . I haven't gotten that far."

As Xhex measured the cut of his jaw, she could feel the tension in his body, sure as if it were her own.

"You deserve to be happy," she murmured.

He shook his head. "Don't waste time pitying me. I'm fine."

"It's not pity." She thought of her relationship with her mate—and wanted him to find that with someone. "It's only fair."

He frowned and lowered his eyes again. "I have a question."

"Talk to me."

When a silence stretched between them, she thought about where they had started out, two people in a club in the '90s, drawn to each other because they had been the only vampires there. A one-night stand had turned into a habit—which had somehow gotten back to her *symphath* kin. And then chaos and torture and dark, dark places for them both.

No way she would have put them here, in the Brotherhood's training center, her mated, him interested in a human.

"That stuff that was done to me." He motioned around his head. "Up in the colony. The things that they . . . uncovered and leveraged against me."

Xhex closed her eyes and cursed her bloodline. "Yeah."

"Is it permanent. The damage, I mean. Did they break me or just wound me?"

Fucking *symphaths*. Their weapons left no outward scars, no tears in the skin that bled, no bones that were broken, no disfigurements that didn't heal. But the destructiveness of what they wrought was almost worse than all that.

The mind was a delicate, dispositive instrument in any person's life, capable of defining their entire mortal experience.

You fucked with that shit? Most people ended up a wasteland.

Murhder's voice dropped to a whisper. "They took me to places . . . even as my body wasn't moved."

She could only imagine.

"Of course they didn't break you," she heard herself say.

When she reopened her eyes, she found him staring at her, and she was struck by how strong he had to have been to get over the torture as much as he had.

"You never lied to me before," he said grimly. "Given what's at stake, I'll ask you to pay me the respect of not starting now."

Xhex took a deep breath and felt like the floor was opening beneath her feet so some version of *Dhunhd* could swallow her down. She was responsible for everything that had been done to him.

"The truth is . . ." Xhex wished she had a better answer for him. "I don't know. Everyone's different. Some people rebound, eventually. Some . . ."

"Stay insane, right?" When she didn't reply, he muttered, "Jesus Christ, Xhex, I need to know where I stand. I got a brief return to what seemed like normal when I was getting us out of that lab, but now . . . I don't know whether that was a hiccup or a trajectory out of this hell I've been in."

"I can't answer that. No one can."

"I've been twenty years off the planet, unable to connect. I guess I was just hoping that the way I felt on that evac means I'm . . . okay."

The sadness in his voice was backed up by fear, and Xhex found herself wanting to punch the concrete wall. "This is all my fault—"

"No," he snapped. "You don't own any of this. I decided to come after you, and your relations did what they did to me. Did what they did to you, too."

"But you had no idea what you were walking into. And that is on me. And then you protected me after I burned that first lab down by letting the Brotherhood think it was you."

Murhder went back to focusing on the floor, and as things got quiet, she knew he was replaying all kinds of bad scenes in his head.

"When do we ever know what we're walking into," he said in a low voice. "Destiny is not a straightaway. It's cluttered with corners and all of them are dark. We make the turns we do . . . and find ourselves where we are."

As he stopped talking, she became very aware that she owed him.

The question was, how did she repay the debt he refused to acknowledge or entertain.

◆   ◆   ◆

The next time Sarah looked at the clock—the one on the lower right-hand corner of a computer screen—the lineup of numbers read five eighteen. Sitting back in the office chair, she cracked her spine and wondered whether that was five in the afternoon or five in the morning. It had to be afternoon, she decided, as in late in the afternoon, almost twenty-four hours after she had driven to BioMed with her backpack and those credentials from the safety deposit box.

As well as some vague idea of rescuing someone she wasn't sure actually existed.

What a day. After hours and hours of studying John's case, her mind was spinning with everything she had learned. After studying slides and test results, and talking with the staff, and processing it all through the filter of her own training and experience she was . . .

Jazzed.

It was the only way to describe the feeling. She was alive. Excited. Focused.

She did not like the fact that John had something wrong with him. Or that his loved ones were worried. But the idea of solving the problem, getting him cured, returning him to full health? In this new landscape of anatomy and immune system? Given that no one was really sure what the pathogen was?

It was the chance of a lifetime in a totally new horizon.

And of course, in the back of her mind, she was wondering how all of this could help humans with cancer. Vampires were apparently like sharks. They didn't get the disease. So why not? Especially as so much about them was the same.

Although so much was different, too.

"You hungry?"

The sound of the deep male voice behind her made her nape tingle—and not because she was frightened.

Spinning her chair around, she looked up at her commando. He'd taken a shower and changed clothes, although now everything was black, just like the other men—males. His long red-and-black hair was damp on the ends and he smelled . . . heavenly.

"Is Nate still okay?" she said.

"He's doing very well. He ate something and now he's resting."

"What did he have?" Like he was her kid or something. "That ginger and rice—"

"Roast beef."

"Oh, that's great! A serving or two of that can help his iron counts."

"It wasn't just a serving. He had a whole roast beef. As in . . . a bone-in, standing prime rib roast. I believe they said it weighed sixteen pounds."

Sarah blinked. "Jeez, what was dessert—an entire pie?"

"Vanilla ice cream."

"Oh, that's more reasonable. It's not like he ate a whole half gallon."

"And the pie."

"What?"

"He ate a half gallon of vanilla ice cream with an apple pie. He's in a food coma now."

Sarah threw her head back and laughed. Part of it was relief. Part of it was lack of sleep. Part of it was . . . the smile on the commando's face: Because he felt the same way she did, that connected them.

And she liked being connected to him.

"What is your name," she said as she caught her breath. When he hesitated, she shrugged. "Come on, I already know everything. Well, a lot of things, at any rate. Your name is a simple thing, right?"

The commando cleared his throat. "I come from a warrior tradition."

She looked up and down his magnificent body. "Really? And here I thought you were a baker."

The fact that he laughed again made her feel good.

"No," he said. "I don't make bread or rolls."

"Have you ever tried?"

"Ah, no."

"Okay, well, don't feel bad. Neither have I. You were saying? You're a badass?"

That smile got bigger. But then faded into a wince. "So our names . . . the names we are given are meant to inspire fear. They are identifiers of our nature as defenders of the race—"

Sarah put her palm up. "Just tell me. How bad can it be?"

"Murhder. My name is Murhder."

She laughed. And then her mouth fell open before she could catch herself. "Wait, you're serious." When he nodded, she tried to compose herself. "Oh. Wow. Is—um, is that first or last?"

"Last. My first name is Cold-Blooded." As she did a double take, he smiled shyly. "I'm joking. It's just Murhder."

Sarah broke out in a laugh. "Did you make a funny?"

He blushed. "I did. I made a joke."

He was so hesitant, so . . . endearingly unsure of the humor . . . that she wanted to hug him.

"That's a good one." She got up out of the chair. "And I am starved. Do you know where food is?"

"I do. Everyone's gone up to the big house for First Meal, but there's a break room down the way. And yes, Nate's being monitored by machines with loads of alarms. If he needs anything, people are going to come running, including us."

"Good. Let's do this."

Sarah followed the commando's—Murhder's—lead, heading down the concrete corridor and coming up to Nate's hospital room. Opening the door, she leaned in and reassured herself that he was, indeed, sound asleep, a slight snore rising from his man's throat.

"I still can't believe what he went through," she murmured.

Murhder's voice was quiet. "It's just the way it works for us."

Making sure the door closed silently, they continued down the hall, walking side by side—and it felt normal. Natural. As if she had been striding next to him for years.

"So how's your work with John?"

She exhaled. "Well, they refuse to tell me how he was injured. It's the one piece I don't have, but I'm working around that. At the end of the day, the 'how' is not as important as the 'where.'"

"Like in the shoulder location?"

"No, as in the status of the wound. I mean, on a molecular level, where are we—is it getting worse? What can I do to make it better? This kind of thing." She glanced around. "Speaking of which, where are we?" And then she held her palm up. "I know you probably can't tell me, but I'm just . . . who paid for all this? Where does the money come from?"

"Here, let me get the door for you."

As he jumped ahead and opened the way into a cafeteria-like space, she knew he wasn't going to answer any of those questions—and it was a reminder that she was just a visitor here. Not a new resident.

Sarah stopped abruptly and stared at the dorm couches, the tables with chairs, the vending machines and the hot and cold buffet that was stocked with food that smelled delicious.

"I won't remember anything," she said in a rough voice.

When she looked over at Murhder, he met her eyes. "No. Nothing."

In the silence that stretched out between them, she tried to memorize everything about him, from the fall of his incredible hair to his strong, handsome face, from his broad shoulders and heavy chest to his long, long legs. When her stare returned to his, the air between them changed, that electric current igniting, the sexual attraction not returning so much as resurfacing because it had never really left her: With all distractions pushed aside, and the fact that they were alone together, she became keenly aware of her own body . . . and his.

"Sarah," he said in that way he did, in that low growl of his.

The first thing that went through her mind was that if she wouldn't remember this anyway, why not pursue the attraction? She had never judged people for having casual sex, and God, who could blame her for wanting him? But more to the point, there were going to be no aftershocks, no regrets, because she was going to have no memory of being with him, however the sex went.

Yet the instant those thoughts went through her mind, she threw them out. She had more self-respect, for one thing—she was going to own her decisions, whether or not she had any memory of what the sex was like. And for another, that kind of thinking dehumanized him, reducing him to a kinky sex toy she used in a proverbial hotel room while away on a business trip—nothing more than a romp outside her normal bandwidth that she didn't need to feel guilty about because it was out of context and didn't count.

Wait, "dehumanized" wasn't the right word, was it. More like . . . "devampired him." Or something.

Shit.

"I won't hurt you," he said.

In the back of her mind, she realized it was the second time he'd said that to her. And she believed him. Down to her core, she had this strange, abiding faith that, regardless of whatever else was being kept from her, when it came to keeping her safe, he was speaking the truth.

Sarah reached her hand up toward his face. And as if he knew what she wanted, he leaned in from his great height, giving her the warmth of his skin, the rasp of his five o'clock shadow, the cut of his jaw.

The instant the connection was made, she knew that she would do this anyway. She would choose him, this man—this male, she corrected—even if she would have memories that made her miss him for the rest of her life. And the strength of that conviction was such that she wished she *would* remember him. In fact, she wished for things even further along than that, things she was not going to get out of this . . . whatever it was.

Things like a future. A relationship. A partnership.

Which was nuts. She barely knew him—and had only just learned his kind even existed.

"Anywhere," he groaned. "Touch me anywhere you want."

When she glanced at the door and wondered if anyone was going to interrupt at an inopportune time, there was a subtle click, as if it locked itself. Before she decided whether that was alarming or not, he pointed to his chest.

"I did that—so we won't be disturbed. But you're free to go. The lock's on this side and I will never stop you from leaving."

"You always read my mind."

He opened his mouth to reply—except as her fingertips brushed over his lower lip, the contact seemed to make him lose all thought.

"I'm not using you," she told him. "I just want to be clear."

"I wouldn't care if you were."

Sarah put her hands on the pads of his pecs and rode the big muscles up to his shoulders. Waves of that cologne he wore got into her nose anew, as if the sexual connection was turning up all her sensory receptors and amplifying everything.

God, he was big. And hard.

Everywhere.

"Kiss me," she said as she tilted her head up.

In spite of his obvious strength, he was gentle with her, his hands slipping around her waist and pulling her against him just enough so that their clothes brushed. Thanks to the proximity, body heat ricocheted and magnified in the space between them, and then she wasn't thinking about even that.

Murhder lowered his head . . . and kissed her.

Oh . . . wow. His lips were velvet on her own, all summer-breeze soft and slow as an August sunrise as they caressed hers. And she would have called the contact sweet, except no. His enormous body . . . his mysterious, other-than-human, incredibly powerful body . . . trembled, and that was what made everything utterly erotic: The subtle shaking meant he was holding himself in strict control, clamping down on his drive, chaining, jailing what was inside of him.

There was a beast on the far side of his will, a wild creature rattling at the iron bars of his restraint, a force so much greater than she could understand.

And she wanted the monster in him. The unleashed. The crazed.

Against everything that made any kind of sense, she wanted him to devour her, master her, take her down onto the hard floor right here, right now, and pin her under his naked, pumping body until she had no thoughts of who or even what he was.

Who or even what she herself was.

"Wipe me clean," she heard herself say against his mouth. "Take everything away for me until I know only you. Make everything disappear . . . but you."

She had been stewing for two years in pain, isolation and disillusionment, stagnating and tied to a past that her present wouldn't release her from and her future couldn't uphold. And then there was what she had found out about that lab, and the boy, and the rabbit hole she had gone down to be here, in this strange place with Murhder, with his people.

She was exhausted with feeling lost. And questioning herself over Gerry. And wondering where to go in a world full of opportunities that had once been exciting, but now seemed consolations to a death she was not over.

This man—this *vampire*—could make all that go away. Even if it was only for a brief spell, she wanted the weight lifted, the toxic swill pushed back, the path cleared of debris.

Her soul, buried under damp blankets of grief she could not seem to shed, needed to breathe.

"Why do you cry?" he whispered.

"Am I?"

His thumb stroked over her cheek and he turned it toward her, the gleam of her tear on the pad catching the light.

"I don't want to think," she told him. Begged him.

After a moment, he nodded gravely, as if they had forged some kind of pact. "Then I shall make you feel . . ."

CHAPTER THIRTY-TWO

Murhder told himself he should hate the pain inside of this human woman who stood, trusting and aroused, before him. He told himself that he should vanquish whoever had caused her the marrow-splitting grief that he had not, until this moment, sensed within her. He told himself that her tears meant that she was not ready for what they were about to do.

And all of that was true.

But there was another layer to it.

As he stared down at her face, he felt like he was looking into a mirror at himself. She was where he had been—and still was. He knew exactly the agony of the burden of loss she carried—sure, not the particulars of what had caused it, not the descriptions or details, but certainly the crushing sadness and confusion that came when your world was turned upside down and you had no idea where you could safely land.

They were separated by a species divide.

Identical in destiny.

This time, when he kissed her, he knew they were not going to stop because what she wanted from him was the very thing she represented *to* him. He wanted to be wiped clean as well. He needed a break from the past that haunted him, too. He was as exhausted with grief and regrets as she was.

And dearest Virgin Scribe, the feel of her: Her mouth moved against his like they had been made to fit together, and then her body was flush to his own, her curves accommodating his straightaways, her much smaller stature belying all the power she had over him.

Murhder drew her over to a couch in the corner, and the idea that they were going to make love in this cafeteria, with a TV on mute, and a bank of soft drinks in a cooler, and an industrial dishwasher quietly humming across the way, made him pray that this would not be the only time.

Not that he wouldn't have asked for that anyway: He hadn't even had her yet and he was desperate to take her again.

They sat down together at one end of the sofa, all tangled legs and arms, and to cure the contortion, he rolled back and pulled her on top of him—oh, *yeeees*. His hips arched up, his erection seeking the pressure of her weight and wanting more of the friction as they shifted against each other. And then his hands learned her body, stroking her back and cupping her hips . . . before slipping onto her thighs.

When he eased under her shirt, finding warm, smooth skin, he groaned and she backed off from the kisses.

"I haven't done this in a while," she said.

"It's the same for me."

They both smiled. And then it was back to the lips and the tongues, the surging of hips, the twining of legs. She was the one who swept her fleece and her shirt off—

"Sarah," he breathed.

She sat up on his hips, her legs splayed over him, her bra hinting at what was underneath. With hands that shook, he stroked up her ribs and drifted his fingertips over her breasts. Just as he was ready to beg to see her, her eyes bored into his own and she sprang the clasp, removing the barrier.

Groaning, Murhder took things from there, rising up, holding her against his hungry mouth, teasing and taking one nipple in to suck and then the other.

"Let me see you, too," she said.

No asking twice on that. He ditched his borrowed shirt so fast, he ripped one of the sleeves. And they enjoyed the exploration part of things for a little longer, her hands branding his chest muscles and stomach as she touched him—but as good as the preamble was, his blood had a roar in it, anticipation morphing into hard-edged desperation.

She clearly felt the same way as she backed off of him, stood up and went for the waistband of her pants and underwear. Inch by inch, she took them both down her legs, kicking them away and peeling off her socks.

"You're beautiful." He rubbed his eyes. "Good God . . ."

Except when she went to straddle him, she stopped abruptly. "Shoot."

Talk about giving him a heart attack. "What is it? Are you okay? Did I do something—"

"I don't have a condom. Do you?"

"I . . ." He shook his head. "I can't . . . you're not fertile. So I can't get you pregnant—I also can't give you . . . you know, anything."

Well, wasn't he Mr. Smooth with the STD talk.

Her head tilted to the side. "Really? So is virus transmission impossible between us or are the two species susceptible to different things? I wonder if we could study—"

Capturing her face in his palms, he licked his way back into her mouth, refocusing her.

Laughing in a husky way, she murmured, "Not the time for science talk, huh."

"How about after we're through?"

"It's a date."

That was the last thing they said to each other. Her hands found the fly of his borrowed combats and she released his erection. By the way her eyes peeled, she was surprised by his size, and he tried not to take too much satisfaction in that.

"I want to taste you," she moaned.

Well, didn't that just about send him over the edge.

But he pulled her back onto his hips. "Yes. Later, though—"

"No, now."

As her hand circled his shaft, he nearly snapped his spine as he jerked back into the sofa. Then she was between his knees on the floor, her open mouth going down to his head.

"Now is also good," he mumbled as he watched her swallow him deep. "Oh, *shit*, now is so good."

His hand clenched onto the arm of the couch as she retracted back up his shaft and then her pink tongue extended and did a dance around the most sensitive place on his entire body. After that heady show, she took him in again, swallowing him whole, everything warm and slippery and—

In the back of his mind, he was aware of a creaking sound that seemed ominous. Worried for her safety, even as he didn't want her to stop EVER—

Great. He was about to snap the arm off the sofa.

Releasing his iron grip, he arched back and his hips worked with her to find a rhythm. Everything about her was the most erotic thing he could imagine, from the way her lips stretched to accommodate his girth, to her hair falling on his lower belly, to her gleaming stare.

Murhder started to breathe heavily, and then he was purring deep in his throat. When there was a pause mid-stroke, she seemed curious about the sound he was making, although she soon returned to her efforts.

Fuuuuuck, he couldn't let her go on much longer . . .

. . . but maybe just a little more.

◆   ◆   ◆

Sarah's vampire was completely undone.

His tremendous body was sprawled awkwardly on a sofa that should have fit three people, but barely held one of him. His red-and-black hair was loose and wild over his bare shoulders. His rock-hard abs were clenched like they had been carved out of stone.

And his pants were wide open, the biggest erection she had ever seen standing up straight at his hips.

His eyes burned as he watched her.

And it was about that purring sound.

As she licked her way up his shaft again, he hissed, his upper lip peeling back. Fangs. He had real, live honest-to-goodness fangs. And as she got a close look at them, so sharp, so white, she wondered what he was going to do with them—and had no fear. She wanted to know everything, feel it all, be a part of him, and not just for research purposes.

Because it was him.

God, the idea that he hadn't been with anyone for a while made her feel again like they were connected. More similar than dissimilar. In spite of the obvious differences.

"Enough," he groaned as he sat up in a rush and pulled her on top of him. "I need in you."

The next thing she knew she was on her back on the couch and he was on top of her, his great weight bearing down, her thighs split wide around his pelvis, that sex of his a firebrand at her core. With some trick of the hips, he angled himself properly, and she braced herself for a powerful penetration.

No regrets, she thought.

She had no regrets about any of this. If anything, he was a blessing she never would have had the guts to pray for.

"I'm ready," she told him as he hesitated.

"I just don't want this to be over."

Funny, she knew exactly what he meant.

With a groan, he dropped his mouth to hers and kissed her as he slid inside, inch by slow, delicious inch. No pounding after he'd filled her, either. Just a retreat and re-advance, gentle . . . sweet. And she was glad. As much as she wanted the raw passion, he was very large and it had been a long time.

The self-control cost him, however. Sweat broke out across his shoulders, and the muscles in his arms tightened up until they spasmed, the veins in his neck looking like ropes.

It was incredible, though. The in and the out, the friction, the heat—

Pleasure, already at a stinging level, grew inside of her and snapped free in a glorious release, the waves of sensation radiating outward from her core, sure as if her body were a vessel catching golden rays.

Against his mouth, in the middle of the orgasm, she whispered, "Don't hold back. I can take it."

Because she wanted him to experience the same thing, at the same time.

But he just held his course, slow and steady, letting her ride out her release.

When it was over, he closed his eyes and dropped his head into her neck. "I don't want to hurt you."

"You won't." Sarah cleared her throat. And then tilted her head to the side. "Do you want to . . ."

"What?"

"This," she said as she stroked up her own throat.

As he stared at her in alarm, she said it again. "Do you want this?"

That purr came back, louder, deeper, more urgent. And the sound of it was what put her over the edge again, especially as she imagined those razor-sharp points buried in her vein. Throwing her head back, she moved against his static body, stroking herself on his arousal, riding out the pulses until he started to orgasm along with her.

As he kicked inside of her, filling her up, her sex gripping and releasing his erection, he started to move again, faster now. Faster and harder.

The next thing she knew, he had locked her in a tight hold, one arm under her shoulders, the other wrapping around the back of her knee and pulling one of her legs up. His power, his strength, his heavy body, was an erotic cage that she nonetheless knew she held the key to: She was unafraid of him while she soared.

She trusted him.

And he did not stop.

Whereas a human man would have stilled after his first orgasm, Murhder just kept going, more of the releases coming for him as they did for her, the pleasure seemingly unending, the sex suspending them both in an infinite now that was full of sensation.

Eventually, though, he locked against her hips one last time, and then he collapsed, draping his torso over the back of sofa as if he didn't want to smother her.

In the silence, they both breathed hard, their bodies throwing off heat, their limbs entwined.

The peace that followed was as profound as the passion had been.

Except when he finally looked over at her, there was a sheen in his eyes that had nothing to do with happiness.

"What's wrong?" she whispered, running a hand up his biceps.

All he did was shake his head and she knew exactly what he was thinking about. There was no happily-ever-after for them, no long-term, no this-is-just-the-beginning.

"Don't think about it," Sarah told him roughly.

"You're right."

But the way he gathered her into his arms—as if she were precious, as if she were liable to break—told her that those were just words to placate her.

How long did they have, she wondered.

She wasn't going to ask, however. Even if they had a year, a decade, a century, none of that felt long enough.

For passion like they had just found? Only forever would do.

CHAPTER THIRTY-THREE

Murhder didn't want to put his clothes back on. And he really didn't want Sarah to get dressed again, either.

Having her skin covered by anything but his mouth and hands, his very body, was a crime as far as he was concerned. Except they couldn't pretend they had true privacy down here. Sooner or later, First Meal or not, someone was going to want to come in here for a Coke from the refrigerator or one of those Florida grapefruit in that bowl over there.

And even though it was no one's business, he didn't want it to look like he and Sarah had just banged. She wasn't some floozy he didn't care about, for godsakes.

So they pulled their shirts on, and she her sweatshirt as well. Then she used the bathroom across the way, shutting herself in, water running. When she came back out, her pants were back on and his were done up.

As her eyes sought him out, he could have sworn there was a small, secret smile on those lips he had kissed so thoroughly. Or maybe he was just telling himself that. Dearest Virgin Scribe, what a female—woman, whatever. And she'd wanted him to take her vein, too?

Closing his lids, he relived the moment her hand had drifted down the column of her throat, and lingered right over her jugular vein. He'd been desperate to taste her, take her into him, feel her essence go through his own veins, but he hadn't fed in a while and it would have been too dangerous. He didn't think he was hungry enough to hurt her—if there was even a chance of that, though, he was not going to risk it. Sometimes, when males were really into the sex and you added feeding on top of that? They could go over the line without meaning to, and because she was human, he couldn't offer her his blood in return to make sure she was replenished.

"Well . . ." she said. Then she took a deep breath and went over to the vending machines. "Fancy anything? We have a stunning array of salted munchie-crunchies at our disposal and there is dessert. Lots of dessert. And hey, wow, it's all free."

She pointed to the keypad where you made your selections and glanced over her shoulder at him.

Except then she frowned and shifted her eyes up to the TV in the corner. Craning around, he went to see what she was focused on. But it was just a local nightly news report on mute.

"Do you know where the remote to that is?" she murmured.

Without waiting for an answer, she walked across the break room to see about finding it herself, and he took the opportunity to unlock the door with his mind. Not that people weren't going to know what they'd just done. Males would scent him all over her, and damn if that wasn't satisfying.

As a soft patter of talk grew to one that was fully audible, she crossed her arms and stood right under the flat screen. Someone in a suit and tie was talking about something political, and then there was a report on a stolen car.

"It's not in the news." She flipped to some other channels and then looked across at him. "What we did last night is not on the news— BioMed is a national corporation with a billion-dollar valuation. There is no way a break-in would not be all over the broadcast even here in Caldwell. Hell, it would make CNN. Do you have a phone on you? I want to see if anything was reported anywhere."

"I don't even have a cell phone. I'm sorry—"

The door swung open, and Xhex strode in. His first thought was she looked hassled.

"Do you have a phone?" Sarah asked the female.

Xhex blinked as if she were translating the English in her head letter by letter. "Ah, yeah, sure."

She took the thing out of her back pocket, put in the code, and met Sarah halfway. "Help yourself—Murhder, can I talk to you?"

Frowning, he nodded and followed her back out into the hall. "What's going on?"

"You see John anywhere down here?"

"No, but I've mostly been sitting with Nate in his room. I know that Sarah and the doctor met with your *hellren* a while ago, but they've been down the hall on the computers ever since, I think."

"I don't know where he is." Xhex pushed a hand through her short hair. "After I talked to you, I went into his room and sat with him. I guess I fell asleep at some point. When I woke up about fifteen minutes ago, he was gone. I went up to the big house, figuring he would have gone there for First Meal, but no one's seen him. I checked our bedroom and I just went through the gym and the weight room down here. He's not anywhere."

Murhder leaned back into the break room. "Sarah, when was the last time you saw John?"

She looked up from the phone in her hand. "It was about an hour ago, maybe longer. He said he was going to the big house, as he called it, to get a change of clothes?"

"Shit," Xhex muttered.

"What's going on?" Sarah asked as she walked over.

"I think he's gone."

✦   ✦   ✦

Sarah was worried as she handed the phone back to John's mate, as they called their spouses. The woman—female, rather—took it and seemed to be checking for texts. Then she typed out a message and the swoosh-ing sound of something being sent rose up from the device.

"What condition was he in?" Xhex asked.

"He was as he'd been." Sarah shrugged. "I mean, the infection hasn't improved, but he didn't seem to be in any distress—certainly not medi-cally speaking, at any rate. He did seem—well, it's not like I know him, but he was distracted and with good reason."

Xhex stared at her phone as if she were waiting for a text back. When one didn't come, she put the phone away. "He's off rotation. They won't let him fight."

"So the Brothers won't be looking for him," Murhder added.

"No, they won't." Xhex turned to walk away. "No one will be looking for him."

As the female strode off, she moved with purpose, her boots pound-ing across the concrete floor. It was obvious what she was planning on doing. She was going to search for him herself.

Murhder stared after her, his arms down at his sides, his fists tight-ened, his jaw hard.

"Go," Sarah told him softly. "I'll be fine here."

"It's okay—"

"You want to go, and she needs the help. Plus I feel totally safe. Jane is supposed to be coming down again after she eats, and we're going back to work."

He looked over at her. Pulled a hand through his long hair. Shifted his weight back and forth.

"Go on." She patted his chest. "I'm not leaving—hell, I don't even know where I am, and no one's looking for me, either. Xhex really needs a friend right now—and I don't blame her for being concerned."

Murhder started to shake his head. Then he cursed, dropped a hard kiss on her mouth, and said something really fast.

Before Sarah could decode the syllables, he ran down after the fe-male. Xhex had made it quite a distance, so that when she paused as he came up to her, there was no hearing what they said.

As the two stood together, it was clear they had known each other for a long time: There was trust between the pair of them, even as they started to argue, arms being crossed, brows going down, faster words getting traded.

And then Xhex rolled her eyes and shrugged in a classic suit-yourself kind of way.

After which the two disappeared through a glass door.

Sarah went back into the break room and helped herself to a Snickers bar, a bag of Snyder's of Hanover pretzels, and a Coke. She ate the calories systematically, and thought about all the times she and Gerry had wolfed down bad choices between classes and seminars and stints in university labs . . .

Back during their schooling years, he had been so young and full of ideals and ideas. So had she.

Now, she was alone in a subterranean, vampire-run clinical environment.

Having had the sex of her life with another species.

Over on that sofa. Like, right. Over. There.

As she glanced at the couch they'd made love on, it was impossible not to note that one arm and part of the back made things look as if it had been in a car accident. The poor thing was bent off whatever frame held the cushions together, all cockeyed and crooked.

She checked the TV again. *Wheel of Fortune* was just coming on and she muted Pat and Vanna.

She couldn't believe that there was nothing on the news or online about what they had done in Ithaca the night before. Kraiten had been yelling about criminal trespassing. His own car had been stolen, for godsakes. But maybe he had realized that getting the authorities involved would be tricky. You'd have to explain why they were needed, and experimenting on a human subject—

Nate wasn't human, she reminded herself.

As she thought about the billions and billions of dollars that Big Pharma competed for, she had to wonder if Kraiten would want the details of his company's secret experiments kept quiet not because of any criminal implications—did human laws even cover non-human species? Was this an ASPCA issue, for godsakes?—but because then the other for-profit research corporations would try to get their own vampires for testing.

It was a sick way of looking at it, but drug breakthroughs were worth incalculable amounts of money, and BioMed's CEO was that greedy—

Wait. His memories had been scrubbed, hadn't they?

She slowly turned back to the TV. What if the man didn't even know the raid had happened? Except how would that work? Did Murhder erase Kraiten's recollections of everything, including the secret lab? In that case, what was going to happen when the researchers in Gerry's department showed up to work on something that the CEO didn't believe existed?

Jeez, the implications were like an LSAT test that strained the capacity of the human mind.

Where did the memories start and stop?

She thought of Gerry's death. And that of his boss, Dr. McCaid.

Kraiten had done many things wrong, and she had the proof. Plus the vampires were back in their own world now, safe and sound. When she returned to her side, she needed to go to the authorities with—

Once again, that blazing headache pounded through her skull on steel horseshoes, the pain eclipsing all thought about where she needed to go with that she knew. Rubbing her face, she abruptly remembered why it wasn't a great idea to eat boatloads of sugar, salt, and caffeine on a oner once you were out of your late teens and early twenties.

"You okay?"

Sarah jumped as someone spoke up, and it was miraculous. As she opened her eyes and focused on Jane, the headache essentially disappeared.

"I brought you guys food." The doctor put a large tray down on one of the tables. "Do you like lamb? It's Wrath's favorite. We've also got baby new potatoes broiled in the oven and boiled carrots."

As a cloche was lifted off, and all kinds of rosemary heaven wafted around, Sarah decided she needed some real food.

"Your timing couldn't be better," she said as she sat down and took one of the two plates.

Jane eased into a chair and smiled. "I should have had Fritz send it down from the big house as soon as we sat at the table. We haven't been very good hosts."

"You've been great." Sarah tucked into the dinner, starting with the potatoes which were proof that God existed as far as she was concerned. "Hey, you didn't happen to see John while you were there?"

"No, why?"

Shifting her knife into her right hand and the fork into her left, Sarah thought about how she could answer that as she cut into the lamb.

"No reason. Wow, this is delicious—and as soon as I'm finished, I'm ready to get back to work."

"You sure you don't want to have a sleep? We have a room you can use. Is that where Murhder is? Catching some z's? I figured he'd be with you."

Keeping her eyes down, Sarah nodded and then pointed at the crumpled wrappers, the crushed bag and the Coke can. "As for me, I'm wired."

She also didn't know how much more time she had. Any moment not working on John's case seemed wasted, although realistically, she didn't know that she was going to be able to offer him any kind of solution the medical staff hadn't already considered.

Breakthroughs didn't just happen; they had to be earned through sweat equity.

At least that's what she and Gerry had always believed.

As a wave of sadness came over her, she beat back the emotion with a reminder of what he'd done in that secret lab. How could he have tortured Nate like that? In the name of making money for a man like Kraiten? It broke her heart to think the student she'd loved had turned into a man she didn't recognize.

A man who did evil things to an innocent boy.

Refocusing on the present, she knew she needed a plan for when she got back to her real life. She was not sure it was safe to return to her house, given that she didn't know what Kraiten remembered of the previous night. But where would she go? And how was hiding from a billionaire going to work?

Kraiten had endless resources.

She had a year's worth of expenses saved, a small inheritance, and her 401(k).

Not really the size wallet you needed if you were going to try to disappear for the rest of your life.

Abruptly, she realized that it was more than just Kraiten she might have to evade . . . because something dawned on her as she looked across the shallow table at the doctor who'd brought her dinner: There was no way of going to the authorities without exposing all of these people and their secret way of life. After all, how could she share the experiments and the test results without providing humans with proof that another species lived among them?

As she considered the ramifications of such a revelation, she knew they would be potentially catastrophic. Given how the human race typically treated things viewed as "other"? The idea of vampires being widely known made her heart pound with panic for the species' safety.

And in this regard, she realized, she and Kraiten were in the same place for completely different reasons. Neither of them could really bring in law enforcement, could they.

Too bad he was the one with the experience killing people, and she was just a scientist.

Where was Iron Man when you needed him.

"Penny for your thoughts?" Jane said softly.

"Do you read minds?"

The doctor shook her head. "No."

"Oh, I forgot, you're not one of them." Sarah wiped her mouth as she swallowed the truth. "And as for my thoughts, I'm just wondering what I can do for John. By the way, this mint jelly is fantastic, is it homemade?"

Jane smiled a little. "As a matter of fact, it is."

CHAPTER THIRTY-FOUR

The wind was cold on John's face as he walked up the rise and looked across the municipal park toward downtown's forest of skyscrapers. He was right on the shore of the Hudson, by the boathouse where rowers put their sculls into the water during the warmer months. Over to his left, there was a playground with brightly colored tubes that kids could scramble through and several sets of vacant swing sets, the seats of which had snowpack-passengers that did not travel far.

Everything was blanketed in winter white, only the shallow, shuffling print-trails of squirrels having crossed the open area disturbing the pristine fall.

When the mournful wail of an ambulance sounded out on the highway, he glanced to the bridges that went over the river and saw the flashing red lights in the midst of the traffic. The emergency vehicle was heading toward him, instead of away, which made sense. The St. Francis ER was on this side of the waterway.

He wondered who was in the back. What their ailment was. Whether they were going to live.

His shoulder hurt more as the thoughts went through his mind, but he didn't think it was because things were suddenly much worse with the wound. Or maybe they were. Who knew.

John refocused on the snow and thought back to Christmases when he'd been at the orphanage—which was an unusual place for his mind to go. Before he'd found his way to the vampire world he belonged in, he'd refused to dwell on what his childhood had been like—nothing good could come of those memories. And afterward, when he'd found his true home and people? He'd told himself none of his human past mattered anymore because he was where he belonged.

Just let it go, he'd always told himself.

Now, though, his brain insisted on digging up a golden oldie from the holiday season. He'd been placed in a Catholic orphanage—because Our Lady of Mercy was pretty much all Caldwell had for unwanted kids outside of the state-sponsored foster program—and he could remember being told all the time that he was one of the lucky ones. The chosen ones.

Nobody had ever told him who had done the choosing, and given that he'd been found in that bus station as a newborn, it wasn't like he had any memories of being rescued. And as for the special status? He'd always had the sense that the people who worked for Our Lady said that to the kids because they themselves wanted to feel part of an elevated platform, a righteous, better-than-anything-else kind of thing.

Performance piety, he thought.

But whatever, fine, he'd been one of the chosen ones, kept out of the foster care system, saved from some terrible fate that clearly had Charles Dickens–in–the–twenty–first–century written all over it.

In reality, he'd found growing up without parents, and waiting around in a valiant hope that some couple would come and declare they wanted to adopt a scrawny kid who couldn't talk, to be pretty grim, even if he'd had a warm place to sleep, three squares a day, and free dental.

And then there had been the Christmas season.

For reasons that, in retrospect, now totally escaped him, every December the orphans were loaded onto a bus and taken to the local mall. They weren't allowed to sit on Santa's lap, because the season wasn't about all that—but they were instructed to walk around and see all the presents they would not be getting, and all the families they were not a part of, and all the normal that, through no fault of their own, they could not participate in. And this was back before online shopping, when throngs of people crowded into those shopping centers, carrying out bags and bags of Christmas morning loot into parking lot sections that were standing room only for new car arrivals.

He'd never understood the why of that trip.

Reaching up to his shoulder, he pushed at the wound and rotated the socket. The pain made him remember something else. Back when he'd been growing up, he could recall the nuns and adults at the orphanage telling the children that youth was wasted on the young.

Like the Christmas mall trip, he'd never understood why they felt compelled to point a blaming finger at something a kid couldn't fix and didn't get. You were the age you were, and death was just not a preoccupation for somebody who'd been on the planet for only eight years. Ten years. Fifteen years.

More to the point, if you'd already lost your mom and dad and had no one who cared for you in the world, what did anything else matter? If dying meant you lost everything, hello. John hadn't even had clothes of his own. Books. Toys. Even the pillow he put his head on every night had "Our Lady of Mercy Orphanage" stamped on it in ink.

No possessions. No control over his destiny. Nothing ahead of him.

He might as well already be dead, he'd always thought.

As the cold wind off the river curled around his legs, the chill made the scene in front of him replace the images of the past. And for some reason, he thought about how old he was. In calendar years, he was not even thirty. For a human, that was the tail end of the transition into proper adulthood. For a vampire, it was a drop in the bucket, a blip on a centuries-and-centuries-long lifespan.

Assuming you didn't die young.

He thought about his wound and the spread of the stain in his skin. Death had taken ahold of him. He knew this without any doubt.

So now he understood about the youth wasted on the young thing. It was hard to fully comprehend the prospect of dying, the way it consumed the mind and the soul, the way it eclipsed previously "important" preoccupations, the way it reordered your priorities . . . until you were forced to stare your grave in the eye.

Children had no capacity not just to appreciate mortality, but to see clearly that they had made a bargain at birth that, even though there was no consent, was nonetheless an enforceable agreement with a payment due.

All things that lived died.

The best that anyone who breathed could do was a skate-by into old age, dodging the slings and arrows of biological failings and accidents, until you could sit back with your aches and pains and mourn the loss of your relevancy, your generation, your place in the population pecking order.

He had never expected to die. Ironic, given that he hunted the enemy every night as his vocation.

But here he was, standing out in the open, a sitting duck for a *lesser*, not worried that he had no weapons, no phone, and no backup.

Then again, he'd already decided his life was a moot point. The question was, with whatever time he had left, what did he want to do?

What was important to him?

Who mattered?

◆   ◆   ◆

Privacy in a partnership was a tricky thing.

As Xhex re-formed downwind from her mate, and stared across a snow-covered park at his back, she didn't know what to do. He wasn't answering her texts, he hadn't told her he was leaving the house, and he was alone not just in fact, but on an existential level.

And no, that wasn't extrapolation. Her *symphath* side knew this as fact: His grid was lit up around his core along the lines of separation and isolation.

Though his body was no more than a hundred yards away from her, he was virtually untouchable.

"You going to go talk to him?"

Murhder's voice made her jump, and reminded her that, unlike John, she was not alone. She and the former Brother had left the training center via the underground tunnel's evac route, pausing only to help themselves to the parkas and gloves that were part of the emergency supply of equipment and provisions stacked by the reinforced steel door.

Probably a security breach, using that exit, but she knew what was in Murhder's heart and soul thanks to his grid—and he would do no evil nor cause any to be done to the Brotherhood or their household.

Once they had emerged on the far side of the mountain, she had located John downtown thanks to her blood in his veins from feeding. And so she and Murhder were now here, standing far behind her mate, John's preoccupations so great, her presence did not register on him.

"Xhex? You going to go to him?"

She shook her head. "He needs some space."

It killed her to say that. But if she crossed the distance between them, John was going to view it as an intrusion, not as support.

Sometimes you had to sit on the sidelines while the one you loved worked their shit out. And she reminded herself that he knew she was there for him, always.

"This isn't about me, is it?" Murhder said.

"No. It's about him."

"Shit. The injury."

"Yeah." She shook her head. "I think I better just go to work. But I'll take you back first. You won't be able to get through the *mhis* otherwise."

When Murhder didn't respond, she glanced over at him. He wasn't looking at John. He was staring at the tall buildings of the city.

"I don't want to head back yet," he murmured.

Well, there was no reason he couldn't stay out and about. He might not be welcome in the mansion, but that didn't mean he was being held in an official capacity. Or even an unofficial one.

"I'm at shAdoWs." She gave him the club's address. "Find me there when you're ready to head back. I'll let my bouncers know to expect you."

"Thanks. I won't be long. It's just been a while since I've seen Caldwell at night."

"Don't engage." As his hard stare shifted over at her, she rolled her eyes. "And don't give me that look. It is perfectly reasonable to assume you'd want to fight. You're a Brother, remember."

"Used to be," he muttered as he went to dematerialize. "I used to be."

His words lingered as his form disappeared, like a ghost had spoken.

Xhex crossed her arms and wondered whether she was doing the right thing—or if she should interrupt. When John did not turn around because he sensed her, she got out her phone and texted him.

As the message showed that it was delivered, he didn't make a move to check his phone. Maybe his cell was on mute. Maybe he hadn't brought it.

Maybe he just needed to be left alone.

In the end, Xhex put her phone away and closed her eyes. It was a while before she could dematerialize.

He knew where she was; she had texted him that she was going to work. And she had faith he would come and find her.

Fate was not going to have it any other way.

At least . . . that was what she told herself.

CHAPTER THIRTY-FIVE

Shortly after Murhder dematerialized away from the park, he re-formed at the base of a forty-story skyscraper that had a glass-fronted lobby the size of a small country and the name of a bank spelled out in glowing letters over sets of revolving doors. Inside, behind a granite desk, there was a guard on duty even though things were clearly not open for business.

The building was new to him. So was the name of the bank.

So were a lot of things downtown.

Picking a random direction, he started strolling down the plowed sidewalk, looking around, seeing the night sky above all the towers full of windows. There were so many new constructions, and there were new names on the eateries. Starbucks. Bruegger's Bagels. Spaghetti Factory.

Nothing like it had been when he'd lived here twenty years ago.

As he went along, he imagined the streets busy in the daylight with men and women in business clothes, all of them hurrying to and from meetings after they dumped their cars in parking garages that were two or three times the size he remembered.

What was the same? Not many humans out and about now on a

cold night like this. Sure, from time to time, a random SUV would go by. A sedan. A Caldwell municipal truck. But other than that, there was no one around as he walked in the cold.

Still, even though he was alone, he had a sense of a great many lives being lived in these tall, thin constructions, boxes of day-dwelling humans layered upward, stacked one upon the other. It was an incalculable crowd, especially when he considered how there were city centers like this all over the nation. Over the world.

He thought of John standing in that barren field alone.

He had walked that particular stretch of loneliness himself these past two decades.

But in the last twenty-four hours, he'd gotten a glimpse of another way. Shit, Sarah *had* to be able to stay in their world. For godsakes, there were humans all over the place now—or at least inside the Brotherhood's facility.

Surely she could stay. If she wanted to.

On that note ... surely he could talk her into staying? She'd said she had no one who was waiting to hear from her. If that was the case, what did she have to go back to ... ?

Crap. The instant he thought that, he felt like an arrogant ass. As if he were offering her some great existence down in South Carolina? At a B&B? She was a scientist. The last kind of forever after she needed was staring at him over that table in the third-floor attic of the Rathboone House—

Murhder stopped dead. Turned his head to the left. And breathed so hard in through his nose that his nostrils hurt.

Instinctually, his body turned of its own volition, and he scented the cold air again. Just in case he'd gotten it wrong.

As a set of headlights swung around and spotlit him, he was dimly aware that he'd once against halted in the middle of a street. This time, he moved away before there was any horn, any impact.

But not because he was avoiding the nuisance of another hit-and-run. Nope, as his feet found a jogging pace, and his body lithely carried itself down an alleyway, he was going after prey. And the sickly sweet stench he tracked was more than a guide. It was a thickening agent for his blood, a source of heat for his aggression, a jolt of awareness that made his brain come alive.

The enemy was not far. A member of the Lessening Society . . . was not far at all.

In the back of his mind, he was aware that he hadn't fought in a very long time. That he was unarmed. That no one knew he was out here by himself and he had no phone to call somebody for backup.

Hell, he had no idea what number he could call, even if he had something to dial.

None of that mattered.

As with all members of the Brotherhood, he had been part of the Scribe Virgin's breeding plan, designed even before the womb to hunt and kill, manufactured like a product to render death to those who threatened the species.

And however rusty and out of practice he was, the siren call of the purpose for which he had been bred was not going to be denied.

Even if it killed him.

✦   ✦   ✦

Far from downtown's alleys, in the enclave of Caldwell's private mansions, Throe unlocked his bedroom door and leaned out into the hall. After looking both ways, he slipped out and relocked things with an old-fashioned brass key.

As he started for the first floor, he had the Book pressed to his chest like a bulletproof shield—and he told himself he had become paranoid.

Then stopped to look over his shoulder.

Nothing was in the corridor behind him . . . except for the console tables with their silk floral displays. The brocade drapes pulled closed over windows. The portraits that hung in the centers of the molding pattern between the entrances to the bedroom suites.

Resuming his stride, he found it ironic that after he had ordered the deaths of all the *doggen* who had worked upon the estate, he now wished he were not alone beneath the great house's roof.

He stopped again. Checked the hallway behind once more.

Nothing.

The grand staircase in the front of the mansion had a gracious turn to it, the better to show off the females of the bloodline as they came down in gowns to formal dinners. No gowns tonight. No formal dinner, either. And unlike the *shellans* and daughters who sought attention, he flattened himself to the wall and debated the merits of sneaking this way as opposed to using the staff stairs in the back. But he'd decided the latter were more troublesome because they were a narrow space for conflict.

He had a gun hidden in the folds of the smoking jacket he'd put on over his fine dress shirt and slacks.

When his monogrammed house slippers finally hit the black-and-white marble tile at the bottom, he looked around. Listened. Listened . . . even harder. There was nothing that seemed threatening: The heating vents at floor level offered whistles as warm air was forced up through the cellar's ducts. A creaking sound that was deep inside the walls suggested January's cold had gotten into the bones of the old house.

Water was running.

In the kitchen.

Throe palmed the gun inside the pocket and proceeded through the formal dining room. In the far corner, there was a flap door for staff to bring out food and drink during service, and he kept out of sight of its small, eye-level glass window, putting his back to the panels.

When he was ready, he quick-shifted over so he could see through it into the kitchen.

One of his shadows was at the sink washing dishes, its balloon-like form split on the top half so it could do its work.

That was when he smelled the turkey.

The shadow had prepared the dinner he had ordered the night before. Just as instructed.

This was good, Throe told himself. This was . . . as it should be.

No more independent thinking.

Pushing his way into the kitchen, he was prepared to shoot—even though he had seen that bullets had little effect on his ghostly soldiers. Still, what other weapon did he have if they turned against him?

"Stop," he ordered.

The shadow didn't hesitate. It froze where it was, bent over a deep-bellied sink full of soapy water.

"Resume."

The shadow went back to work, cleaning the roasting pan with its pair of arm-like extensions. The food that it had cooked was laid out upon the butcher block counter that ran the length of the industrial kitchen, the fine porcelain serving dishes covered with their lids, the turkey under a large cloche. The tray that was to be taken up to his bedroom when he called for it was set with his favorite Herend dishes, a sterling silver fork, knife, and spoon, and a linen napkin that had been folded and pressed.

The bottle of wine he had requested was chilling.

There was a wineglass and a water goblet yet to be filled.

The shadow brought the roasting pan up out of the suds and rinsed it with the sink's hose. Then it set the pan aside on a drying rack, water dripping from its translucent form, falling unimpeded through the lower half of its body onto the floor.

His soldier, born of his own blood from that incantation, turned to face him and waited for an order. Nothing but a vessel for his will. Utterly obedient.

Mayhap he had been mistaken, he thought as he lowered the Book. These entities of his, deadly or docile upon his command, surely had no independent thought.

So why had he assumed they had snuck up upon him?

"Others," he said out loud. "Come hither!"

In a lower voice, he said to the one before him, "You shall protect me against any threat. From no matter the source. Do you understand?"

The shadow nodded its upper half, the movement causing its buoyant form to bounce a little as it hovered over the kitchen floor.

"No matter what the other three do, you must always protect me. This is your sole purpose."

As the entity bowed to him again, he pivoted around and backed up against the still warm stoves. He didn't know exactly what he was worried about, however, as he brought the Book into place once again over his vital organs.

Like it was a bulletproof shield.

But these shadows had no will of their own, he reminded himself as one by one the three entities entered the kitchen and stopped obediently. Patiently.

Stupidly.

These translucent smoky killers were his creations, to do with as he pleased. The Book had promised him this army for his ambitions—and it had delivered. Everything was going to be all right.

Surely he had been mistaken about what had transpired at his desk.

He must have been wrong about them sneaking up on him.

CHAPTER THIRTY-SIX

Murhder tracked his prey down two streets and into an alley, zeroing in on the slayer without a sound, his senses and his brain working together to adjust for wind direction, change of his position, change of the *lesser's*, so that his scent did not give him away. In pursuit, he was a mortal mechanism, his muscles and blood, his very bones, thickened by a surge of hormones that made him more animal than civilized.

Rounding the final corner, he entered a lane formed by the back end of a skyscraper and the building behind it—

Shit. Humans were performing some kind of municipal night work two blocks down, the glow from their spotlights and clanking from whatever they were doing spilling through an intersection.

His eyes adjusted in the darkness as wind abruptly came around and pushed against his back.

Immediately, the *lesser* halted and pivoted, clearly called by what was carried down to him on the cold gust.

It was young, both in terms of when it'd been turned and how long it'd been under the command of the Omega. *Lessers* lost their pigmentation over time, whatever skin, hair, and eye color they possessed prior to their induction paling out until their bodies were as their souls became: an existential blank.

Just killing machines.

This one had its dark hair still, and its skin had yet to become Kleenex white. It was also dressed badly, and not as in sartorial style. Its leather jacket was ripped and stained, its jeans ragged, its boot laces loose and trailing. It was more orphan than squad leader—

Over at the construction site, a high-pitched, metal-on-metal screech pierced the ambient noise of the dozing city, some grinder set upon something that offered resistance.

It was the perfect bell for round one.

Murhder sank into his thighs and brought his hands up. Focusing slightly to the left of the slayer, as his peripheral vision was the sharpest, he wanted to make sure there was only one. The scents on the wind suggested so, and with the gusts at his back, he would catch anything behind him.

But you could never be too sure.

Murhder tracked where the *lesser's* hands were: Out in front. And that leather jacket was zipped up tight. Harder to get at a weapon— which made Murhder conclude that the slayer was as unarmed as he was. Even with humans so close, knives didn't make much noise. Nunchucks. Guns with suppressors.

No, this one was young. Ill-equipped.

And unsure.

Something has changed, Murhder thought as he leaped forward.

The slayer snapped out of its immobility just as Murhder tucked into a mid-air roll and then sailed parallel to the ground boot-first, the soles of his size fourteens targeting that chest like there was a bull's-eye on it. The kid twisted to deflect, but Murhder had enough agility to shift as well, the impact nailing the slayer in the upper arm and blowing it off its feet. As they both hit the ground, it was a case of who grabbed who first, holds clamping on arms and legs, the grappling game on.

Murhder wrestled around in the snow with the enemy, that leather jacket riding up and revealing no gun holster, no knives at the belt, nothing bulky in the jeans pockets. Before long, Murhder gained control, flipping the slayer on its back and mounting its body as he locked his dagger palm on its throat and pressed down with all his strength.

Its eyes bulged and filthy hands came up to claw at the strangulation.

Curling up a fist, Murhder punched it in the head once. Twice. A third time.

As black blood welled from the shattered eye socket, the roadkill stench got stronger and the slayer began to thrash, kicking up snow. The more it fought, the stronger Murhder became until he was a cage over the former human, locking down, locking in—

The bullet whistled by his head, a fraction of an inch away from his frontal lobe.

Murhder ducked and rolled the slayer over, using its body as a shield against whoever had discharged that silent slug. Digging his heels into the snowpack, he shimmied for cover in the shadows.

The one-eyed slayer slammed a fist into Murhder's own face, payback for its cosmetic realignment, and then it head-butted him—or tried to. Murhder shot to the side and bit the back of the slayer's neck.

That got a holler released.

Not helpful. Over the slayer's shoulder, the second *lesser* appeared, and yup, it had a handgun of some sort with an extra long barrel—and the suppressor did its job again, muffling the sound of a bullet discharged from twenty-five yards away.

I may be in trouble here, Murhder thought as he ducked his head and made sure his vital organs were covered by the slayer on top of him.

The *lesser* with the trigger-happy finger was closing in, striding fast with that muzzle up. No way of knowing how many rounds there were, but what Murhder was clear on was that until you stabbed a *lesser* in the heart with something made of steel, it stayed animated even if it was full of holes. So the fact that its comrade in harm was being used as a shield wasn't going to dissuade it from emptying its clip—not that slayers cared much for each other anyway.

More bullets went sailing and Murhder looked around for a way out—

A blazing streak in his thigh told him he'd been hit.

Dematerializing was now not an option, even if he could concentrate enough to try to ghost out—something that was tough to do when you were distracted dodging lead slugs.

"Sonofabitch!" he barked as the slayer on top of him managed to drive a finger—or maybe its entire arm—into the bullet wound on his thigh.

Jacking upright, he held his PITA cover in place and crab-walked backward into a shallow doorway. But like that was going to help much?

The advancing *lesser* kicked a clip out of the butt of that gun and slammed in another one.

Everything slowed down, and Murhder had only one thought go through his mind.

This is how it happens? This is how I die?

He was more annoyed with his own stupidity than sorry—until he thought of Sarah, back at the training center, working with good faith to save a vampire she didn't know, as she waited for Murhder to come back to her.

Dearest Virgin Scribe, what if the Brothers didn't do right by her? What if they didn't take care of her? What if she went back to the human world and somehow suffered the consequences for Nate's rescue?

True panic flooded Murhder's veins, giving him super strength. Forcing himself up off the ground, he kept one arm locked around the bleeding slayer's torso as he grabbed for the handle of the door—

Locked. Of course.

The *lesser* with the gun raised that muzzle and pointed it at Murhder's head. The slayer was fifteen yards away. Ten yards. Five—

From out of the corner of his eye, Murhder caught sight of a figure entering the alley at the far end, the dark shape cutting through the billowing, backlit steam that rose out of a manhole, white and frothing as a cloud.

Something in the way the figure moved, the size of its shoulders, the short crop of its hair, took Murhder back twenty years.

"Darius . . . ?" he whispered.

✦   ✦   ✦

John Matthew stopped at the head of the alley. Humans working on a sewer main had cordoned off the next intersection of the street, their brilliant lights, clutch of municipal trucks, and official hard-hatted conference around a room-sized hole they'd made in the pavement suggesting that they were going underground with their equipment soon.

But they weren't subterranean yet, and they all had cell phones.

He refocused on the alley. As steam boiled up around his body, obscuring his view, he didn't need his eyes to tell him that there was a bloody fight going on in the darkness. He'd caught the combination of vampire and slayer blood on the wind as he'd walked out of that park, faint at first, strengthening as he closed in.

It wasn't any of the Brothers he worked with.

But he knew who it was. And they were not dying on his watch, goddamn it.

Just as the slayer pulled his trigger at Murhder point-blank, John dematerialized onto the undead and shoved the muzzle of the autoloader away.

The bullet ricocheted off a metal girder on the building, the spark yellow in the night.

And it was on. John fought for control of the gun, two-handing that wrist, grunting, cursing, as he and the *lesser* landed in the frozen snow tracks that were stained with the blood spilled from Murhder's fight.

When you fought in a pair, you had to make sure you knew where your other half was, especially if there were firearms involved. Last thing you wanted was collateral damage that was your fault. And by some stroke of luck . . . or magic . . . he always knew what Murhder was going to do—and vice versa. The former Brother peeled off with his *lesser* and danced behind John's ground game, like they had choreographed the shit.

But why the hell had he thought it was a good idea to come out without any weapons?

And fuck it, he'd had enough of this.

Pinning the slayer facedown, he got up on the *lesser*'s back, slammed a hold on the gun arm's elbow and yanked up on the wrist, breaking all the bones, the snap like that of hardwood thrown on an open fire. When the *lesser* started to scream, John pushed its piehole into the snowpack, the sound muffled.

Talk about your suppressors.

Then he snatched the Glock out of the now lax hand and put the muzzle to its head.

One! Two! Three!

The bullets went through the skull and brains, all knife-and-butter, the arms and legs flopping with each impact.

John jumped off, and double-handed the weapon, pointing it at—

Murhder was back on the ground, holding his slayer down with his superior weight, his arms bowed out, his head down in the bite-zone.

When he came up, he brought a hunk of flesh with him, the whatever-it-was anatomy dangling from his descended fangs, black blood covering his chin, his throat, the front of the parka he had on.

He spit it out to the side.

Beneath him, the slayer was moving in a slow, uncoordinated churn—oh, check it. Most of its facial skin was gone, the cheekbones and curlicued roots of the teeth flashing bright white in the midst of all the glistening black tendons and ligaments.

With his red-and-black hair tangled on his shoulders, his huge body poised to do more damage to what was underneath him, his gleaming fangs and wide, brilliantly glowing eyes, Murhder looked like a demon.

And then he started to laugh.

Not in an evil way, though.

More like someone whose hometown team has just beaten their rivals at the buzzer: The sound was all about the high-five, the cheer, the go-us.

"This was fucking awesome!" he said. "And nice timing, I was almost dead!"

John blinked. It was the last thing he'd expected to come out of the guy's mouth—especially given what had just been in it.

"Let's finish these off—and go get some more!"

As if the field of conflict were a Baskin-Robbins and they had fifty-two more flavors to look forward to.

This is crazy, John thought. He himself was injured—totally red-shirted until further notice or when he took to his deathbed. They had one gun between them—thanks to the slayer with the now-broken arm—and a questionable amount of bullets left. And there were things other than slayers stalking the night, shadows that John had learned about the hard way.

Oh, and this male with the black blood all over his face and chest was known to be insane.

But John started to smile.

The next thing he knew, he'd dismounted his *lesser* and was picking a discarded tire iron up out of the snow. Back at the undead, he two-fisted the thing over the chest of the slayer and drove the dull end you were supposed to work lug nuts with into the hollow cavity where the heart had previously been.

The pop and flash momentarily blinded him. And then he was back to work, doing the same to the slayer Murhder had given a facial to.

After that flash of light and sound faded, John reached down and offered a palm to the former Brother.

Murhder was leaking, the scent of his fresh blood suggesting he'd been plugged by at least one lead slug somewhere. But as the male's eyes shined with an uncontaminated happiness, John knew the guy wasn't going to let that bother or stop him any more than a certain shoulder wound was going to sideline John.

They clapped palms and John dragged the other male off the snow with his good arm. Then they walked off into the night, side by side.

It was almost, John reflected, as if they'd done this before—

Murhder started to whistle a cheery little tune, and John had to do a double take.

After a silent laugh, John joined in, finding a perfect harmony: "Don't Worry, Be Happy." When Murhder started doing a hop'ita-skip'ita every third step, John Fred Astaire'd, too.

Just two vampires, looking for the undead, ready to enjoy some good old-fashioned bloodshed.

Besties.

CHAPTER THIRTY-SEVEN

Tohr had heard that parents had a sixth sense about their young. That even if your kid grew up, went through the change, and came out the other side, ready to settle down with a mate to live their own lives, you still had this radar that pinged when they needed you. When they were off the rails. When something was wrong and they hadn't come to you about it yet.

As Tohr walked the territory that he, as the commanding officer of the Brotherhood, had assigned himself in the field, he couldn't shake the idea that John was in trouble.

The male hadn't been at First Meal. More to the point, Xhex had showed up in the dining room only long enough to look the cast of characters over and leave quick as she came. Which suggested she didn't know where he was.

Plus hello, that wound—

"What's up, my man?"

He glanced across at Qhuinn. In the last couple of months, he'd taken to pairing himself with the brother, even though on paper they didn't make a lot of sense. Tohr had come up in the Old School and was as disciplined as a soldier could be. Everything from the trim of his high and tight to the press of his muscle shirts, his daily workouts to his calorie intake, his fighting stances and his weaponry had to be perfect, and he was ever eagle-eyed for error like a pathologist looking for cancer cells.

Qhuinn? Gunmetal-gray piercings up one entire ear. Tattoos everywhere, a collection he was constantly adding to with V's help. And the brother could take or leave workouts, liked boxes of Milk Duds and bags of Cheetos when he got peckish, and couldn't give two shits about a proper haircut.

He'd colored his black hair deep purple two weeks ago.

In another seven days, it was liable to be hot pink.

But here was the thing. Qhuinn was now the happy father of a pair of twins and totally committed to his *hellren*, Blaylock. He was also a crackerjack fighter, utterly loyal to the King, and fiercely protective of the others in the Brotherhood.

So yeah, core values and all that stuff.

Plus he and Tohr both liked *American Horror Story* and *Stranger Things*. And actually, on his cheat days, Tohr had been known to sneak Cheetos.

Aware that a reply was in order, Tohr stopped and glanced around at the abandoned warehouses, the girded skeletons all that was left behind of Caldwell's previous claim to fame as a vital port of call on the St. Lawrence waterway's turn-of-the-century trade routes.

"I've just got a bad feeling about—" His phone went off with a vibration and he took it out. "Damn it. We need to head downtown."

As he gave Qhuinn an address that was right in the middle of the financial district, the brother didn't ask for any explanation—which was another thing Tohr liked about the guy. Qhuinn was prepared for anything at any time in any form.

Probably explained the hair thing.

The pair of them ghosted out and re-formed in an alley behind Citibank's towering monument to capitalism.

Xcor, leader of the Band of Bastards, was standing next to his boy, Balthazar. The latter had been the one to text, as Xcor was just becoming literate. In front of them, in the dirty snow, were twin scorch marks that had yet to refreeze in the below-zero temperatures.

Tohr walked over to the burns and knelt down. The stench of *lesser* blood was so strong, his sinuses stung from it. "And you didn't do these?"

He knew the answer before there was any reply: Vampire blood had also been spilled at the scene, and he knew whose it was.

"No," Xcor replied. "We came upon them during our sweeps."

"Goddamn it," Tohr muttered as he looked around.

There was gunpowder in the air, too, so someone or someones had a gun. What the hell was Murhder doing out here, killing *lessers* without permission?

As he rose back up to his full height, a jackhammer sounded out at the next intersection down.

"And right next to humans. Just his style."

Xcor frowned. "You know who did this, then?"

"You haven't had the pleasure of his acquaintance yet. If you luck out, he'll leave Caldwell before you have to shake his hand."

"Do you want us to help find whoever this is?"

"No, you go back to monitoring your territory. Call me if you find anything else, though."

He clapped palms with the two fighters and hung back as they took off. Then he looked toward the bright glow of the humans' construction zone.

"So who is it?" Qhuinn asked.

"A blast from the past. Come on, we've got to find the idiot before he gets himself killed."

◆   ◆   ◆

Sarah took a break from looking at spreadsheets of data, stretching her neck and then standing up from the stool she'd been using. It had been a long while since she'd enjoyed the amnesia that came with getting deep into scientific study, her brain lit up with extrapolations and questions, her body left behind as she fell into an intellectual vortex.

Linking her hands over her head, she arched left. Leaned right.

All over the exam table in front of her, spread like the snow that covered everything else in New York State, were pages and pages of patient files. The species evidently had an issue with the storage of its blood, both for transfusion and for feeding purposes. Unless the stuff came directly from the vein, it was all but clinically worthless. So . . . if someone had an arterial wound and experienced a sharp drop in blood volume? Or if they were giving birth and had a uterine bleed? Unless someone of the species was standing handy with an available jugular, the patient was going to die. And the same was true for feeding, especially when it came to transitions. If you were trapped indoors because of sunlight, and no one could get to you when the change hit? You were dead.

It was a fascinating problem, and it related to John's wound in a couple of different ways. For one, transfusions for vampires were trouble. The white blood cell count in the recipient inevitably exploded after blood was given intravenously. Every time. So there was something in transfused blood that turned it into a foreign body to be defended against, and she'd wondered initially if this wasn't a solution for John: Give him some blood vein to vein and have his immune system ramp up all over his body. Unfortunately, any transfusion under those conditions was potentially fatal—so no-go there, given that she wasn't sure it would help him.

The risk/reward equation just didn't work.

But maybe there was another solution somewhere.

And the other way the studies were tied to John was on the feeding side. She assumed he was fully fed.

But maybe, she thought, we need to make him take his mate, Xhex's, vein—

Sarah stopped. Looked around at the exam room. Stared down at the spreadsheets.

Amazing to think in just over twenty-four hours she'd gone from "they" to "we."

On that note, she went over to the door and let herself out into the corridor.

Nate's room just two doors down and she knocked before she entered. When she heard his voice, she leaned inside.

"Feel like some company?"

The boy—um, man—sat up higher in the bed. "Please."

Sarah entered and brought a chair over with her. Sitting down, she crossed her legs and smiled. "You look great."

"They said I'm free to go at nightfall tomorrow." Nate frowned. "But I don't have anywhere *to* go."

Yeah, I get that, she thought.

"I'm sure you'll find a . . ." She cleared her throat. "I wish I could help. But I'm on the other side of things."

Funny how disappointing that was now.

"How did you know?" he asked. "That I was in there, I mean. You never said."

"I work at BioMed. Well, worked. I'm very sure I'm out of a job by now."

She had remote-accessed her home phone, and there weren't any messages from HR or her supervisor. But she hadn't showed up for work, and if that trend continued—given that there was still nothing about the BioMed raid on the news—she had to imagine someone would start trying to find her.

She hurried to fill the silence. "I want to assure you that I wasn't involved in . . . I didn't have anything to do with the experiments on you."

"I know." He fanned out his large hands as if still marveling at the changes he'd been through. "But how did you find me?"

"Did you know the people who worked on you? By name?" Sarah's heart began to pound. "Did you know them?"

"They always had masks on and they tried not to speak around me. Sometimes they slipped up, but never about names."

Sarah took a deep breath. "My fiancé worked in the department." As Nate stiffened, she shook her head. "He's dead. He died two years ago—actually, he was murdered. I'm not with someone who hurt you."

Any longer, she thought to herself.

She thought about Gerry sitting at that computer of his, his back to her, all holed up in that home office. Keeping secrets, bad secrets.

"He was murdered?" Nate asked.

As Sarah nodded, her temples started to hum with pain and she winced, rubbing her head. "He was a diabetic. But I believe he was killed."

"By who?"

"I don't know who exactly. It's a dirty business he was in, though. We didn't know that when we started, of course."

"Are you in danger?"

Yes. "No." She forced a smile. "I'm perfectly fine."

"They're not going to let you stay, are they."

"Here, you mean? I don't think so. I'm going to help for as long as I can, but then I guess I have to go back where I belong."

"You belong here."

She thought of being with Murhder and found herself agreeing. But that was emotion talking, not reality.

"I wish that were true." She patted Nate on the foot. "But enough about me. I just want you to know that I will be sure to say goodbye before I go, okay? And I will not leave until I'm satisfied that there's a plan for your future that you're comfortable with. You're what's important here. Not me."

There was a long pause. And the boy—man, rather—shook his head gravely.

"No, you also matter. A lot."

As tears came to her eyes, she ducked her head and blinked fast. That was what had been missing from her relationship with Gerry at the end, she realized: She had not mattered any longer to him, and since his death? She hadn't mattered to anybody—including herself.

If you were loved, if you had people who cared about you, you could be by yourself and never feel alone. But if no one cared? You were isolated even in a crowd.

"Don't cry," Nate said in his now deep voice.

"I'm not," she lied in a whisper.

CHAPTER THIRTY-EIGHT

Robert Kraiten fought his mind for as long as he could.

His thoughts, long the sound and logical road to follow, had taken him into a forest of threatening chaos that he could not find his way out of. And now he was stumbling through his actual glass house, tripping and falling on his face, dragging himself across polished marble . . . circling the second-story rooms before funneling, like dishwater, down the front staircase.

On the first floor, he caught his breath and tried to resist the impulse that controlled him, but his body refused to stop its forward progression.

He was naked, and his bald elbows and knees, his sweating palms, squeaked over the glossy tiling that he had a vague memory of installing two years ago: Alabastri di Rex by Florim. In Madreperla.

His recollections of spending months choosing the stone were like a distant echo, a pin dropping in the middle of a cheering stadium. Everything was like that. His business. His money. His secrets.

He had secrets. Terrible secrets. Secrets that . . .

The firestorm in his head whirled around faster, words forming and disintegrating, torn apart by the raging fury that surely his skull could not contain any longer.

He did not want to go to the kitchen. He did not want to go in search for what his brain was telling him he needed. He did not want to use the object for what his mind was telling him he wanted it for.

Instead, he wanted to go . . .

Robert Kraiten, long the master of his destiny and that of others, could not hold an independent thought.

After a lifetime of self-determination, something had come un-hinged deep inside of him. He had only the vaguest sense of when it had started: Leaving the labs the night before. In a car that was not his own . . . in one of the security vehicles that he'd made a guard give him the keys to.

And he had come home.

The security vehicle was still in his garage. He did not know where the keys to his actual SUV were, nor did he have his wallet or his cell phone. But he had gained access to his house by fingerprint.

He had come home.

He had come home to—

Something had happened at the lab last night. He had met with someone he needed to control in his office, and he had a vague idea that the meeting had gone satisfactorily—the deflection of their interest had been effective. But then, before he could leave, an interruption. A dangerous, Level I infiltration that had—

His body froze. His head reared back.

With a vicious strike, his forehead slammed forward of its own voli-tion, his frontal lobe hitting the alabaster so hard, a crack like lightning striking a tree echoed into the high ceilings above him.

Blood dripped, red and glossy, off his nose, onto the floor.

He smeared it as he crawled onward, creating handprints and smudges in his own blood. Red blood. Drop, drop—now flowing. A river down his face, getting into his nostrils, into his mouth, copper-tasting drool now.

The going became harder, his purchase on the glossy stone compromised by the slick mess he was making.

With relentless fixation, his mind drove his body forward even as his conscious self, his actual will, the true north on the compass of his sentient being, said, *No! Go back! Do not do this!*

The disintegration and degeneration of his mind had started as soon as he'd gotten home. Standing in his back hall, by the alarm center and computer systems that ran the entire house, he had inexplicably become bombarded with childhood memories, the images and sounds and smells hitting him as cannon shots, rocking him internally until he had collapsed onto his knees.

It was every bad thing he had ever done: All the joy he had taken at the expense of others, the shame and humiliation he had puppet mastered on his younger brothers. On his classmates. On teammates. On opponents.

Lost in the morass of memory, he had watched his younger self ride the ugly, but ultimately triumphant, tide of his own creation, his prominence sustained by the power structures he created and leveraged on his behalf. He had cheated on tests. Gotten his papers written by smarter students who had secrets they needed to keep. He had falsified his SATs and gotten into Columbia on an application written by a fellow senior who had been sucking off their English teacher. In college, he had sold drugs, and he had used women, and he had sparked a campus riot just for the fun of it. He had gotten a physics professor fired for sexual harassment she did not commit just to see if he could. He had blackmailed a dean for swinging because he was bored.

Kraiten had graduated having learned nothing of substance academically, and everything that mattered in terms of exploiting weakness.

Five years later, he had founded BioMed. And seven years after that, he had been driving home from his summer house on Lake George late at night, and come upon a car accident on the rural road halfway between Whitehall and Fort Ann.

He had never understood why he had stopped. It was not in his nature.

But something had compelled him.

Behind the wheel of the wreck, he had found a woman who was not just a woman. She had been a female of a different species: The deer she had hit was still struggling on the ground, and as it expired, her open mouth had shown him the kind of anatomy that he was unfamiliar with.

Fangs.

She had coded in his car on the way to the lab. Twice. He had pulled over and revived her both times.

As soon as he had her in secure custody, so to speak, he had talked to his partner, who had instantly seen the possibility. And as they had worked on her, he had discovered where to find others. Make deals.

Seven of them. Over the course of thirty years. Males and females. Then one who had been born in captivity, the result of a breeding.

He had learned so much. He had . . .

Robert Kraiten abruptly realized that he was up off the floor, on his feet, in the kitchen. Blood was all down his chest and his belly. And as he looked down at himself, he noted that he hid his old man body under well-tailored suits.

Pudgy, flabby, gray hair on his chest.

He had been fit once—

His hands were moving, pulling open a drawer that revealed things that flashed, mirror bright, under the overhead lights.

Knives. Chef knives. Freshly sharpened, state-of-the-art, knives.

Tears formed in his eyes, flowing down, mixing with the blood that drip, drip . . . dripped from his forehead into the drawer, onto the blades.

His right hand, the hand he wrote with, reached in and gripped one of the fourteen-inch Masamotos. The blade at the tip was tiny. At the base, it was two inches. This was the knife that was used to cleave slices off turkeys and roast beefs.

He had always been in control of everything. His whole life, he had ruled everyone around him.

Now, at the end of his mortal coil, he could control nothing.

"No . . ." he said through the blood in his mouth.

Robert Kraiten watched as his hand turned the knife around and the other one joined its mate in steadfast grip, all ten of his knuckles standing out in stark relief under the skin that covered them.

His lips peeled off his teeth as he gritted and fought and tried to stop the stabbing. Fruitless. It was like fighting a foe, a third party, an attacker who had snuck up on him.

Veins popped down his thin forearms as they shook.

There was sound all around him now, a loud sound that was echoing around the closed, smooth cabinets and empty counters and chrome appliances.

His scream was that of bloody murder . . . as he drove the knife into his abdomen and jerked it side to side, over and over again, turning his digestive tract to soup held within the tureen of his pelvic cradle.

He died in a crumbled mess three minutes later.

CHAPTER THIRTY-NINE

Some two hours after the killing party started, Murhder stabbed a third *lesser* back to the Omega. With that tire iron. And then he tossed the tool to John Matthew, who dispatched number four.

They were blocks and blocks away from where they had engaged the first pair, at least a mile and a half, maybe two, to the west, and as they'd gone along, he'd been shocked at how few of the slayers were out and about. Kind of frustrating when you were looking for quantity—and P.S., the quality of these fighters sucked. Every one of them was newly turned, unequipped, and ragged as the first had been.

But beggars/choosers and all that.

As John's pop and flash lit up the vacant street, Murhder laughed.

Just threw his head back and laughed as loud as he wanted to.

Across the street, lights came on in a walk-up, humans stirring, not that he cared.

John straightened and flipped the tire iron end over end, catching it in a snap and smiling. Murhder nodded without the guy having to ask anything: More. They needed more.

The freedom was intoxicating, the city spread before them, a field to hunt and find the enemy in, a playground in which to eliminate those who sought to kill innocent males and females—for no other reason than the Omega wanted to destroy that which the Scribe Virgin had created.

Murhder double-checked the sky. The position of the stars suggested a number of hours had passed, but there was time still left before the dawn came and robbed them of their pursuits. Not enough though. He wanted night after night after night of this buzz, this deadly hunt and peck, this sense that he was doing meaningful work.

"Where have they all gone?" He motioned around the street. "There should be dozens of *lessers* out tonight, but we've seen only four?"

John made a slicing motion across the front of his throat.

"They're dying off?" When the male nodded, Murhder frowned. "The Omega can't die. It's as immortal as the Scribe Virgin."

John shook his head again.

"Wait, what?" He was vaguely aware of humans moving around in those lighted windows, and he sank back into the shadows at the head of an alley. "I don't understand. The Omega is gone?"

More of that shaking.

"The *Scribe Virgin* is gone? What the hell's been going on here—"

"You two have gone rogue. That's what the fuck's been going on."

Murhder looked over his shoulder and grinned. "Tohr! What's up! How're you?"

The Brother with the levelheaded reputation was not looking particularly even-keeled at the moment. He was hair-across-the-ass mad, his lips thin, his stance tilted forward as if he were on the verge of punching someone.

And hey, ho, what do you know, Murhder appeared to be first in that line.

"John," the Brother said, "go back home. Now."

Murhder frowned. "Excuse me?"

Tohr jabbed a finger at the center of Murhder's chest. "Stay out of this. John, get the fuck out of here—"

"Don't talk to him like that."

"That's an order, John!"

"He's not a young, you know. He's a grown male who can do what the hell he wants—"

Tohr stepped up to Murhder, putting their faces nose to nose. "He is injured—and you are way fucking out of line bringing him into the field. You think it's a fucking joke that the two of you are working outside of the system, taking risks you can't handle and putting the rest of us in jeopardy, too?"

"Outside of the system? What system?" Murhder tilted his head to one side and raised his voice. "And we didn't take any risks we couldn't handle. We're still standing and four *lessers* are back to the goddamn Omega. What the *fuck* is wrong with you? Back in the day, we didn't need a system—"

Tohr punched at Murhder's shoulders. "We don't work without a coordinated plan anymore. And in case you haven't noticed, we're finally winning this war—without your help."

Murhder punched the guy back. "You sanctimonious piece of shit—"

"How many weapons do you have between the two of you."

When Murhder took a pause to try to answer that in the best way possible, the Brother said, "Cell phones? Either of you? Because I know that people have tried to reach him so I'm thinking he's either ignoring his own *shellan*, or he left his phone at home. She's worried about him, but here you are, leading him on a death mission out here alone—"

A loud, piercing whistle brought their heads around. And as John Matthew got their attention, the male stamped his foot in the snow. Then he nodded at Tohr and gestured with his thumb that he was leaving.

"At least one of you is making sense," the Brother muttered. "Son, please get yourself back to the clinic. You shouldn't be out here and you know it."

John nodded. And then stuck his palm out to Murhder.

As Tohr cursed, Murhder clasped what was offered. "It was a good time. Thanks for reminding me how much I used to love this job."

But instead of letting go, John tugged at him.

"Oh, no, you don't," Tohr said. "He's not going back with you. As of right now, he is not allowed on Brotherhood property ever again."

◆   ◆   ◆

"What did the transition feel like?"

As soon as the question left Sarah's mouth, she shook her head. "I'm sorry, Nate. That's invasive—"

"No, it's okay. It's just . . . I don't remember a lot of my transition, to be honest." The boy looked down at his now-long legs. "I'd felt off for a while beforehand. I mean, I had this weird craving for chocolate and bacon? I could get one or the other at the lab, but not both at a time. They fed me well, but I couldn't put requests in. And anyway, I couldn't eat much."

Sarah's stomach clenched at the idea of him in that cage. Alone. Suffering.

The experiments. The tests.

"By the time we came here from that house?" he continued. "I felt hot all over. But it was in my inside. Like a fever. And I just got hotter and hotter, until these waves went through me. I felt like every part of my body was blowing apart, and my blood was racing . . ."

Abruptly, Sarah's attention split. Half of her kept listening to Nate talk, so that she nodded in the right places and made murmurs of support. Another part of her, however, retreated to the data she'd been reviewing.

Including John Matthew's blood tests. Which showed that he had a normal level of white blood cells for a vampire—

"—wound healed up just fine."

"I'm sorry," she said, shaking herself. "What was that?"

"My wound is healed." Nate pulled back some of the blankets on his leg. "I tripped and fell in the cage, and cut myself. They bandaged it— but it kind of didn't do well. Now, it's all okay, though."

Sarah winced at the further reminder of his captivity. Then she leaned down and looked at the smooth, hairless expanse of a very powerful leg. On the outside of the calf, there was a faded line, jagged and rather long.

"And you said it healed?" Sarah glanced up. "After the change."

"Yes, but from what the doctor said, that's the way things are. Vampires who are fed properly have incredible healing powers."

Sarah sat back. "So I've heard. And I'm really glad you're okay."

"Me, too. I guess." Nate pulled the sheeting back over himself. "The doctor here said that the healing thing is to make up for no longer being able to see sunlight. Not that I ever had the chance to."

"You were never let outdoors?"

"No."

Sarah closed her eyes and tried to imagine what his life had been like. What it was going to be like as he went through another kind of transition, one of captivity to freedom.

"Nate, I am so sorry about everything you've been through."

"It is what it is. The question is . . . what now?"

"I get that one. Trust me."

They sat in silence for a while, and it was . . . well, she wouldn't say that it was necessarily good that the two of them were both at a loss for what the rest of their lives was going to look like. But it was nice to not be alone.

Disliking the direction of her thoughts, she refocused on that leg, now hidden.

"Did you heal because of the feeding or because you got through the change," she said to herself.

Nate shrugged and then smiled. "Maybe it was the transition itself. You know, wiping clean all blemishes. Starting fresh—"

Sarah sat up so fast, she nearly knocked the chair over. In a flicker of images, she thought of the way his body had grown during the change, and the kind of cellular storm that transformation had to represent . . . down at the molecular level.

"What?" he asked her.

When she didn't reply, Nate sat up as well. "Why are you looking at me like that?"

As the scientist in her went forward a hundred miles, the human she prided herself on being stayed put.

No, she thought. *It's not right.*

"What's not right?" he asked.

Sarah shook her head. "Sorry. I just . . . you've been through enough."

"Enough of what?"

"Ah, you know, experiments. Being poked and prodded and stuck with needles for the purposes of someone else."

"What are you talking about?"

"It's okay. It's nothing—"

"Sarah," he said in a tone of voice that suggested not only was he twenty, and not twelve, he was a lot older than even that. "What's on your mind?"

CHAPTER FORTY

I owe you," Murhder said an hour later. "Big-time."

As he and Xhex walked over to a stand of boulders on the side of a mountain, he paused and looked around. The snowy landscape was distorted, *mhis* making it hard to determine exactly where they were.

Vishous, he thought. *Up to his old tricks.*

But she'd been wrong about him not knowing where they were. He knew exactly the place: Darius's mountaintop mansion. The Brotherhood must have finally moved into it, just as Darius had always wanted them to. Murhder could remember coming to the construction site back in the early 1900s and watching as the magnificent house had been erected, steam cranes setting I-beams, great walls laid stone by stone, the whole of it built by fine vampire craftsmen to commercial specifications.

So the manse could last centuries.

"No, you don't owe me." Xhex slipped in between the car-sized rocks. "But you are lucky we had a change of clothes in Trez's office."

And that shower, he thought as he squeezed himself into the shallow hideaway. As he'd come off the field of conflict, he'd been covered with all kinds of blood and the last thing he wanted was for Sarah to see him like that. Looking for exactly what he happened to find, he'd gone to Xhex's club and ID'd a vampire among the security staff monitoring the entrance. The male had been good enough to get Xhex without asking a lot of questions.

She hadn't asked for any details, either. Especially as he'd told her he'd been with her mate. It was obvious her feelings were hurt, but typical of the female, she hadn't let any of that emotion through.

Leaning forward, she hit a hidden button and a small fake "rock" panel slid back to reveal a keypad. After she entered in a code, the lock was released and part of the entire cave wall opened.

But she didn't step aside so he could go through. Instead, she leveled those gunmetal-gray eyes at him.

"Listen," she said, "you need to get straight with the Brotherhood and take care of that human woman. She can't stay here in our world, Murhder. Say your goodbyes, wipe her memories and then get her back where she belongs. Or they're going to do that shit for you."

"She's going to help John." As the female looked away sharply, he put his hand on her shoulder. "Xhex, she's going to figure it out."

Those hard eyes swung back to him. "I don't want to be cruel here, I really don't. But you don't know that woman. You're attracted to her so that sizzle of chemistry makes you think you're on intimate terms, but you don't have a clue about what she's really like—and I refuse to put my faith in some human who incidentally worked for the company which has been torturing members of the species for over two decades."

Anger curled in his gut. "So you're just going to let John die?"

"Excuse me?" Xhex glared at him. "Not believing in a pipe dream does not equate to letting my *hellren* die. And fuck you for bringing that up."

He let his head fall back as he took a couple of deep breaths. When he righted things, the female had crossed her arms over her chest and was staring over his shoulder.

He was willing to bet in her mind, she was kneeing him in the balls.

"I apologize," he muttered. "That was a low blow."

Her eyes returned to his again. "Thank you. Now go make things easy on yourself and do the right thing. It'll be better for everybody."

When she went to walk off, he reached for her hand. "Xhex . . ."

It was a while before she glanced at him. And when she did, there was too much emotion in her normally composed face.

"Let me go," she said. And yet she didn't fight his loose hold.

"Talk to me. You look . . ." Too much like how he felt. "Just tell me what I can do to help you."

"God, Murhder," she said in a voice that cracked. "I'm just so tired. I'm . . . so fucking exhausted from being in pain. It's like I can't shake the hits. They keep coming at me, and anytime I feel like I've bounced back, I get nailed again—and this one? With John's injury? It's a mortal wound for the both of us if I lose him."

As she rubbed her eyes, Murhder cursed and pulled her in against him. There was a hesitation, and then her arms went around him and she held on tight. And that was when the fantasizing stopped for him and reality fell on his head.

He was going to lose Sarah.

She was going to lose John.

They had always had things in common. Too bad it was only the stuff that hurt.

When they eventually stepped apart, Murhder said, "When it comes to Sarah . . . I'll do the right thing."

"You always do," she murmured with defeat.

After a moment, she stepped away and he slipped through the heavy steel entry, making sure things closed up tight behind him. Walking forward, he came up to the shelves of weapons, nonperishable food, water and outerwear.

This was the place to be if the zombie apocalypse ever went down.

Striding through the tunnel, he shoved his hands into the pockets of his borrowed slacks and entertained a brief folly of him and Sarah living at the Rathboone House—and of course, in his version of reality, they were like all the other romantic couples who cuddled in old beds and enjoyed the fires in the fireplaces and held hands for absolutely no reason. But all of that was ridiculous. He couldn't expect her to sacrifice her scientific work for a nocturnal existence with a vampire rattling around in that B&B.

You don't know that woman.

But he did. He'd seen her with Nate. With John . . .

She was a female of worth.

Except, even as the conviction came to him, Xhex was right about one thing. He knew nothing about how Sarah had come to be at BioMed and how she had "discovered" the terrible secret experiments. Had she been involved with them somehow? He didn't know how that was possible, but what if she were lying to everyone? He'd been inside her mind, true . . . but could he trust himself to have seen clearly?

He was, after all, insane.

When he got to the entry into the training center, he put in the code Xhex had given him and walked through the supply closet. No one was in the office, which was a bonus, and he didn't run into anybody as he strode down to the clinical area—another bonus, as he was technically banned from the premises. But fuck that . . . and fuck Tohr.

Murhder was halfway to the treatment area when Sarah stepped out of Nate's room, a stainless steel tray in her hands, all kinds of test tubes filled with blood standing upright on it in a holder.

"Is he okay?" Murhder asked in alarm.

"You're back." She smiled and walked over. "He's great. He's a great man—male. He's a really good person."

"What are you doing with all that?" He tacked on a smile so it didn't sound as suspicious as he suddenly was. "I mean, just checking him, right?"

"Actually, I'm working on a theory about John's case. I'm wondering if—" She frowned. "Where are your clothes?"

He glanced down at himself. "I, ah, I had to change."

"I get that. I wish I had some of my own clothes, too."

As he looked at her face, as he stared deeply into her guileless golden eyes . . . as he probed for signs that she was misleading them all . . . his heart told him what he did not trust his mind to know: She was a healer, not a destroyer.

His fingertips lifted to the open collar of the button-down shirt he'd borrowed and found the sacred shard of seeing glass.

No, he thought as he rubbed the talisman between his thumb and forefinger. Xhex was wrong. She just had to be. Sarah's was the visage he had seen in the glass long ago, the woman he was supposed to be with.

And as soon as he grounded himself on that fact, he thought of one and only one thing: How in the hell he was going to be able to take her memories, release her out into the human world, leave her to live the rest of her life without him?

Sadly, however, the sacred glass had showed him only her face, not some kind of a future for them as mates.

Destiny had dictated only that they meet. Not that they be together for long.

"Are you all right?" she said. When he didn't immediately answer—because his throat was too tight to let speech through—she nodded to the left, toward a doorway. "Let me give this to Ehlena for testing in the lab. And then let's—is there anywhere we can go for a walk or something?"

"There's a gym?" He motioned over his shoulder. "Back that way."

"Give me a minute."

◆   ◆   ◆

The facility was a lot larger than Sarah had initially assumed, and she learned the footprint firsthand as she and Murhder strolled down the corridor away from the clinical area. As they went along, they passed by locker rooms. A weight room. That gym he'd mentioned. An office. There was also a pool complex with what certainly seemed to be an Olympic-sized body of water.

"Big place," she murmured as they kept going.

"Yeah."

She glanced over at Murhder. His head was down, his brows cranked tight over his eyes, his big shoulders tense.

"You look like you're trying to take *pi* out to thirty decimals."

He looked at her, his beautiful red-and-black hair hanging forward. "What?"

"Sorry. Scientist joke."

"So you were saying you've got an idea for John's treatment?"

Sarah stopped. "What's going on? Just tell me. Whatever it is, I'll deal with it."

Murhder reached out and brushed her cheek with his fingertips. As silence stretched between them, she got the feeling he was trying out lies to her in his head.

The truth, however, was what he eventually spoke: "We're running out of time."

Her first thought—her only thought—was that she couldn't leave him. Nate. John. And logic told her that that desperation was because she had no other life to go back to anymore. It couldn't possibly be because . . . she'd fallen in love with a vampire. In like, twenty-four hours.

Oh, God . . .

"I know," she said sadly.

"Come here."

When he put his arms around her, she went willingly up against his body. And the next thing she knew, they were kissing, lips melding, tongues meeting.

When they were both breathing hard, he took her hand and drew her over to a door. She had no idea where they were going and didn't care. Whatever was on the far side was dark, and that meant they could steal some private moments.

Really dark, that was.

As they were shut in together, she could see absolutely nothing, the room they had entered pitch black and then some—and oddly, she was reminded of what it was like to skinny-dip at night, your body floating in a void.

At least she didn't have to worry about sharks in this case. In fact, she wasn't worried about anything attacking them. Murhder would take care of it—and defend her.

His hands were rough as he peeled off the top half of the scrubs she'd borrowed after she'd taken a quick shower during the day . . . his nimble fingers shedding the baggy layers, finding her skin. The fact that she was blind in the darkness meant every stroke of his was magnified, and when he captured her breast in his palm, she gasped against his mouth.

She was sloppy with the buttons of his fine silk shirt, impatient, fumbling. When he helped by yanking the thing off, a tear sounded out. And then they were kissing again, the bottoms to the scrubs disappearing, his slacks getting unbuttoned at the waist and falling down to his shoes.

Murhder picked her up and she straddled his hips, his strong arms holding her off the floor. His penetration was a firebrand, nothing slow and gentle this time, his arousal entering her on a one-stroke that went so deep, she nearly orgasmed then and there. Desperate to find a good rhythm, he shuffled them over to a wall, the hard, cool surface hitting her bare back as he braced her against it. Then he pumped into her, his body working hard, churning, dominating.

She held on for dear life.

And only wanted more.

Linking her arms around the back of his neck, she put her face in his long hair. He'd shampooed it, and it was still damp underneath, and she breathed in the scent of—no, that wasn't shampoo. That was him.

And he was making that erotic sound again, deep in his throat, part growl, part purr.

When he started to release, she went along with him, their bodies going over the edge together, the pleasure so intense it was painful, the.

line between orgasm and agony mixing, the explosions inside of her racking her to the soul—

All at once, lights came on, rows of caged fixtures in the long, low-ceilinged room illuminating sequentially toward some kind of terminal point.

Target range. They were in a target range.

As they both froze in surprised blindness, Sarah shifted her arms and started patting around behind herself, trying to find the switch they'd hit.

"Oh, my God!" She pushed against Murhder's shoulders. "What happened to you!"

Staring down at his magnificent pectorals, she saw the leather thong necklace he wore with its piece of quartz in it—but that was not what she was looking at. Bruises. There were big bruises all over his chest and shoulders, the deep purple welts staining his tan skin.

"It's okay—they don't hurt."

He must have found the switch himself because they were instantly back in the dark. But when he tried to keep kissing her, she turned her head aside and pushed at him again.

"You're hurt," she said into the void. "I want to know what happened."

CHAPTER FORTY-ONE

Murhder hadn't even thought about the black and blue marks. He'd seen them in the mirror as he'd undressed in Xhex's boss's bathroom, but they were no big deal. By morning, they would already be faded—and even the bullet wound on his leg was nothing more than a surface graze. He was perfectly fine, the battle bruises nothing more or less than he'd ever gotten when he'd headed out into the field and engaged with the enemy.

"Murhder, seriously." Sarah's voice was brimming with concern. "What happened? You're hurt."

"No, I'm not."

"So that's what, paint? Come on."

He wanted to track what she was saying and respond appropriately. But she was wriggling around in his hold and that was causing the kind of fiction that males had a hard time focusing through: His cock was hard and ultra-sensitive, her core warm and tight, the slip and slide going right to his head and fritzing out his higher reasoning.

As much as he tried to hold himself back, he started to come, his arousal ejaculating in a series of pumps deep inside of her. He fought it as best he could, gritting his teeth and cursing, and when that got him nowhere, he attempted to pull out—but she squeezed her legs on his hips and arched against him, saying his name in frustration and pleasure.

He didn't mean to start pumping again, but the next thing he knew they were straining against each other, their bodies taking over, the need for the release, the joining, the connection, overriding everything else.

At least temporarily.

When they finally stopped, he relied on the wall to help him stay upright, his breath punching out of his mouth, his body throwing off all kinds of heat as he braced his weight on his arms so he didn't crush her.

He felt her hands make their way up his throat . . . to his face.

"How did you get hurt?" she said in the dark.

Not a demand. A worried plea.

Murhder closed his eyes. He wanted to lie to her and tell her he got distracted and was hit by a car—not exactly a fib, given what had happened in front of Wrath's Audience House. But that was just going to alarm her more, and he already knew that lying to her was never going to sit right with him.

Abruptly, the lights came on again, the punches of their ignitions echoing in the concrete facility. Glancing over his shoulder, he saw a lineup of shooting booths and then paper targets hanging at various distances down a target range.

When he looked back at Sarah, she was blinking in the glare, her human eyes requiring more time to adjust than his did.

With reluctance, he loosened his hold on her waist and let her disengage and slide down to the floor. She picked up her scrubs and got them back on with an efficiency that he respected. He didn't want anyone to see her naked, either.

As she yanked up the bottoms, she stared at his bare torso. And then looked into his eyes with a very clear you-better-start-talking-now-mister glare.

"I was trained to fight," he said in a dull voice. "And I fought tonight."

He pulled up the slacks and did the fly thing. Then he picked the borrowed shirt off the concrete floor and pulled it onto his shoulders. Unable to stand still, he paced up and back by the shooting stations. Each booth had ear protection hanging on a peg. Boxes of ammo stacked on the left. Yellow-tinted eyewear.

"We're hunted," he muttered with his back to her. "And not by humans. I was trained to protect the species. It was what I used to do."

"No longer, then? You're doing something else now?"

She sounded almost relieved, as if she recognized the danger he had faced.

"I'm not fighting anymore." He focused on the target straight ahead of him and hated himself. "I had a problem."

"Physically?"

Could he still shoot well, he wondered. That target was fifty yards away. There was a time when it would have been no big deal for him to hit a thimble at that distance.

He thought about that first slayer's backup nearly killing him at point-blank range. If John hadn't come along when he did, by some stroke of luck . . . Murhder would be dead now.

"What kind of problem did you have?"

"A mental one." As he touched the side of his head, he could not bear to turn around and look her in the eye. "I lost my mind. Just cracked."

"Because of PTSD? From fighting."

"No." He shook his head. "I just couldn't pull myself together anymore."

"That's not uncommon for people who—"

"It wasn't related to my job." He paused. "Xhex was sold to BioMed—you remember, she told you she'd been experimented on? Well, I was determined to find her . . . a lot of things went wrong. She ended up getting herself out and then I couldn't—I just didn't let it go, you know. I needed to make sure they didn't do anything like that to anyone else. So I kept hunting the humans who hurt her, the humans you work for."

Now, he glanced over his shoulder. "That's how I knew Nate's *mahmen*. I knew her. I failed to rescue her. But she ended up getting out and eventually found me."

"So that's why you were at the lab that night."

"Yes."

He went back to staring at the targets. It was a safer bet for keeping his composure. Sarah's eyes were too . . . kind.

"You and Xhex . . ." she started.

"We were lovers. Not any longer, though. Those times are far in the past for she and I, and there are no regrets on either side. We're just friends."

"I'm glad. Even though I have no right to be."

"You have every right."

"We both know that's not true." Before he could say anything else, Sarah crossed her arms and stared down the target range, too. "What kind of enemy does the race have?"

"Sarah . . ."

"I can't talk about us right now. I will break down in tears and I'm too tired for that. Please . . . just tell me who your enemy is."

Murhder cursed under his breath and tried to remember something, anything about the Lessening Society. "It's all a source of great evil. And by that, I'm not talking about a human with a mean streak. The Omega is much, much worse, and he can turn men into killing machines that are as immortal as he is until you stab them home. He is pure malevolence and has special powers to act on it."

When she didn't say anything, he rubbed his aching head. She was just staring straight ahead of herself, but obviously not seeing anything.

"This really is a different world," she mumbled. Then she shook herself and looked at him. "Is that what's in John?"

"I don't know. Maybe it's some version of the Omega. They aren't really telling me much."

The shake of her head was not encouraging. "I wish I had more time."

Murhder thought about what Xhex had said about Sarah, about him doing the right thing by the woman. Erasing her memory. Sending her back to her own world.

Then he touched the sacred shard of glass at his throat and looked back at the targets. He thought about getting Sarah out of that lab. He would have fought anything that came at her, protected her with his life.

Why was the Brotherhood's decision about her staying any different?

This was bullshit. She didn't have to go back, any more than the other humans working here did.

"I'm going to go talk to the King," he announced. "And change his mind. You should be able to stay here as long as you like."

There was a tense silence. And then she said the words he wanted to hear.

"I would like . . . to stay." Her eyes were pools of warmth as she looked at him. "With you."

Striding over to her, Murhder kissed her and brought her in close to his chest. "I'll change their minds. I don't know how, but I'll do it."

"Can I come with you?" she said into his shirt. "I've got some stake in all this—especially because Kraiten is going to want to take care of me—and by that, I don't mean a conventional severance package. More like my head in a box."

He pulled back. "You think you're in danger?"

◆   ◆   ◆

Fucking finally, Xhex thought as her phone went off with a text from John. It was the work of a moment for her to peel off from shAdoWs and dematerialize back to the mansion, and as she re-formed on the front steps of the Brotherhood's great Gothic manse, she didn't feel the cold at all. A combination of anger and relief made her numb.

He was back home apparently. Had been for a little while and had only just now thought to check in.

Like it was any other night. Like he didn't have that shoulder wound no one could explain or heal. Like he hadn't taken off without telling her a goddamn thing.

Racing up to the entrance, she yanked open the heavy door and shoved her face into the vestibule's security camera. As soon as Fritz opened things wide, she burst into the grand foyer, the multi-colored, Russian tsar–like interior making absolutely no impression on her at all.

"Are you looking for the sire?" Fritz said as he jumped back so he wasn't mowed over.

"John—yes, I'm looking for John."

"He's in the playroom."

Xhex stopped. "What's he doing there?"

"He just sent down an order for hot cocoa."

Xhex thanked the *doggen* and took the palace-worthy staircase two at a time. As she hung a left in front of the closed doors of Wrath's study, she could feel her temper rising, and the anger got worse as she hot-footed it down the Hall of Statues and punched through the double doors at the end. On the far side, there was what had originally been solely a staff wing. In the past few years, however, things had been renovated extensively, first to accommodate a state-of-the-art movie theater . . . and then, with all the babies that had come along, a playroom.

Striding past the entrance to the theater, she headed toward the two-bedroom suite which had recently been converted into a land of plush toys, dancing robots, iPads, Legos, art supplies—you name it, the Uncles Brotherhood had ordered it off Amazon.

She even knew what Melissa & Doug was now.

As she closed in on all the cheerfulness and whimsy, she didn't need her vampire hearing to pick up on the sounds of cooing babies and adult talk. The door to the space was wide open, and the scents suggested someone had cut up strawberries and someone's diaper was fresh: She could smell the sweetness of both—and scent her mate.

John was in there. And for fuck's sake, she wanted to march in and interrupt whatever oochie-poo, cutesy-pie conversation he was having to point out that she was being strong, she was being brave, she was trying not to freak out and give him space over the very thing that John himself was terrified about—but goddamn it, he needed to answer his motherfucking phone.

And not go out hunting *lessers* with fucking Murhder, goddamn it. When he was unarmed and injured.

And could you fucking answer your fucking phone, fucker!

But even though she had the maternal instincts of a heavyweight boxer on a good night—and this was *not* a fucking good night—she didn't want to scare the young.

"—remember, John, yes." It was Bella, Z's *shellan*, who was talking. "Mary introduced us. And I called the Brotherhood. So mysterious how it all happened."

"But how great it is." Now Beth, the Queen. "That we all ended up here."

"It was meant to be." Mary, Rhage's mate. "Speaking of which, mind if I hold His Lordship?"

"L.W. loves his auntie Mary."

Xhex slowed down. And when she got in range, so she could look through the jambs, she froze.

In the midst of a scatter of colorful bouncing balls, John was sitting up against a wall that was painted a cheerful pale blue with clouds, the depiction of a maple tree growing in bright green grass seeming to sprout out of the top of his head. With his legs stretched out in front of him, and his hands in his lap, he was nodding at the three females around him, smiling with his lips . . . but not his eyes.

His emotional grid was stained with sadness as he sat among those who had been so instrumental in getting him to the Brotherhood: Beth, with whom, as her blooded brother, he had always had some kind of special connection. Mary, who had answered his call at the Suicide Prevention Hotline. Bella, who had brought him to the training center because of that scar he'd been born with.

Only Wellsie was missing.

The females had no idea he was saying goodbye to them, Xhex thought. But he did.

She took a step back. And another. When she hit the wall across from the doorway, she linked her arms around herself and felt her heart pound with pure terror. It was one thing to read his grid and see into his soul. It was another altogether to witness him begin to get his affairs in order.

He really was dying.

As Xhex felt a pressure on the lower half of her face, she realized that her palm had somehow known that it was a good idea to cover her mouth. In the event the anguish in the center of her chest somehow escaped.

Abruptly, John shifted his eyes and looked at her.

The three females continued to reminisce about the past and the mysteries of destiny. And they passed their young around. And they smiled.

John stared out of the happiness around him with sadness in his eyes.

As Xhex's anger dematerialized as if it had never been, she reflected on the fact that when you were out of time, you found forgiveness and acceptance so much easier to give.

Bringing her hands up to the center of her chest, she moved through finger positions with deliberation.

I love you, she signed to him. *Come find me when you're ready.*

He nodded, and she took off before any of the others saw her.

It wasn't that she didn't love the females.

It's just, when you were trying on grief for size, you wanted privacy.

Kind of like when you tried on your own death.

CHAPTER FORTY-TWO

S o where are we going?"

As Sarah put the question out there, it was because she only knew part of the answer: She and Murhder were in a borrowed Volvo, and after they'd left the underground facility and proceeded through a series of very impressive gates—as well as a strange haze that was nearly impossible to see around—they were now headed toward a city which she understood to be smaller than the Big Apple, but much larger than Albany, the New York State capital.

She'd only ever driven past Caldwell before.

"The King has a place where he meets with people." Murhder glanced over. "It's in a nice part of town, don't worry."

"Is it like a court?" Images of Buckingham Palace went through her mind. "Does he have a throne and everything?"

As she pondered the possibilities, a childlike wonder came over her, but the flush of curiosity didn't last. They were going by strip malls now, and the restaurant chains that anchored the lineup of stores—Panera, Zaxbys, Applebee's, TGI Fridays—reminded her that real life was still happening, all around her.

She couldn't keep her head in the sand. She had a house. Bank accounts. Bills. Taxes, insurance . . . a car—which was still in the parking lot at BioMed. If this worked, and she could stay in his world, she was going to have a lot to clean up first.

"Do they know we're coming?" she said.

"It'll be fine."

She looked at him. "Are you sure about that?"

Eventually, they got away from the retail centers and into neighborhood territory—not that the houses on either side of the street had anything in common with where she lived in Ithaca. These were big places, set back a ways from the road, all kinds of brass fixtures hanging from porches with lots of molding and flourishes around them.

Not exactly the crib you'd expect a vampire king to hang out in, but not slumming it, for sure.

The house Murhder eventually stopped in front of was a Federal beauty that certainly looked authentic, as opposed to the result of modern builders copying the best of the past.

As Murhder turned off the engine, he stared out of the front windshield. His profile was striking, all the masculine lines of his cheek and nose and jaw an arresting composition of male beauty. And then there was his hair.

And everything he could do with his hips when they were—

Okay, not the time to think about that.

"What's wrong?" she asked.

Even though she could guess. She had the feeling that he had "borrowed" the car—as in taken it without permission on the theory that apologizing would work if they were caught in it. And she also was pretty sure this was going to be a surprise visit.

"We don't have to do this," she said. Even though she wasn't sure what their other option was.

"Yes, we do." He turned to her in his seat. "But I don't want you to find out who I really am. I want you to believe that I'm a hero. That I saved you and Nate. That I'm worth something—because I feel like if you think it, it will be true. And it's really not."

"I know who you are—"

"You don't. But you will."

At that, he opened his door and got out. As the cold air rushed in, she tried not to find portent in it, but as a tremor went through her, she had to remind herself the deep freeze was just the winter temperature. Not a hint at the future.

He waited for her as she came around the front of the car, and then they walked up a shoveled path to a door that she expected to be answered by a butler in uniform—

The heavy panel swung wide. Not a butler on the other side, though. Nope. Not unless they were arming Mr. Carsons and sending them out into combat zones fully weaponized: The male had a military haircut—with a white streak in the front of all the dark—military clothes, military boots. And dark blue eyes like laser cannons.

She had some vague memory of seeing him down in the underground facility.

"And your bright ideas just keep coming tonight," he snapped. "Are you going for some kind of award?"

"I need to talk to Wrath."

"No, you need to take her back where she belongs." He glanced over at Sarah. "No offense, ma'am."

Murhder's upper lip began to twitch. "You can't keep me from the King—"

"The hell I can't—"

Murhder stepped up into the male's face. "What is wrong with you, huh? What the *fuck* is your problem—"

"You took my adopted son out into the field when neither of you were prepared or armed and you went rogue with him." The male bared his fangs. "My *son*. Do you have any idea how important that kid is to me? There's only one person on the planet who means more to me than John does, and I'm mated to her. *That* is why I'm pissed off at you."

Murhder cursed. Stepped back.

The other male's voice dropped. "Look, I don't actually have a problem with you. What I have a problem with is the chaos you bring wherever you go. We've got real issues to deal with. Serious shit. And here you are on the sidelines, kicking up drama. It's not what any of us needs, and it's not doing you any good, either. Now, please, take her and yourself, and do what's right in both cases. Which is get gone."

Sarah opened her mouth. But before she could speak, Murhder cut in.

"Everything you say is true. All of it. And I'm sorry I took John out in the field. Just let us see Wrath and we'll go peacefully. You have my word."

"Your word isn't good around here anymore."

Sarah put her hand on Murhder's arm in case he decided to get aggressive again, and waited until he looked down at her. "It's okay. I can tell Jane everything I'm thinking in terms of John's care and she can take it from there. She's a good doctor and she'll be able to do it all." Then she glared at the military guy. "And excuse me, but you might consider the fact that he saved a boy from a human torture factory, got me out of there safely, and is the only reason your son has even the hint of a clinical solution to his mortal wound. So back the fuck off, Sergeant Know-It-All."

◆   ◆   ◆

Annnnnnd now they were in Darius's formal parlor waiting for Wrath.

As Sarah went over and inspected the floor-to-ceiling portrait of that French king, Murhder hung back and had to smile to himself.

There were not a lot of grown males who would get up into the face of Tohrment, son of Hharm. Especially when the Brother was armed and in a bad mood. Sarah, on the other hand, had been willing to risk great bodily harm to stand up for what she believed in.

Who she believed in.

Too bad the faith was so misplaced.

"This house is amazing." She pivoted on one foot. "And who would have guessed? I mean, that vampires are in a neighborhood like this. You know, I expected the King to live in a big castle up on a mountain, with gargoyles on the roof and a moat. Instead, this is something out of *Town and Country* magazine."

How am I going to let you go, he wondered.

Sarah walked over to him and took his hands. "Okay, sphinx. You need to talk to me before we go in and see the big guy. Let's just lay it all out on the table. I can tell you're uncomfortable here and around those males—"

"It's not about them. I don't care about them anymore."

"Anymore?"

"They were my Brothers. All of them. But that was a long time ago. A forever ago."

She frowned. "Family doesn't stop. There is no past tense to family, Murhder."

Murhder just shook his head. He didn't have the energy to argue the point or explain himself. Instead, he was oh, so very aware that time was passing fast and this mission to see the king, which he had started out on with such purpose, was devolving into a rock-solid hell-no that he was going to be unable to counter.

"I need you to know something," he whispered as he stared down into her golden eyes. "Even if you can only know it for now and a little bit longer."

"What?" she breathed.

"I love you." He brushed the smooth skin of her cheek. "I've fallen in love with you, and I just . . . some things need to be said, even if they're wrong."

"But it's not wrong." She turned her head and kissed his palm. "It's not wrong between you and me. None of this is wrong . . ."

Her eyes, as she looked up at him, made him wish he still believed in a higher power. Life had taught him otherwise, however, and there was no un-learning the lesson that destiny was a douchebag and loss was more likely than gain.

He placed her hand over his heart. "I am yours. And that is forever, even if your memories of me are not."

"I refuse to believe you can take all this from me." She shook her head. "How can you reach so deep into my mind, into me? You are permanent in my life. In me. And I love you, too."

They met halfway, her rising up onto her toes, him lowering himself down. And as their lips met and melded, the kiss was a kind of vow, a promise of ever after that would ultimately not be kept by her, and always kept by him.

Murhder wouldn't have had it any other way.

He would rather bear the pain of all that could have been for the rest of his nights than have her suffer even a day of that burden of grief.

Besides, he told himself that even though their love would be one-sided, better that than never-have-been.

The paneled doors slid open. Tohrment looked grim, but then again, the Brother had never been a party.

"Wrath will see you now."

CHAPTER FORTY-THREE

Okay, wow, Sarah thought as she was led into a vast, empty room that had a chandelier the size of an SUV hanging from the ceiling and a rug like a park lawn in the center. Not that she spent a lot of time checking either of those two out. Nope, pretty much the only thing she saw was the massive male sitting beside a crackling fire. Now *that* was what she'd expect the king of the vampires to look like. The male had long, straight black hair falling from a widow's peak, black wraparound sunglasses, black leathers and a muscle shirt, and a face that was cruel and handsome by turns. Tattoos ran down the insides of both his huge forearms and a large black stone glinted on one of his fingers.

The golden retriever who was curled up at his feet was a little surprising, and sure, that armchair he was parked in wasn't exactly a George R. R. Martin–worthy throne, but the impression he made was so overwhelming, you could have put him in a *Finding Dory* kiddie pool and he'd still have looked like a badass.

Oh, and the males lined up around him were no slouches, either, and she recognized the handsome blond one from her arrival at the training center. Next to him was another male with a goatee and tattoos on his temple, a stocky one in clothes that were straight out of *GQ*, and a third with mismatched eyes, purple hair, and a lot of piercings.

No one was smiling. No, wait, the blond guy with the electric-blue eyes gave her a little wave.

"So this is your human," the King said in a deep voice. "What's your name, woman?"

Sarah cleared her throat. "Dr. Watkins. Sarah Watkins."

"Nice to meet you. I understand you met our boy here when you were in the process of busting one of my civilians out of that lab. I'd like to thank you for your service to the species and for what you're doing with John's case."

"You're welcome." What the hell else was she supposed to say? "Listen, if you could just—"

The King spoke right over her—which was better than getting beheaded, she decided. "You can't stay in our world, however. I cannot allow you to do that—"

Murhder cut in. "There are humans all over your training center—"

"I *know* you did not just interrupt me," the King bit out at Murhder. Then he refocused on Sarah. "Now, I realize you mean us no harm. I can scent you." He touched the side of his noise. "You are without ulterior motive and you do not lie. But—"

"She's in danger," Murhder interrupted. "They already killed her fiancé for what he learned about the hidden lab. They're going to do the same to her. She's seeking asylum from that CEO—"

The male with the tattoos on his face turned his cell phone around. "That boy's dead. Assuming you're talking about Dr. Robert Kraiten, CEO of BioMed, he was found on the floor of his kitchen with a knife in his own hand and his lower intestines all over the place about two hours ago. So if that's the threat you're talking about, it's been neutralized."

"Goddamn it," Murhder said under his breath.

Sarah blinked. "He killed himself?"

"Gutted, I believe is the term," the vampire with the cell phone said. "And yup, did the handiwork all by his little lonesome."

"Is there anyone else you can think of from that company who'd want to hurt you?" the King asked.

"Not that I know of." Sarah shook her head. "But who can say for sure. I'll tell you one thing, I'm not working there anymore."

They weren't going to want her anyway—

"No one's going to be working there anymore." The vampire with those tattoos shrugged and put his phone away. "The whole thing is closing down. That guy with the abdominal leak closed up everything yesterday. Shut the two campuses. Sent everyone home."

Sarah could only blink as the ramifications of it all spun in her head.

"So I don't need to worry about meeting with HR," she muttered.

Shutting the whole corporation down? Made sense, and apparently, Kraiten wasn't going to be doing anything in the future but pushing up daisies. Still, what if there were other labs around the country run by other people, doing the same thing?

As she fell silent, Murhder started to argue for her safety, and immediately, the tenor in the room got aggressive, male voices raising, male bodies leaning forward. It was all the same arguments, that other humans were allowed in the world, that she was helping John, that nobody wanted attention from Homo sapiens, but exceptions had been made; they'd been through all of it before.

"This is bullshit," Murhder spat. "And it's more to do with me than her, isn't that right."

The male with the tattoos spoke up over the debating. "Finally, you get it. You're not sticking around here, big boy. So she's not. It's really just that simple."

"I can take care of her—"

"You can't take care of yourself—"

"Fuck you!"

"Stop it!" Sarah said in a loud bark. "Just *stop*."

With her head pounding and her emotions on the brink, she took a couple of deep breaths in the silence that followed. All of the men—males—were focused on her. She stared at the King.

This was going absolutely nowhere. Even though they knew she had no ulterior motive, it was very clear that they would never trust Murhder, and it was for that reason she wasn't going to be allowed to stay.

With a heavy heart, she thought about what he'd said in the car outside. That he didn't want her to know what he was really like.

The problem was more that these males didn't know who he was. But have fun trying to convince them otherwise.

"I don't want any trouble," she said to the King. "And it's not for us to second-guess your decision. I'll go back where I belong. I just— I promised Nate I would say goodbye before I left, and I want to hand over my idea about John's treatment properly. Will you permit me to do both of those things before I leave?"

The King inclined his head. "Yes. And as for the young, we will make sure he has a place in the species."

"He needs a family," she heard herself say. And then she thought of the reality that he'd never been outdoors. "Please remember, too, that he has no frame of reference for the world at large or the freedom we all take for granted. He's been in captivity his entire life. You're going to have to give him a hell of a lot more than room and board if you want him to come through what was done to him and where he was kept. That is all on you, not him. He's been through enough."

The King cracked a smile, flashing enormous white fangs. "I like you."

"Thanks," she said with resignation. "I appreciate that."

"Go back to the training center. Do your goodbyes. And then you have to go."

"Okay," Sarah said with a heavy heart. "I will."

◆   ◆   ◆

John resumed his corporeal form in the driveway of the Audience House just in time to see Murhder and the human scientist leave out the front door. As they headed down the walkway to Mary's Volvo, neither of them was saying anything, but they were holding hands, both of them focused on the shoveled snow beneath their feet.

They were not happy, and he could guess why. God, he wished he could help.

Entering through the kitchen in the back, he greeted both of the *doggen* who were making cupcakes for the waiting room, and then proceeded through to the front hall. There were no civilians hanging out in the parlor on the right, which was kind of a surprise. There was still plenty of night left for Wrath to see people.

But with Murhder here? Accompanied by the human? No doubt the place had been cleared out of an abundance of caution.

The archway into the dining room was open, the doors wide on their brass hinges, and he felt a surge of envy as he looked in. Tohr, V, Rhage, and Butch were clustered around Wrath, the five of them clearly discussing "Brotherhood business."

Tohr looked up. Smiled. Motioned. "Come on in, John."

There was a part of him that wanted to no-thank-you the invite. But what point was he proving by that and to who?

Stepping into the dining room, he looked up at the twinkling chandelier, and then down at the fancy Oriental rug, and then over to the sconces and the heavy, closed drapes.

Helluva a long way from that shitty flat he'd been able to afford for himself as a dishwasher.

"How are you?" Tohr phrased the question casually. But his eyes were too direct to carry off the no-BFD. "You look good."

Well, he'd had a shower before he'd made arrangements to see Beth, Mary, and Bella.

Wrath glanced up even though he couldn't see. As those nostrils flared, John had a moment of anxiety—and sure enough, those brows disappeared behind the wraparounds.

Could he smell the death, John wondered.

"I heard you were out in the field tonight," Wrath said. "Not the brightest idea, but I gather you were successful."

John brought up his hands and signed, *Murhder is an incredible fighter. We made a good team.*

As Tohr looked away sharply, and V translated into Wrath's ear, John continued, *Why do you all hate him so much?*

"Let's not focus on the past." Tohr presented a composed face. "I want to know how you're feeling?"

I came to see you, actually, John signed.

"Oh, yeah. Of course. You want to talk?" When John nodded, Tohr stepped away from the King, from his Brothers, and came across. "Something wrong?"

When Tohr put a heavy arm across John's shoulders, John kept a wince of pain to himself and let the Brother lead the direction—and soon enough, they were shut in a study that seemed out of an Agatha Christie novel: The oak-paneled room with the crackling fire was exactly the place all the suspects would gather at the end to hear the whodunit conclusion.

He'd learned about Agatha Christie from Mary.

"What's up?" Tohr took a seat on an oxblood leather sofa. "What can I do to help?"

John paced around. In his mind, when he'd drafted his list of people he wanted to make sure he connected with, he'd envisioned this meeting with Tohr to be all father-son poignant, the pair of them embracing. Sucking back tears. Throwing around all kinds of manly expressions of love and respect, I-was-honored-to-have-been-your-son statements volleying with you-were-the-best-son-I-could-have-had exclamations.

But now that he was here? It was sort of like it had been with the females. He'd wanted to make transcending pronouncements to Beth, Mary, and Bella, but instead, he'd just sat with them and reminisced about the beginning of things, the start of the connect-the-dots that had brought him into the household.

In these failures of dramatic emotional apexes, he felt like a kid who had imagined his own funeral—and then actually showed up as a ghost to discover that all of the gnashing and wailing he'd anticipated hadn't happened. Instead, there were just a couple of hankies out and some runny noses, and then everyone beat feet back to the house for food.

No, wait, that wasn't quite right. The failures with Beth, Mary and Bella had been on his side. Not the females'. They didn't even know he was dying, and he'd lacked the courage to tell them.

Emotion was so much harder outside of the hypothetical. When you were actually standing in front of someone you needed to say difficult things to, when your throat got tight and you felt like you couldn't breathe right, and your brain—previously spitting out sound bites that belonged on Instagram posts of beach sunsets and mountain peaks with clouds—went blank as a snow field . . . all of the Hollywood-perfect Moments That Mattered stuff ended up in the crapper.

And on that note, here he was with Tohr—and he was frustrated more than in the mood for a soul-wrenching goodbye.

Just so you know, John signed. *Murhder didn't take me out into the field. I found him fighting and I joined in. If you're counting me on the list of things he's done wrong, you need to change that.*

Tohr muttered something and looked over at the fireplace. "I swear this guy is like a bad penny. I can't get rid of him—"

John whistled so that Tohr would look back. *Why would you want to? You know there's a new enemy out there. We need fighters—we need Brothers.*

"It's not that simple, John."

Then explain the complexities to me. Explain to me why a guy who's done nothing but help people is being treated like a criminal. And as for making Sarah leave—Rhage's shellan was a human. V's, too. Payne's hellren still is a human. Even Assail was allowed to have his Sola. Why are you not letting—

"Have you ever considered the idea that Dr. Watkins is a plant? Someone who's here to gather intel on the species and use it against us?"

Wrath can scent liars. She was just here to see him. He would know that.

"Things change. People change. And Jesus, John, your own mate was in those labs for a while. You know what those humans are capable of. Why are we arguing about this?"

I was there with Sarah. I saw her with Nate. She came out of the hidden lab with him—she was saving him. Someone who wants to use us for research is not going to aid and abet an escape.

"Okay, fine, so let's pretend there's nothing wrong with her. She has no sponsor in our world. Murhder is not going to stick around Caldwell, and we do not need a random human kicking around."

He's bonded with her.

"Maybe for this ten minutes. Look, John, you don't know him like we do. Murhder is totally unreliable, and I'm not going to argue about this with you any further."

Why, because it's Brotherhood business?

"John, you know it's not that. Where's all this coming from? What has Murhder been feeding you?"

I know what it's like being on the outside looking in. It's been my whole life—and it's still true. So I feel for the male. More to the point, I don't know what the hell happened in the past, but he has been nothing but a straight-up guy to me. I'm not sure how much time I have left so I've got nothing to lose and I'm going to speak my mind, goddamn it. You all are treating him like he's the enemy.

Tohr rubbed his face like everything under his skull was aching. "John. You're not going to die from that—"

With a quick movement, John ditched his parka and yanked his long-sleeved shirt off. As Tohr hissed in shock at the ugly black wound, he leaned in, just to make sure the Brother didn't miss a thing.

Don't tell me this isn't going to kill me, okay, he signed. *And don't tell me Murhder doesn't belong back with the Brotherhood. 'Cuz both are fucking lies.*

CHAPTER FORTY-FOUR

Sarah walked into the training center holding Murhder's hand, and the feel of his big palm against her own seemed right on a lot of levels: Us against the world. We are a couple. An I Love You on both sides, not just one.

Too bad they were counting down the time.

As they were both aware of what was coming, they hadn't said much on the way back, and when they'd arrived at the series of gates, she'd distracted herself by watching as the wintery forest landscape had gotten hazy again. So strange. Like an optical illusion.

It was a shame she didn't have more time here. There was magic in this part of the world, supernatural things that she would love to have learned about, lived around, experienced for herself. In comparison, the human world seemed one-dimensional. Uninteresting. Unremarkable.

Or maybe that was the prospect of her life without Murhder.

"I'll go sit with Nate while you talk to Doc Jane," he said.

"I'll come find you when I'm done—"

Far ahead, a door in the clinical area was thrown open and the doctor in question skidded out into the hall. When she saw Sarah, she came running down, her Crocs slapping against the bald concrete floor, her scrubs and white coat flapping behind her.

"Oh, God, Nate," Sarah said. "Is he—"

"You were right!" Doc Jane took Sarah's free hand. "The blood samples were exactly what you wanted to see! The white blood cell count is off the charts, the immune activity is so strong—it's what you were hoping to find!"

Sarah released Murhder's palm. "Show me."

The two of them ran off to the clinic and all but pile drove their way into the pocket lab the facility used for rudimentary testing. Ehlena, the nurse, was smiling over by a refrigerator with a biohazard marking on it.

Doc Jane pulled a sheet out of a printer that sat on the counter. "Here are the values."

Sarah took the readings, and as she reviewed them, she had to remind herself that what was normal for vampires was not anything close to what she was used to.

"Okay," she murmured to herself. "So the immune response is striking. Evolutionarily, that would make sense. Given the amount of change in the body during the transition, infection could easily occur through leaks in the digestive tract or from the lungs being flooded. And then the white blood cell count must return to normal—let me see if I can get Nate to give us one more sample. If the count is even lower, my theory may be correct. In which case . . . we could try and trick John's body into believing it's going through the change and stimulate his immune response in that way."

Jane whistled under her breath as she leaned back against the counter by a microscope. "That could be catastrophic."

"Are you aware of the growth hormone that triggers the transition?" Sarah tapped the sheet. "I'll bet there's a pituitary trigger. It's the same for humans, except for us, HGH is secreted over time and allows for maturity to occur gradually. As you told me before, there is a similar mechanism for vampires, only it happens all at once. If we're looking to juice up John's immune system, we could synthetically trigger the change."

"What if it works, though?" Jane rubbed her neck like it was stiff. "One thing I've learned about vampires is the normal rules of medicine don't always apply. What if it kills him? Or deforms him?"

Sarah stared at the columns of numbers without seeing them. "Too bad we can't somehow test it first—"

"I'll do it."

All three of them looked over to the door. Murhder was standing just inside the lab, his big body dwarfing the space between the jambs. His eyes were calm and steady, his face composed.

Like he hadn't just volunteered to try out something that could put him in his grave. When he was perfectly healthy.

"What?" he said as Sarah and the two females continued to stare at him. "You need somebody to try it out, this transition thing. You've got to know whether it works and whether it's safe, right? Before you use it on John. So I volunteer."

Sarah cleared her throat. "This is a highly speculative theory. There are huge risks involved, and I'm not even sure I'm correct."

"So."

She put the sheet aside and went over to him. "Will you excuse us for a moment," she said to no one in particular.

Out in the corridor, she made sure the door was closed behind them. "This is inherently dangerous."

"I know."

Looking up into his handsome face, she was struck by the need to protect him from her own idea. "I can't let you do this—"

"You're not making me do anything. And by the same token, you can't prevent me from helping."

"Murhder, I don't want to be responsible for killing you. Bottom line. I can't live with that—"

"You won't remember it." He reached out and touched her face. "My love . . . you will not remember it."

Tears flooded her eyes, everything she had been holding back coming out all at once. As she collapsed against him, she cried for the loss that was coming, and the bravery he was showing, and the fact that of all the near misses she could have had in life, why . . . why did hers have to be true love?

Murhder held her until she was cried out, his hand making circles on her back, his body warming her even as she felt cold to the bone. When she finally eased back, he kissed her softly.

"Sarah, listen to me." His eyes drifted away from her, so he was focusing over her shoulder, down the corridor toward the parking area. "When I came back to Caldwell, to ask the Brotherhood to help me find what turned out to be Nate . . . I knew that afterward, I wasn't returning to where I'd been staying. I was very aware that this was the end of me, and I welcomed that. I haven't had much of a life these past two decades, and it's clear I don't fit anywhere anymore. Living in an attic in an old house, talking to bats, watching humans live their lives around me? That's all I have, and it's all I can handle. Meeting you . . ." His stare came back to her. "Oh, Sarah. You have been the best thing that has ever happened to me. But as much as I want to fight for you, for us? The King and the Brotherhood won't have it, and even though you and I could run, they'd find us. They're like that. Hell, they found Ingridge. They can find anyone. You're going to go back to the human world you're from, and I'm not going back to that attic and rot."

Wait, was he suggesting suicide? she thought with horror.

Before she could say anything, he gathered her hands, his thumbs stroking over her palms. "So let's do this one thing together. Let's you and I see if we can save John's life. And if I die? I will be at peace that I went out on a good deed, and you won't remember any of the pain. You'll be free, too. This can be our thing, our mark on this world. Even if I'm gone, and you have no memories of us, if John lives? He's proof that you and I existed."

Sarah blinked away more tears. And it wasn't enough. They spilled from her eyes and ran down her cheeks. For many couples, having a child was the way they cemented their love. She and Murhder would never have that immortality.

But if they saved John's life? His children would be theirs, in a way.

"Don't cry, my love," he said in his accented voice. "This is a better ending than I could ever have had."

It was a long time before she could speak.

Reaching up, she stroked his face and tried to remember each of his features with such clarity that maybe something of him would be left after they took her memories.

"Just so you know," she said hoarsely. "You are *exactly* the male I think you are."

CHAPTER FORTY-FIVE

G uns going off. Tight corners in alleyways. Lack of clarity in the
chaos, death a consequence of bad decision making—

"Watch out, John!"

Up on the flat screen, his avatar got drilled in the head, animated
blood going flying in a spray, the zombie who'd nailed him a good one
heading off to stalk Blay and Qhuinn.

The former was in charge of payback, leveling his virtual weapon
and drilling the animated corpse until it was so full of holes, the bitch
could have drained pasta. And the death was lit: The surround sound
speakers played a symphony of enhanced bullet discharges, all movie
magic with a deep bass and a high, tinny treble.

As John sat back against the foot of the bed, he extended his legs on
the carpet and thought that real-life gunfire sounded nothing like that.
Hollow pops, dull and flat in the ear, were more what you'd hear if it
was a handgun or a rifle. Shotguns were a little more dramatic, but
again, nothing like what TV or the big screen portrayed.

Glancing over at his best friends, he reflected that when the three of
them had started playing these kinds of video games, they hadn't known

about actual warfare. They had been pretrans in the training program, excited about the prospects of learning to fight, and getting out and engaging the enemy, and realizing their potential as males of worth.

John had been the scrawniest of them all, and a target for Lash— God, what a pain in the ass that male had been. And meanwhile, Blay and Qhuinn had already been best friends at that point, with no hint that they'd end up together permanently as mates. Which they had. After all, some things just made sense, and the redhead with the serious, earnest disposition coupling up with the hardcore, pierced wild male was one of those equations the solution of which was just inevitable.

And they were still awesome at gaming. The two of them were both leaning over their controllers, brows down, cranked thumbs and forefingers flying as they jerked from side to side.

They should be good, though. The three of them had spent countless hours sitting together just like this, on the carpet, at the base of someone's bed, bowls of nachos, bottles of Mountain Dew, and bags of M&M's littering the floor. As John remembered those times now, he reflected that it was nice to think he'd gotten some of a normal childhood after all.

Sure, it had been with vampires, as a vampire—surprise! But courtesy of Blay and Qhuinn, he had found a place to belong.

And they'd stuck with him through the transitions and their matings . . . just as he had been with them through Lyric and Rhampage's births.

As his buddies continued to play, he sat back and watched them. At least he knew that they were going to be okay after he was gone. They had each other and the twins.

"John?"

When Blay said his name, he shook himself back to the present and whistled in an ascending way, his way of throwing out a *Yeah?*

"You all right?" the male said as he put down his controller. "You're awful quiet."

I'm mute, remember, John signed with a smile.

"Ha-ha."

Qhuinn was still playing—and like a boss, shifting left and right, running his avi back and forth, coordinating his finger movements perfectly to control action on the screen.

He's really great at this, John signed.

"That's why they made him a Brother."

As Blay looked at his mate, his eyes shined with a shy love and an obvious affection, and John tried to think of the last time the three of them had hung out together. Months? Longer? There was always so much going on, especially for them with the young. There was also the rotation schedule that sometimes put them together, sometimes did not.

I've missed you guys, he signed.

Blay unscrewed the top of a fresh Mountain Dew. "It's been a while, hasn't it. Why don't we do this more often?"

Life gets in the way, John signed as he refocused on the screen.

They both started cheering for the last man standing, as it were.

It was such a shame, John thought to himself, that it took death to make him appreciate the living so much.

When he'd assumed that he had an infinite amount of time in front of him, there had been a lack of urgency to catch up and connect with those who mattered. Thanks to the sense that he could do something like this on any given night, he'd fallen into a complacency that allowed the unimportant to overshadow the truly critical.

Youth wasted on the young.

Life on the living.

"Are you sure you're okay, John?" Blay asked.

◆   ◆   ◆

"The good news is that night is almost over," Murhder said as he closed the door to the patient room. "They can't make me take you back now. I won't be able to drive you to your house in Ithaca in time."

God, he hated the idea of letting her go.

Sarah smiled a little. "No sunlight for you."

He didn't like the dark circles under her eyes, or how pale she was. As she and Jane had worked in the lab, analyzing samples and consulting with Havers, the race's longtime healer, Murhder had brought them a proper meal made to his exact specifications by Fritz. Chicken. Rice pilaf. Green beans. Rolls, and pie for dessert. Coffee.

That had been an hour ago . . . right around the time they had confirmed with Havers that a synthetic version of growth hormone, human in derivation, would at least theoretically work—and "work" apparently meant "might not completely kill the guinea pig." Not that Murhder particularly cared one way or the other.

He had fought for so long: *Lessers*, humans if he had to, his Brothers if there was an argument. After that, he had fought Xhex's relatives. Those scientists.

Insanity.

That last one had been the longest-lived of his foes.

Now, though, he was ready to put down his swords, his shield. He was prepared to lay himself bare to fate's decree for him, the life-or-death outcome not anything he had any control over—and not something he was overly worried about.

It was breathtakingly easy. And calm.

A placid acceptance smoothing choppy waters.

He refocused on Sarah. She was pacing around the patient room, and though he wanted to bring her ease, he knew better than to try to quell her nervous energy.

"Havers is sourcing the somatropin from a confidential contact at a New England hospital." Sarah put her arms around herself and continued to walked back and forth in the short space. "We should be able to get it by three in the afternoon. If you . . ." She stopped and cleared her throat. "Assuming you can tolerate it, and depending on what your body does, we can get a second dose for John."

She stopped abruptly and faced him. "Are you sure you want to do this?" When Murhder nodded, she came forward with urgency. "I need you to understand the risks here. We have no idea how you're going to react to a dose sufficient to simulate what goes on during the transition. I know you've arranged for a feeding beforehand, but this is—"

Murhder stepped up to her and put his finger on her lips. "Shh. We have some time now. Let's not waste it."

"Murhder, I'm serious. I'm worried about this. All the logical conclusions in the world sometimes make no sense—"

"There's hot water over there." He pointed over his shoulder. "How does a shower sound. I'll wash your back, you wash mine?"

She leveled a stare on him. "You're not going to talk to me about the experiment, are you?"

"Nope. My mind's made up."

Her face was still all intense, her eyes flashing, her lips pursed, but she let him draw her into the tiled bathroom. And then he was checking out the shower. The stall took up one whole wall and even had a bench. Handrails. Grips to steady oneself.

He couldn't have designed it better himself.

Sliding the glass door back, he fired up the hot water and turned to his female. "I want to taste you. All of you."

She had put on a lab coat at some point, and one by one, he unfastened the three big buttons down the front. Dropping it off her shoulders, he went for the scrubs underneath, pulling the boxy blue top up and over her head, easing the loose blue bottoms down past her thighs.

Her underwear was gone. She had a sports bra on and nothing else.

"I borrowed this," she murmured as she snapped the tight nylon band around her breasts. "They have extra ones for the trainees in case something snaps during the drills."

Murhder was totally distracted by the sight of her sex, but he got back to work with the undressing of her, sliding his thumbs under the sports bra and moving it up. As her breasts popped free, he couldn't resist. He latched on to one of her nipples, licking, sucking, kissing.

As she speared her fingers through his long hair, and urged him ever closer to her naked skin, he tore the shirt he'd borrowed in half, buttons popping off and bouncing over the tile floor, the silk ripping. He was no kinder with the slacks, yanking, jerking—

Finally, they were naked.

Under the warm spray, he found her lips again as his hands coasted over the curves of her body. Knowing this was probably his last time with her—even though it was only his third, if he counted right—he took his time, cupping her ass, kneading the flesh.

His fangs extended, and he wanted to go for her neck. But he held off.

Kneeling in front of her, he kissed his way down her abdomen, teasing her belly button with his tongue, cupping her breasts as he stared up at her.

"My Sarah . . ." he groaned as he circled her thigh with his hand. "Give me what I want."

Lifting her leg, he put it over his shoulder and went in, leading with his tongue, delving into her sex, worshiping her with his mouth. Over the fall of the water, he heard her cry his name and then she fell back into the bench.

Perfect. He had more access this way.

He pleasured her with his mouth until she orgasmed against his lips, her hips undulating, her core kissing him back as she came. And he didn't let her stop. There was too much to learn, especially as he added his long fingers, penetrating her, finding a new rhythm.

He watched her the entire time, her head back, the water falling, warm rain, on her closed eyes, her open mouth, her tight nipples and full breasts.

She was the most beautiful thing he'd ever seen.

And he wished they had more time.

CHAPTER FORTY-SIX

S arah stretched her arms up the warm tile of the shower and let her head go loose. She could not remember ever being so free with her body. She wasn't thinking about whether her breasts had fallen off to the sides, or when she had shaved under her arms last, or if the man between her legs was pleasuring her because he thought he needed to in that way as opposed to actually wanted to.

She had nothing in her mind except the sensation of his fingers going in and out of her and the way that incredible tongue of his lapped around the top of her sex . . . and then she looked down to see what he was doing.

As she met his bright peach eyes, there were too many orgasms to count that followed.

And then he stopped.

Rousing herself, she lifted her seven-hundred-pound head and tried to focus—

He was smiling at her. And not in a Mr. Lover-Lover way. In a you-are-beautiful way.

She wanted to smile back. But she noticed how long his fangs were. How hungry his eyes were. How intense his scent was.

Sitting up, but keeping her legs spread, she parted his mouth with her forefinger and stroked one of his long canines.

"I want to know what it's like." When he immediately shook his head, she said, "This is my only chance. And I know you want it, too."

His broad chest, with its strange circular scar, started to pump, and that purr vibrated up his throat. "Sarah . . ."

Resuming her sprawl on the bench, she tilted her head to the side, exposing her jugular. "Take me."

There was no way to adequately describe the erotic way his lips parted and the razor-sharp tips of his fangs flashed in the overhead light.

"I won't take too much," he vowed in a guttural voice.

"I know. I trust you."

"You shouldn't."

She shook her head sadly. "I will always have more faith in you than you do."

His eyes glowed neon as he moved up her body, taking her mouth in a bruising kiss. And then, between her legs, she felt him enter her again—but not with his arousal. It was his fingers, again. Two of them. Sliding in and out.

She should have been satiated by now, but he made her ravenous all over again.

And just as she began orgasming once more, he broke off from the kiss, and she braced herself for the penetration at her throat.

The strike did not come at her neck.

As the rhythmic constrictions of her sex filled her whole body with starbursts of ecstasy, she felt a blazing pain on the inside of her leg, where her thigh joined her torso . . . barely an inch from her pulsating core.

Crying out, her lids popped wide and she looked down to see his head lowered.

He was in her skin, in her vein, and oh, God, he started sucking, his satin lips pulling at the puncture wounds, his red-and-black hair fanning over her hips, his fingers still going in and out of her—

There were no words to describe what she felt, the overload of sensation taking her to another plane of existence, liberating her out of her corporeal form, sending her to heaven. The pain where his fangs had entered her was sharp as a knife and it reignited with every swallow he took, but the pleasure was a roar, a wildfire, all-consuming in its intensity and duration.

Sometime later, he lifted his head. His eyes were worried.

"More . . ." she said roughly. "I want more . . ."

That purr from him was so loud, it drowned out the fall of the water, and then he peeled back his lips and flashed his fangs.

This time, when he struck, she knew what to expect and she was greedy for the twin stings, well aware of the incredible pleasure that came next. He did not disappoint. More of that volcanic passion came back, otherworldly, unbelievable.

She was with another creature, something other than human. An entity capable of killing her.

Vampire.

And she loved him.

◆   ◆   ◆

Murhder only wanted to keep going. He wanted to drink from his Sarah, right next to her sex, so close he could taste her core along with her blood, for the rest of his life and hers.

But he would never endanger her.

He had to force himself to release her sweet flesh, her delicious vein—but he was rewarded with an incredible sight. Lifting his head, he found her in the thralls of ecstasy, her breasts tight, her cheeks flushed, her boneless legs loose and totally open to him.

He would keep this image of her for however long he had.

But then he had to take care of her. Her blood welled at the puncture marks he had made—the second set—and he felt the hunger for her vein rise in him again. But no. He would seal her up and give her more pleasure and then they would sit together under the warm water, holding on to each other . . . until the time came for him to try the drug.

Lowering himself back to where he had been, he extended his tongue and drew it up the twin marks he'd made in her. Lapping. Sucking. Making sure that they had closed and then licking into her sex some more just because he couldn't get enough of there, either.

Then he reared up over her, his much larger body dominating her graceful form, the predator claiming what he wanted, what he needed.

Gripping his cock, he put his head at her core and sank in deep, pushing in hard. Her breasts registered the penetration, gleaming under the spray as they moved with a bump, and he touched them, caressing the nipples with his thumbs.

Gritting his teeth, he pumped hard into her, her sex's hold tight on him even as the rest of her was lovely-loose. Reaching up to one of the rails screwed into the wall, he grabbed on tight, using it as a way to go even harder.

Just before he started to come, he pulled out and sprayed her sex, her lower body, even her breasts with his scent. Marking her. And then he reentered her and filled her up from the inside, too.

Murhder went for longer than he ever had. And when he finally kicked out a final last release, he collapsed without warning, clonking himself a good one in the head on that rail. Not that he cared.

He was breathing hard. He was dizzy. He was lost and found at once.

Sarah's lids slowly opened. And her smile was the sunrise he would never see outdoors.

Except then she frowned. "Why are you crying?"

Funny, he thought. It was the same question he had put to her before they had been together for the first time.

"Am I?" he whispered in return.

Without waiting for a response from her, he gathered her in his arms and sat them together on the tile, her in his lap. As she held on to him, and put her head on his pec, he settled back against the shower's wall.

With the warm water falling on his head, his vision was blurry and he told himself the hot trails flowing down his cheeks and off his jaw-line were just the shower doing its job.

He also reminded himself that the click fit of their bodies was momentous, but momentary.

Their meeting of souls was forever.

No matter what happened next.

CHAPTER FORTY-SEVEN

I 'm *not* going to let you say it."

As Xhex spoke in a pushy, kind of bitchy, manner, she was marching into the bedroom she shared with John. He was across the way in their bathroom, naked in front of the mirror over the sinks. He was poking at that goddamn shoulder wound, flexing his arm, turning this way and that as if attempting to measure the progression.

The area of infection—or whatever it was—was so much larger, there was no question it was getting worse.

"Did you hear what I said," she snapped.

He stopped the prodding and looked over.

Walking across to him, she put her hands on her hips and was well aware she was spoiling for a fight.

"There's *no* goodbye for you and me," she announced. "So you can just cut that shit out right now. I am very aware of what you're doing, checking in with the people in this household, going around, seeing them one by one or in groups. And that's fine. But you're *not* going to do it to me because I refuse to believe you're going to die from that thing."

When he lifted his hands to start signing, she slapped them down and shoved her forefinger in his face. "I am going to fight for you. I don't know what I have to do or where we have to go, but that"—she jabbed her finger in the direction of the wound—"is not getting in our way. It is not ending us. And you need to get on board my fucking optimism train, John Matthew. I love you. You love me. We are survivors. Do you hear me!"

Her voice got louder and louder, and she might have even stamped her boot once or twice. But goddamn it, if your mate was giving up, sometimes you needed to kick them in the can—

They think they've found a new approach, he signed. *Doc Jane and Sarah, the human. They think that maybe they can trick my body into thinking it's in the transition again, and that as a result, my immune system will respond aggressively and kill the infection.*

His hands moved super fast, his fingers flying through the positions—as if he knew damn well she was going to get on her high horse again and talk over him if he didn't get the news flash out quick.

"Wait, what?" she said, shaking her head. Like that would help with her translating the ASL. "What about the infection?"

Sarah, the scientist, believes that my own immune system—if, like, properly motivated, I guess—will win. It'll kill this. It'll fucking stop it. They just called me.

It was the very last thing she had expected him to say.

"When . . . what . . ." She rubbed her eyes to take the sting away. "I'm sorry, I—did you say they're going to try and put you through the transition again?"

That's the plan.

Xhex dropped her hands. "Won't that kill you?"

They're trying it out on someone first.

"Who?"

Murhder. John reached for his T-shirt and pulled it over his head. *Even though they're kicking him and that human woman out of here, he's still willing to put his life on the line for me. That is a male of worth right there.*

Wait . . . *what?* she thought.

"He's going to allow them to experiment on his body?" Okay, fine, totally rhetorical there. But still. "He's got to be out of his mind."

As soon as she said it, she wanted to take the words back even though she and John were alone. It just seemed disrespectful, after everything Murhder had been through. And P.S., what the fuck was he thinking?

But . . . what if it saved John's life?

"I guess he's determined to be a savior," she said in a voice that cracked.

Without realizing she'd decided to move, Xhex went over to the edge of the inset Jacuzzi and sat down. When she still felt wonky, she put her head between her knees and breathed slowly and evenly through her mouth.

Holy shit, the world was going around and around . . . and around.

John came across and sat with her. When he put his arm around her shoulders, she leaned into him, which was not something she did very often. She had always preferred to stand on her own. But God . . . she couldn't believe Murhder was rushing in and saving something again. Someone again.

Her mate, this time, instead of her. The male either had the biggest conscience in the world or he was determined to be a martyr. A *rahlman*.

"We've got to help him," she said. "I don't know how . . . but we have to help him."

◆   ◆   ◆

After Murhder dressed in some scrubs and left the patient room to go feed from a Chosen, Sarah dried her hair at the sink—and was interrupted when Ehlena knocked and came in. As Sarah cut off the dryer and got the report that the drugs were in early, she wanted to slow down time. Everything seemed to be moving so fast—which, granted, was what the scientist in her needed.

Her heart, on the other hand, just wanted things to go at a crawl's pace.

"The powder is being compounded right now by Jane," the nurse said.

"Okay. Is the OR ready?"

"Yes."

"Thank you so much."

As Ehlena left and the door eased shut, Sarah looked back at the shower and thought of what Murhder had said about the vein he was going to take from that other female. He had assured her that, as it had been at Nate's transition, there was going to be nothing sexual in the encounter, and he had even invited her to watch if that would reassure her. She'd declined that offer for two reasons: One, she trusted Murhder; and two, she was liable to get jealous.

Even though, come on, it was a medical thing, like a transfusion, for godsakes. Still, now that she knew what it was like? Watching him do that with anyone else was more than she could handle.

Heading for the door into the corridor, she found it hard to leave their patient room. There just seemed to be such a hard divide between what she and Murhder had shared here and all the unknowns that waited for them—

Murhder opened the door wide.

She stopped short. And then jumped back. "You cut your hair! Oh, my God!"

Murhder brought his palms up to his new haircut, all of his red-and-black glory gone, just a tidy little trim left behind that was lighter than what had grown out for such a long time.

"What have you done," she whispered as she put her hands to her mouth.

As he explained things—something along the lines of not having had a haircut for twenty years—all she could think of was *Steel Magnolias*. When Julia-frickin'-Roberts cut off her gorgeous mane before her transplant. Because she wanted to "simplify things."

Shortly after which she collapsed and was hooked up to all kinds of wires and her mother ended up sitting at her bedside, reading articles about makeup to her.

And then she died.

"Sarah?"

She shook herself back into focus. "I'm sorry. You're right. It's only hair."

He brushed his big palm over the short length. "It feels so silky. Try it."

She obliged, and he was right about the softness. But all she could think was that he wouldn't be around to grow it back out.

No wonder the Food and Drug Administration had such stringent rules about drug trials. What they were about to do to him was nuts— and would never happen to a human. Yet . . . even as she thought that, she had to consider the courageous cancer patients who volunteered to take the drugs she and her colleagues developed in the immunotherapy field. This was no different.

Except Murhder was not the sick one.

"It's going to be fine," Murhder said. "It's all going to turn out exactly as it needs to."

Sarah threw her arms around him and held him tight. As she put her head over his heart, she considered how she was going to feel if this test killed him: Like a murderer.

"I'm going to be fine."

She looked up at his chin and didn't want to say what she was thinking: *You don't know that.*

"Trust me," he said. "And wait, there's something I want to give you."

He eased back and reached up behind his neck. When he brought his hands forward again, the necklace he always wore dangled behind his fingertips.

"I want to give you this," he murmured as he tied it onto her.

The quartz gleamed in the midst of the leather crisscrosses that kept it in place, hanging much lower on her than it did on him. As she picked up the stone, she looked down—

Sarah recoiled and stared up at him. "It's a painting of you."

"What?"

"See?" She turned the flat stone to him. "Your face."

Murhder leaned in and stared at the thing. And then a smile, slow and sad, pulled at his lips. "That is me. And when I wore it . . . it showed me you."

"What?"

He tucked the necklace inside the scrubs' top. "It's a little piece of magic to take with you after all this."

"But what about my memories?"

"It will be a special souvenir that you were given by a mysterious man you never got to know. Every time you look at it though . . . your mind will tell you that you are loved."

Sarah grasped the thing through the scrubs.

"Come on." He held open the door. "Let's do this."

She was numb as she went down the corridor with him, and only snapped out of the dissociative state when they entered the operating room. Ehlena, Doc Jane, and their medical partner, Manny, were there, and the facilities were ready, the hospital bed under the brilliant fixture in the center of the room surrounded by monitoring equipment.

Murhder greeted the medical staff. Got up on the bed. Stretched out.

He had on scrub bottoms and a muscle shirt. When Jane suggested his chest should be bare, he sat up and peeled off the top.

Sarah went over to the bed and picked up the folded sheet that was under his ankles. Shaking it out, she draped his lower legs in it. Then she took his hand.

"The compounding is done?" she said to Jane, who nodded. "Okay, let's get a line in, the EKG set up, and the blood pressure cuff on. Ehlena, you're ready for the blood draws?" As the nurse nodded, Jane addressed Murhder, stroking his hand with her thumb. "We're going to give you a series of injections and monitor your body's response between each one. We want to see what your immune system does, but we have to be careful not to give you pancreatitis."

Or worse.

"I trust you," he said as he stared up at her.

He was so calm. So at peace.

When they'd been resting after their marathon sex session in the shower, he'd told her that if something happened to him, he'd requested that Xhex be the one to take her back to Ithaca and deal with her memories. He'd said he trusted the female. He'd also sworn that Sarah would be watched over for a while, just to make sure there was no fallout from the BioMed raid even with the corporation going under.

As she contemplated his contingency plan, she found it ironic as hell that she hoped he himself was the one who robbed her of her memories and their relationship.

Yay. What an upside.

I love you, he mouthed as he looked at her.

"I love you, too," she said as the medical staff began to hook him up to the machines that would tell them whether or not he was dying.

As she contemplated the lulls between doses being administered, Sarah truly wished she was religious, because prayer seemed like the only way she could help affect the outcome. But that was nuts.

Squeezing his hand one more time, she touched the necklace he had given her and nodded at the medical staff. "Let's begin."

CHAPTER FORTY-EIGHT

Murhder turned his head to the side so he could watch what was happening on his arm. The needle they inserted into a vein at the crook of his elbow was very small, just a sliver of metal that bit delicately into his flesh. After the thing was taped into place, tubing that ran up to a bag suspended on a pole was hooked on.

"I taste salt in my mouth," he said after a minute.

"It's the saline." Sarah smiled a little. But the lift to her lips didn't last. "Are you ready?"

"Yes."

She took a syringe out from behind her back and inserted it into a break in the IV tubing. As the plunger found home and the drugs went in, he felt nothing. Tasted nothing new. Took a deep breath.

It turned out he'd braced for naught. After twenty minutes, they took a sample of his blood from another port they'd put in his opposite arm. Behind him, a subtle beeping noise, tied to the compressions of his heart muscle no doubt, was a metronome without a symphony. Just beep ... beep ... beep ...

His back became stiff as he lay on the flat surface—no doubt everything he had done in the shower with Sarah had activated muscles that hadn't been used in a very long while. He wanted to turn on his side, but that was a no-go.

"Let's increase the dosage."

Sarah gave him more of the somatropin, as she called it, and he cleared his throat, like he was getting ready to give a speech. Sing contralto in an opera. Recite something by Robert Burns.

More waiting. From time to time, he looked over at the two physicians, the human man with the intense eyes and the female with the short blond hair. The latter had a strange scent—nothing unpleasant, but not really something that was a vampire, either. Curious, the case of this Doc Jane. She wasn't a vampire, but neither did she read as Homo sapiens. He wasn't going to ask for details, however. It was rude and none of his business.

More testing. A third dose. More waiting. More testing again.

And then a knock on the door. The human man went over, cracked things only an inch or two and spoke to someone softly. Then he went over to Doc Jane. When she nodded, he approached the bed.

"John and Xhex are outside. They want to come in and pay their respects if that's okay with you?"

"I'm not dead yet, you know." Murhder smiled. "Let's not plan my . . ."

Funeral, he thought. The word was "funeral."

For some reason, he couldn't get the syllables out. He tried again, forcing his mouth to move while he pushed air up his throat and through his voice box.

Dimly, he was aware that that metronome tied to his heart rate had sped up suddenly, the sound it released more like beepbeepbeepbeep-beeeeeeepbeep. And right after his brain registered that increase in intensity on a strange kind of delay, a wave of heat flooded his arms and legs: Starting at his fingertips and toes, the blaze rode his limbs as if they were the wicks for dynamite sticks . . . like somebody had put a match to his extremities and the TNT they were charged to ignite was stored in his torso.

His body jerked up from the table. Fell back.

So much thrashing came next.

The human man raced over and threw his heavy weight across Murhder's seizing muscular load, and straps, black and wide and linked around the table, were added before the doctor could remove himself.

A ring of fire.

Murhder was consumed in a ring of fire.

His last conscious thought was that he should focus on his Sarah. But it was too late for any kind of coordinated anything. He was riding a bucking bronco . . . and holding on for dear life.

◆ ◆ ◆

Sarah wanted to get in there. Do something to ease Murhder's pain. Give him chest compressions—even though he wasn't in the kind of cardiac distress that would benefit from that kind of thing.

And that last impulse was why she needed to hang back. Scientists who studied the immune system were not medical doctors, even if they had an MD after their names courtesy of their joint degree program back at uni.

And as for the cardiac arrest, she feared it was a case of "not yet." That heart monitor was practically tap dancing.

Sinking back against the wall, she covered her mouth in her hand and gripped his necklace with the other. Murhder was pulling against the arm restraints, great veins snaking down into his clenched hands and standing out in stark relief under his skin. His neck was the same as his head craned up off the pillow, the cords on either side like ropes pulled taut in the effort of securing a vessel against violent seas. Under the sheet she had pulled up over his legs, he was kicking and not getting far with it, the restraints down there keeping him on the table.

Jane shouted something. Ehlena rushed over with a syringe. Dr. Manello looked at Sarah.

"We need to stop. Right now. We can't take him any further without risking damage."

"I agree—"

"No!"

They all turned to the word that exploded out of their patient. Murhder's eyes were wide open and locked on Sarah. Through gritted teeth, he let out a growl of pain.

And then he said, "You keep going. You keep going . . . you keep . . . going."

The force of his will had a physical impact on her, sure as if he had stood up off the bed and rushed at her.

"*You don't stop this, Sarah . . .*"

His face was beet red, sweat beading on his brow, his jaw so tight, it seemed like it was going to snap free the tethers of its joints.

"Last . . . thing . . . I do."

Sarah looked deeply into his peach eyes, searching for the right thing to do. But then she knew that any calculation of hers was wrong. The choice had been, and was, his to make.

"Ehlena," she said roughly. "What are the blood results showing?"

"His white count is rising."

Are you sure, she asked Murhder in her head.

As soon as the thought crossed her mind, she could have sworn she heard his voice in her mind, clear as day.

Yes, I'm sure.

"Do the final dose," she said. "Now."

CHAPTER FORTY-NINE

S arah stayed right by Murhder's side. After the last push of the somatropin, he disappeared into the suffering, no longer able to meet
her, or anybody else's, stare or respond to anything. His heart rate
was all over the place. His blood pressure was sky-high. The seizures
were so bad, he snapped two of the restraints.

Eventually, the big blond warrior with the bright blue eyes had to
bring chains.

It was shortly after those metal links got put on that Sarah felt herself crumble on the inside. A trembling overtook her, as if she were following his lead in that regard, and then she couldn't breathe.

"Excuse me," she mumbled as she lurched for the door.

Out in the corridor, she wobbled and started to fall.

Hands caught her. Strong hands.

She looked up into the face of the female commando.

"I've got you," Xhex said.

Sarah wasn't thinking right. Wasn't thinking at all. She grabbed
onto those shoulders, and felt herself get hugged in return.

John was standing behind his mate, his arms crossed over his chest as if he were hugging Sarah as well, just virtually. His eyes were dark with emotion, and she could understand why. With the chains rattling as they were, it was clear Murhder was suffering—and either the male in there was going to die or John was going to have to go through it.

Calling on her professionalism—because it gave her a job, something to focus on other than the nightmare in that operating room—Sarah pulled back and cleared her throat.

"The blood tests are showing what I was hoping to see. So don't focus on how hard it is going to be for you—think about how the cure—"

John's brows dropped low, and he started to sign, furiously.

A male voice spoke up behind her. "He says he doesn't care about anything other than if Murhder is going to be okay—"

Sarah cut off whoever was translating. "I know what he said."

She turned around and was shocked to find that . . . there were a dozen males standing around in the corridor. She hadn't even noticed them, which was a surprise, given how big they all were.

In the back of her mind, she marveled at how so many different faces could show the exact same expression.

Grim terror.

"We're not giving him any more," she told the crowd. "So now we have to see how he rides it out. The white blood cell count is doing what . . . it's what I thought." She looked at John. "It's what I believe you need."

"Is he going to die?"

She glanced over at the male who had spoken. He was the one with the military haircut and the white streak in the middle of his cowlick. The one that, if she remembered correctly, she had called Sergeant Know-It-All.

"I don't know." Abruptly, she threw her shoulders back. "But I can promise you this. I'm going to do everything in my power to make sure he lives through this."

Amazing how being in service to others gave you strength you didn't know you had. Repurposed and refocused, Sarah pushed open the door and went back to the bedside.

The chains were cutting into Murhder's ankles and she grabbed two towels from a stack. Waiting until his legs went loose for a split second, she slipped them into place on both sides so the metal links wouldn't chafe his skin.

Then she resumed her watchful pose up against the wall. As he continued to seize, the medical staff monitored everything—and even though she didn't doubt their competency, nothing felt like it was enough.

◆   ◆   ◆

"We've got to kill those motherfuckers."

Out in the concrete corridor, John glanced across as Vishous spoke up. The Brother was lighting a hand-rolled, his teeth holding the cigarette in place, his glowing hand doing the duty of a Bic. His slashing brows were so low, they distorted the tattoos on his temple.

"Those fucking shadows need to be over," he muttered.

John refocused on the closed door of the operating room. It was impossible for him not to feel responsible for what Murhder was going through. Even as John knew he hadn't volunteered to get stung, his reaction to the wound . . . this shit with Murhder . . . he was never going to forgive himself if the male died on his account.

"John." Xhex's voice was low, barely above a whisper. "This is not your fault. You did not do this."

Turning his back to the crowd, so no one could translate, he signed, *They did the right thing.*

"What are you talking about?"

The rattling of chains coming through the closed door made him close his eyes. It was all he could do to keep from screaming.

Refocusing, he signed, *Not letting me into the Brotherhood. They did the right thing.*

Xhex shook her head and said softly, "What are you talking about? Every one of them has gotten injured at one time or another."

Not like this.

"Just stop," she said with exhaustion. "You're not making any sense."

He turned back around and faced the door. The bumping and slamming, the rattling, the barked orders of the medical staff on the far side of the wood panel—it was the soundtrack to a nightmare. And as he listened to the different noises, separating each component of the suffering, he felt a shift in the center of his chest.

Xhex was right. He was being ridiculous. He had fought with courage and strength, and what he had happened to him could have happened to anyone. What did it matter whether or not he was a Brother?

Murhder wasn't one any longer, and look at the male of worth he was, sacrificing himself for somebody he barely knew, putting his life on the very line.

I will fight in your honor, he vowed to the male on that operating table. *I'm going to take this cure after they're done with you, and if I live through it, I will evermore fight for you.*

Xhex tapped him on the shoulder. "I'm sorry, I didn't mean to be harsh."

I love you, he signed. *With all my heart. Always.*

His *shellan* gave him a strong hug. And then as she tucked herself against him, she trained those gunmetal-gray eyes on the door. As he studied her profile, he decided he'd been very lucky in his life. In spite of all the setbacks and the hard start, his female was his luck. She was his good fortune. She was his risen star that guided him to a safe harbor.

Looking around at the Brotherhood, at his friends, at the *shellans* who had showed up in support, he decided that, whatever higher power was up there after the Scribe Virgin's disappearance, surely it would respond to all this collective worry over what was, without a doubt, a male of worth.

Surely it would help.

Surely the one overseeing them was a savior instead of a foe.

CHAPTER FIFTY

Murhder was totally unaware of the passage of time. The roaring heat inside of him stripped everything away, and yet, as he burned in the fire, he knew he would come through. He had been here before. He had lived through what the *symphaths* had done to him, had survived the torture of his mind turning against his body—and even though this was the reverse, his body turning against his mind, he knew he was going to make it.

Strength did not exist unless it was tested.

And he had been tested before.

There was no end in sight, no hint of an easing, no relent to any of the present suffering, but there had been none of that before. That was the nature of torture—it was not just the pain; it was the not knowing when, or even if, the end was coming. But he knew better than to be-lieve in all that forevermore nonsense. There was going to be a terminal event: Either the agony stopped or he did.

And until either of those happened, it was just a miserable waiting game—that he could withstand.

Hell, the chaos in his brain caused by the *symphaths* had been much worse than all this. At least now, in the center of the firestorm, he was still himself. Even though he was blinded, unable to hear, lost in the sea of suffering, he still he knew who he was. He knew where he was. He knew why he was putting himself through this.

Most importantly, he knew who he loved.

When the *symphaths* had played with him, when they had filled his head full of terrible images and thoughts—triggers, triggers, everywhere—he had lost himself and his way. Anchorless, with nothing really significant to live for, he had floated off into an ether of madness. And afterward, when it was over, he had not been able to find his way back.

No matter how hard he had tried to *ahvenge* Xhex.

Now, however, this kiln of incredible heat, coupled with his bonding for Sarah, forged him like steel, the remaining scattered parts of him uniting and hardening . . . baking into an unassailable whole . . . sealing up, the cracks gone.

His foundation once again became solid and strong in this second transition of his.

The instant the conviction arrived unto him, he snapped free from his spasming body, his soul floating up over the table he was tied down on, his closed eyes nonetheless seeing his arms and legs strain and jerk, his ribs pump from hard breath, his head thrash.

He watched himself.

And the medical staff. And especially his Sarah. She was right by him, standing next to him, hand on his shoulder no matter how much his torso twisted and pulled. She was his angel, making sure he came through.

I'll be back soon, my love, he said from his lofty observation. *I'm here with you now—*

Sarah looked up abruptly, sure as if she heard him.

I'm coming back. I promise . . .

◆   ◆   ◆

The next thing Murhder was aware of was silence. Stillness.

He came awake, but it was inside the cage of his body. His eyes were closed—either that or the blindness he'd experienced was permanent—and he couldn't really feel the bed under him. He did even know if he was having seizures anymore or not.

Beep. Beep. Beep—

His lids lifted slowly. All he saw was white, and for a moment, he thought, *Goddamn it, I've died. This white landscape is the Fade.* After all his "I'm going to make it through this," he'd ended up dying—

Sarah's face appeared above his own, and blocked out the brilliant light. "Hi," she said softly. "You're back."

Murhder started to smile. He wasn't sure exactly how well he managed it. His mouth felt loose as yarn.

"Back . . ." His voice was like sandpaper. "Back to you."

She was gentle as she brushed his newly shorn hair at his temples. "You were so brave."

"What . . . happened? Results?"

"It looks good. It looks really promising. We've ordered a second set of the drug. Havers said he should have it by nightfall. If I'm right, it's John's best shot at a cure."

"You're . . . going to be . . . right."

As Murhder's eyelids became heavy as garage doors, he fought to keep them open.

"It's okay," he heard her say. "You rest."

"Stay . . . with me?"

"You bet your life I will."

◆   ◆   ◆

Second time was the charm. This time, when awareness returned to him, his sensory functions were much more normalized: He knew he wasn't having seizures, he could feel the bed underneath his body, and his hearing was back.

His eyes popped open. He took a deep breath. And he sat up, rising off the thin pillow, the hard mattress.

"Sarah?"

He glanced around—ah. There she was. On the floor, curled on her side against the wall, hands tucked up under her neck, a security blanket of her own making. Her hair had fuzzed out from her pony-tail, wisps touching her face, and her features were tense as if, even in her repose, she was waiting for bad news. Worried about him. Worried about John.

Murhder looked down at his legs and wondered whether they were going to hold his weight. There was a sheet covering him, and he lifted it aside—only to stop. There were terrible marks on the front of his calves, the twin lines of bruises standing out bright purple and deep red.

It made him remember the fire. The kiln.

He smiled. After two decades of floating, he was now firmly on the earth, thank you very much. Granted, he wasn't sure he could stand up, but that was only one measure of being grounded.

His thoughts were clear as they had been before everything had happened up at the *symphath* colony. The artificially stimulated change had been the last part of the cure he needed, the final piece to making him whole, the unexpected blessing that had finished the job.

Now, let's try for some footwork, he thought as he moved his legs off the table one by one. His joints felt like they'd been over-oiled. And he had wires still attached to his chest. Glancing over his shoulder, he checked out the front of the monitor and located the off button. The machine went silent and dark when he pushed the thing, and he re-moved all the sensors that had been clipped on his chest via pads that had been stuck on him.

They'd already removed the IVs. Good.

The tile floor was cool under his bare soles, and he was relieved when his legs held him up. Baby steps. Little, shuffling baby steps. And as he lowered himself down next to Sarah, he used the wall like it was crutches, buttressing himself on the way to the tiled floor.

Sarah woke up just as his butt hit proverbial pay dirt, and she sat up like an alarm was going off.

"Hi," he said. "That's the first word you spoke to me afterward, by the way. Or at least, the first one I heard."

"How are you feeling? Do you need me to get the—"

"Just you. That's all I need."

He lay down with her, spooning her body so that he was her wall to lie against. Sure, they could have moved to that room they'd been in before, or gotten up on the bed under the bright lights. But all that was too much like work. He was bone-tired.

As she settled in against his chest, using his arm as a pillow, she said, "They're administering the drugs to John as we speak."

"God, I hope it works."

"Me, too."

"Murhder?"

"Hmm?"

"You were very brave."

"I'm going to will the lights off, 'kay?"

At his command, the big eight-light chandelier in the center—the one that had made him think he was in the Fade—extinguished. And then the ones along the ceiling followed. He kept the line under the cupboards as it was, the glow making everything seem a little less medical.

"You were so brave," she murmured.

"So were you."

Murhder closed his eyes and let out a long exhale. He only had some vague memory of his first transition; it had been centuries ago, after all. But he did recall this loose, logy feeling after it had been over, like post-feeding satiation times a thousand. What he hadn't had back then, though, was a female like Sarah to cozy in against, to hold, to love—

Woman, he meant.

Not female.

The reality of their situation, eclipsed by all the medical drama, returned in a rush, as if it were pissed at him for having been distracted. And as Sarah let out a yawn, and pressed a kiss to the inside of his elbow, his eyes popped open again.

The dimness was no longer a reassuring camouflage that smudged the fact that they were in an operating room.

It was a reminder that night would fall, if it hadn't already. And they would have to go their separate ways.

His recovery might buy them an extra twenty-four hours. But courtesy of the Chosen who had given him her vein, he was fully strong and he would be fully recovered very soon. Whether or not John was cured of his infection, Sarah was going to have to go home.

And so was he.

Closing his eyes again, he drew his woman to him and held her even tighter.

This was the longest goodbye he'd ever had. Then again, it was going to last his lifetime.

CHAPTER FIFTY-ONE

As night fell the following day, Sarah wiped the tears from her eyes and knocked on the patient room next to the one she and Murhder had moved into after they'd left the OR. At the moment, her male was taking a shower, and then . . .

Well, she didn't want to think about that.

"Come in."

Pushing things wide, she stepped into the room. Over at the bed, a clutch of medical staff in blue scrubs was around John's head, with Xhex and Tohr on the other side. Everyone was leaning down over the recumbent patient, and the tableau reminded her some of the pietàs she'd studied during her one art history class in undergrad.

I am not part of them, she thought.

But she was involved, and she thought of her work with the war on cancer. Her drugs, her theories and experiments, brought her into countless scenes like this around the country, around the world.

It was important work. Even without Murhder, she had important work to do.

As a hollow feeling sunk in at the center of her chest, she took a deep breath and—

Xhex looked up. Motioned urgently. "You've got to see this!"

Sarah gathered herself and went over to the bedside. As she approached, everyone straightened and she had a full view of John. The male looked like he'd run a marathon and then bench pressed a couple of houses: He had dark circles under his eyes, he seemed to have lost forty pounds of body weight, and his face was waxy. But he was smiling. Oh, how he was smiling.

The wound on his shoulder was half the size it had been, the black infection retreating like enemy forces being overrun by a strong defense. In the area where it had previously extended, the skin was puckered, as if it had been burned, but the color was normal—and that ring of healing seemed to be increasing in size before her very eyes—

John extended his long arms, and at first, she was confused who he was reaching for. But then she realized it was her.

The medical staff backed up and smiled as she went to him, bent down and gave him a hug.

"I'm so glad you're getting better."

As she straightened, he started to sign and she focused on his hands as they smoothly moved from position to position.

Xhex started to translate, but Sarah stopped her. "He says he owes me his life and he's grateful." She shook her head. "You don't have to repay me anything. I'm just glad the hunch paid off."

Xhex cleared her throat. "I'm grateful to you, too."

"Make that three of us," Tohrment said roughly.

Sarah felt her face get hot. "Like I said, I'm just glad my extrapolation worked out."

There was conversation at that point, with John looking at Tohrment and signing, the other male smiling and saying that yes, John would be allowed out in the field as soon as he was medically cleared. Then Doc Jane and Manny talked about John's test results, all of which were trending positively.

Sarah said some things back to everyone. She wasn't sure exactly what came out of her mouth because it was hard to internalize all of the gratitude that continued to come her way. And then she was very aware of needing to depart before her composure cracked.

As she took her leave, she was also very aware that it was a goodbye instead of a see-you-later situation. But she wasn't going to bring any of that up. They were all having a profoundly happy moment and there was no reason to darken it. Besides, she didn't imagine they were going to miss her much after tonight, and no, she wasn't being mopey. The reality was, she was an outsider, whereas they were family.

Back out in the corridor, she paused by the door to Nate's room. He was staying in the training center until housing arrangements could be made, which was fine. But she was a little concerned that he didn't seem to want to leave the four walls he'd been in since he'd arrived at the facility. It wasn't like she didn't get it. He had been kept in a small space his whole life in that lab. The room he was in now replicated that experience to some degree. He had to branch out, though.

"You can come in," his voice said through the door.

She pushed the panel wide. "How did you know it was me?"

Nate touched the side of his nose. "Good sniffer."

Sarah went over to the bed and took his hand. As she smoothed his big palm, she worried about him as if he were still the young boy she'd assumed he was when she first saw him in that cage.

"I'll be okay," he told her.

"The Brotherhood will take good care of you." She'd just learned what they were all called. "You will not be alone."

"I wish you could stay."

"Me, too."

The next thing she knew, she was giving him a hug.

"I'm scared," he said hoarsely. "I don't know how to be in the world . . ."

"You're among friends." She eased back and put her hand on his shoulder. "You're stronger than you know. Trust me."

There were tears on both sides as they fell into silence. And then she had no choice but to hug him one more time and leave.

Outside his room, she took a moment to pull herself together and she thought of something she had heard about friends. Some were in your life for a season. Some were in your life for a reason. And then there was, of course, the third grouping: The lifelong relationships that you carried through all seasons and all reasons.

Murhder stepped out from the room they'd shared.

He was dressed in surgical scrubs again, as was she, the default wardrobe doing absolutely nothing to conceal how well he was built, how tall he was . . . how strong his shoulders and heavy his thighs were. She was still having to get used to his short hair, but she found him as handsome as ever.

"Hi," he said quietly. Like they hadn't just parted twenty minutes before.

"Hi."

They both opened their mouths to speak at the same time, but no words came out on either side. And then John's door opened and Tohrment stepped out, pulling things shut behind himself.

Murhder threw up his hands. "Christ, I'm going, okay. I'm leaving and taking her with me, just like you want, so you can back off as we wait for the car—"

The Brother marched up to him and Sarah stepped back, intending to go for the medical staff when the fight broke out.

Damn it, this was not how she wanted to leave things.

◆   ◆   ◆

As Tohr came at him like a tank, Murhder fell into his fighting stance. He couldn't believe, after everything the last twenty-four hours had brought, that the Brother was going to run at him like this—in front of Sarah, right outside from where John was apparently surviving that infection, right next to Nate's room—

The powerful arms that shot around him did not twist him into a choke hold. They didn't throw him against the concrete wall. They weren't a precursor to punches thrown.

Tohr embraced him, bringing him up against a body that was trembling so badly, it was a wonder the male could stand.

"My son . . ." the Brother said hoarsely. "Dearest Virgin Scribe, my son . . . you saved my son."

The scent of the male's tears was like the seashore had come into the underground training center, and as Tohr dropped his head on Murhder's shoulder, the Brother wept openly.

Murhder slowly raised his hands and put them on the other male's back. And then he was not just holding Tohr in return, but holding him up as he sagged.

"Your son is all right," Murhder whispered. "Your son is going to be okay . . ."

The outpouring of the Brother's relief was so extreme, it was hard to comprehend. But there was no reason to question its sincerity. And Murhder was more than willing to be patient with all the emotion. Even though he and Tohr had had their conflicts lately, how could you not give the guy a break?

Eventually, Tohr eased back. Stepped back. Scrubbed his face.

When he refocused on Murhder, he looked a thousand years old. "I lost one young. I lost . . . one son." His voice cracked. "I couldn't have withstood losing another. I know John was Darius's by blood, but he's mine in my heart."

"Wait, he's Darius's son?"

"Yes."

"God . . . no wonder." He thought of the male emerging from the darkness in that alley . . . and how he had mistaken the son for the sire. "He fights like Darius did. And, ah, I didn't know . . . I didn't know that you and Wellsie . . ."

Tohr wiped his shirtsleeve over his eyes. "They killed my *shellan*. The *lessers* did. And she was pregnant with our son when they put their bullets into her body."

The strangest feeling came over Murhder, a combination of ice-cold numbness and hellfire passion.

"Oh . . . shit. Tohr . . . I didn't know."

"John is the only living son I may ever have. That's why . . . when I found you out with him in the field when he was injured as he was— that's why I lost it. I'm sorry about that. My emotions got the best of me."

Murhder reached out and put his hand on the warrior's shoulder. "It's all forgiven. I totally understand."

Absently, he was aware that Xhex had joined them in the hall. No doubt the *symphath* had felt the disturbances outside John's room, and now she was on the sidelines, watching everything.

Down at the far end of the corridor, by the parking area, the steel door opened and Fritz came in, his hoppy little stride as he approached them suggesting that he remained full of youth in spite of his deeply lined face. And his approach seemed to reset the emotions in the group, everyone reining themselves in.

"I have brought the car around for you, sire." The butler smiled as he stopped in front of Murhder and bowed. "When you are ready."

"Thanks, Fritz."

Xhex looked at Sarah. "Do you have everything?"

"Yes. Except I left my backpack in the—"

"I'll go get it," Murhder said, and ducked into their room.

There was an awkward moment. And then he was back with her things.

Sarah seemed to force her smile at Xhex. "Doc Jane and Manny know everything I do. Havers is on call to consult if there is any change. But I really think everything's going to be fine."

As those names rolled off her tongue—like she'd known the cast of characters for her whole life—Murhder was struck by a profound sadness.

Then there were hugs. Between the two females. Between him and Xhex. Not the *doggen*, though. Fritz would have fainted at that kind of attention. There were also official words of thanks to Murhder from the King, from the Brotherhood. To Sarah, as well.

Next thing Murhder knew, he and Sarah were walking off alone. Heading for that steel door. Leaving the rest of them behind.

He could feel the stares on his back, but he didn't turn around.

Instead, he reached for Sarah's hand. At the same time she reached for his.

CHAPTER FIFTY-TWO

When Sarah and Murhder drove out from the training center, she took solace in the fact that the drive from Caldwell to Ithaca was a good two hours. At least. One hundred and twenty minutes. At least. Seven thousand two hundred seconds.

At least.

And yet, all that time later, as she pointed out her little house on her quiet street, and he pulled into her short stack driveway, and put the fancy Mercedes in park . . . it seemed like the trip had taken only a nanosecond. No longer than a blink or the beat of a heart.

"So this is my house," she said. Stupidly.

Except even as she spoke the words denoting property ownership, she felt like she didn't recognize anything about the arrangement of windows, the peak of the roof, the bushes which she herself trimmed once a year in August.

Had she really been living here? Had she actually bought the place with Gerry?

God, Gerry. Her life with him was a century ago. Or longer.

"Do you want to come in—"

"Yes," Murhder said. "I do."

They got out together and walked up to the front door. She'd cleared the pathway a couple of days before she'd left and there was new snow buffering the previous hard cuts she'd made with her shovel. Opening the storm door, she propped it wide with her hip and started to unzip her backpack.

"I've got to find my keys." She glanced at Murhder. "It'll just take me a sec."

"I'll bet I can open it."

As she stepped aside and kept rummaging around, she didn't particularly care if he shouldered the door open and broke all kinds of things in the process. Nothing about the house seemed to matter—

The door opened of its own volition, the lock retracting itself, the wood swinging wide from the jambs. Inside, her alarm started to beep.

"Wow," she said as she hustled in and went for the kitchen. "You're very handy."

The security pad was in the back, by the door into the garage, and as she came up to it, she wondered whether or not she'd remember her code. But then her fingers made the familiar four-digit pattern: 0907. The day she and Gerry had met in a biomechanics class.

Hitting the pound key, the beeping was silenced, and she looked around. Walked around. Was so surprised to be in the house at all.

She'd expected to get arrested when she'd left. Or worse. Who'd have thought what actually happened would be so much more dramatic than either of those anticipations.

Murhder was standing by the front door, which he'd closed, and she wasn't sure who was following whose example with the taking-in-the-four-walls-and-a-roof routine: He was looking all around at her things.

Sarah shook her head and went over to the sofa. The throw blanket was wadded up from one of her sleepless nights, and she folded it carefully, laying it on the back cushions.

"This is like being in a furniture store," she remarked as she plumped the pillows.

"I'm sorry?"

She wandered over to the armchair that faced the gas-powered fireplace. "I've never been big into decorating or anything. Gerry and I . . ." She cleared her throat. "He and I got that couch with these two chairs and the coffee table when we went to Ashley Furniture. They were having a sale and we both thought it was so much more efficient to buy a room's worth of stuff. I can remember walking through the store and looking at the displays. It was totally overwhelming and utterly banal at the same time. Eventually, my eyes just glazed over and thank God he happened to stop in front of all this." She looked up at the ceiling. "Same thing with the bed set. Two side tables. A dresser. Headboard."

"You're ahead of me already," he murmured. "I've never bought furniture."

"Sometimes you luck out." She couldn't keep her smile going for very long. "Anyway, coming back here feels just like being in that store. It's nothing but a space crammed with useful objects I don't feel connected to. Except . . . I live here."

When he didn't say anything, she looked his way. "I'd give you a tour, but . . ."

Murhder came at her on long powerful strides and she was ready for him, lifting her mouth for his kiss, throwing her arms around him. They were desperate and rough with the scrubs they'd borrowed, yanking, pulling, throwing, and then they were on that anonymous couch she'd gotten so many years ago with a different man.

Who turned out to be a stranger.

Her hands stroked through Murhder's downy soft short hair. Then she ran them down to his shoulder blades. Caressed the ridges of muscle that wound themselves like rope around his torso. Gripped his hips.

As she split her legs and offered herself to him, he thrust in hard, going deep, making her cry out.

The rhythm was punishing. Just as she wanted it to be.

She was hoping that if the sex was heavy-duty enough, it would make it impossible for him to erase their last time together.

* * *

Murhder felt Sarah arch as he penetrated her core. He was too rough, he knew he was being too rough ... but he couldn't stop, and she didn't want him to. She was talking in his ear, begging ...

"Harder ... do me harder."

He pulled her leg up, and shifted the angle, going even deeper. And as he pounded into her, the sofa moved across the rug, leaving tracks in the nap. Something fell with a crash. Her hair tangled.

She orgasmed. He did. They did together.

He wanted it to last forever. But the sex was over way too soon.

To make sure he didn't crush her—something he always worried about—he put his weight on the arm of the sofa, and he stroked her hair back. Her honey-colored eyes were sad even as her face was flushed from the pleasure and the exertion.

"I'm sorry," he said.

"For what?"

"Everything."

As they both became very still and very silent, her eyes searched his face. "Don't do it. Don't take my memories from me."

"I have to—"

"Says who?" she cut in. "I promise I will not reveal anything I saw or learned. I don't even know where that training center is. I am going to go my own way and will never bother the race again. I swear to it."

"Sarah ..."

"Listen to me. If you take my memories, you're the only one who suffers. That's not fair. But more than that, if I can't be with you? Let us be united in our grieving. Let us be together that way."

"It's easier for you if I—"

"I don't want easy. I want you. And if I can't have you, then I want to remember you for the rest of my life. Besides, you're taking something that doesn't belong to you in service to people who you're no longer tied to."

"I don't care about them. All I'm thinking about is how much I'm going to miss you—and how I can spare you that."

"Don't do it. You have my word. I will not look for you. I will not look for them. So in this regard, no one will ever know." She held up his necklace with its sacred shard of glass. "But I will know who gave me this. And I will know who loved me."

Murhder sat back, his softening arousal slipping from her and hating the cold of the outside. As she closed her legs and tucked them up, she pulled the throw blanket she'd just folded over her nakedness, and though he wanted her warm, he hated that he could not see her body.

"I've taken some of your memories already, Sarah."

She sat up. "When? And which ones."

Murhder looked across the sofa. She was upset and he didn't blame her. And instead of explaining, he entered her mind with his will and found the patches, releasing them.

She hissed and dropped her head into her hands as if it ached. After a moment, she raised her eyes to level again. "The FBI agent. Who came by my house and asked me about Gerry."

"I couldn't risk you contacting him while you were entering our world. I didn't know what your motivations were and there was too much risk. Too much to be exposed."

"Is there anything else that you hid?"

"No."

She seemed to wait for him to say something. When he didn't, she murmured, "You're not going to do it, are you."

He had to look away. His ties to the Brotherhood were deeper than he'd realized; the idea that he'd given his word to Tohr, to the King himself, still meant something even if he wasn't one of them . . . even if he wasn't in their world any more than Sarah was.

Old habits died hard.

But Sarah meant more to him than his word to those males. And even though he knew damn well it would be so much easier on her— better for her—to resume her life without any conscious knowledge of him or his species, he would not, as she had rightfully pointed out, take something from her that was not his to remove.

That was a violation.

"No, I'm not going to."

"Thank you," she breathed.

"I can't come see you, though. I will always want to and I will always miss you. But the Brotherhood would know. They know everything. They'll check on your house to make sure I'm not around. They might even monitor you for years to come—I mean, you've seen the training center. You know what kind of technology they can afford. If I show up in your orbit and you recognize me? God only knows what they'll do."

"I won't bother anyone, I promise."

There was a pause. And then he asked, "What are you going to do?"

Sarah's eyes went to the fireplace and fixated on it as if there were flames in there. "I have a standing offer to interview out in California. I may go work there. I don't want to be here in Ithaca anymore—and I'd kind of reached that decision before . . . you know, all this."

Everything in him wanted to say that he'd go out west with her. That he'd find her there. That he'd . . . be with her there.

"With Kraiten dead," she continued, "and BioMed closing, all I was worried about is a non-issue."

"If the FBI comes to you, you can't—"

"I know." She looked back at him. "I mean, I feel like I have friends in your world. Jane and Manny and Ehlena. John and Xhex. Nate. And then there's you . . . I would never endanger any of you. Ever. I've seen how the human race treats your kind, and it's an abomination."

As she stared at him, he felt so responsible for how this was all ending. Maybe if he hadn't so impulsively gone looking for Xhex all those years ago. . . if her relatives had not taken control of his mind . . . if he hadn't come out of the colony obsessed with finding her . . .

If he hadn't taken responsibility for what she'd done at that first lab and then done the same kind of thing himself at the second.

Maybe the Brotherhood wouldn't be so . . .

What did it matter. However he and Sarah had come to be at this point, here they were.

"I should go," he said in a voice that cracked.

They leaned in and met halfway, their mouths finding a kiss that shattered his soul. Then he cradled her to his chest.

Of all the suffering he had ever been through, nothing compared to this.

CHAPTER FIFTY-THREE

D awn arrived in the way of the winter season, the sun on a quiet, slow approach low on the horizon, as opposed to summer's brilliantly streaming pop-up sunrises.

As the weak frosty light bled in through the drapes in Sarah's living room, she turned her head and played a little game trying to guess what time it was. Not that she really cared.

Seven-ish, she decided.

As things got brighter outside, she continued to stay where she was, on the sofa, still wrapped up in the blanket. She had some vague sense that her toes were cold and her shoulders, too. But she was disinclined to do anything about it.

Next door, she heard her neighbor's garage door go up. Moments later, their sedan putt-putted down their driveway in reverse, the tires crushing the ice pack of treads. She couldn't see out into the street from where she was sitting, but she knew when the car went by her house and sped off, another workday ahead for them.

What day of the week was it, anyway?

Dragging herself to her feet, she went around the sofa and nearly burst into tears as she saw the track marks the piece of furniture had left in the carpet from when they had made love and things had gotten pushed out of position.

She left the sofa where it was even though the thing wasn't lined up properly anymore and ordinarily, wonkiness wasn't something she could tolerate.

Tucking the blanket around herself, she headed for the stairs, but stopped by the front door. Her backpack was set down by the jambs. He'd obviously brought it in for her, not that she'd noticed.

Even though there was a temptation to leave the thing where he had last put it, she picked the backpack up and carried it to the second floor. As she got to the top landing, she looked into Gerry's study. Seeing the desk where he had done his work was a reminder there were things she had to take care of. Obligations. Loose ties.

Phone calls to make. A few personal things to pick up at the lab.

And then there was her car in that parking lot.

The former she could maybe leave behind, but her car she was going to need.

In her bathroom, she dropped the backpack on the counter and started her shower. She should probably eat something. But God, that felt like an insurmountable obstacle course of what to choose, where to find it—and then, fuck, the chewing.

Too much like work.

Under the spray, she tried not to think about what she and Murhder had done in that hospital room's shower. And when she stepped back out and toweled off, she tried not to think about everything she had just washed off of herself.

Little by little, she was losing pieces of him. Of them together. Of her happiness.

She was familiar with this phenomenon. After Gerry had died, she had monitored the gradual forgetting. Like the first night she was able to sleep through. Or the first day she didn't think of him at all. Or the first week she went without tearing up.

This was going to happen with Murhder, what she had refused to let him do to her mind on a oner occurring anyway because of time's passing.

But at least now it wasn't going to be a complete erase.

As she got dressed in front of her bureau, she felt as though she were putting on a stranger's clothes. And as she brushed her wet hair out and tied it back, there was a stranger staring at her in the mirror. And when she went over and sat down on her bed to use her landline, she didn't remember what the switchboard number at BioMed was.

That last one wasn't a very material lapse as it turned out. She managed to recall the digits after a couple of pattern tries on the number buttons, but just got a recorded message stating that the laboratory was closed.

She did find something interesting on her own voicemail. Her colleague from Stanford was looking to meet with her, and not just for networking. He had a real-life lab position that was opening up.

She'd have to think about that.

Before she left her room, she went over to the duffel and decided to empty it so she had something to put the few personal effects she had at her workstation in. And there might be employee severance packets or something.

Who knew. Who cared.

Unzipping the top flap, she—

Murhder's scent, that incredible dark spice that she loved so much, wafted out and she had to blink quick as her eyes watered from sadness. It was a good minute before she could start the unpacking, and as she took her clothes out, the shirt and the pants, the sweatshirt, the bra—

"Oh . . . God . . ." she choked.

With a hand that shook, she reached in and pulled out a thick length of braided rope.

It was black and red, and tied on both ends with leather strapping.

Murhder's beautiful locks.

Running the heavy weight through her hands, she collapsed backward onto the floor and lowered her head. He had cut it off for her, she realized.

He had wanted to leave her something more of him, even if they could not be together.

There was no blinking away anything as she cradled the unexpected gift to her heart and then touched the necklace he had tied around her neck. The talisman and the braid were all she had of him.

Sarah wept until she felt sure that her soul cracked in half.

◆   ◆   ◆

The attic in Eliahu Rathboone's house still smelled the same.

As Murhder sat at the trestle table, his sole companion was a single candle in an antique holder that burned steadily before him. The small flame that hovered at the top was unmoving, the yellow glow perfectly round at the bottom where it fed upon the wick, the tip like that of a paintbrush's fine point.

The softness of the light made him think of the head of a dandelion gone to seed, downy and gentle.

Down below, he could hear humans moving around in the house. Doors shutting. Voices trading places in conversation. Footsteps. The fact that this was their active time, that these daylight hours he could not safely enjoy were the basis of the men's and women's lives, was a reminder of the divide that existed between the species.

The divide that could not be crossed in his and Sarah's case.

There was a cheap pen on the old wood panels of the table and he picked it up. Blue ink, its plastic body marked with the logo of an orthodontist's office in Virginia. The thing had been left behind by a guest, and he had used it to sign those papers Wrath had wanted executed.

The guests did that often—leaving things behind, that was, the incidentals forgotten in their haste to repack what they'd brought with them on their break from their normal lives. The lost-and-found down at the front desk was a series of Rubbermaid bins tucked under the check-in counter into which all manner of human detritus was stored in the event the owners called looking for their sunglasses, reading glasses, regular glasses. Sweaters. Socks. Retainers and bite plates for teeth. Keys. Belts. Books.

He had always told the people who worked for him to send the things home as requested, no matter if the postage required was greater than the intrinsic worth of the object.

As an exhile from what he considered his home in the Black Dagger Brotherhood, he had always felt badly for the objects left behind.

Staring into the flame, he pictured Sarah's face with all the specificity his memory could provide, everything from the curve of her lip to the arch of her brow, her nose, that beauty mark on her cheek. He had never seen her with makeup on. Her hair done up with false fancy. Her body clothed in the distraction of "fashion." She had never presented herself as anything other than exactly what she was, and he had loved her for that and so much more.

But what would have happened to them in the far future, as his much longer lifespan outpaced hers? And what of her family? He knew her parents had both passed—she had shared that with him during one of their quiet times—but surely she had friends. More distant members of her bloodline. Acquaintances.

As his mind churned over everything she would have had to give up to be in his world, he knew he was trying to find footing in the reality that they were not together.

Great loss, like death, required time to become real. The brain needed to get trained in the absence, the never again, the there-but-now-gone.

Emotions, after all, could be so strong that they could warp reality—not in the sense that mourning could resurrect what had been lost, but more like grief could sharpen recollection to such painful degrees that it was as if you could call the person to you, touch them . . . hold them.

The brain had to learn to accept the new reality.

Sarah, his love, was a human he could not have. She might as well have died.

And he should have taken her memories. That had been a mistake. She had weakened him with her logic, but he should have done the right thing even if she hadn't wanted it.

Except Tohr was right.

Murhder's nature was that of impulse, and it was because of this, as much as his insanity, that the Brotherhood had kicked him out: He had never bowed to even their loosest rules, even as he had fought beside them in service to the race.

He had been born a loner.

And he would die one, as well.

Sitting back in the spindle chair, the creaking wood was a loud, familiar sound in the silent attic and he reflected on how he had been right. When he had headed up to Caldwell, summoned by Ingridge's letters, he had known he wasn't coming back . . . that he was on his final mission.

His premonition had proven to be too right.

As a bonded male without his mate? He was dead, even as he had a heartbeat and could still draw oxygen.

The fate he had known was coming had in fact been realized. And as for committing suicide? Given how numb and cold he was . . . that seemed just plain redundant.

CHAPTER FIFTY-FOUR

I thought this place was closed? Didn't you see the news?"

As the Uber driver pulled up to BioMed's gatehouse, Sarah sat forward in the backseat. "I used to work here. I have to be able to get in to pick up my car. They can't just lock everything and walk away."

"Did you hear what the guy did to himself?" The older woman made the sign of the cross. "My granddaughter showed me some pictures from the Internet. Who does that to themselves?"

"I can't even guess."

"Well . . . what do you want to do?"

There was clearly no one in the guardhouse, and it wasn't like Sarah was going to climb up the gate's fencing and pull a gymnastic move over all that barbed wire. And on the security note, she couldn't see the complex from here, something that never had struck her as significant because hey, she'd always had her pass card and never spent any time parked at this entrance. But clearly, there was a rise and long drive for a reason.

Shoot. "I guess I'll go back—"

"Someone's coming up behind us."

Sarah twisted around. It was an unmarked sedan. Dark gray. And she recognized the man behind the wheel.

"I know him. Gimme a minute?"

"Yup, sure thing."

Opening her door, she got out of the Camry and was careful to show her hands as she walked forward. Special Agent Manfred immediately disembarked from his vehicle.

"Well, if it isn't Dr. Sarah Watkins. You're a hard lady to get ahold of."

"I'm sorry about that."

"I've been calling your home phone. And your cell."

Given that he worked for the frickin' FBI, she figured it was stupid to ask him how he'd gotten the numbers. Besides, she had more important things on her mind.

Like whether or not he was going to arrest her for trespassing or something worse.

Except as she waited for him to Miranda her or something, he seemed content to wait for her to answer his implied where-have-you-been question.

Huh. Guess there weren't any handcuffs in her future. At least not for this ten minutes.

"Again, I'm sorry I haven't returned the calls." She pointed to the closed gates. "Do you know how I can get my things? And my car?"

"Yeah, you were here Sunday night, weren't you." He smiled, but the expression did not make it to his eyes. "Working late on a weekend."

"No doubt you know what that's like."

"You can bet your life I do."

There was a pause. And Sarah shrugged. "Well, if you can't help me, I guess I'll go back home—"

"Where have you been, Dr. Watkins."

As a cold breeze whipped around, her ears stung. Or maybe that was her anxiety. "Nowhere."

"So you routinely do not answer calls from federal agencies? When the CEO of the company you work for is found dead?"

"I've never had them before. Calls from the Feds, that is."

"Tell you what, how about you and I go in together. You can answer some questions, and give this Uber driver the opportunity do some actual driving instead of parking."

"Am I being taken into custody for something?"

"If I were arresting you, you'd be handcuffed and in the back of my car."

"You have such a way with people, Special Agent Manfred. Has anyone ever mentioned this?"

"My ex-wife. For about ten years straight."

❖   ❖   ❖

Sitting shotgun in Special Agent Manfred's unmarked, Sarah couldn't help but lean into the dashboard as they rounded the drive and BioMed's low-profile, windowless expanse came into view. With all the snow on the ground, its white walls and gray roof blended in. What did not? All the FBI and other law enforcement vehicles parked right up next to the entrance, without regard to the yellow lines for parking spaces or even the arrows that directed traffic on the lane.

Manfred stopped cockeyed next to a blacked-out SUV, put his engine in park and turned things off. "That's your car over there, right?"

Sarah looked out the passenger side window. Right where she'd left it. God, with everything that had happened, she almost expected the thing to be turned on its roof with its wheels spinning and flames all over the undercarriage.

"Yes."

"It's been here awhile. Look at the snow covering the hood."

She thought of her front walkway, no longer cleanly shoveled. "Yes."

"Tell me something, if you came here Sunday night to work and you left your car here, how did you leave? I mean, I'm assuming you didn't decide to walk all the way back to your house. Nine miles is a long way to go. At night. In weather like this."

As Sarah turned to face the federal agent, she was amazed at how calm she was. Then again, she didn't really feel like there was a whole hell of a lot for her to live for. And that kind of made you unimpressed even by someone with arrest powers.

"Do you want to go inside?" she said. "It's getting cold in here."

"Sure." His tone was dry. "I'd hate to be accused of false imprisonment."

The two of them met up at his front bumper and walked to the entrance together. A member of the New York State police was guarding the interior door and Manfred flashed his ID to the officer.

"I've got a witness," Manfred announced. "We're walking through the scene."

"Yes, sir. Head right in, sir."

Sarah walked through into the lobby, but she didn't proceed down the hall. Instead, she went to Kraiten's photograph. As she stared at the portrait, she remembered him under the thrall of Murhder's mental control, by turns combative and threatening . . . and then foggy and acquiescing.

"Is he really dead?" she murmured.

"Do you want to see the pictures?"

As she shook her head, she recalled everything about that night: Coming out of the secret lab with Nate. Seeing Murhder, John, and Xhex. Escaping with them and taking Kraiten along to the loading dock. Using Kraiten's SUV to—

"Dr. Watkins? Hello?"

Sarah turned to the agent. "Who owns the company now?"

"No one. Kraiten shut everything down the day before he killed himself. Weren't you here working?"

The shrewd light in his eye suggested she needed to step carefully.

"Will you take me to my lab?"

"Sure." Same dry tone. "I'd be happy to."

They proceeded down the corridor, going past all the divisions with their opaque glass walls and their closed doors. From time to time, they passed a cop or another agent. Sarah just kept her eyes straight ahead.

When they got to her lab, she stopped. Looked at him. "Do you want me to use my ID to get in?"

He smiled a little. And pushed the door wide. "Locking systems are turned off."

Sarah stepped by him and stopped. The work area was exactly as she remembered, the cubicles with their desks in the same setup, the chairs where they had always been, the wastepaper baskets down on the floor.

But all the computers were gone.

"My pictures are in a drawer here," she said as she went over to her assigned area. "Is it okay to take them?"

"Sure."

She put her backpack down. Unzipped it. Took the photographs out. She found it impossible to look too closely at the images of her with Gerry. The fact that they were all from their uni days had never struck her as significant—until now.

No pictures of them together after they'd moved to Ithaca.

"So how'd you like to tell me about Sunday here." Manfred hopped up on one of the bare desks. "And be creative, why don't you. I like a challenge."

Sarah frowned and looked over her shoulder at the man. It was hard to read his expression, but professional implacability was no doubt part of his training. And yet . . .

He didn't know about the raid, did he. Somehow, the vampires had in fact managed to disappear all evidence of the infiltration and extraction—including Sarah's role in it.

"All I did was check on some work and the order of a new microscope. That's it." As Manfred looked away, there was a hint of frustration on his face. "You said Kraiten shut the company down? What do you mean, exactly?"

"He dissolved it. Legally, RSK BioMed no longer exists."

"What about all the patents? The research? The people who worked here?"

"Let's refocus. After you finished your work, how did you get home if you left your car in the lot?"

"Look, you already know I didn't kill Kraiten, right. He was one of the most paranoid people on the planet. Do not tell me you don't have security feed of how he died."

"As a matter of fact, we do. But what I'm wondering about right now is why you think you're a suspect."

She thought long and hard about what to say. "I'm going to be honest with you."

"Great way to start. I commend you."

She took a deep breath. "I think Robert Kraiten murdered my fiancé two years ago. And I think he killed Gerry's boss, too, but I don't know why exactly on either account. Gerry was very private about his work. He didn't talk to me about what he was doing, ever. I have no idea what the Infectious Disease division was working on or why Gerry would be a threat to Kraiten or this business. But I know that Gerry had managed his diabetes well, and I don't believe for a second that he died of natural causes."

Manfred's eyes narrowed. "Why were you really here Sunday night?"

"I told you. I was just checking up on a couple of my protocols. I've been working on tumor markers in renal cell carcinoma. Sometimes I can't turn my brain off for a whole two days."

"When did you leave?"

"Around eleven. My car didn't start in the cold."

"So who'd you catch a ride with?"

Sarah paused. "Kraiten. I rode home with Kraiten."

CHAPTER FIFTY-FIVE

After night fell over Caldwell, John Matthew did cartwheels down the grand staircase of the Brotherhood mansion. Like, literally. Hand hand, down—feet in the air. Land, shitkicker shitkicker. Hands in the air. Land, hand hand. Feet in the air. On the red carpeted steps.

He was doing very well, calibrating the stairs perfectly, balancing like a boss—except then he slipped up and bowling-ball'd it, banging and crashing all the way to the bottom. Whereupon he sprawled on the mosaic floor like a crash-test dummy.

Laughing his ass off.

Silently, but still.

Tohr's face entered his field of vision from above, blocking the lofty painted ceiling of fighters on warhorses. "You okay there, big guy?"

John shoved two thumbs up so high that the Brother had to jerk out of range or get his nose plugged.

Then again, John had made love to his *shellan* for about seven hours straight—Xhex was still in bed, sleeping the marathon session off—and he'd followed that with a tray brought up from the kitchen by Fritz himself.

Four cheeseburgers. Double set of homemade fries. A gallon of organic milk.

And three frozen Hershey chocolate bars. The one-pounder size.

John leaped up, landing solidly on his shitkickers. Pulling his dagger holsters back into place, he saluted Tohr and then stomped his foot.

Tohr smiled. Pulled him in for a quick, hard hug. Pushed him back. "Okay, okay. I heard from Doc Jane that you're cleared to fight, so yes, you can go out into the field." As John pumped a fist, the Brother frowned. "Actually, why don't you come with me to the Audience House? We had a strange voicemail during the day, and we're following up on it. A lot of the guys are already there. I'm just running a little late."

John nodded. Like, a hundred times.

Then he nearly skipped his way to the door out into the vestibule, all full of the joys of spring in spite of it being January. And he would have Easter Bunny'd it out of the mansion—except the sense that he was being watched made him quit the fun-and-games. Just as Tohr opened things for them to leave, John glanced into the billiard room.

Past the pool tables, over by one of the leather sofas, a tall figure stood in the shadows. Staring his way.

A shiver went through him.

"John?" As he jumped, Tohr said, "Is there something wrong?"

John shook his head and walked through the vestibule, doing the duty on the heavy outer door. As he and Tohr emerged into the night, he closed his eyes and tried to concentrate to dematerialize. The fact that Tohr ghosted out first was not a surprise.

Why had Lassiter been looking at him like that?

The blond-and-black fallen angel was rarely serious. And certainly never in the shadows.

Casting off an eerie sense of foreboding, he forced himself to calm down . . .

. . . and soon enough was flying through the cold air in a scatter of molecules, zeroing in on the gracious old house that Wrath held his meetings with civilians in. Tohr was waiting for him around back as John re-formed, and they both went into the kitchen.

"Oh, yeah, danish," the Brother said as he headed over to a silver tray set on the counter. "I need some danish right now."

As Tohr helped himself to four of the cherry ones intended for the waiting room, John had to smile. He had a feeling that the Brother had missed First Meal and was "a little late" for exactly the same reason John had been.

Sometimes, a male just needed alone time with his female. And after all the ridiculous stress lately?

John reached across his chest and massaged his shoulder. There was some residual stiffness where the wound had been, but the infection was gone, as far as Doc Jane and Manny were concerned. No more discoloration. And the puckering that had appeared as the retreat had intensified had cleared as well.

All thanks to Murhder. And Sarah.

A piercing sadness went through him. It still seemed wrong that they couldn't stay. But like so much in the Brotherhood world? Not his call.

"You want any?" Tohr asked as he held out his dinner plate full of danish.

When John shook his head, the Brother took one more, thanked the *doggen* pastry chefs, and together they went down to the dining room. As they approached, deep voices rolled out of the open doors, filling the foyer sure as if the males were actually standing by the front doors.

Tohr went in first.

And then John entered—

Everyone stopped talking and looked over at him. When no one moved, he glanced at Tohr, thinking maybe the Brother had been wrong about the meeting? Maybe it was only for—

"John."

As the King's voice rang out, big warrior bodies parted to reveal Wrath sitting in one of the armchairs by the fireplace.

"Welcome back, son."

That was when the hugging started. Rhage and Butch. Phury. Blay and Qhuinn, his very good friends. Z gave him a high five, which was a miracle considering that the male didn't really touch other people all that much. Even Vishous came over and pulled him into a hard, brief embrace.

With each connection, each contact, John felt his face flush more and more. And then the King himself came over, George leading him across the Oriental carpet.

"I'm glad you're okay." Wrath smiled, revealing enormous fangs. "Things wouldn't be the same around here without you."

Funny how it all worked out. John would never have volunteered to get injured as he had. Certainly wouldn't have chosen to walk the lonely path of mortal disease, finding out what it was like to realize your friends and family were going to keep living without you on the planet. Clearly hadn't wanted to go through a version of the transition as an adult.

But he'd needed this moment of communion with the Brotherhood. He'd needed this. . . validation from them.

This you're-one-of-us-even-if-you're-not.

And in retrospect, he could understand that with the Murhder stuff, it truly was Brotherhood business. Given all the history that male had with the rest of them? Well, sometimes even the most intimate of friends still needed moments of privacy.

But Murhder was gone now, and sad as that was, things had been recalibrated, taken back to normal.

John didn't need to be a member of the Brotherhood officially.

This was more than good enough for him.

◆   ◆   ◆

Night had fallen by the time Sarah returned to her home. Then again, January in Upstate New York meant five p.m. was dark as the inside of your hat, to borrow a phrase from her father.

She turned to Special Agent Manfred. "Thanks for the ride."

He put the unmarked sedan in park, but kept the engine running. "Do you think if this whole federal agent thing doesn't work out, I could be an Uber driver?"

"Absolutely. I'd totally use you again."

In the close quarters of the front seat, with the glow of the dash illuminating his face, she decided he was handsome enough. For a human.

"What?" he said.

"I'm sorry?"

"You're smiling."

"Just thought of something funny. Gallows humor. You know how it goes."

"Too right. Listen . . . you have my card. You see anyone around your property, get any strange calls, feel like you're even in the slightest danger, you call, okay? I'll be checking in with you in a couple of days anyway."

"I'm not going to take any chances. Thank you—oh, listen, I might have a job interview out at Stanford University. In California. Is it okay for me to travel? I mean, I'll let you know where I am and when I'm expected back and everything."

"Sure." No dry tone anymore. "I just need to know where to find you in case I need you."

"Okay." She picked her backpack up from between her feet. "Thanks again for the ride. I'll send a tow truck for my car tomorrow or the next day. Guess that cold really drained the battery."

"Winter'll do that."

Sarah got out and closed the passenger door. She was not surprised that he waited until she'd unlocked things and was in safely in her home before he drove away.

He was a good guy, she thought as she locked herself in. A good guy in a tough job.

Refocusing, she went back to her kitchen and intended to eat something, but there was nothing very inspiring available. Stouffer's Lean

Cuisine in the freezer. Ramen noodles in the cupboards. She settled for a bowl of Frosted Mini-Wheats and didn't eat much of it.

Probably for the best. The skim milk was twenty-four hours away from a "Best By" violation.

As she sat at her little table in her silent house, the magnitude of her isolation was terrifying. No family. No friends, really.

No Murhder.

The only person she might call if she needed something? An FBI agent.

To keep herself from hyperventilating, she thought about everything she had covered with Manfred. He'd been utterly shocked when she'd told him she had ridden home with Kraiten. He'd even questioned her as to why in the hell, if she believed the man might have killed her fiancé, she would ever get into a car with him.

Sarah had lied and told Manfred that she'd wanted to see if Kraiten brought up the deaths. If the man had anything to say about Gerry or his boss.

Pretty reckless, the agent had said. *Downright dangerous is more like it.*

Sarah had looked him right in the eye. *When the love of your life is gone, nothing is all that scary anymore.*

And that was that.

When everything was said and done, it turned out the FBI had nothing to contradict her story about Sunday night. No evidence. No tapes. No security guards with different versions of the truth. Manfred hadn't exactly told her as much, but the more comfortable he became with her and her story, the more his frustration with the case had started to come through. And it wasn't hard to guess that there was nothing that got members of law enforcement more twitchy than lack of evidence.

Especially when their guts told them that a crime or crimes had been committed.

If she hadn't known what Murhder could do to the human brain— if she hadn't experienced his tricks herself—she would never have understood how it was possible for three individuals to break into a secured location, rescue someone, and leave without a trace.

Although Kraiten had certainly assisted them in all that by killing himself. Which was lucky . . .

Or was it? For all she knew, Murhder could have programmed Kraiten to get rid of all of the evidence. Erase not just the footage, the servers, the logs, but the company itself.

The CEO, himself.

Neat and tidy.

Like none of it had ever happened.

Sarah put her hand on her heart and massaged the pain there. She was going to have to get used to a perpetual heavy weight behind her sternum again, wasn't she.

As she thought about that secret lab and what had been done to innocents there . . . she prayed that there were no other vampires held in captivity by other research companies.

Dear God, what if there were? How would anyone know, though. Kraiten had been careful to keep what he'd been doing a secret, and so had the people who had worked in the lab. Other corporations would do the same.

With a curse, she looked up at the ceiling and thought of Gerry at his desk in his study above. She had spoken the truth about him to Agent Manfred: Gerry had never told her what he was working on. Never once.

And not even in the evidence he left behind after his death: None of it, after all, had been directed toward her or left for her.

Getting to her feet, she went across to the door into the basement and descended into the cool dark cellar. When she got to the bottom, she flipped the switch.

The fluorescent lights on the low-slung rafters flickered to life and she glanced at the remnants of her college days in those containers. Then she went in the opposite direction away from all that, over to the washer and dryer. Bending down, she pulled the lower panel under the dryer loose and put it aside. With a stretch, she reached in, all the way to the back, pushing through dust bunnies.

She took out the USB drive Gerry had left in the safety deposit box. The credentials that had been with it, the ones she had used to get into her own lab, had been left in Doc Jane's office area back at the training center—an oversight on her part when she'd been packing up her clothes, one that she'd only noticed earlier in the day.

What did they matter now, though?

Next to the washer/dryer was a shallow wooden worktable that had never been used by her or Gerry. Putting the USB drive on it, she looked around for something hammer-like.

Over on the floor, there was a gallon of Benjamin & Moore latex paint left over from when she and Gerry had done the downstairs. A full gallon.

She picked up the can and held it over her head.

Then she slammed the flat bottom of the thing down on the drive.

Over and over again.

CHAPTER FIFTY-SIX

In the dining room of the Audience House, after all the hugging was done, John Matthew took up res next to Butch, the former homicide cop, and Vishous, who as usual had lit up a hand-rolled. Wrath and George had returned to armchair position to the left of the fireplace, and Saxton, the King's solicitor, was at the desk off to one side. Apart from the Brotherhood and other fighters, there was one further notable addition to the group. Abalone, the King's First Advisor. From what John understood, the male had deep roots in the aristocracy, but he was a good guy, the opposite of those tight-ass, judgmental types that typically propagated the *glymera*.

His blooded daughter had even gone through the training program, and was mated, with the male's blessing, to a civilian.

There was no one else in Audience House, other than the receptionist. Unusual, given that it was the start of the evening. Civilians were typically lined up in the waiting room, ready to present their issues to the King.

"Sire," Abalone said with a bow to Wrath, "with your permission, I will bring your subject in?"

"Yeah. We're ready."

Abalone passed through the open doors and disappeared into the waiting room. When he came back, he had a male with him whom John recognized.

"May I present Rexboone, blooded son of Altamere."

Boone, as the male was known, bowed deeply even though Wrath could not see him. "Thank you for allowing me to come, my Lord."

The guy was built big and strong, and was classically handsome in a clean-cut kind of way, reminding John of the marble figures in the Hall of Statues back at the house. He'd gone through the training center's program and not made a lot of waves, a quiet, watchful presence who, as John understood, had done particularly well in physical challenges.

But other than that, John didn't know much, although he wasn't on the ground floor of the training program, either.

"What can we do you for," Wrath said as he bent down and picked up George. Settling the golden retriever in his lap, he stroked the long blond fur that grew out of those flanks. "And listen, I've heard you're working hard for us out in the field. You've taken two *lessers* down. I like that. Keep it up."

As Boone flushed and bowed again, his response was mumbled, but his blush was loud as a holler—and John liked the humility.

"I'm not sure this is . . ." The trainee cleared his throat and looked around at the Brothers. "This may be nothing, but my father has been invited to this dinner party. Tomorrow night."

"What are they serving?" Rhage chimed in. "If it's lamb, I'm coming, too."

Wrath sent a glare in Hollywood's direction, then refocused on Boone. "G'head."

"Well, it's being organized by an aristocrat that goes by the name of Throe?"

Instantly, the mood in the room changed, the Brothers straightening, shifting in their shitkickers.

"I know that the Council was disbanded by you." Boone glanced around again. "But that the *glymera* is not prohibited from congregating, provided it is for social purposes only. However, my father doesn't know this male well, and when my sire asked who else was invited, he learned that the other remaining Princeps were on the list."

"So it's basically a meeting of the Council," Wrath muttered.

"Called by a known agitator," someone else piped in.

"My father is not going to go, and he asked me to come here and tell you about it because I'm in the training center program and he figured it would look less suspicious for me to have an audience with you. As I said, my sire doesn't want to get involved in any intrigue, and he certainly does not want a civil war within the species."

The King's nostrils flared. "Is that all that you've come to say to me?"

"Yes, my Lord." There was a pause. "I beg of you, send someone out there. You must . . . this is not right. They should not be gathering like this. It is sowing seeds of revolt, I just know it."

"Anything else?"

"I can provide you with the address."

"Can you. And what is it?"

Boone gave a street that wasn't far from the Audience House. "It is at midnight, my Lord. They gather at midnight on the morrow."

John looked at the King. And then checked out the expressions of the Brothers. When no one said or did anything, he was confused. This was a possible coup in progress—

"Is that everything?" the King prompted Boone once again.

"Yes, my Lord—except . . . please don't tell anyone that my father sent me or that this word came from him. He does not want any trouble. He wants to stay out of it."

Wrath continued to stroke George's fur, his dagger hand moving over the dog's golden hair. "Son, I appreciate you coming here and all. Giving us a heads-up."

"So you'll send people. And stop them—"

"But you and I have a problem."

Boone shook his head. "There is no problem. I am utterly loyal unto you. There is nothing I would not do to serve you."

"Then why are you lying to me?" Wrath tapped the side of his nose. "I may be blind, but all my other senses work just fine. And you are not being truthful here."

Boone opened his mouth. Closed it.

"Why don't you take another stab at this, son."

The trainee crossed his arms over his chest. Stared at the floor. Then he paced back and forth.

"I know you're in a helluva spot," Wrath said quietly. "So you take your time. But I'm going to be clear here. Consequences are going to fall where they do and there is no carefully crafted version of reality that is going to stop that. Do you understand what I'm saying?"

When Boone finally halted, he was facing the King, and his voice was reedy as he spoke, like his throat was tight.

"My father . . ."

"G'head. Just say it. This is not your fault, okay? You are not going to get blamed for anything as long as you tell the truth."

Boone took a deep breath and closed his eyes. "My father is going to attend. He's going to the dinner. He's . . ."

"Not as loyal to me as you are."

The male dragged a hand over his features. "I've been telling him he shouldn't go. That this isn't right. I'm doing everything I can to talk him out of it—I believe he'll come around. He has to—he just has to. And in the meantime, I couldn't let this happen—it's wrong. I don't know for sure what they're planning, but why are they meeting like this? My sire doesn't know this male at all. Throe showed up from out of nowhere, and was part of that meeting to overthrow the throne a while ago. And now he's living in the mansion of that older male?" Boone shook his head and started pacing again, his words coming faster and faster. "We know who owns that house. He's related to us. Why is he letting Throe stay with him and his *shellan*—who, by the way, is just ten years out of

THE SAVIOR   397

her transition? And why is he allowing Throe to be the host of the party? It's not Throe's house, it's not his position of authority. I mean, in the *glymera*, it is a tremendous breach of protocol for any other person to issue an invitation to a home for so much as an afternoon tea, much less a formal dinner." Boone stopped and faced the King again. "It makes no sense. None of this makes any sense."

Wrath's nostrils flared once more. And then the King nodded. "This is the truth as you know it. Now you are being truthful."

Boon threw up his hands in defeat. "I keep telling my sire not to go. I'm trying to talk to him—but he is . . . he has never really been interested in my opinion." Boone looked around at the Brotherhood again. "And listen, I could be wrong. This could all be paranoia on my part—in which case I've embarrassed myself, called into question the loyalty of my father, and brought shame upon my bloodline."

"I don't think you need to worry about any of that, son." Wrath shook his head. "We're pretty goddamn familiar with Throe and his little party planning committee. Even if there's nothing going on, you have not wasted our time, and your loyalty to me is never going to be forgotten."

"I didn't know what else to do," Boone said baldly.

Jesus, what a position to be in, John thought. In the Old Laws, treason against the King was punishable by death.

So this son might well have put his father's head on the chopping block.

"Come here, solider mine." Wrath extended his long arm, the tattoos of his lineage flashing on the underside. Switching into the Old Language, he said, "*Approach and present your fealty, young male.*"

The trainee strode over and lowered down onto his knees. Bending forward, he kissed the enormous black diamond on Wrath's hand.

"*My allegiance unto you and your throne, forevermore,*" Boone said in a voice that cracked.

Wrath sat up and reached around his dog. Placing his broad hand on the side of Boone's face, he said in his deep voice, "*Your loyalty brings honor upon the quick and the dead of your bloodline. This shall not be for-*

gotten by me, and shall be held as a service unto both the throne and my personage. Go forth and know that you have performed a vital function unto your King, about which I shall not forget."

Switching back into English, Wrath continued, "This really is not your fault, son. So don't blame yourself. No matter what happens, you did the only thing you could."

"I would beg for you mercy on my sire's behalf," Boone mumbled as he stared up into the King's face. "But I'm afraid he may not deserve it."

"That's his choice. Not your responsibility."

Boone nodded and got back to his feet. After bowing again to Wrath, he turned to the Brotherhood and did the same. Then Abalone escorted him out, closing the doors behind the two of them quietly.

No one spoke. The Brothers all just stared at Wrath, who sat there with his dog in his lap, stroking, stroking . . . stroking.

After the front door to the house opened and shut, Abalone came back into the dining room, and re-closed things even though there was nobody else except for loyal *doggen* in the mansion.

"Go scope out the place tonight," Wrath ordered. "And I want a full complement of fighters there tomorrow."

Vishous stabbed the hand-rolled he'd been smoking out on the sole of his shitkicker. "I'll plant some mics around the exterior right before dawn."

"What do we tell Xcor?" Tohr said. "My brother is going to want to know about this. I mean Throe was his second in command for a century."

"Xcor can be there tomorrow if he wants." Wrath cursed. "But the rest of the Band of Bastards needs to be downtown. We can't let off the Lessening Society even for a night. We're so close to the end of this fucking war."

"The trainees can cover territory, if they're supervised by the Bastards," Tohr said. "We definitely need the full Brotherhood at that house and John and Blay, too. If this is a coup, it's going to have to be dealt with then and there."

"You're goddamn right about that." Wrath looked around at the group. "If it turns out they're plotting against me? I want them all dead. Are we clear? You kill them where they stand. I'm done with this *glymera* shit."

John whistled so that everyone looked at him. *How about Murhder? He could help if we need more fighters.*

There was an awkward silence. And then Tohr said, "I appreciate your loyalty to the guy. But—"

I've seen him fight. He's a total badass.

"What's John saying," Wrath snapped. "Will someone please fucking translate."

CHAPTER FIFTY-SEVEN

Standing off to the side of shAdoWs's dance area, Xhex was smiling. Even though the purple lasers pierced her eyeballs, and the music made her eardrums pound, and the humans who were drunk, high, and hyper-sexed required constant oversight, she was Glo-Lite happy. Positively radiant on the inside. Downright fucking cheerful.

Like, greeting card cheerful.

She might as well have a pink bow in her hair and be wearing fuzzy slippers—

As a fight broke out between two men, one of them got shoved in her direction, his arms pinwheeling, his balance going off-kilter, his sloppy feet tap dancing to the tune of "Too Much Coke, and That Wasn't My Girlfriend I Just Grinded On."

Xhex caught him with both hands and stood him back up. "You want to stop or go back in?"

The guy looked across at the steaming hot pile of I'ma-fuck-you-up who was waiting for round two. "I want to fight him! I can do what I want! She weren't nothing—"

"Roger that. Have at it."

Xhex obligingly shoved him back at the guy who was probably going to use his face as a punching bag—oh, yup. Here we go, melee time.

"I thought you were supposed to stop things like this?"

She turned and looked up at Tohr. "Hey! How are you?"

"Aren't you security?" They clapped hands. "I mean, not that I'm complaining. I love watching amateurs—oh, ground time."

The two combatants hit the floor, all sloppy, flappy hands, and bronco bucking butts.

"I'll give you five bucks on the one with the yellow shirt," Xhex said.

Tohr took out his wallet. Checked his money. "You got it, but you're going to have to break a hundy. It's all I got."

"No worries."

They hung back and waited for the outcome to arrive. Which it artificially did when one of her bouncers stepped in and pulled apart the two snarling tomcats.

"Damn it," she muttered as she pulled her fold of bills out of her ass pocket. "Why do I only hire people who insist on doing their job."

As a second bouncer came over and the two combatants were ushered out to the Buck Stops Here room in the back, Tohr put her fiver into his wallet.

"So you wanted to see me?" he said.

"Yeah." Fun time was now over. "Let's go upstairs."

"Trez around?" the Brother asked as they headed over to the staircase to the office. "I haven't seen him for a while."

"He's here and there."

"That Selena thing . . ."

"Horrible. Just awful. If there actually is someone running this show from up above, they need to make that right." She stopped halfway up the steps. "I'm sorry. I don't mean to suggest that Wellsie's death isn't . . . shit. Fuck."

Tohr took her hand and gave it a squeeze. "It's okay. I know what you mean. And everything is the way it's supposed to be."

She squeezed back and then kept on going, opening the door to Trez's office. When she shut herself and the Brother in together, the music was buffered to a dull thud.

Tohr wandered over to the bank of glass and stared down at the humans. His reflection was one of sadness, and she gave him a moment to come back from the past and his unfathomable loss.

Hell, after getting as close as she had to losing John Matthew, she couldn't imagine how Tohr handled the death of his *shellan*. But the Brother had somehow continued on in his life, meeting and falling in love with Xhex's *mahmen*, Autumn.

It was possible to go on.

The Brother turned around and tucked his muscle shirt into his leathers, even though it wasn't loose. Then he straightened his leather jacket.

"Okay," he said in a normal voice. "So what's up?"

"I need to make something right." She planted her boots and braced herself, even though there was nothing coming at her. "It's been long overdue and . . . it's time."

◆   ◆   ◆

Murhder left the attic out of the window, dematerializing onto the snow dusted lawn. Huddling against the chill, he walked off down the allée of live oaks, imagining the fruit trees in the side garden blooming, the grass green, the sky twinkling with stars and a fat summer moon.

He wondered if Sarah would have liked the house. The bustle of humans. The people who worked on the estate. Maybe she could have found work at a university close by. There were some good ones in the state that had all kinds of . . .

The thought drifted and disintegrated, like his breath over his shoulder.

Paring off from the two rows of ancient trees, he crossed the thin layer of snow, heading for the thicket of trees that grew next to the rushing stream. As he closed in on the little river, the burble of the water was soft, barely audible. Off to the left, two deer were startled by his presence, kicking up their white tails and loping away through the brush.

Murhder stopped on the shores and stood over the water.

After a period of time—it could have been a minute or an hour—he unsheathed the black dagger from where he'd tucked it into his belt at the small of his back. Putting it in his dominant hand, he regarded the weapon, tracing the blade with his eyes, remembering how many times he'd used it. Vishous had made the dagger just for Murhder, its hilt custom-fit to his palm, the weight just as he preferred, the razor-sharp cutting edge maintained by the other Brother.

Previously maintained, that was.

He thought about what Kraiten had done to himself, courtesy of Xhex's very wise suggestions. And he had to wonder if losing Sarah had been some kind of existential punishment for that human's death. But that didn't make sense. The Scribe Virgin had been all about balance when she had watched over the race. Good with the evil. Price and payment. Alpha and Omega.

Just like her and her brother in the world, the pair of them established by the Creator to keep things level.

Kraiten had been pure evil. He had gotten what he deserved.

Glancing over his shoulder, Murhder could see the lights of the main house in the distance. It was too cold for anyone to be out tonight. And tomorrow? He'd checked the forecast. Cold and clear.

Even though winter sunlight was not as strong as the rays in summer, it had enough firepower to disappear his body.

No one would be any the wiser. And he'd left a directive on that trestle table as to what to do with his money and the B&B.

All was in order.

He put the blade to his throat. One advantage to being a vampire was that he knew neck anatomy like the back of his hand.

It was helpful when you were looking for the big fat vein that fed your brain.

One streak was all it was going to take. A pull of his arm. A left-to-right with that viciously sharp, Vishous-ly honed blade. And then his blood would empty sure as water from a tub.

Just a quick move with his dagger hand.

Something he'd done countless times as a fighter to *lessers*.

Gritting his teeth, closing his eyes, he tilted his head back. "Do it . . . just do it . . ."

His whole body started to shake and sweat bloomed over his brow in spite of the cold breeze. A hoarse moan rose up and breached his lips.

"Fuck!" he yelled into the woods. "*Fuck* . . . !"

Dropping his arm, he breathed hard and cursed some more. It was so goddamn simple. All he had to do was kill himself right here, in this hidden glen. Sun comes out in the morning. His body is gone.

Suffering done.

He put the blade back where it had been.

This time, he was going to fucking do it.

CHAPTER FIFTY-EIGHT

Throe walked around the dining room table, putting the place cards down in their proper arrangement. Twenty-four place settings of the very best: Royal Crown Derby's Old Imari plates, Tiffany's Chrysanthemum sterling flatware, Baccarat wine and water glasses. And down the center of the table, sterling candelabra were set every four feet with spaces left for the flowers. There were also plenty of blue glass salt holders sitting next to sterling pepper shakers.

When he was done assigning seats, he stepped back and regarded the entire room with a jaundiced eye, searching for faults and imperfections. The oil paintings in gilt frames depicted aristocrats who were not part of his immediate bloodline, but they looked like him—because all of the *glymera* were distantly related anyway. The hearth was dark at the moment, but it would be crackling with dried hardwood on the morrow. The sideboards were prepared to receive vases of flowers and bottles of wine.

The latter never to be served.

In fact, none of the seats would be sat upon and none of the plates would be filled with the food that would be cooked starting at nightfall.

But everything needed to look the part and the house had to smell right. And besides, vis-à-vis the meal, he himself would need to eat after everything was done.

Satisfied, he left the stage set and went across to the parlor.

As he entered the gracious room, the antiques were all old in the best sense of the word, and the sofa and chairs were covered with a lovely silk that matched the damask-covered walls. Nice Aubusson on the floor. Stupendous Russian chandelier hanging from a plaster medallion in the center of the room.

He'd had a large folding table brought up from the basement and covered with a monogrammed tablecloth. Glassware was set up off to one side. Liquor bottles and mixers were in a line. There would be lemon and lime slices set out before guests arrived, as well as a bowl of ice.

Self-serve.

He hated it. But as he'd had to kill all of the estate's *doggen*, he had no servants to orchestrate the evening, and there was no reason to try to hire any just for tomorrow night—especially given the attack he had planned. Further, the only thing more entrenched in the vampire world over and above the *glymera* were the *doggen* who worked for aristocrats.

There were never short-term hires in that sector.

So yes, his guests could pour their own libations. And then he would make sure that his shadows performed their show of aggression soon after all of the invitees had glasses in their hands. The breach in etiquette with regard to the cocktails would soon be forgotten as they scattered for their lives.

He needed two of them to die.

Not the females of course, and not because he cared about the weaker sex. It had to be two of the males because they had the power, and if the others witnessed a pair of their own kind being murdered by an enemy the Brotherhood couldn't protect them against?

Well, that just took things up a notch, didn't it.

Back in the foyer, he looked toward the grand staircase.

Then he turned and stared at the front door.

A feeling of unease rippled through him and he quickly glanced over his shoulder. Nothing was there. Or rather . . . nothing that shouldn't have been. Just a marble statue. And the hall of paintings that led to the back rooms of the home. And the side table with the antique mirror over it.

No shadows where he didn't want them.

All was as it should be.

In fact, all was as it had to be. He deserved to be in a house like this, making a power play like this. He had returned to his blue-blooded roots, to the money and the prestige—

Throe quick pivoted and looked into the parlor.

Nothing was there.

Loosening his ascot, he breathed through his nose, and reassured himself that there were no scents that should not have been in the air.

As the tension in his shoulders refused to ease, his ambitions wobbled. Listening for footsteps, for creaks, for the clicks of gun triggers, his mind played tricks on him, pulling out of the silence soft-decibel'd noises that funneled through his filter of fear.

There was no one he could call, he realized.

No one that would come to his aid.

He thought of Xcor. Back when Throe had been a part of the Band of Bastards, there had been fighters who aided him. And he them.

No more the now.

Of course, the corollary to his loner status? The throne would be his and his alone. No need to share or divvy up anything. He would be king—

A fluttering made him jump, but then he recognized the sound.

"My darling?" he said.

Going back to the dining room, he found the Book at the head of the table. The tome had opened itself, and its pages were flipping as they did, an infinite number of folios between its ancient covers.

When they settled, he smiled as the ink rearranged itself into the symbols of the Old Language.

"I have my love," he translated, "and my love has me. I have my love, and my love has me . . ."

The words came out of his mouth, not as an expression of conscious thought, but as a chant that sprang from a great well within him, his soul.

Picking up the Book, he closed it and held the weight to his heart. As he continued with his chanting, he went to the stairs and started the ascent, moving as if on autopilot.

It wasn't until he got to the top landing that a thought struggled to find purchase in the midst of the repeated words.

How had the Book gotten to the head of the table?

He had left it upstairs.

◆   ◆   ◆

In the end, Murhder could not kill himself.

He tried a number of times. By that river.

But in the end, he had turned away, retucked the black dagger into his belt, and wandered off toward the house. Back down the allée. Over to the front porch this time, where he mounted the wooden steps and stood in the darkness out of the way of the security lights.

Looking through the wide old-fashioned windows, he had a clear view of the main sitting room which was candlelit. Over on the sofa, there was a human sitting, a woman. She was in her thirties, he guessed, with long dark hair, and beautiful dark eyes. She was fidgeting in her pretty blue dress, fussing with the skirt, tugging at the sleeves. Then she got up and walked back and forth.

He had seen her and the man who had come with her go out to dinner. He had watched them get into a car and drive off to somewhere in town. They must have come back from wherever they had shared a meal while he'd been almost committing suicide out in the woods.

Talk about two different kinds of nights—

Abruptly, the woman turned to the archway. And her hands went up to her face. And surprise flared in her eyes.

The man who was staying with her entered with a bouquet of red roses. Murhder had smelled them when they had been brought into the house during the daylight hours, and he had wondered whom they were for. Question answered.

The man lowered himself onto one knee before the woman. The woman's eyes watered, her happiness a sunrise in the candlelight.

As she accepted the flowers, her beau held out a small black velvet box. His lips moved as he opened the lid.

She gasped. She smiled. She nodded. Many times. And then she bent down and kissed him.

"That was why I couldn't do it," Murhder said into the cold air.

As long as Sarah was alive, he would live, too.

Even if he could not be with her, his world had a distant sun, and that was just enough to sustain him. Life support as opposed to health, it was true. But he would not be a coward to take the easy way out. That diminished him—and disrespected his woman.

He would follow her brave example, and love her from afar for however long he had—

The creak on the stairs behind him had him wheeling around. When he saw who it was, he frowned.

"Tohr?" He shook his head, wondering if his mind wasn't playing tricks on him. "What are you doing down here?"

"I wanted to talk to you." The Brother came up the old wooden steps slowly. "I would have called, but you don't have a phone."

Out of training and instinct, Murhder tracked the powerful male, searching for signs of aggression or impending attack.

Maybe he'd use his black dagger tonight after all.

"Nice house." Tohr glanced around. "Never been down here before."

"Are you really a tourist right now?"

"No, I'm here on official business."

Christ. How the fuck did the Brotherhood know? They must have bugged Sarah's house. "Listen, I'm not looking for trouble, and frankly, I'm a private citizen, so it's none of your concern—"

"Why didn't you tell us what you did?"

Murhder threw up his hands. "It's not going to affect anything. Seriously, what consequence does it really have on all of you? I'm living my life, I'm out of your hair, and if she never crosses your path, why does it matter? Do you have to take everything from me?"

Tohr frowned. "I don't understand."

"So I didn't scrub her memories! It's none of your fucking business—or the Brotherhood's or the King's!" Catching himself, he lowered his voice. "I'm not going to apologize for it, and you're not going to do anything about it. Sarah's not in my life, and fuck—it must make you happy. All of you Brothers have been enjoying my suffering these past twenty years and it's going to continue—yay! So get out your popcorn and your sense of superiority and add my true love to the list—but put her at the top, would you. Because she sure as shit hurts the worst."

Murhder shut his mouth with a clap and linked his arms over his chest. He almost hoped the Brother came back with something. He was in the mood to fight—especially if it got really physical.

"That's not why I came," Tohr said slowly.

"What?"

"Not even close."

Murhder whistled under his breath. Rolled his eyes. "Great. Sooooo . . . any chance I can take all of that back?"

"I, ah—" The Brother shook his head like he was changing mental tracks. "Let's start with why I'm actually here. Why didn't you say what really happened with Xhex? With that first fire at the first lab? Or that you were taken captive by her relatives?"

Oh, boy.

Tohr continued, "You let us think for two decades that you flaked off when we needed you. Instead, you were getting tortured up there in the colony. For months. And then when you got out, thanks to Rehvenge? You went looking for her. That's what you were doing. And she set that first fire and killed that scientist. Not you."

"I did the other shit, though," Murhder said roughly. "At the second location. Wait, where are you getting this from?"

"Xhex talked to me."

Murhder scrubbed his now short hair. And wondered if Sarah had found the braid he'd left her yet. Back when he'd assumed he'd be scrubbing her, he had planned to tell her brain that it was a prized possession of hers, something she never wanted to lose—even if she didn't remember exactly how it had come to be hers.

A throwback to his time in the Victorian era when lovers gave locks of hair to each other.

"Why'd she do that," he asked the Brother.

"Because she wanted the truth to come out. Because you were being blamed for something you didn't do and catching flak for deserting the Brotherhood when you didn't. Because we were wrong to blame you and didn't know."

Cursing under his breath, Murhder walked over to the railing and stared out over the lawn, to the stream.

"She told me what they did to you in the colony," Tohr said. "The mental torture."

"It's all right."

"No, the fuck it isn't."

"I'm okay now. That's all that matters."

"Murhder. My brother—"

He turned around. "Don't call me that. I'm not your Brother anymore, remember."

"Yes, you are." Tohr came forward. "I'm so sorry. We're all so sorry. I wish you'd told us what really happened—we could have worked with you or . . . whatever, I'm not blaming you for the choice of staying silent. You had your reasons, you were protecting Xhex, and we get that. But we wish we'd known the truth."

Of all the conversations he had ever expected to have? This was not one of them.

Not even close.

"Apology accepted," Murhder said roughly. "I appreciate you—well, thanks for coming down."

Tohr shook his head. "This isn't just an I'm-sorry. We want you to come back. We want you to fight with us again, be one of us—again."

Murhder didn't bother to hide his recoil. "What?"

"We want you back. In the Brotherhood."

"Can you even do that?"

Tohr laughed in a short burst. "The Brotherhood decides on matters of membership. You know this."

"Is Wrath aware you're here?"

"He's the one who sent me."

"Really." Murhder broke off from the Brother and turned back to the railing. "So the King's given his blessing."

There was a long silence. And then Tohr said, "We need the help. We've got a big cover issue tomorrow night. A meeting of probable insurgents."

"So just like this, you think I'm cleared for fieldwork. Back in the saddle. Ready to roll. No more insane."

"Xhex says she's read your grid. She knows where you're at."

Murhder closed his eyes. "Now she's a social worker. Wow."

"We were wrong, Murhder. We were going on the facts as we knew them, but we were wrong and we are sorry. All of us. And then there was what you did for John."

Murhder thought back to being out in those cold alleys with Tohr's son. So alive. So fist pumping, heart pounding, balls-to-the-wall alive. He'd felt like he was following his purpose again. Serving the race. Playing a vital role in the species' survival.

But there was another level to it all. The thing about the Brotherhood was . . . that group of males was united over more than just fighting. There was trust, loyalty, friendship between the Brothers, and those emotional ties were just as important as the fighting skills.

Xhex was right. He was no longer crazy.

But he couldn't go back to Caldwell, and reenter the Brotherhood, and be who he needed to be with them. Who he had to be.

That kind of heart just wasn't in him anymore.

"I can't do it," he said. "I'm sorry. I left that version of me behind a long time ago."

"Are you sure about that?"

"Yes." He glanced back at the Brother. "That's the thing about not being insane anymore. I actually know where I stand. And it's here."

"Is there anything I can do to change your mind?"

What about Sarah, he thought.

Except then he reconsidered that knee-jerk request. Yes, there were humans working around the Brotherhood, but if he were out in the field every night, what kind of life was that for her? Sitting, waiting, wondering if he were injured. And what about her scientific pursuits.

He had gotten online and looked her name up. He didn't know what he'd thought she did, but it turned out she was a world leader in her field. How could he ask her to give all that up just for him?

"Murhder?"

"No," he said. "There's nothing you can do to change my mind. But thanks for coming down."

"Okay. Well."

"Yup. All right."

There was another long pause. And then Tohr said, "I guess I'll head back. You know where to find us if you need us."

As Tohr turned away and headed for the steps, Murhder spoke up. "What are you going to do about Sarah?"

The Brother frowned over his shoulder. "Sarah?"

"You know, about what I told you."

"Did you mention her?" Tohr shrugged and hit the porch stairs. "Huh. I must have missed it. I didn't hear anything about her."

CHAPTER FIFTY-NINE

The following evening, Sarah sat at her kitchen table and laid out her bills: Cable TV and Internet, with her landline bundled in. Cell phone. Car payment. Car insurance. Life insurance. Mortgage. House insurance. She had one credit card, but didn't carry a balance on it.

Her most recent bank account statement was in her lap and she checked the balances in her checking and savings again. She also had her 401(k) and just over a hundred thousand in stocks in an investment account, the result of the inheritance left to her by her father after his death.

Her house was carrying a good two hundred grand in debt. But according to the realtor she'd spoken to in the afternoon, the place was worth three-hundred to three twenty-five. After paying the agent, she was going to walk away with about seventy thousand after taxes on the nominal long-term capital gains were taken out.

She sat back and looked around the kitchen. The agent was bringing the listing forms over first thing in the morning, and there was going to be an open house on Sunday if everything went as planned.

Not a bad nest egg for someone her age. And there was more.

She picked up a FedEx envelope she'd opened earlier. Inside was an official severance package from an attorney purporting to represent BioMed's residual interests. They were giving all employees at her level six months of salary, which was . . . absolutely unheard of from what she knew of the company. Kraiten had been willing to pay for only two things: top talent and top facilities. Everything else was second or third rate, with lower-tier employees receiving crappy benefits.

Gerry's hiring deal, for example, had been far richer than her own.

Then again, his employment had also put him in his grave.

"Oh, Gerry . . ."

Picking up her cell phone, she checked the time. Out on the West Coast, it was four in the afternoon still.

She went through her contacts, found the number for Lorenzo Taft-Margulies and hit send. The man picked up on the third ring, just as she was beginning to construct the message she was going to leave on his voicemail in her head.

"Enzo, it's Sarah Wa—hi. Yup, it's me. What?" She pulled another chair around with her foot and stretched both legs out, crossing them at the ankles. "Oh, God, I know, right? Who could have seen it coming? Me? No, I mean, I was never that high up in things at BioMed. Just a humble researcher, no one that Kraiten would have much to do with— and as my dad used to say, sometimes you luck out."

They chatted a little bit more about the BioMed drama. And then she said, "So listen, Enzo, about the job interview. I am so flattered and I really thought about it—yes, I'm afraid it's a no. Yes, I'm aware I have no job at the moment." She smiled at her friend's joke. "But I've been work- ing straight through since grad school, and while I realize that was the plan, I just need a break. Where? I don't know. I could stick in New En- gland or I might look into something totally new. Teaching at the col- lege level. Maybe an even bigger change. I guess I just want to get off the hamster wheel and see how I feel."

"Sarah," the voice on the other end said. "You're on the cusp of a major career. I know that hamster wheel is hard, but if you leave now, you may never get back to where you are. You have greatness ahead of you. I've always seen it in you."

Sarah blinked. "You're kind to say that."

"I'm not being kind here. Don't throw away everything you've worked for."

After some further back and forth, they changed the subject by mutual agreement and Enzo returned to being his usual self, supportive but gently needling—and when it came time to end the call, she promised to look him up if she changed her mind.

Pondering what the man had said, she wondered how much of it was hyperbole . . . and how much of it was a truth she had never recognized about herself. Enzo had always been a straight shooter. He was ten years older than she and Gerry, but a fellow Harvard/MIT program alum in Sarah's field, which was how she'd gotten to know him. He'd been impressed with Gerry—God knew everyone had been—but he'd been more interested in Sarah.

Just professionally, that was. And she could remember being flattered that he'd pursued her for work. It had been a nice change from being in Gerry's shadow. Not that she'd ever resented Gerry back then.

No, the resentment had come later. And not because they'd been competing for jobs or notoriety.

Was Enzo right? Was she letting everything go if she took time off? She had spent a lot of time downplaying her accomplishments—because she hadn't been on Gerry's level. But maybe that was more her own insecurities, as opposed to an accurate assessment of her professional standings.

Getting up, she rinsed the plate she'd eaten dinner on and put in it in the dishwasher. Nothing else to clean up because she'd had one of those Lean Cuisines out of the freezer. So actually, she could have just put her plate back in the cupboard because it had functioned more like a china tray for the plastic tray she'd put in the microwave.

Heading for the living room, she debated binge-watching something, but she'd never been all that into TV and had no frame of reference for the shows people were talking about now. *Ozark. Supernatural. Making of a Murderer 2.* And what the hell was a podcast, anyway?

Sure, falling into the vampire world had been a shocker, but like she knew much about the human one she supposedly lived in?

At university, she had studied all the time. And after her degree, during her employment at BioMed, she had worked all the time. And then Gerry had died. So she'd worked even more than all the time.

Yes, that was possible.

There had to be another way for her. And there was certainly going to be a different place to live.

She'd already mourned the loss of one man in this house.

She was not going to do that here again.

◆   ◆   ◆

"Does everyone understand their positions?" Tohr asked the brothers as everyone gathered in the mansion's grand foyer. "Is everyone clear?"

He was aware of a sense of foreboding creeping up the back of his neck and he rubbed his nape, trying to convince himself that he'd just slept funny.

"Actually, I'm confused." Rhage bit down on a cherry Tootsie Pop. "Am I devastatingly handsome tonight facing here to the left." He shifted to the other side. "Or the right? Left . . . right. Left. Right—"

"I'm going to break his nose," Vishous said. "I swear to God, I am going to bust his fucking septum just so we can stop this conversation."

"I think left *and* right," Rhage announced. "I think there are no bad angles."

"You sure about that, Barbra Streisand?" someone called out.

The voices of the Brotherhood filled the space as much as their huge, leather-clad bodies did, and Tohr let them all go with the verbal jabbing. It was typical nervous energy bubbling around, and he knew better than to try to quell the chatter.

Instead, he went over to his half brother. Xcor was still as a statue, his face too composed. His body too tense.

"How you doing?" Tohr asked quietly, making sure his back was to the group so no one overheard them. But like they all didn't know what the male was facing tonight?

Xcor kept his voice down, too. "Just so you know, I will kill Throe myself if he's going after the throne. I will not hesitate. I know where my allegiance lies."

Tohr put his hand on the male's shoulder. "I never doubt it, brother mine. Ever."

Xcor's eyes shined out of his brutal, harelipped face, and, not for the first time, Tohr was glad that the fighter was on their side. Xcor was formidable on a good day. A night like tonight? He was beyond deadly.

And what do you know, they had another thing going for them. Wrath was not heading down to the Audience House. Thank God. In a rare change of habit, the King had actually listened to reason. He was staying put here at the mansion, with Phury and Z on guard along with Payne. Rehvenge, with all his tricks as a *symphath*, was also hanging in for the night. Just in a case.

And *symphaths* had special weapons.

As Murhder had learned firsthand, Tohr thought with regret.

"Okay, let's do this," he said as he headed for the grand door.

Pushing his way through the vestibule, he was aware that a piece was missing. But Murhder was free to make his own decisions, and at least John was back and ready to fight—

Tohr stopped short without any warning, and John, who was right behind him, slammed into him, bumping his body out over the threshold.

A tall, powerful figure stood on the stone steps in the wind, unmoving in spite of the gusts that rushed the top of the mountain. Feet planted, hands down, head up, the male was prepared for what he had been bred to do.

Fight in defense of the species.

Tohr started to smile as he resumed walking forward. "You have a change of a heart, then?"

As he put his dagger hand out to Murhder, he had not expected to see the other male ever again.

Sometimes, separation was what destiny provided, regardless of what you wanted. Tohr had lived, fought, and loved long enough to have learned that lesson the hard way. But shit . . . it would be really god-damn good if in Murhder's case, things didn't go down like that.

It would be really good to have him back.

CHAPTER SIXTY

Murhder had not been able to sleep all day long. This was not unusual. What had been a fresh change to his chronic insomnia was that instead of his mind racing around how crazy he was, he'd spent the hours reviewing his life and all the people he had known, loved, and lost. Especially that last one.

There were new names on that list. Sarah, obviously. But also Nate. John.

The Brotherhood and the King.

What are you going to do about Sarah?

Did you mention her? I must have missed it.

That exchange with Tohr, just as the Brother had been leaving the B&B, had haunted Murhder the most—in a good way. It was a reminder of the loyalty he'd once had with the Brotherhood, and also a powerful statement that such fidelity was clearly still available to him.

Of course, Tohr wouldn't have kept a secret that jeopardized the King's security or that of the Brotherhood's or the race's. But he'd backed Murhder in that moment, and it had been a long time since someone had done that. More importantly, among males of worth, loyalty was like trust and respect: earned and reciprocal. With Tohr's pledge, Murhder was inclined to offer the same, and not just to the one Brother.

To all of them.

And that was what you needed in the field. That was what he required before he could even think of returning. The door, unlocked. The final missing piece of himself, found.

That wasn't all he'd ruminated over, however. He had also thought about the centuries he had fought. First in the woods and around the villages in the Old Country. Later, down turn-of-the-century streets of Caldwell. And more recently, in the modern world.

It had dawned on him that if he was who he believed himself to be—a warrior—then why in the fuck was he not fighting for what he wanted. What he needed. What he had every right to have.

Sarah.

You have a change of heart, then? Tohr had said.

As the Brother's dagger hand still waited for his own in the cold breeze, Murhder glanced over at the Brotherhood who were hanging back. John was with them, the younger male looking optimistic—and also worried.

Murhder looked up at the menacing façade of the great gray mansion he remembered Darius building so very long ago. It had aged in the past twenty years, but not by much. A few more streaks down the stone, bigger trees, new plantings around the grounds.

The Brother had built the massive house to last. And now, just as Darius had always wanted, the Brotherhood and the King were living together under its roof.

"Yes, I have had a change of heart," Murhder said roughly. "I want to come back. But I need two things from you all and the King."

Tohr's palm lowered. "Tell us."

"I need Sarah. My life is nothing without her. I'm not coming back without her being allowed in our world if she so chooses. This cannot be a news flash."

Tohr inclined his head. "We're on the way to a potential engagement and Wrath is on lockdown at the moment. Would it be acceptable if we address this as soon as we return? I am prepared to offer my full support. If anyone is going to get behind the importance of a female in a brother's life, it's me—and I'm sure the King will agree with me in your case now."

The King was locked down? Murhder wondered. *What the hell is going on here?*

"What's the second request?" Tohr prompted.

Murhder looked over the Brotherhood and focused on John. Then he dropped his voice to a whisper. When he was done speaking, Tohr closed his eyes.

"Yes," the male said hoarsely. "I agree."

Now Murhder put his own hand out. "Good. We have a deal."

As they shook, he was aware of a swell of emotion in his chest. There were too many loose ends to start celebrating, however. The King had to sign off on Sarah, for one.

And that was the big deal breaker. But somehow, he had a feeling which way things were going to go on the demand. The rest was going to be up to her.

"Do you want to wait at the Audience House?" Tohr indicated over his shoulder. "We are not going to be back here for a while—"

"Do you need another dagger?"

Tohr started to smile. Then he turned to the group, who immediately sported thumbs-up, fist pumps, high fives.

So Tohr hadn't lied. All of them did want him back.

It made a brother feel welcome, it truly did.

◆   ◆   ◆

Amazing, how quickly old habits returned.

As Murhder re-formed in the side yard of a gracious old manse, his body was drumming with strength and power, and he had the kind of weapons and equipment a fighter needed to back that shit up: The holster of daggers he'd been quickly fitted with crisscrossed over his heart, a familiar weight. He had guns around his waist. Hard boots on his feet. A Kevlar vest. Leathers.

His brothers had outfitted him in the work of a moment, everything a backup of what everyone else wore, brought out by a positively skip-happy Fritz.

And now he was here, in the snow and the cold, looking up at windows which revealed a typical *glymera* cocktail party, all kinds of well-dressed, high-chinned, arched-browed superior types clustered around . . .

Was that a serve-yourself bar?

Murhder shook his head. He'd been gone awhile, but he had to believe some things hadn't changed that much: Aristocrats never served themselves. Not even drinks.

They barely blew their own noses.

Going by the haughty looks exchanged as males in tuxedos filled cut crystal wineglasses for their *shellans* and gave themselves scotch on the rocks, the assembled were likewise not impressed.

A quick head count totaled just over twenty, and he guessed who the host was by the amount of carpet the guy crossed: One male, a handsome, blond-haired number with a cravat, was going back and forth across the parlor, leaving the room to answer the door, returning with guests, making introductions.

Where were the *doggen*? After all, house like this? Male like that? Party like what?

Murhder had been told the male's name was Throe, and that he had recently come over from the Old World. Long story and not relevant to this particular event, so they hadn't spent a lot of time on it. The only thing Murhder cared about was this guy had had bright ideas about the throne in the very recent past—and was likely at it again.

Without looking away from the view inside, Murhder said softly, "Are they discussing the weather in there? Or the lack of good help."

Vishous's voice was dry. "Both. I swear to fucking God, I'd rather binge-watch *Bubble Guppies* than be at a party like this."

Murhder looked at the brother. "Guppy what?"

"You don't want to know. The things you learn when there are—"

"*You* live with young? I mean, I guess I've heard there are lots of young around now."

"I'm not talking about the toddlers. It's that fucking Lassiter. The Fallen Angel. You'll meet him at some point. Hell, he probably already knows you're here." Those diamond eyes shifted over. "I'm glad you're back, by the way. All the way back."

Murhder glanced at the fighter again. Vishous had always been the most intelligent of them all, and also the most cynical—so it was kinda touching that he'd ditched the snark for once.

"Thanks, man," Murhder said.

"My brother."

As a leather-gloved fist was presented, Murhder pounded it. And then they both went back to work.

Just like old times.

CHAPTER SIXTY-ONE

There was one couple who had yet to arrive, and under any other circumstance, Throe would have told the butler to send them away. Thirty minutes late! What disrespect.

Alas, there was no butler, but the offense still stood.

Over at the bar, he poured himself a sherry, and downed it in two pulls. Other than the tardiness, however, things were progressing well. Following the initial hellos, all of which were as disingenuously warm and effusive as ever, talk had shifted to the attacks in the alleys downtown. How they all knew a family who had lost a son to some nefarious new foe. How the Brotherhood had not made it to the rescue in time. How it had happened again. And a third time.

Yes, this was precisely why Throe had sent his shadows after the offspring of these people. Set the stage. Then create the chaos here at this gathering.

Whereupon he would save the attendees, except for the two who had to die to give it all teeth. And then the tide would begin to turn.

In the direction he dictated.

Before he got things truly going, he made sure to take a mental snapshot of it all, and it was a sustaining sight for a male such as himself: the remaining members of the *glymera's* best cut of bloodlines talking with animation, the jewels of the females winking under the chandelier, the fire crackling, the ambiance matching the prestige of the decor.

A shame the way the evening was going to have to end.

"That's a bit quick, is it not?"

Throe turned to the gentlemale who had spoken. "I beg your pardon."

"Your sherry is too fine to take that fast." The male smiled smoothly. "But I suppose we all have our different ways of doing things."

Altamere, Throe thought. The male's name was Altamere.

"Cat got your tongue, old friend." Altamere put his hand on Throe's shoulder and pushed down. "Although old is a bit of a stretch for us, isn't it. You have only just arrived."

Throe narrowed his eyes. "Our bloodlines have mingled for centuries."

"But not you and I. You're a newcomer here in Caldwell. An upstart, as it were." The male indicated the grand room. "Tell me, where is the true master of this house. Does he know you're using his estate for your own purposes? Or will he be joining us."

Throe smiled coldly. "No, he will not."

"A squatter playing sire." The male leaned in. "Such a cliché."

"Will you excuse me?" Throe said. "I must go check on the meal."

"Why? Because you cooked it for us?"

As the male smiled slyly, Throe put his glass down on the makeshift bar. "Your son is in the training center program, isn't he. Don't you find that beneath you? I mean, fighting is no longer something that people in our class do. Unless you're trying to teach him a lesson in social humility?"

The male clamped his teeth together. "It is Rexboone's honor to serve the race. And with our sons dying in downtown Caldwell, I would say it's an excellent skill for a male of my class to have."

Nice little dig there, wasn't it.

Now Throe was the one leaning in. "If you truly believed that, you would announce that he's in training. That he's fighting. That he's working for the Brotherhood. The only way I found out was through the female that plays tennis with your *shellan*. Not exactly shouting it from the rooftops, are you."

As the male's pale eyes shot across the way and locked on his mate, Throe felt a stab of satisfaction at causing mated strife. After all, the aristocracy was centuries away from any fighting tradition. In this modern era, it was shameful to have any male in one's bloodline wield a gun in defense of the species.

"Things get around in society, don't they," Throe murmured as he turned away. "It's hard to keep secrets. Now, if you'll excuse me."

Walking out of the rear of the room, he went into the study which he had deliberately kept dark—and all he wanted to do was stab the fucker himself.

But that was not how things were going to go.

"Come here," he commanded into the darkness.

His favorite shadow, the one that he had tasked to protect himself, materialized beside him, a bobbing void with the slightest shimmer denoting its contours.

"You see that male?" He pointed to Altamere. "That is the one they start with. Are we clear?"

More bobbing, not that he'd expected any kind of disagreement. And to hell with waiting for the remaining two people to arrive. It wasn't as if they were going to make it to the table, anyway.

Throe checked his watch.

Regarded his guests for one last time.

"I think now. I think we shall commence . . . now."

◆   ◆   ◆

John Matthew had been paired with Qhuinn and Blay on the stakeout of the party, the three of them clustered halfway down the flank of the house in the dark wedge between spotlights that shined out onto the rolling, snow-covered lawn. They were to wait for a signal to infiltrate, and as he watched the people circulate in a room that was so elegant, he wouldn't have wanted to try to sit in a chair there, he really hoped these fancy types weren't planning to make a move on Wrath.

John had dispatched a lot of *lessers* back to the Omega. But he hadn't killed members of the species before. Not that he would hesitate if they were committing treason.

Tohr's directive was clear. If the signal was given, the Brotherhood and the fighters on the property were going to burst in and take the assembled guests into custody. Things were only going to get deadly if somebody did something stupid.

Throe, on the other hand, was a different story—

John frowned and leaned forward. Speak of the devil. The host with the most had just taken his leave of the gathering and walked into a totally dark room. Silhouetted in the light streaming in from the parlor, his dark form tilted forward, as if he were speaking to someone.

Tapping Qhuinn on the shoulder, John pointed to the window.

"Yeah," the Brother whispered. "I see it, too. What the hell?"

A sense of foreboding had John reaching for his gun; he had a really bad feeling about all this: Throe was not alone in that room. And yet there didn't seem to be a corporeal figure with him.

When the male returned to the party, John moved with him, tracking the aristocrat from window to window. Coming up to V and Murhder, John tapped them both.

Something's wrong—

The attack happened in slow motion. One moment, the cocktail party was in full swing, people talking and gesturing with the exaggerated politeness of the *glymera*—the next, a figment of John's nightmares wafted into the room.

A shadow.

Vishous barked into his shoulder mic. "Now. Now. *Now!*"

Without thinking, John took two running strides and leaped into the air, tucking his head and rolling forward such that his leather-covered shoulders shattered the glass. Swinging his feet over his head to complete the somersault, he landed on his boots with his gun up.

But it was too late for the male who was attacked. Before John could squeeze off a round of the Brotherhood's sacred bullets, the shadow entity lashed out at a guest, piercing him through the chest, the male's screams bloodcurdling until they were cut off by a throat slash.

Blood flew from an open artery in the aristocrat's neck, the arc as graceful as the violence was terrible.

John set his position, leveled his gun . . . and squeezed off two rounds as soon as he got a clear shot. But that was all he could do. In the panic typical of laypeople, the party guests fell into a disorganized scramble, tripping over gowns, over each other, running in all directions like the spooked sheep they were.

He'd hit the entity at least once, though: Its high-pitched squeal cut through even the yelling and the pounding of feet.

And then the shadow turned on him.

As the crowd scattered away, John smiled. And pulled his trigger again. Two more times. A sixth—

With each bullet, the shadow was forced back, the slugs of lead that were treated with holy water from the Scribe Virgin's fountain driving the entity into a retreat. Even as fins licked out of its translucent black core, and those knives flew around, John was too dominant as he pursued the thing.

Smaller. The outer edges of the shadow were shrinking in, its size diminishing. And fortunately, the crowd and the other fighters were staying out of range, so he had the room he needed to finish the damn thing off.

John kicked out the clip he'd emptied. Slammed in a new one.

He was careful not to get too close.

He had no intention of getting stung—

"John! Watch out!"

Before he could look in the direction of the voice, a massive body tackled him, throwing him off his shitkickers. He kept shooting even as he headed for the floor, focusing only on his target. Just before he slammed into the carpet, the shadow became lit from the inside, an evil glow emanating from the center of its bulbous form. In the blink of an eye, that glow rippled outward—

John hit the floor with Murhder on top of him, the breath exploding out of his lungs . . . at the same time the shadow blew apart, a black wash, part tar, part congealed blood, spackling the previously perfect wall behind it as well as the rug, a painting, a sofa.

It was like sewer sludge had been blown out of a cannon.

John could only stare at the spectacle. And it was as his brain replayed frame by frame what had gone down that he recalled seeing another shadow coming at him from the side.

Murhder had undoubtedly saved his life.

For the second time.

CHAPTER SIXTY-TWO

S tanding on the far side of the parlor, next to the guns and knives he had discreetly stashed in a bookcase, Throe had been ready to arm himself to defend his guests against the "threat." But just as he was about to reach for the weapons, he heard the sound of breaking glass—at the exact moment one of his shadows attacked Altamere.

He could not comprehend what had shattered and why such a thing would occur.

And then it was all too clear.

His plan, to be the "defender" of the aristocrats in the face of the shadows, to be the one to save these useless members of the *glymera* so they would back him, to set the stage for an overthrow of the King after the Brotherhood had not rescued their targeted sons, was utterly shattered—just like the glass of the windows the Brothers and fighters broke through to jump into the room from the outside.

Throe hit the ground so he didn't get struck by the cross fire, and he watched with stunned disbelief as the Brotherhood took over the attack, protecting the civilians, engaging the shadows . . . saving lives.

Throe didn't stick around for more than a minute.

Scrambling across the carpet on his belly, he pushed with his slippery tuxedo shoes and dragged himself forward with his bare palms to go around the corner and get away from the chaos. As soon as he was in the foyer, he jumped up into a crouch, put his arms over his head, and ran for the stairs. Taking them two at a time, the gunfire, the screams, the squeals, receded some as he made it to the second story.

When he got to the master bedroom, he took out his key. Vampires could unlock anything but copper with their minds which was why the master of the house had made sure his suite was properly protected.

Throe dropped his keys. Fumbled them again—

Finally, he was through the door and he wheeled around to slam the heavy oak panels shut with his palms—

Throe froze as a strange breeze brushed over his hair.

A breeze that had a pull to it.

As his instincts pricked in alarm, a nauseous fear goosebumped his skin and his breath got short.

Don't look behind yourself, a voice deep inside his head ordered him. *Get out of here, now!*

Throe didn't waste a heartbeat. He didn't care what was on the other side, he grabbed for the doorknob—

"Ow!" Retracting his palm, he shook out a sensation of burning. "What the hell?"

Ripping off his tuxedo jacket, he wrapped his hand up and—

A hollow moaning sound rippled through the room, and the lights flickered. And even though he knew he should not look, should never look, he found his head cranking to the side.

When he saw what was behind him, Throe screamed.

✦   ✦   ✦

Murhder didn't jump off of John, even though he knew damn well he was crushing the male. With this many guns being discharged? You made any quick vertical moves and you lost your fucking head.

Bullets whistled by, taking out lamps, turning oil paintings to sieves, blowing up porcelain bowls and gold-speckled plates. Grabbing John by the shoulder, he rolled the two of them out of the way, taking cover behind a sofa the color of a buttercup.

Jesus, it was like *Die Hard* only shot in a museum instead of a high-rise. And what the fuck were those shadow things?

Murhder took aim at the nearest one, which was lashing out at Rhage, and as he pulled the trigger on a gun for the first time in twenty years, his aim was really fucking bad. He ended up drilling a crystal sconce to the left of the fireplace, the lightbulbs exploding into sparks as they vaporized.

He didn't make that mistake twice.

Finding a groove, he squeezed off multiple rounds, and thus gave Rhage the chance to rescue two females who were holding each other and cowering behind a silk armchair. With the brother as protection, they ran off, high heels twisting ankles, their gowns held up to their waists, their once-neat chignons now birds' nests full of tangles.

John swung his own muzzle around, and doubled down on the shadow that Murhder was working on, discharging his own bullets—

There was an unholy squeal, a sound higher than a piccolo's best note and louder than a jet engine. And then the entity blew apart like the first one had, oily mud flying out and hitting the mantelpiece as well as what was left of the window Murhder had broken with his own body.

It was like someone slinging fresh cow flops around.

Two more to go.

Except . . .

The remaining shadows weren't attacking anything. The entities were side by side and stationary in the archway of the darkened study beyond, like smog balloons tethered to a fixed point in the floor.

He and John leveled muzzles on their direction.

Nobody moved: Not them. Not their targets.

That was not true elsewhere in the house. The other brothers and fighters were rushing to get the guests to secured locations, all kinds of shuffling feet, hushed voices full of fear, and barked orders radiating into the parlor from a distance.

"We need to kill them now," Murhder said softly. "It's the only—"

Poof! Poof!

The entities disappeared, one after another.

As a scream lit off somewhere on the second floor.

◆   ◆   ◆

Throe tried for the doorknob again, but it burned through the tuxedo jacket—and then getting out of the bedroom suite was no longer an option. What started out as a breeze morphed into a vacuum, the pull dragging him away from the door—

He dropped to his knees. Grabbed onto anything that he went by: A spindly chair. The edge of a side table. The bureau. He fought and clawed, churned his legs, locked eyes on the door into the bathroom as if that would give him a redirection.

He did not want to look again. But once more, his head turned as if controlled by someone else.

The Book had opened itself on the writing desk, and the perfectly cylindrical black void had reappeared, that which Throe had witnessed previously happening anew, that which should have been no deeper than the three-foot drop to the bedroom floor under the blotter funneling into an unfathomable depth—

Something stung his hand. And then his other one.

He swung his head back around. Two of his shadows were before him, and they were lashing out, punishing his grips as he tried to keep himself in the realm of reality.

Throe screamed one last time as he lost all purchase against the powerful draw.

And then his body was sucked feet-first into the void.

Falling. He was falling, the cold damp air becoming more and more frigid. Colder, faster, colder . . . faster. Ice forming on his upraised hands, his eyelashes, his cheeks.

As his velocity continued to increase, his tuxedo frayed off his body, the fibers brittle from the indescribable freeze, the speed of the fall, the pressure that began to bear down on him. Naked . . . he was naked now, his skin frosting over, turning black.

And then fraying as his clothes had.

His flesh was next. That which had contained his insides stripped off his bones, and though his eyes disintegrated, he could somehow still see the white of his skeleton—until that turned black as well.

All of his corporeal form was torn away, nothing but his spirit remaining.

And that was when he landed at some kind of bottom, sure as if he still had a physical body, pain lancing through him as if vital organs had been pulverized and his spine destroyed from the impact.

Throe lay on his back, and stared up at a circular stone construction that glistened in torchlight. A well. He was at the bottom of a well.

And that was not torchlight. His path, his descent, had left a glow in the darkness and he traced its path until it seemed to disappear at some far-off place way up above—

Metal clanking brought his head up, and he looked down his naked body which had somehow regenerated. Shackles had clamped on his wrists and his ankles.

"What . . . what is this?" His voice was hoarse. "What e'er is this?"

He pulled at the metal bands and found no give in them at all. He was on some kind of ancient wooden table, the stains of which made him more than merely squeamish.

"Where am . . ."

He did not finish the thought.

A woman entered from the walling, as if there was a break somewhere therein. She was naked and gloriously so, her high firm breasts and perfect nipples, her flat stomach and lovely hips, her long legs and hairless sex, the very picture of beauty. And it was only after he had made his impression of her body that he looked at her face.

She had brunette hair that curled, long and luscious, around her shoulders, and her features were bold and arresting.

Her smile was paradise. And so was the sound of her voice: "Welcome."

"Who are you?" As he felt himself harden, she looked at his erection. "Is this a dream?"

The woman came over to him and trailed her fingers up the inside of his thigh. "No, this is a trade."

". . . what?"

The female stroked his arousal, her touch going through his body, his blood thickening instantly. As he moaned, she smiled again.

"A trade," she murmured as her hand went up and down his shaft, nice and slow.

The pleasure she called out from him seemed familiar. In fact . . . her scent was familiar. He knew her. Somehow, he knew—

The Book.

She was the Book.

"That's right," she said. "And I have enjoyed our dalliances even though I was only able to participate up to a point."

Dread, fast and powerful as the lust, came onto him like the pall of death, but somehow did not cancel the erotic swell that was taking him to the very knife edge of release.

Throe struggled, but there was no getting free. Not of the terror that curdled his gut, not of the orgasm that was just about to explode out of him, not of his restraints.

Not of her.

She released his erection right before he could find his relief from the rising tide of pleasure. And as she took a step back, he protested even though he was frightened of her. But she couldn't stop now. She couldn't leave him on the verge . . . could she?

"It's been fun, Throe. So glad you came looking for me. You showed up just as I needed a way out."

With that, she tilted her head up. Raising her arms, she bent her knees and propelled herself into a jump.

That took her airborne.

Throe's scream echoed around the slick walls of the well as the female followed the trail he had lit with his body and soul, her graceful escape taking her up, up, up . . .

. . . and leaving him in her place.

CHAPTER SIXTY-THREE

Murhder and John took the stairs two at a time as Vishous stayed down below with the corpse of the male who had been killed by the shadow entity.

The brother seemed to be standing guard over the remains, as if he expected the dead aristocrat to sit back up and have a conversation or something. But Murhder didn't argue as Tohr assigned the second floor to him and John.

On the top landing, he covered right. John covered left.

There was no more screaming, however. No moaning of someone injured. Nothing moving.

But only the inexperienced would take all that as dispositive. There were countless explanations for why someone would scream and then shut up. Especially if that someone was Throe, who had taken off running up here—

The whistling was soft, the kind of thing that could be generated either by an air vent or someone who was having an asthma attack.

Murhder looked to the right again.

But then John nodded in his direction and Murhder fell in behind the male, the pair of them crossing to the opposite side of the corridor so they went down the wall that was solid, as opposed to the one that had all the door breaks in it. Guns up, instincts on fire, they moved in perfect coordination, and Murhder had to smile, even though it made him a freak.

Except John looked over his shoulder. And winked.

Murhder lost his step.

He hadn't seen that expression in years. Not since he and Darius had hunted slayers together—and wasn't it great to see that male of worth live on through his blooded son? All you had to do was look at John and know that D was still alive and well . . . and with the brothers.

Abruptly, the whistling ended, and they both stopped. Without a word of communication, they split and back-flatted on either side of a closed door.

Inexplicably, the panels had a black rim around the jamb, as if there had been a fire inside and smoke had escaped. But there was no heat. In fact, it was noticeably colder here, a draft coming out from under the gap at the bottom. Which explained the sound they'd tracked.

Murhder pointed to himself and John nodded. Then he held up one finger . . . two . . .

On three, John swung around, kicked open the door, and Murhder went in first with his gun up—

"What the fuck," he muttered as he hauled up short.

The window across the bedroom suite was wide open, the winter night barreling in on a stiff wind, the drapes billowing. And everywhere else, the antique furniture was in disarray, the bureau, the bed, the side tables . . . all crammed in a circle around an old writing desk with a burn mark on it.

John went across and punched open the door to a walk-in closet. When he shook his head indicating it was clear, Murhder proceeded further into the room, zeroing in on that desk as John checked out the bathroom.

Murhder lowered his weapon. The burn mark on the leather blotter was perfectly square, about two foot by one foot.

The size of a book—

A high-pitched whistle sounded out down the hall, and John sent three short bursts in reply. Moments later, Tohr came in with his guns up.

"What happened in here?" the brother said.

"No clue." Murhder looked around again, searching for . . . fuck knew what. "Did you find Throe—"

Three gunshots went off directly below them on the first floor.

"Shit!" Murhder lunged for the way out. "The shadows are back—"

Tohr caught him and prevented him from leaving. "No. That's . . . the male who died and did not stay that way."

"What are you talking about?"

Tohr didn't reply to that—verbally. Instead, the bald look in the brother's eye stated plainly that nightmares could come true—and suddenly, Murhder knew without a doubt where John's injury had come from.

"Shit," he breathed.

◆   ◆   ◆

After John had cleared a second closet, he came over to Tohr and Murhder and signed, *How many injured downstairs?*

"Xcor got shot, but at least it was just through the thigh," Tohr answered. "I had to hold him back from going after Throe. We've also got a female who probably has a dislocated ankle. And then there's you."

John looked down at himself in a panic, his brain going a thousand miles an hour into the brick wall of another wound like the one he'd had.

Except then Murhder said, "Huh. What do you know. I got hit."

The Brother poked at his shoulder, and that was when John started to smell the blood in the air. Sure enough, there was a round bullet hole in Murhder's leather jacket—and John breathed deeply in relief. Conventional wound. Totally treatable—

Headlights flared across the walls of the room, the beams flashing through the open window.

"Surgical unit is on-site," Tohr said to Murhder. "Let's get you down there. You coming John?"

John pointed at the open window and then went over to close it. As the other two left, he gripped the sash and . . .

Leaning out, he looked down to the snow in the side yard. In the otherwise perfectly undisturbed blanket of white, there was a set of tracks that went from just below the window across the property. At the tree line that separated the estate from its splendiferous neighbor, the prints seemed to disappear, but it was hard to know if that was because whoever had made them had dematerialized or just walked into the evergreens.

All of that was odd, for sure. First of all, if Throe had wanted to leave the scene, he could have just ghosted out. Why open the window? There was no steel mesh. And if the male were injured and therefore couldn't dematerialize? There would be blood—or the prints would have been messy, indicating a shuffle.

But none of that was what really got John's attention.

The true weirdness made him rub his eyes and refocus, just to make sure he was seeing things properly.

The footsteps appeared to glow like phosphorus.

John shut the window and strode out of the room. Downstairs, he entered the secured area in what turned out to be a library. Rhage, V, Blay, and Qhuinn were guarding the assembled civilians, all of whom appeared shaken in their formal evening clothes. Doc Jane was assessing each of the guests with Manny no doubt doing procedures as necessary in the mobile surgical unit.

Tohr was talking on his phone, and John waited for the Brother to end the call. "Hey, son, what's up."

John indicated the front door with a nod of his head, and the pair of them went out and around to the side yard. There was no reason to point at the tracks. They were still glowing.

"What the hell is this?" Tohr muttered.

The Brother strode forward, getting down on his haunches as he checked out the start of the prints under the second-story window. Then he and John followed them to the tree line, ducking under the pine boughs and looking for signs that they continued through the undergrowth.

Nope.

They ended.

Back out from under, they watched as the glow dimmed. And then disappeared altogether.

"This makes no damn sense." Tohr got out his phone again and triggered the flashlight. Lowering himself down, he shook his head. "On too many levels to count."

John bent over and stared at the prints, also.

WTF?

Up close, it was clear they weren't made by loafers or boots, but what they seemed to be from . . . well, it was a case of no damned sense, as Tohr said.

The print had a triangular front pad and a point for the back.

As if whoever had made them had been wearing stilettos.

CHAPTER SIXTY-FOUR

Back in Ithaca, Sarah was wide awake and busy, busy, busy. Then again, a whole lot of her life was off course from the path she'd set for herself, her ship blown into unfamiliar waters, her map lost overboard, her compass broken.

So yes, she was packing up her house at—what time was it? Ah, one thirty a.m.

She'd tried the whole sleeping thing. First upstairs in her bed with Murhder's plaited hair underneath her pillow; then two hours later, down on the couch in front of the TV. Neither had worked in the slightest. Eventually, she hadn't been able to stand herself for one more minute longer.

She was in so much emotional pain, she couldn't stay still, her body moving, jerking, shifting in whatever position she stretched out in. She missed Murhder so badly it hurt, and she was struck by the fact that it was all so much more painful than the aftermath of Gerry's death.

By an incalculable degree.

Thus, a Mr. Clean kind of thing had struck her as a productive use of her insomnia. And initially, she'd decided to start with Spic n'

Span'ing the kitchen, on her hands and knees, going all Joan Crawford in *Mommy Dearest.*

Helga, when you polish the floor, you have to move the tree.

God, she couldn't believe she still remembered that quote.

But when she'd opened the cupboard under the sink for the Bona, she saw a clutter of containers, and steel wool packages, and paper towels. Getting to her feet, she'd ended up going through every drawer, every shelf, each nook and cranny.

Only to become overwhelmed by the amount of stuff she was going to have to organize to move out. And in a way, it was a relief to have a big job, even though compared to most people, she probably didn't have a ton of extra things. Not like, if she'd had a child—

She'd thought of Nate at that point.

Which was how she'd ended up here on the second floor: She'd tried to leave the mourning for that young male in the kitchen where it had kicked off. Besides, start at the top, work your way down, right?

Except what awaited her upstairs turned out to be worse.

Going through her clothes seemed like a good idea, the out, safe, giveaway decisions the kind of thing that her exhausted, yet wired, brain could handle because, hello, it wasn't brain surgery. Plus, she'd saved some of the U-Haul boxes she and Gerry had used when they'd moved in up in the attic, so she could bring that whole touch-only-once efficiency to the endeavor.

Feeling like she was back on "a" course, if not "the" course, she pulled down the ladder steps from the ceiling in the hall and walked herself up into the cold, raftered attic of her house.

At which point, she got kicked in the chest again.

Sure, there were empty boxes, the lids unfolded, their bellies open. But there was also one that was closed up.

"Damn it."

Still standing on the ladder, her body half in and half out of the attic, she told herself to keep with the plan. Get the empties and drop them down. Go to her closet. Organize.

Instead, she ascended the last three rungs, and went over to the box with the taped lid. Before she knew what she was doing—and thereby could block the impulse—her fingers pulled up the masking tape and popped the folded sleeves free.

The box was one of U-Haul's wardrobe varieties, a dowel running across the top so that you could put hangers on it.

There was only one thing suspended within its four sides. Sometime in the last two years, the jacket to Gerry's wedding suit had slipped off its hanger and slid down its matching slacks to pool in the bottom.

Sarah closed her eyes and sagged.

After he'd died, his parents had insisted on coming over from Germany to claim the body and visit the house which they had not yet seen in person. Sarah had invited them to go through Gerry's things, thinking that they would want to keep a few of his belongings. She had left the house to give them some privacy—and returned an hour later to find that they had packed up all his clothes and anything that he had had with him through college.

She'd had the sense that his mother had viewed this as a service to Sarah. A way of tidying up the mess that his death had caused in all their lives.

The only thing the woman could have done to keep herself in one piece.

Sarah had known that he still had a few things at work, little mementos on his desk. She figured she would keep them, and then she had pictures on her phone, her computer. Her memories. Plus, how did you fight with someone's mother over their socks, for godsakes.

So she had let it go, and they had taken everything with them, including his laundry out of the clothes hamper. She'd never forgot those suitcases they'd bought at Target. It had been kind of sad to think that all of Gerry's worldly possessions could fit into three medium-sized Samsonites. Then again, he'd been a thinker. Possessions had not been a priority for him.

It had been a surprise a week later, then, to go into the closet in their bedroom and find his wedding suit tucked behind her one long dress, two dress blouses, and her own interview suit that she'd last had on when she'd come for an on-site visit to BioMed.

Gerry's mom had missed the jacket and slacks because everything else of her son's had been in his bureau outside.

Sarah had put the matching set away up here a couple days later. It wasn't that she'd wanted to forget him. It was the wedding. The almost-made-it reality of that ceremony and reception had been too painful, although not because she was mourning the fact that they'd never made it to the altar due to his death.

It was more that she hadn't been sure they were going to make it if he'd lived.

And so . . . up here.

In this box.

Hanging from a dowel on a Macy's hanger.

She took the hanger out and smoothed the slacks. There had been a Black Friday sale the day after Thanksgiving, and she'd made him go to the mall with her to take advantage of the savings in the men's department. He hadn't even owned an interview suit. He'd gone to BioMed in jeans and a Harvard sweatshirt with a hole in the sleeve. Then again, when you were a genius and people were not hiring you for your sartorial sense, what did all the navy blue and the lapels and the pinstriped ties in the world matter.

Gerry could be odd. Disinterested in things other people normally did.

A pain in the ass, to be honest.

But God, his brain. He had had the most magnificent brain. And as she thought about what he had been like, she realized that his intelligence had been a huge part of his appeal to her. He'd been an outlier as sure as a male model was, an unusual combination of attributes that resulted in a spectacularly special human being.

Except boy, the shopping trip. That excursion had been the first tip-off that things were really bad between them. Or rather . . . the first tip-off that was a conscious thought of hers instead of a weighty feeling she had resolutely ignored.

He'd never worn the suit, obviously. Had barely tried it on before they'd had to come back here so he could return to his study, his computer, his work.

Running her hand down the slacks, she found the fine wool smooth. There were no cuffs yet on the bottoms of the legs because they'd needed to get it fitted, but she'd known better than to try to get him to wait until the in-store tailor had been done with another customer.

There would be time, she'd told herself.

Nope. No time.

With a curse, she bent down into the box and picked up the jacket, pulling it out—

Something dropped to the bare floorboards.

An envelope.

◆　◆　◆

Nate had no idea where he was or what he was doing.

Okay, he was outside in the woods somewhere and it was cold. Oh, so very cold. He had on a borrowed parka that was puffy as a cloud. Borrowed shirt and pants that were huge in terms of size and yet fit him. Borrowed underwear. Borrowed boots.

He had been out here for now three hours and forty-five minutes. Give or take.

So in a way, he had grown used to how much he didn't like looking around. Too much of a vista, and everything was overwhelming: the spindly trees, the fluffy trees, the spiky undergrowth, the sense that there was an incalculable distance to be traveled in any direction. And he *really* didn't like looking up at the vast sky above: The incalculable number of little pinpoints of light shining through a dense blackness made him worry he was going to fly off the earth and get lost up there.

And the smells. The complex bouquet of earth, animal, and air was just too much for his brain to handle. His heart was pounding like he was being chased, he was too hot under the parka, his eyes were darting everywhere and making him dizzy.

Then again, he had been working hard.

As his eyes watered, he brushed at them with impatience. The cold dry wind. Yes, that was it.

He absolutely was *not* crying. From fear of how big the world was. From anger that he had been cheated out of twenty years of his life. From sadness that he was out here for his *mahmen*.

"They should arrive soon," a female voice said. "Any minute."

Nate looked over his shoulder. Xhex, the female who had been kept in the same lab as his *mahmen*, stood with her back to the wind. Her short hair was smudged by the gusts, moving this way . . . another way. She was dressed in black leather, and her face was grim.

He wondered, if his *mahmen* had survived for another two decades, whether she would have turned out to be as tough as this female clearly was. Or would she have remained as he remembered, kind, gentle, but scared.

He wanted to ask what Xhex recalled about his *mahmen* and the lab, but he had a feeling he didn't want to know. He'd seen enough for himself. He'd had enough done to him.

"Are you over it?" he asked roughly. "What they did to us?"

It was a while before the female answered. "No. I don't think about it much, but I don't believe it's because I'm over it."

"Am I going to be okay?"

"Yes, you are. I promise you that."

Nate shivered and braced himself . . . and then looked over at the simple pine coffin that had been put on a platform in the clearing. He had hammered himself the latter from trees that he had cut down with an axe and honed as best he could. His palms were torn up. His work was shoddy. And the scent of pine sap was still thick in the air.

But he had made the pyre himself. As was proper.

The coffin had just appeared, about twenty minutes ago. Murhder and John had driven it into the clearing on the back of a beautiful truck, and they had just taken the vehicle back to wherever it had come from—

One by one, two figures materialized in the clearing. Murhder and John reappearing.

"Hey, son," Murhder said as he came over.

They embraced, and the older male said, "You did fine work with this. Very fine."

Nate took his hands out of his pockets. He meant to say something, but he choked. His torn up palms spoke for themselves, though.

Murhder squeezed his shoulder and then John was giving him a hug, too. As the males stepped back, he wished Sarah were here. Even though that made no sense, he supposed.

Yeah, except for the fact that she had found him. Helped get him free. Taken care of him.

He missed her presence from this like a family member's.

Nate took a deep breath and stared at the coffin. While he'd been staying in the training center, he'd asked everyone who came by to visit him how they honored their dead. The humans had one way. The *symphaths* another. The vampires a third. After a couple of nights, people had started to seek him out to share their stories. *Doggen* had come to him. Two Shadows.

And then a blond-and-black-haired male who had seemed like a vampire, but who, he later learned, was actually a fallen angel.

A real, live fallen angel. Which was pretty magical.

He'd never met an angel before. Other than his *mahmen*, of course.

Actually, he hadn't met many people.

The fallen angel had given him the best advice. He'd said that there was no right or wrong way to honor the dead. The living could pay their respects in any way they chose. The important thing was that the deceased was sent unto the afterlife on a wave of love.

Because it helped the departed souls find peace in their new place.

At least that was what the fallen angel maintained. And if anyone was likely to know about these things . . .

In the end, Nate chose the way of the Shadows. He didn't like the idea of his *mahmen's* remains rotting and disintegrating in the ground.

And the heat would carry everything to the heavens, to where he'd been told the Fade was.

Off to the side, he had a torch that he'd stuck, handle first, into the snow. The top of it was kerosene-soaked cloth wound tightly around a steel-and-wood shank. He lit it with something called a Bic that one of the Brothers—the one with the tattoo on his temple—had given him.

Flames burst to life, orange and yellow, bright in the darkness of the woods.

As he approached his *mahmen*'s remains, he decided the clearing he'd chosen was almost made for this kind of thing, a near-perfect circle barren of growth.

As he touched the flame to the supports of the pyre, the gasoline he'd splashed onto the fresh-cut lengths of pine caught fire in a blaze that spread all around the construction in a matter of moments.

The resulting heat multiplied and multiplied until he had to step back.

A hand was laid on his shoulder. Murhder. And then Xhex held his hand. And John put his palm on Nate's back.

The three of them stood together and watched the coffin and the body burn, the white smoke rising up into the black night in curls that carried countless sparks ever higher.

Unto the Fade.

He desperately wanted to know if she thought he'd been a good son. But he was never going to have the answer for that. What he could do, however: Live his life in honor of her. Even though he wanted to lock himself in that patient room in the training center for the rest of his nights because it felt safe and familiar, he would not do that.

In service to his *mahmen*, he would try to live the freedom she had been so cruelly cheated of. He would force himself to acclimate to this too-big world. He would conquer the fear that dogged him.

Everything he did would be for her.

"Goodbye, *Mahmen* . . ." he whispered into the cold wind.

CHAPTER SIXTY-FIVE

Up in Sarah's attic, all she could do was stare at the envelope as it lay facedown on the floorboards. When she was finally able to think, she looked stupidly at the jacket. The thing must have fallen out of one of the pockets.

Her hand shook as she bent down to pick it up. Bracing herself, she turned the envelope over, expecting to see Gerry's name on the front and a receipt inside. A business card to contact the tailor. Or—

Sarah.

In Gerry's handwriting.

Her name, written by him.

As her legs got wobbly, she sat where she stood, dangling her feet out the folding steps' hole in the ceiling. She trembled so badly that she almost dropped the thing as she opened the flap. Inside, there was a single piece of paper, folded in three, and she needed to breathe for a bit before she could flatten things and try to read.

He'd handwritten the entire note. Something she had never known him to do.

Her eyes could not focus. Part of it was tears at the sight of his scribbles. Part of it was fear at what he was about to tell her. Most of it was the idea that he was communicating with her. After all this time, after her recent searching . . . he was answering her from the grave.

Dear Sarah,

If you are reading this, it means things did not go as I hope they will. It means I'm gone. It means I will not have a chance to wear this suit proudly and stand with you at the altar to become your husband. This breaks my heart.

I know I have been distant these past few months. Maybe even longer. Please forgive me. I am not even sure where to begin. About a year into working at BioMed, my security clearance was increased. You remember this. We felt it was a promotion. Shortly after I had more access in my division, I learned of an inhumane experiment being conducted in secret on the premises. It is not the first time BioMed has done such and I gather that at least one researcher has been killed because of it.

Without going into specifics, because the less you know, the safer you will be, I have to try to stop them. I am exporting information and will be going to authorities as soon as I can be sure that I can do so without endangering the subject's safety. Believe me when I say this, I am afraid for my life—and by extension, yours. They will stop at nothing to protect their interests and their research. This is why I have not been talking to you about my work anymore.

If I am dead, know that Dr. Robert Kraiten either killed me himself or had me killed on his behalf. There is a safety deposit box at our bank under my name. Go there. Take the disk and the security clearance out and go to the FBI with them. This is an interstate crime of incomprehensible scope and implication.

Please know that I love you. I wish there was a way to open

up to you now, but I cannot risk your safety. I miss you. I love
you. Every night, while you sleep, I stand in the doorway of our
bedroom and cry. How has it come to this?

Love, Gerry

Sarah could not stop reading the words, tracing the messy penman-
ship, looking at the jacket. The release of the tension she had carried for
two years was so tremendous, she got dizzy and had to throw out a
hand to catch herself from falling backward.

Gerry was still gone. This much was true.

But he was back now, too. The letter resurrected the man she had
always thought he was, replacing the version of him she had feared he'd
become.

If only he had known the other half of the story. Had he been aware
that the boy he wanted to protect was of a different species? Or maybe
he had realized that from the scans . . .

Bringing the jacket across her lap, she put the letter back in the envelope and returned everything to the inside pocket. For some reason,
she wanted to leave it all exactly as Gerry had. It was like their last embrace.

There was no bringing him back. And no going back to who she'd
been when they'd been together. Murhder had changed her. Nate had
changed her. Her knowledge of that species had changed her.

Time had changed her.

But this . . . brought a measure of peace that she desperately needed.

Shifting up onto her knees, she hung the jacket over the slacks and
set the suit back on the dowel inside the box. There was no re-sticking
the tape on the top. It was two years old to begin with, and had lost a lot
of its adhesive properties. She tucked the four flaps into each other,
however, and she would return with better tape later.

Sarah stood at the box with her palms on the closed top for a while.
It seemed appropriate to take a moment. And she would make sure that

wherever she went, the suit came with her. She would not leave him behind, even if Gerry was not a part of her future.

He had played a substantial role in her past, for sure.

The loss of Murhder was still going to hurt like hell. But at least it wasn't compounded by the sense that the man she had almost married hadn't been who she'd believed him to be.

Fucking Kraiten. She was glad he'd stabbed himself in the gut and had bled out all over his no doubt fancy kitchen. He deserved worse.

And in a way, Murhder and his kind had avenged Gerry's death for her—

A knocking on her front door, loud and insistent, brought her head up. Then . . . silence.

More knocking now.

Why didn't she have a gun in the house?

"Because you don't know how to shoot one," she muttered as she went down the ladder.

Heading to the dark guest bathroom in the front of the house, she peeled back the curtain and—

Now, her heart raced for a different reason. What was . . . was she seeing things?

Knocking on the glass, she waved and then turned around so fast, she slipped on the throw rug and nearly broke her arm catching her fall on the tub edge.

She hit the stairs on a full scramble, and almost did a roadrunner through her own door. Fumble . . . fumble . . . fumble with the dead bolt—

Sarah nearly ripped the door off its hinges.

There on the other side was her short-haired, beautiful vampire, with a bouquet of evergreen boughs gathered in a satin bow.

The instant he met her eyes, he dropped down on one knee and held up the fragrant, fluffy branches. "These should be roses. I'm sorry that they're—"

"What—what are you doing here—"

"—not roses. I understand that human males present their females with red roses—"

"Murhder, how are you here?"

He stood up slowly, his eyes traveling around her face as if he were re-memorizing her features. "I fought for us. I am a warrior, and I fought for us."

"What?" she breathed.

"Here, let's go inside, it's cold for you."

"Is it?" she whispered as she backed up.

Murhder shut them in together, she couldn't believe he was standing in front of her.

"Am I dreaming?" she asked.

"No." He touched her cheek. "This is real."

"Kiss me, then?"

He closed his eyes in reverence. And then leaned down and pressed his lips to hers. Once. Twice. Again.

Sarah wrapped her arms around as much of his shoulders as she could manage—which was granted not much given his size. "How are you here?" she repeated against his mouth.

"I feel like I haven't seen you in a lifetime." Those incredible peach-colored eyes of his bored into hers. "I ached for you."

"And I ached for *you*."

There was babbling at that point. Both of them were speaking, but no one was making sense, and none of it mattered anyway. She had been trying to get used to the emptiness of his absence, swimming in the cold murky waters of loneliness—and yet now he was here. They were together, they—

She pushed him back. "What happened?"

"I realized that I needed to fight for you. The Brotherhood, they wanted me back with them, they asked me to fight for the race with them again as one of them. But there was no way I was doing that without fighting for us first. And Wrath had a change of heart."

"So I'm allowed back?"

He stepped away and held up his hands. "I looked you up on the Internet."

"Well, at least I don't have to worry about any naked pictures surfacing."

"You are not just any scientist. You're a very important—"

"No more important than anyone else. I don't believe in the ego stuff."

Murhder's slow smile made her blush. Then again, that expression on his face was telling her without words how much he respected her.

"Be that as it may," he said, "I'm not going to force you to come with me. I can come to you, if you don't want to leave your work—"

Sarah tucked his bouquet under her arm, grabbed his face, and kissed him. "Oh, my God! So I can continue my research at the training center? Because I need to work with Doc Jane on the storage of blood. I'm not sure you're aware of this, but you have a critical issue as a species when it comes to blood storage . . ."

◆   ◆   ◆

God, he loved this female. He loved her so damned much.

Only his Sarah could embrace him and kiss him, and look like he had delivered the entire world to her just by showing up on her doorstep—and then promptly get excited about the science she was going to do.

Murhder's smile was so great, his cheeks stretched wide. And he was oh, so content to let her go on for however long she wanted to.

"—looking at me like that?" she said with a grin.

"Because I love you, Dr. Sarah Watkins. I love you so much, and I just . . . want to be with you."

On that note, he took his "bouquet" from her, set it aside, and got serious with the kissing. The next thing he knew, they were on her couch again, this time with her on top, her thighs split over his hips. She lifted her shirt up and over her head, and then . . . the bra. Her bra disappeared on a oner. Naked, so beautifully naked. And as he cupped her breasts, and then sat up to worship them with his mouth, he knew he was home.

And that would have been true no matter what house he was in with her. The key was her. For tonight and the rest of his life, the key to everything was going to be her.

"So Wrath is okay with all this?" she asked breathlessly.

"We can live with the Brotherhood or get a house."

"I'm selling this one, so I'm free."

"You are?"

"I was going to let you know where I went." She kissed him some more. "I was always going to let you know where to find me."

He pictured her in his attic down at the Rathboone House and decided that might be a good retreat for them. He was going to have to move a nice big bed in, though.

And she must never know how close he came to killing himself. He didn't want to think of that ever again, either.

"I'd like a house of our own," she said as she dismounted and tore off her jeans like they'd burned her. "That would be great."

He meant to say something coherent. He truly did.

But then she was up on him and working his fly. The second his erection was sprung, she was on him. Literally.

"Oh, God . . . *Sarah* . . ."

They made love for a good hour. Maybe more. And then they wrapped up in her blanket and held each other close.

"Sarah," he said.

"What's wrong." She sat up. "I can hear it in your voice."

"I have to go."

"Oh, right, before the sun shows up. This house really isn't safe for you, is it. Can I come with you?"

Murhder smiled. "Yes. Please. Fritz is getting a bedroom ready for us at the big house. And there's going to be a party at dawn."

"Really?" She smiled. "What perfect timing. I feel like I have all kinds of things to celebrate."

"Me, too, my love." He kissed her again. "Me, too."

Murhder intended on things stopping there. But it was Sarah. So naturally, the kissing led to all kinds of other stuff. And he wouldn't have had it any other way.

CHAPTER SIXTY-SIX

B ack at the Brotherhood mansion, John Matthew stepped out of the shower and toweled off. As he tucked the terry cloth around his hips, he looked over at the double sinks and smiled. Xhex's wet towel had been ditched on the counter and he took care to hang it up on the peg by the alcove. She'd seemed to be in a hurry to leave after they'd had sex under all that hot water: Kissing him goodbye while he'd been shaving. Dressing fast.

All but running out of their suite.

She'd lost a lot of time at work lately, though. There was probably stuff she had to take care of at shAdoWs—

The pounding on his door brought his head around and stopped his heart.

There was only one kind of fist that made that kind of sound, and he hustled to answer things. Opening the—

John Matthew froze.

Standing outside of his room, in the Hall of Statues, which had been plunged into darkness, the Brotherhood had gathered in a semi-circle. He could not see their faces because they were covered from head to foot in black robes, their features hidden by hoods that had been pulled up. But their scents. He knew their scents.

He blinked. Tried to take a breath.

Either someone had died or—

"John Matthew, blooded son of the Black Dagger warrior Darius, adopted son of the Black Dagger warrior Tohrment, you are going to be asked a question. You may give one and only one answer and it must stand for the rest of your life. Are you prepared to answer?"

It was Murhder. Murhder was speaking.

Even as John Matthew nodded, he could not believe this was happening. Maybe this was a mistake. Maybe they were—

Tohr's voice now, loud and clear. *"Mine son, will you join us this night and for all others that Fate provides you?"*

John Matthew bowed low. As he straightened, he mouthed the word "yes" at the same time he nodded and signed.

You know, just in case there were any doubts.

"Put this on."

A black robe was shoved at him and he whipped that thing over his head so fast, he almost tore it. Putting the hood up, he found himself trembling. But not from fear.

No, it wasn't fear.

"Lower thine eyes and keep them thus. Your hands shall be clasped at the small of your back. You are not to look up until told to do so. You are not to respond unless prompted to do so. Your bravery and the honor of the bloodline you and I share by virtue of adoption shall be measured in every action you take. Do you understand this?"

As John Matthew nodded, he did as instructed, and felt his arms get gripped on both sides. Tohr was on his left. Murhder was on his right.

The two males, one the only father he had ever known, and the other, a new acquaintance that he knew only too well, led him down the grand staircase.

Everything was dark, all the lights in the mansion seemingly extinguished.

And then he was outside, and being put into a van.

◆   ◆   ◆

The next thing John knew, he was being drawn out of the back of the van, his bare feet hitting frozen ground that was covered in fallen pine needles. The air was bracingly cold, and full of the scents of the forest.

They had taken him somewhere on the mountain, but he would not look around. He would do nothing he was not told to do. His arms were gripped again by Tohr and Murhder and he was led forward, his footfalls mirroring theirs, his trust in them absolute, the frigid ground not even registering.

And then they were out of the gusts, in a space that smelled like damp earth. A cave. They were in a cave.

Pause. And then a procession along a gentle decline. Another pause.

He had the impression that a second gate was being opened. More forward going.

He could sense the other members of the Brotherhood behind him, the large bodies moving in succession, the power in the group magnifying by proximity.

Warmth came after further walking, and now underneath the hem of his robe . . . candlelight. And no longer a packed dirt floor or one of rough stone, but fine honed marble.

He was jerked to a halt.

All around him, there was a shifting of fabric. The Brothers were disrobing, he thought. And then a heavy hand clamped on the back of his neck and the deep growl of the King's voice shot into his ear.

"*You are unworthy to enter herein as you are the now. Nod your head.*"

John nodded his head.

"*Unclasp thine hands and say that you are unworthy.*"

I am unworthy, John signed.

"*He states that he is unworthy,*" Tohr translated.

Immediately, there was a shout in the Old Language, a protest uttered by every one of the Brothers.

Wrath continued, "*Though you are unworthy, you desire to become as such this night. Nod your head.*"

John nodded.

"*State that you wish to become worthy.*"

I wish to become worthy, John signed.

"*He has so declared that he wishes to become worthy,*" Tohr said.

Another shout in the Old Language, this time a cheer of support.

Wrath went on to say, "*There is only one way to become worthy and it is the right and proper way. Flesh of our flesh. Nod your head.*"

John nodded.

"*State that you wish to become flesh of our flesh.*"

I wish to become flesh of your flesh, he signed.

After Tohr translated again, a low chanting started up, and John heard the Brothers shifting their positions, big feet whispering over the glossy marble, a line of bodies forming in front of, and behind him. And then they were swaying. Back and forth, back and forth, in rhythm with their deep bass voices.

John did not struggle to find his place, his movement, his echoing of the larger group.

Sure as if he had done this before, he fell immediately into the groove.

And then they were all going forward.

Together. As one body—

Without warning, there was a great change in acoustics, the booming voices blooming in a vast open space and echoing around, the chanting redoubling on itself, expanding . . . exploding. And just as abruptly, tears formed in John's eyes and he blinked quickly but could not catch them. As he swayed along with the others, the tears landed on the tops of his bare feet.

But he was smiling.

In the strangest way, he felt like he'd come home.

He even somehow knew when he needed to stop even before some-one's hand on his shoulder halted him.

The chanting silenced, the tail ends of the voices trailing off. Both of his arms were clasped, and then he was led forth once again.

"Stairs," Murhder said softly.

John took the marble steps one by one, and though his hood and his lowered head prevented him from seeing anything, he knew that he was being moved onto a stage. And even before he was positioned so that his toes touched something and he was left by himself, his mind told him that it was the wall.

The Wall.

CHAPTER SIXTY-SEVEN

Deep within the Black Dagger Brotherhood's *sanctum sanctorum*, Murhder stepped off the dais and stood shoulder to shoulder with his brothers, the whole lot of them staring up at John Matthew as he faced the great wall of names. Every single member of the Brotherhood who had served had had his name inscribed in the marble expanse in the Old Language, and the torchlight that glowed in the subterranean cave played over the beautiful characters.

Breathing in deep, he braced himself for the appearance of the Scribe Virgin—except no, the mother of the race would not be coming. Wrath would be performing her part in the ceremony, and sure enough the King was being led up to the marble steps by Tohr—

All at once, a brilliant light blazed through the cave, so bright that it had a white-hot blast to it. Everyone covered their eyes, and even John, who was still hooded and facing away from its source, had to duck his head into his shoulder.

When the blast of illumination faded some, Murhder dropped his arm, looked over his shoulder . . . and gasped along with many of the others.

A male figure had materialized at the entrance of the cave, his body glowing from within and without, an aura surrounding his naked body. Draped in chains of gold, from his neck to his nipples to his hips, he had long hair that was blond and black, and an unearthly beauty that defied description.

But none of that was what truly awed.

Rising behind his shoulders, a magnificent pair of iridescent angel wings glimmered with all the colors of the rainbow.

He did not walk down to the Brotherhood. He floated over the marble aisle that led down to the dais.

Next to Murhder, Vishous slapped a palm on his face and cursed.

Rhage chuckled. "So this is who your mom picked as a successor, huh."

"Yeah, I always knew she hated us," V muttered.

Over by the steps, Tohr leaned into the King, clearly telling him what had arrived and Wrath smiled slowly.

"Yes, I know," the King said.

The angel passed by the row of brothers, and paused in front of Vishous. In a low voice, he whispered, "Who's your daddy?"

Vishous rolled his eyes. "Give it a rest."

The angel blew a kiss and then looked at Murhder.

Abruptly, the angel's voice entered Murhder's mind, "*Worry not over your female's future. I have her in hand.*"

Murhder's eyes flared as he recoiled. "What?"

But the angel merely continued on, stopping in front of the King. With a deep bow, Tohr stepped aside, leaving the sacred male to escort the race's leader up to the great wall's altar.

In a clear, deep voice, the angel called out, "*Who proposes this male?*"

"*We do,*" Tohr answered. "*Tohrment, son of the Black Dagger warrior Hharm.*"

Murhder shook himself back into focus and spoke up as well. "*And Murhder, son of the Black Dagger warrior Murhder.*"

"*Who rejects this male?*"

When there was only silence, the angel spoke again. "*On the basis of testimony from Wrath son of Wrath, sire of Wrath, and upon the proposal by Tohrment, son of Hharm, and Murhder, son of Murhder, I find this male before me, John Matthew, blooded son of Darius, adopted son of Tohrment, an appropriate nomination unto the Black Dagger Brotherhood. As it is within my power and discretion to do so, and as it is suitable for the protection of the race, I hereby give you permission to begin.*"

Wrath nodded. "*Turn John. Unveil yourself.*"

Up at the wall, John pivoted around and removed his robe, keeping his head still lowered as the folds fell to the marble at his feet. As Murhder watched, he remembered his own induction and had to blink away tears. Never had he thought he'd stand here again. And how wonderful this all was.

"*Lift thine eyes,*" Wrath ordered.

The inductee slowly followed the command—only to gasp at the sight of the cave and the Brotherhood before him. His gaze then went to the altar on which an ancient skull was placed, a tangible representation of the great history of the warriors serving the race.

"*Step back against the wall. Grasp that which fits your hands.*"

John Matthew did as he was told, locking fists on two pegs that were mounted in the wall, his position framed by the lines of names.

Wrath brought up his dagger arm, revealing an ancient weapon that was locked on his entire forearm and hand. Made of silver, the flexible glove had barbs at the knuckles, and inside the curl of his fist was the handle of a black dagger.

Tohr led him over to the altar and positioned the King's other wrist above the silver cup that was mounted in the top of the skull. With a vicious streak of the blade, Wrath cut himself and let his sacred pure blood flow into the reservoir.

"*My flesh,*" the King said. Then he licked his wound closed, put the blade down, and approached John.

After Tohr made sure he was in correct alignment, the King grabbed onto the inductee's jaw, wrenched the male's head to the side, and bit him in the neck, clearly sparing none of his strength. In response, John's body spasmed from the pain, but he gritted his teeth and did not so much as exhale, his hands using the pegs to control his response. Like a Brother should.

Wrath stepped back and wiped his mouth, smiling with aggression. "*Your flesh.*"

Then he curled up a fist within the silver glove, drew back his powerful arm, and pounded the barbs into John's pec . . . directly over the scar that was already present there.

As if John had previously been through the ceremony.

What a birthmark, Murhder thought.

Tohrment was next, scoring himself with the black dagger, mingling his blood with the King's in the sacred skull cup, biting John, and brutally marking the male's chest in the same place Wrath had.

And now it was Murhder's turn as the second nominator.

Trading places with Tohrment, he accepted the glove and slipped it onto his own hand. Over at the altar, he picked up the black dagger, the candlelight flashing on the blade. For a moment, his eyes clouded once more with tears.

He thought of Sarah, waiting for him when this was through.

He thought of Nate, with her now.

He thought of what he hoped for the future.

For no particular reason, he glanced over at the angel who was far off to the side. The male was watching him, and the smile that came at Murhder was full of love and acceptance, as if the angel had had a hand in all this.

In everything.

The angel's hand lifted and swept through the air—and Murhder jumped as he felt a stroke on his cheek, a tear being wiped away. Then the angel made a fist and opened his palm. Something caught the light, sending out a sparkle.

Shaking himself, Murhder refocused and turned back to the skull. "*My flesh.*"

The pain as he opened his vein was sharp and sweet, and his blood glowed red in the candlelight as it dropped in to join Wrath and Tohr's. Licking the wound closed, he went up to the inductee. As he approached John, his eyes went to the list of names . . . and as he found his own, he felt a flush of pride.

"*Your flesh.*"

He didn't have to tilt John's head to the side. The male did it by himself.

The bite marks on John's throat were bleeding, leaving a trail of blood down his collarbone and his chest, the side of his torso and his hip. The male was unwavering in the pain, his face composed and his body strong, even as his jaw spasmed from the agony he was in and his arms trembled from how hard he was gripping the pegs.

Murhder curled up a fist in the glove and spared none of his strength. To do so would have been disrespectful to John.

◆   ◆   ◆

John took all of the bites and all of the strikes, adrenaline running through him, keeping him upright even as the pain magnified and threatened his vision and hearing.

When it was Qhuinn's turn, his best friend seemed to tear up as their eyes met. John did the same.

And then Zsadist was the last one to approach him from the lineup. John stared into the male's yellow eyes as a pair of massive fangs dug deep into a wrist still marked with a slave band. And then came the impact on John's chest, all breath knocked out of him, his upper body going limp such that he nearly lost his hold on the grips.

But he remained standing.

His hollow belly pumped in and out as he refused to lose consciousness. And when next he was fully aware again, he saw with clarity the lineup of males that had gathered around the altar, proud warriors, all with the same mark on their pec as he had.

Wrath picked up the skull and held the ancient relic high. *"This is the first of us. Hail to him, the warrior who birthed the Brotherhood."*

A roar of triumph and respect echoed around the candlelit cave, and then the King turned to John and was brought over by Tohr.

"Drink and join us," Wrath said.

John released the pegs and went for it, taking the skull and putting the silver rim of the reservoir to his mouth. Opening his throat, he drank it all down, the blood blazing a trail to his gut, scorching him.

The King took the skull back, and said softly, "Better hold on to those grips, son—"

The firebrand of power that came unto him was like nothing John had ever experienced before. It was a rush of incalculable dimension, sure to blow him apart—and yet in the midst of it, he recognized each of the Brothers within it, their individual characteristics entering him, nourishing him . . . strengthening him.

Teeth chattering, muscles jerking, heart pounding, he hung on . . . until he could no longer. Falling . . . he was . . . falling . . .

✦   ✦   ✦

. . . John opened his eyes and blinked . . . blinked again . . .

He was on the marble floor, facing the wall of names, his body spent as if it had been used to run a hundred marathons. His head was like a balloon, his spinal cord the string that tethered it to his torso, his legs useless—

Abruptly, everything became focused.

Below the inscription of his best friend Qhuinn's name . . . was his own. John Matthew. In the symbols of the Old Language.

Pushing up against the marble floor, he started to smile as he reached out and traced the deep carving.

Clapping brought his head around.

The Brotherhood was standing behind him, re-robed, their hoods down. All of the fierce males were smiling as they cheered for him.

Tohr extended his dagger hand. "Let me help you up, my brother."

John looked into the male's face and was reminded of the first time he'd seen the one he would call "father." As tears threatened, Tohr's eyes became misty, too.

John stood up on his own, and the two embraced, holding each other tightly.

It had been a long road from that bus station where he'd been born and left for dead, so much of it full of terrible losses. But there had been amazing surprises, too, and blessings that had been both prayed for and unexpected. There had been laughs and sobs, illness and health, confusion and clarity.

Throughout all of it, John had questioned his path so many times. Had felt for sure he would never recover from countless problems. Had worried he would be alone for his days and nights.

But that was not how things had ended up, had they.

If he'd only known to put a little more faith in Fate.

Just before he broke away from the only father he had ever known, he caught Lassiter's strange silver gaze. The fallen angel smiled at him.

And then pulled a Taylor Swift move, making a heart of his forefingers and thumbs over his pec.

"Oh, for fuck's sake, did anyone bring a tissue?" someone muttered.

As multiple brothers started to sniffle, somebody else said, "Use your robe. I did."

"Goddamn it, I hate crying."

"So why do you watch *Grey's Anatomy?*"

"It's the angel's fault. Fucker is a glutton for punishment . . ."

As the Brotherhood talked and laughed, John and Tohr separated and then he was hugging Qhuinn. Murhder. Everyone.

John could not stop smiling. He was one of them for reals.

And wasn't that awesome?

CHAPTER SIXTY-EIGHT

Sarah got out of the Mercedes slowly, rising from the warm interior without noticing the cold. At all.

The structure before her was more castle than house, a monolithic stone construction with gargoyles on its roofline, a thousand diamond-pane windows, and multi-story'd wings that went on forever. The magnificent expanse was anchored by a courtyard with a fountain that was shut down for winter, and there was also a carriage house off to one side and a lineup of very different cars and trucks across the way.

"So this is where we live."

Sarah jumped as Xhex came around from the driver's side. "You know . . . this is the kind of place I assumed the King of all vampires would live in."

"Wait'll you see the inside," the female murmured. "You ready?"

Sarah nodded, but didn't walk forward. She couldn't seem to move.

Xhex took her arm. "Come on, they don't bite—okay, maybe that's not the best choice of words."

Together, they started up a shoveled set of stone stairs toward an entrance that belonged on a cathedral. Overhead, the moon was full in a clear sky, and the night was still. Sarah's breath left her lips in puffs of white, and she had to put her hands in the pockets of her parka because she didn't have gloves.

Xhex opened a heavy door into a vestibule and looked down into a camera mounted next to a computer monitor. "Hey all, it's us—"

The inner door was opened by a tall dark-haired woman—er, female—with a dark-haired baby on her hip. "You must be Sarah! This is so great! Hi!"

Before Sarah knew it, she was wrapped in an embrace, the baby going for her hair, a bunch of women—er, females—stepping in close.

And then Sarah lost track of everything. On account of the holy-shit-will-you-look-at-that.

The vast space on the far side of the double doors was so luxurious, so colorful, so overwhelming, she couldn't take it all in. Everywhere she looked there were crystal chandeliers, and gold leafed mirrors and balustrades, and columns made of claret marble and—was that malachite? Glancing down, she found an intricate mosaic floor depicting an apple tree in full bloom and three stories up, there was a domed ceiling sporting a fresco of warriors on stallions.

The staircase made Tara's look like a frickin' step stool.

There was also a grand dining room off to one side and a pool room on the other, and in the latter, she could hear male voices . . .

Sarah shook herself as she realized all of the females were looking at her with indulgent smiles.

"It can be a little overwhelming," the dark-haired female with the baby said. "But I promise you, you'll get used to it. I'm Beth, by the way, and this is L.W."

The baby looked at her with the clearest pale green eyes she'd ever seen—and reached for her.

"Oh, he wants to say hi. He likes you."

And that was how she ended up with a baby in her arms.

The little one was warm, and he smelled like fresh soap and sweetness, and as he smiled at her, her eyes pricked with tears.

She had forgotten about her dream of having a family. Just left it behind after Gerry's death. Decided it didn't really suit a scientist anyway. But now, as she held this vital weight against her body, and felt him move, and saw him respond to her, she found the spark reigniting. Except...

"It's okay," the mom said gently. "You can have one with Murhder. My mother was human. It happens, if you try enough times, and somehow, I'm thinking your man is going to be up for practicing."

Sarah looked at the female. "Really?"

"Yes, I promise." She turned to the others. "Now, let me introduce you around. This is Bella and Nalla. Mary. Cormia and Autumn. Marissa . . . Payne. Ehlena. And of course, you know our Doc Jane well."

Jane smiled and raised her wineglass. "You're handling the future King very well over there."

Sarah paled. "What?"

"He's the King's son. This is our queen."

Sarah immediately held the baby back out to his mother. "Oh, God. Too much—too much responsibility. Nope, not going to be the one who drops him."

Everyone laughed, and before she knew, she was talking to them all, answering questions about what she did, what she hoped to do, where she and Murhder wanted to look for a house. They were the most welcoming group of females, and then there were more people to meet in where the pool tables were.

It was a whole community.

Family, was more like it.

And after having lost her mother and father, and then Gerry, and being prepared to live her life alone, she couldn't wait to get to know—

From around the base of the stairs, the old butler with the happy face brought someone very familiar into the grand space, and Sarah started to smile.

"Will you excuse me?" she said before all but running across the mosaic tile.

Nate seemed as shell-shocked as she was as he looked around at the grandeur. But the second he saw her, he exhaled in relief.

She wrapped the boy up in a hug so hard, she had to force herself to release him before he couldn't breathe—except he didn't let her go. He held on, dropping his head into her shoulder and sighing.

Stroking her hand up and down his back, she remembered finding him in that cage, in that lab. She couldn't believe they were here now, standing in this awesome place, with a group of strangers that felt like family.

She inched back and took his face in her hands. His eyes were tired and his smile more determined than honest.

"Hi," she said.

"Hi." His pseudo-happy expression lost some of its traction. "You came back."

"I did. And I'm not leaving. Come here."

She pulled him in again and had to get up on her tiptoes to hold more of him. "It's okay," she murmured.

"I did my *mahmen's* Fade Ceremony tonight. I wish you'd been there."

Sarah closed her eyes. "Oh, Nate. I'm so sorry I missed it."

"It's okay."

"I didn't know."

"I maybe could have waited. But I just . . . I needed to get through it."

"I was the same when my father died."

Now Nate was the one easing back. "You lost a parent?"

"Both of them." She smoothed his hair. "It's hell. No matter when or how it happens. It just . . . sucks."

As he nodded, he looked beyond lost.

And maybe she should have talked to Murhder first, maybe she should have thought things through better, but no. Some things, you just knew.

"Nate, Murhder and I are going to get a little house just outside of

Caldwell. It's going to have an extra bedroom. How'd you like to come live with us?"

The boy—male, that was—blinked a couple of times. "You mean it?"

"Yes. I want you to come . . . stay with us. And listen, if you don't like it, or if you don't like us, you can—"

Nate's face lit up. "Really? You're serious? I could . . . live in a house? With you guys?"

"Yes." She started to smile. "We'd love it. We love . . . you."

Now he hugged her hard enough to crush her, not that she minded in the slightest. And when he set her back, he said, "I don't have any money. I don't have a job. I can't really read all that well—"

"Not to worry. We'll figure it all out together."

His smile became real, his eyes glowing with true happiness. "So you have a house already picked out?"

"No, we haven't started looking yet."

"But wait, how do you know it'll have an extra bedroom."

Sarah clasped his hand and gave it a squeeze. "Because we aren't going to buy something that doesn't have room for you."

◆   ◆   ◆

Murhder nearly broke the mansion's damn doors down. He'd only been away from Sarah for what, like an hour? But it was too long. Waaaaay too long—

As the inside door of the vestibule was sprung by Fritz, Murhder nearly ran over the poor *doggen*. And then he was instantly frustrated because there were frickin' people all over the frick. Some he recognized, like Rehvenge and Trez and iAm, others were new, like some of the females, and four huge males who were draped in weapons.

None of them was who he was looking for, though, and he had a moment of panic. Where was Sarah? Xhex was supposed to—

"She's over there, buddy," Xhex said.

His friend the *symphath*'s dry tone belied the grin on her face—and

Murhder had to give her a hug as he looked into the billiard room and saw his Sarah standing with Nate by a pool table.

"Thanks for taking care of my female," he said.

"And thanks for nominating my male." Xhex grew serious. "It meant a lot to him."

"He deserves it. He's a helluva fighter." Murhder leaned in and dropped his voice. "And brace yourself."

"For what?" When he didn't respond, she frowned. "What am I bracing for?"

Murhder winked at his old friend. "Let's just say the era of the Brotherhood being a boys' club only is officially over. And I understand you're pretty damn good with a *lys*."

It was so satisfying to stun the *symphath* into silence.

"That's right," he said as he saw John Matthew come for her. "We've got our eyes on you, soldier."

Murhder stepped aside as John swept his female up and the two kissed like they hadn't seen each other in years.

Good example to follow. Murhder strode through to the billiard room, and the instant Sarah saw him, the glow of love in her face was a beacon he would follow to the ends of the earth. Pulling her into his arms, he held her up off the floor and twirled her around.

After he kissed her, he reached around and drew Nate in. "Group hug!"

The young male folded into the pair of them as if he were an essential piece of their unit, and Murhder thought about Ingridge reaching out to him all those months before. Thank God, she had. Thank God for . . . everything.

"So I've invited Nate to live with us," Sarah said as they stepped back from the huddle. "I hope that's—"

"Fantastic!" Murhder put his hand on the boy's shoulder. "You up for that, son?"

"Yes, please." The hope on that face was almost painful to witness. "I promise not to get in the way—"

"You are welcome always." Murhder tucked his Sarah into his side. "We're your family. All of us here, are your family."

Someone offered him a beer and he accepted it with thanks, and then he just hung back and enjoyed the view into the foyer. Fritz and some *doggen* brought in a sheet cake, and bowls of punch, and then balloons were falling and people were cheering.

It felt so good to be a part of it all. Once again.

So many familiar faces, laughing, talking. He missed Darius, though. The male should have been—

Through the grand archway into the dining room, John returned from the back of the house, his robe still on, his face still shining with pride and happiness. He was carrying something—no, two things. One was a black dagger, and the other was . . .

A green apple.

The newest member of the Brotherhood started peeling the Granny Smith as he wound through the crowd and went over to Zsadist, who was standing next to a beautiful female and holding a young in his powerful arms who looked just like him. The brother was laughing and smiling at his *shellan*, until he saw what John was doing with the apple.

Instantly, his face grew serious, especially as the two males locked eyes.

After John had peeled the apple in one long strip that fell on his bare foot, he cut a piece of the white flesh with the black steel of the dagger—and offered it to Z on the blade.

Zsadist reached out and accepted the slice, popping it into his mouth.

His smile was ancient. And beautiful, even, if not especially, because of his scarred face.

John ate the next slice. And then the young got the third.

No words were spoken between to the two, and Murhder was pretty sure that the party all around them was totally forgotten as some sort of debt was repaid with happiness on both sides.

"Oh." Sarah stiffened as she looked out into the foyer. "Oh . . . my."

At first, Murhder wasn't sure what she was focused on. There were all kinds of couples hugging and friends laughing and Wrath had picked up his dog, who was so excited at being reunited with his master that his tail was going a mile a minute—

But then Murhder saw what the issue was.

Lassiter, the fallen angel, had come into the billiards room after a clothing change . . . and he was wearing gold lamé on his golden body. Which wouldn't exactly have been a problem, except . . .

"Are those ass-less chaps?" Sarah asked. "Or am I seeing things wrong."

Murhder put his big body in the way so she and Nate were spared the vision of two golden globes making waaaaay too much of an appearance.

"Um, yeah," he muttered, "I don't think you need to get your eyes checked. Unfortunately."

"Who is he?" Sarah asked as Nate started to laugh.

"That's our deity. You know, the one who runs things from above? He's a fallen angel."

His mate did a double take. "You're not serious."

"No, he really is magical. I know it's hard for humans to understand the magic in our world, but there is another realm, and Lassiter does live there. According to what Tohr told me, he took over from the Scribe Virgin who—"

"Oh, I get all that. I don't have a problem with the paranormal." She laughed and kissed him. "I mean, hello, I'm going to marry a vampire. But how are you guys ruled by something that would wear ass-less chaps?"

Murhder glanced over his shoulder. Yup. Still butt all over the place.

"Well," he said, "you know, it's probably best to have a god with a sense of humor, don't you think? I mean, all that stuffy stuff just gets tiresome, and sometimes, you do have to pray for crazy things. Plus, he does have a good ass. I mean, honestly, if you look at it objectively, he doesn't have a thing to apologize for."

As Sarah and Nate started laughing together, Murhder put his arms around the two of them, and decided that all was right in the world.

After all, if you had the love of your life, your friends, and your family . . . and a god who watched over you lovingly—even if he was only partially dressed?

What else was there to the mortal coil?

Except then the angel in question came over, and Murhder wasn't so sure those golden globes needed to be so—

The angel held something out to Sarah. "A gift of welcome to you."

"What is it—" Sarah flushed. "Wait . . . this is a diamond."

"And you know what they say about them."

Murhder's breath caught. "Forever. A diamond . . . is forever."

All at once, a glow suffused Sarah's body, and she looked down at herself in alarm.

Lassiter smiled. "Another gift as it were. Enjoy your long life with your males. Both of them."

Sarah gasped. "What did you do to me . . ."

But the fallen angel was already walking away. Flashing that ass.

In the wake of Lassiter's departure, Murhder wasn't sure whether he should laugh or cry. So he gathered his true love to his heart . . . and did both.

"I think we just got our happily ever after," he whispered in her ear. "And we owe that angel . . ."

Sarah inched back. "Can we start by getting him a real pair of pants?"

"Excellent idea, scientist mine . . ."

And then Murhder kissed his eternal *shellan*.

ACKNOWLEDGMENTS

With so many thanks to the readers of the Black Dagger Brotherhood books! This has been a long, marvelous, exciting journey, and I can't wait to see what happens next in this world we all love. I'd also like to thank Meg Ruley, Rebecca Scherer, and everyone at JRA, and Lauren McKenna, Jennifer Bergstrom, and the entire family at Gallery Books and Simon & Schuster.

To Team Waud, I love you all. Truly. And as always, everything I do is with love to, and adoration for, my family of both origin and adoption.

Oh, and thank you to Naamah, my Writer Dog II, who works as hard as I do on my books!

From the #1 *New York Times* bestselling author of the
Black Dagger Brotherhood series.

Get ready for a new band of brothers. And a firestorm ...

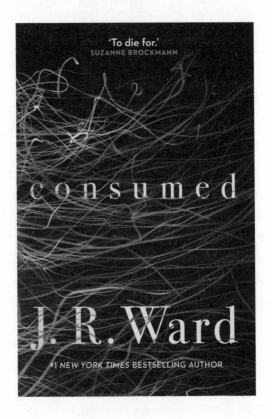

Anne Ashburn is a woman consumed –
by her bitter family legacy, by her scorched career as a firefighter, by
her obsession with department bad-boy **Danny McGuire**, and
by a new case that pits her against a fiery killer ...

Available now from Piatkus!